T0198717

Greywolf Down

RUSTY CASH

authorHOUSE®

Other books also written by **Rusty Cash**
Havana Moon
By Author House

Book Cover Artist
Evelyn Camby

AuthorHouse™
1663 Liberty Drive
Bloomington, IN 47403
www.authorhouse.com
Phone: 1 (800) 839-8640

Published by AuthorHouse 06/20/2018

ISBN: 978-1-5462-3484-5 (sc)
ISBN: 978-1-5462-3485-2 (hc)
ISBN: 978-1-5462-3483-8 (e)

Library of Congress Control Number: 2018903837

Print information available on the last page.

Any people depicted in stock imagery provided by Getty Images are models, and such images are being used for illustrative purposes only. Certain stock imagery © Getty Images.

This book is printed on acid-free paper.

Because of the dynamic nature of the Internet, any web addresses or links contained in this book may have changed since publication and may no longer be valid. The views expressed in this work are solely those of the author and do not necessarily reflect the views of the publisher, and the publisher hereby disclaims any responsibility for them.

CHAPTER ONE

I watched the green Cuban jungle rushing by my canopy as I flew formation next to Raul's MIG-21. I heard Manuel's voice over my headphones counting down until the bomb release. I watched as the target came into view. I moved the stick a little to the right. I wanted to be clear of the debris when the bombs hit their target. At zero the four bombs were released and dropped onto the target. I watched out the left side of the canopy as a massive orange explosion filled the sky. It was a good drop, target destroyed. I turned to look forward and saw lines of tracers reaching up at us from a Russian ZSU anti aircraft gun. I heard rounds hitting my MIG and warning lights began to flash red across the flight panel as smoke began to pour out the rear of the fighter. The rounds had ripped through my flight controls making it difficult to control. I felt intense heat all around me inside the cockpit as flames began increasing around me.

"Greywolf EJECT EJECT EJECT!" I heard Raul's voice screaming at me through the headphones. My mind returned to the flight training Alexi had drilled into me, my hands moved in coordination. My right hand released the canopy, which was ripped away in the strong wind. Then my hands returned to the eject handles between my legs, I pulled with all my strength and the rocket motor beneath me ignited thrusting me out of the burning MIG-21 and clear of danger. It was a clean separation from the ejection seat and my right hand automatically reached for the D ring to release my parachute but to my horror it wasn't there.

I was freefalling over the Cuban jungle from 2000 feet up without a parachute, the ground rushing up at me. Falling to my death.

"ALI!" I screamed at the top of my lungs as my wife's face filled my mind. The falling feeling consumed my body.

I awoke from the nightmare, my body bathed in sweat as Ali was shaking me trying to rescue me from the nightmare. I lay there in her arms, breathing heavily, my heart pounding in my chest, her arms around me talking to me in low tones until I came out of it.

"The same dream again?" she asked. All I could do was nod. She left our bed and returned with a cold wet washcloth and ran it over my sweaty body, cooling me. This same nightmare had haunted me ever since I had taken part in a bombing attack on the Chinese electronic intelligence gathering station in Bejucal Cuba. I had been part of a hand picked group of international mercenary fighter pilots who flew updated MIG-21s disguised as Cuban Air Force fighters. It was a successful mission. We eliminated the Cuban leaders while they were having a top-secret meeting with Chinese officials inside the installation. The Chinese had wanted to increase their influence in the Western hemisphere. They had moved in when the Russians decided to abandon Cuba. China was giving the communist Cuban government military and monetary assistance. We hit them while they were meeting with Chinese representatives discussing further military assistance in exchange for allowing them to eavesdrop on American military and civilian radio and telephone traffic.

The nightmares began two weeks after the Cuban government collapsed, which was replaced with a non-Communist type of government led by a no nonsense anti communist military general. Later after surviving the mission, I was offered a position in the new Cuban Air Force by the new government.

Getting out of bed we both walked out onto the patio of our house that was right on the beach. We sat there holding each other under the stars watching the waves roll in.

CHAPTER TWO

The next morning I went to the airport in Havana to pick up my friend and former wing man from my Navy days. We had flown together off the carrier USS Grant. He had been an unplanned partner in the attack on Bejucal covering my ass helping us fight our way out. It had been almost a year since his last visit to Cuba. He was coming for a week of Cuban sun, fun and sand. Or as he always put it the three Bs, broads, booze, and beaches. His name was Wally but I always called him by his call sign Boner.

The International Airport in Havana had been modernized since the changeover, and almost doubled in size to handle the massive amount of tourists that were flying in daily from around the world. We saw each other at the same time as he entered the concourse. He was wearing his Navy whites and I was in my Cuban Air Force uniform. He had been promoted since the last time I'd seen him. He was a now Lt. Commander. He threw me a quick salute. I saluted him back, grinning. We shook hands then walked to the carousel to retrieve his bag.

"I'll never get used to seeing you in a Cuban uniform." He told me looking at the Cuban flag on my shoulder.

"You should see my dress uniform, it has US Navy Wings, Indian Flight Wings, Cuban Air Force Wings, the emblems signifying I'm a Colonel in the Indian Air Force, my Cuban Colonel insignia, it's quite a sight I'll tell ya," I told him as he shook his head grinning at me.

He had to walk through processing, show his military ID, and have his bag searched. Boner had to verify how long he was planning to stay and the nature of his visit. I stood quietly as he finished. Walking out into the warm Cuban sun he laughed as we approached my vehicle. It was a green Hummer, the driver standing there with the door open saluting us.

As a Colonel in the new Cuban Air Force, I was allowed a driver who doubled as my bodyguard. The new government took security very seriously.

The driver saluted Boner then loaded his bag as we got in.

"An air-conditioned Hummer, man you really rate," he smiled as the cool air hit him.

"Well as I remember you did your part. That's why you get an all expense government paid vacation every year here," I reminded him.

"Has it really been two years since our little adventure?" he asked.

"Doesn't feel that long. So much has changed here since the Communist government was thrown out."

"All for the better I've heard. Has anyone discovered our little secret yet?" He asked, referring to our bombing mission that eliminated the communist leaders of the old government. Our participation was a closely guarded secret to prevent any attempts on our lives by former angry family members or Chinese assassins.

"Thankfully no, only a handful of people know, and they realize the possible consequences if it ever leaked out."

"Yeah, I still look over my shoulder wondering," He revealed.

"If we were ever compromised I would contact you ASAP," I offered.

"How's Ali?" He asked referring to my wife.

"Beautiful as ever," I answered.

"How's married life treating ya?"

"It's great. Nice having more to come back to every night than just an empty house."

"Still working two jobs?" he asked sitting back into the seat as the driver pulled out into traffic.

"Yeah, I love it. I get to test flight the updated Migs for Antonio's company and then teach the new Cuban pilots how to fly. Manuel finally finished flight school. He is married and has a baby on the way."

"Manuel a daddy, man if I remember correctly he tried to nail anything that moved," he grinned.

"Yeah, well Maria keeps him happy," I told him.

"Oh man, she is a hottie."

"What's new in your life? Still single?"

"Oh yeah, I'm still too young for the old ball an chain."

"If memory serves me, we're the same age," I reminded him.

"I'm having too much fun right now to settle down. Those women love Top Gun pilots," he explained.

"How is it being an instructor there?"

"It's a blast, I get to fly my ass off as a bad guy. Man they sure have improved the roads around here." He remarked looking out the window.

"Just one of many improvements here. I have to stop at the base before we head to the house," I told him.

"No rest for the wicked eh?"

"Ahhhhh, there are fitness reports, pilot qualification reports, and then write-ups on every Mig I test fly. Not to mention mission drill results to type up. Damn paperwork never ends. I have to keep track of training levels, create training scenarios, maintenance reports on 9 MIG-21s, health records of my pilots. There's more to wearing this uniform than just turning women s heads," I lamented.

"As I live and breath, I never thought I'd hear you of all people talk like a desk jockey," he laughed.

"Comes with the rank I'm afraid. When they made me a Colonel, I never realized how much desk time I'd have to do."

The driver stopped at the gate of the Air base and two armed guards checked our ID cards. They both saluted and waved us in.

"I'll never get used to seeing AKs without getting a chill down my spine," he revealed.

"Amen to that. Took me forever to get used to that too. I'm still not used to a lot of things here yet, takes time," I said as the driver stopped in front of the building. He got out and opened the door for us. Boner followed me into my office. My secretary handed me a folder as we walked past and into my office.

"Mig-21s?" he asked as the deafening roar of jet engines shook the building.

"No, 23s," I told him as I sat behind my desk.

"How can you tell the difference?"

"The pitch is different, the 23 has two engines. Must be the last training flight of the day. The Mexican government has sent some of their pilots here to train in the 23s they are buying from Antonio. It's keeping Alexi very busy," I explained.

"How is our favorite Russian?" he asked.

"Ahhh you know Alexi, he's the Russian version of a jarhead. Stiff as usual." Alexi was a former Russian flight instructor. He had been left stranded in India when the Soviet Union folded. He had been in India teaching their pilots how to fly the MIG-21 purchased from the Soviets. Antonio offered him a job as a combination flight instructor slash test pilot for his company. He had run me through the Soviet designed training class teaching me how to fly the MIG-21 when I joined the company. He was the best pilot in a MIG-21 there was. He was able to do things with the MIG-21 the designers never dreamed of. He had been my wing man during our bombing attack on Bejucal.

"Raul still your boss?"

"Ayep, he's in heaven I'll tell ya. He loves being in the Air Force now that everything has changed," I told him, opening the file on my desk. Years earlier Raul had been in the Cuban Air Force. Disgusted with the Communist way of life he flew his MIG-23 to Key West, defecting. Later he had taken part in our mercenary mission bombing the site where the previous government leaders were holding their meeting. Now he was once again a pilot in the Cuban Air Force, but a Colonel this time, and my superior officer.

I started scanning the fitness reports and signing them in the appropriate places. Boner helped himself to a cup of Cuban coffee and walked around my office looking at the photos and certificates I had on the wall. It was an odd combination, a copy of my US Navy Flight School certificate, the certificate the Indian government had given me for shooting down two Pakistani F-16s, confirming me as an honorary Colonel in the Indian Air Force, the certificate from the Cuban Air force confirming me as a Colonel, and the certificate given to me by Antonio, verifying I was an official test pilot for his company. On my desk was a color photo of Ali and next to it was a group photo of Raul, Antonio, Alexi, Manuel, Perry, Boner and me at our beach wedding, the greatest gang of aerial outlaws ever to help free a country from communism.

"Ali know you have this one?" he asked, pointing to Toni's photo hanging on the wall.

"Yeah, she's not too happy about it, but it reminds me of an important time in my life. Toni was there for me at a dark time in my life. I don't forget people who have helped me," I told him, looking at the photo. Toni was the school teacher I had met in Key West after I was discharged from the U.S. Navy for shooting down two Cuban MIG-21s against orders while flying F-18s off the carrier U.S.S Grant. Later Antonio, the owner of a large aviation company based in Israel, had offered me a position in his company test flying modernized Russian MIG-21s for sale to poorer countries. I traveled to India where during a test flight of a MIG-21, I shot down two Pakistani fighters sent to kill me and ruin the test flight. It was hoped by the Pakistani government that by shooting me down in the updated MIG, the Indian government would refrain from updating their fleet of MIG-21s. Luckily I was able to use the modern updated weapons systems installed in the new MIG-21 I was test flying for the Indian Government to shoot down the two Pakistani fighters helping to secure the contract.

"I can vouch for that one amigo. You shot that Cuban MIG-29 off my ass," he reminded me.

"I'd do it again too," I smiled remembering the Cuban MIG-29 I shot down that was attacking him from the rear two years ago during our mercenary mission. We were interrupted by a knock on the door.

"Colonel, your wife is on the telephono for you," my secretary told me, sticking her head in the door.

"Gracias," I told her, reaching for the phone.

"Damn she is fine," Boner observed after she left.

"Yeah Anna is one damn fine secretary, and she's easy on the eyes too."

"I'll bet Ali isn't happy about her," he remarked.

"She trusts me, but you're right," I told him, as Ali's voice came over the phone in my ear.

"Hi Honey, did Boner make it?"

"Ayep, he's standing right here," I told her.

"Wonderful. Hey why don't you invite Anna to dinner here with us? I'm sure Boner would love to get to know her."

"You're about as subtle as a sidewinder, but yeah I'll ask her, see what she says," I chuckled.

"Whatever do you mean my dear?" her Israeli accent coming through innocently.

"I love you, we'll see you in a bit." I heard her laugh as I put down the phone.

"Ali wants me to invite Anna to dinner tonight so you can get to meet her," I grinned.

"She is just trying to protect her six. I'd love to get to know her though," he told me.

"I recognize that look in your eyes, remember that waitress at the Tropicana? You still keep in touch with her?"

"Yes I do, in fact she is expecting me to get together with her while I'm here. That was a wild night wasn't it?" He said referring to the night Ali and I got married on the beach under the moon. We had all gone to a club afterwords where he had hooked up with a dark red-haired fireball cocktail waitress. No one had gone home sober that night.

"Truly a night to remember," I said with a grin. I signed the last of the reports and stood up to leave. On the way out I relayed Ali's invitation to her.

"Si, Gracias Colonel. I would enjoy that very much sir," she replied, looking Boner up and down with interest. Boner was practically drooling on his uniform undressing her with his eyes. I had to wonder, knowing Ali, if she had called and invited Anna ahead of time.

"Seems like we've been preempted Grey," Boner told me reading my mind. She lifted her phone and called for my driver. Boner stood there making small talk with Anna, trying to slyly look down her blouse.

"Red light there, Commander," I told him. He just grinned. Anna didn't seem to mind a bit.

"So Mexico is buying MIGs now?" he asked in the back of the Hummer as we rode to the house.

"Yeah, they are upgrading their air force and are tying to cut costs buying older MIG-21s and having Antonio's company upgrade them. Antonio convinced them it would be a great idea."

"That man could sell air conditioners to Eskimos"

"Amen to that."

"Is Mexico having money problems?"

"There seems to be an increase of narco-guerrillas in Central America. A group in Guatemala that is being led by former Cuban Communists is infiltrating Mexico. They have hooked up with a Communist group in Chiapa. Get this; the Chinese have been funding them. They hope to replace the electronic intelligence gathering stations they lost when they were thrown out of Cuba. They believe they can help establish a Communist group in Central America." I explained.

"The Chinese? No shit!" he exclaimed. "What's with the Chinese interest here anyway?"

"When the Russians pulled out of Cuba the Chinese moved in, took over the electronic intelligence gathering station here in Bejucal. They listened in on the United States phone and radio traffic. They were paying Cuba millions in exchange for the right to listen in.

Then with our little air raid and the change of government here the Chinese were told to take a hike. Now with the hands off attitude that Washington has concerning foreign affairs, it's likely to get worse"

"Why the hell they elected that asshole to be President I'll never know. He doesn't want to upset other countries to the degree that he'll be kissing the UN's ass every time something happens," he said disgustedly.

"If the Chicoms get a foothold in Central America, it'll be a nightmare."

"I thought the guerrilla days were over in Guatemala" he said.

"Well when the Guatemalan president was assassinated, the military took over. There have been several massacres in the mountain villages. The military there is so heavy handed, the communist rebels are turning the rural people against the government."

"Making it easier for the guerrillas to establish a foothold" he observed.

"Exactly. The Communist guerrillas there have aligned themselves with the drug smugglers providing security in exchange for additional funds to build their forces. Then with China giving them arms and money and training, it wont be long before we have a really bad situation over there."

"Damn, it's the early eighties all over again." he remarked remembering Nicaragua.

"Albert Einstein said as long as there is man, there shall be war." I told him.

"So where does Cuba fit into all this?"

"We have been training Mexican Air Force pilots, ever since the U.S. cut backs there. We have been doing joint flight ops with them. We've got some operatives keeping us informed on what's going on. Other than that, we're staying out of it"

"Sounds weird hearing you say we," he said.

"Yeah, well, Cuba is my home now. I love it here."

"Ya think there might be a place here for an ex US Navy Top Gun Instructor?"

"You're kidding!" I exclaimed turning to look at him.

"My re-enlistment date is approaching. With all the damn military cutbacks imposed by the new administration on us, the future doesn't look all that rosy," he told me disgustedly.

"Well damn. Hell yes. I'll make a few phone calls and see what I can do buddy. Damn. If this works I'll see if I can get you attached to the company here."

"Partners in crime again. God help them" he grinned.

We pulled up to the black security gate that surrounded my house and waited for the gate to open. The driver drove us in and stopped in front of the door. Ali's blue Jeep was in the driveway, I was glad she had gotten home before we did. Consuelo our housekeeper greeted us as we entered. Ali had hired her right after we purchased the house. She was a Godsend, warm, friendly, she acted more like a mother to the both of us and we in turn treated her like she was family. She hugged Boner welcoming him. Ali came in and hugged Boner. She was still in her blouse and skirt from work.

"I've invited Antonio for dinner tonight" she told us.

"That works out well, Boner here asked to join our merry little band of outlaws. We can discuss it with him."

"Oh Boner, that would be wonderful"

"Thanks Ali," he said, giving her a hug.

Boner went to the guest room to change and I followed Ali into our room, playfully pinching her rear. Later after we changed, the three of us sat on the patio watching the waves roll up onto the beach. The gate buzzer rang and I got up and answered it. I heard Antonio's voice over the metal speaker. I hit the green button that opened the electrically operated gate.

Antonio's black armored limo glided quietly up to the front door. His driver and personal bodyguard that accompanied him everywhere got out opening the door for him.

"Welcome Antonio, nice to see you." I told him. He was more than a boss, he was like a second father and he treated me like the son he never had.

He had been the only one to offer me a job when I left the US Navy. Boner had been my wing man then as we were flying between Cuba and Florida. Our mission had been to fly a racetrack pattern. Our ROE were to fire our missiles only if fired upon. We witnessed one of the Cuban Migs shoot down two civilian planes patrolling the area giving assistance to Cubans trying to flee Cuba in boats to Florida. I lost my temper, shooting down the two Migs against orders. After time in the brig and a show trial the Navy discharged me for disobeying orders. After Antonio hired me I was flown to India. There I learned how to fly Russian MIG-21s being upgraded by his company. I became a test pilot for the company. While I was test flighting one of the new MIGs I became involved in a dog fight with two fighters from Pakistan. The modern upgrades and increased performance of the new MIG helped me to shoot them out of the sky. India signed a contract with the company to upgrade 100 MIG-21s for their air force. Later he had offered me a place in the mission he masterminded to eliminate important Cuban leaders, allowing Cuba to end years of Communist oppression. He moved his avionics factory headquarters from Israel to Cuba when the island nation began the transformation into the economic center of the Caribbean. After the government changed I was offered the rank of Colonel in the new Cuban Air Force along with maintaining my contract with Antonio's company as a test pilot flying updated aircraft his company modernizes.

"Boner, wonderful to see you again," Antonio said grabbing his hand.

"Thank you sir, "Boner replied.

"Consuelo drinks on the patio please," I called out as we walked to the patio. We found our chairs, Carlo his giant bodyguard preferring to stand. Consuelo appeared with a tray of drinks for everyone.

Again the gate buzzer rang, and Anna's voice came over the speaker. Consuelo went to the door to greet her and led her out to the patio with us. We all stood as she came out and took a seat next to Boner. He was admiring her low cut green dress that went well with her red hair.

"So Boner, how has the US Navy been treating you?" Antonio asked him.

"Oh I dunno Antonio, I love being a Top Gun instructor, but with the new cutbacks, it's been a real headache. The new administration is gutting the military and shifting a lot of the military's operating funds to domestic programs".

"Ah yes, the American political pendulum has swung to the liberal side again" he observed.

"I'm afraid so. It has made me rethink my commission,"

"Is that so?" Antonio's demeanor suddenly changed as he stared at Boner.

"He was wondering if there might be a position here for an ex Navy Top Gun flight instructor" I threw in taking a drink of my green label beer.

"Coincidentally I have been planning to hire a test pilot for our new A-4 upgrade program I'm starting. The Mexican Air Force has signed a contract with us to upgrade their fleet of A-4 Sky hawks. Since you have experience flying A-4s as a Top Gun Instructor there may be a position in the company for you".

"I think I would enjoy that." Boner told him smiling.

"Yes well things seem to be heating up in Mexico, so I hope to be doing a lot of business there."

"Grey was telling me earlier about the increase in guerrilla groups forming there".

"I'm afraid it is going to become a very serious problem in the next year. With the assassination of the progressive president in Guatemala, their military stepped in to keep control of the country. They have control of the urban areas, but strong rebel forces control the rural areas. When this government here changed over to a freer system, the frustrated Communists left and joined the growing rebel forces in Guatemala. There is a rebel group in the Chiapa province of Mexico who have aligned themselves with the Guatemalan rebels as well," Antonio explained.

"Grey said something about the Chinese aiding these rebels?" Boner asked.

"That's correct. According to our intelligence reports, China is planning to move on Taiwan soon, and they are looking for a way to tie up any U.S. forces that might be used to aid Taiwan's military. What better way to do this than to build a strong Chinese presence in Central America? China plans to help the Communist rebels with funds and arms so they can create a Communist government in Guatemala. Once that has been accomplished, with the help of the Communist rebels in the Chiapa province in Mexico they plan to expand further north".

"A Communist Mexico on the border of the United States would certainly redirect the current administration's concerns," Boner lamented.

"With the new hands off policy of the new administration in Washington, they would be so tied up with a Communist Mexico they might think twice before committing forces half a world away, which would mean dealing with a two front war." I added.

"Especially with a deep water port for the Chinese Navy in Guatemala. China has also completed repairs on the aircraft carrier they purchased from the Russians. Once it is finished the Chinese will have a naval presence off the coast of Guatemala. "Antonio revealed. It brought a silence to the conversation as we all pondered the ramifications of what we were discussing.

"Oh man Antonio, this is going to get very ugly" Boner remarked.

"Cuba is Mexico's ally, I don't see any way we will be able to stay out of it," Antonio told him. "If you are really serious about resigning your commission with your Navy, then yes do come talk with me. I'm positive I'll have a position for you here. How long will you be here?"

"I have a week's leave. I'll be leaving a week from Sunday".

"I'll have a contract drawn up for you to take with you by Monday afternoon. Have Grey bring you to the office and I'll have it for you. I'm afraid we'll need all the experienced pilots we can find once this starts to unravel. Mexico will fight back once they are invaded. Then as you so eloquently said, it truly will get very ugly" Antonio said with a sad voice.

"Dinner is ready," Ali said, walking out from the kitchen. We walked into the dining room looking at the food on the table. Ali and Consuela had created a feast. There were shark and grouper steaks with a salad and wine. Consuelo sat next to Antonio looking at him with a smile. He watched her out of the corner of his eye. Ali and I quietly grinned at each other watching them. Boner was clueless, concentrating on his food. The ocean breeze blew in as the sun fell into the ocean with an explosion of orange light. We talked of lighter things and of the future of Cuba, Antonio's favorite subject. Boner and Anna made small talk. Boner bragged about being a shit hot Top Gun Instructor, trying to impress Anna. She politely pretended to be impressed, while the rest of us quietly watched the exchange with knowing smiles. I wondered who was the hunter and who was the prey was.

Later the three of us sat on the patio after dinner. Drinking wine and looking at the stars as the hushed sound of the waves rolling up on the beach hissed at us.

"It's amazing how different everything sounds at night" Boner observed. The three of us sat there in the darkness smoking cigars and drinking wine.

"It's times like this I wish could be frozen in time," I added. "Good food, good friends, excellent atmosphere. I remember when we were flown to Norfolk after I shot down those two MIG-21s, locked in that dirty cell, waiting for the trial. I thought my life was over."

"Yeah, I remember. It sucked. Worse time of my life," Boner remarked. He too had been locked up, both of us awaiting trial. Boner had been detained as a witness against me. He stuck to my right wing during the entire time I battled against the two Cuban Migs. The Navy considered him an unindicted co-conspirator. In reality Boner was yelling at me the entire time over the radio trying to stop me during the entire fight as he stuck to my wing.

"When I was living in Havana in the seventies, I was arrested and thrown into prison here. It was a filthy existence. There was never enough food. The beatings, the sadistic guards, I swore someday I would get out and escape Cuba. It's what kept me alive all those years," Antonio shared with us. "When I did get out, a group of friends and I sailed a leaky boat at night across the strait to Key West. Everything I did from that moment on, went towards freeing Cuba," he told us, exhaling a cloud of cigar smoke.

"To freedom," I said, raising my glass.

"To freedom," Boner echoed.

"To freedom," Antonio joined in.

Ali, Anna, and Consuela joined us as we talked of happy things, enjoying the warm tropical night. Boner invited Anna for a walk along the beach. Taking off their shoes they walked laughing together under the stars.

CHAPTER THREE

The next morning was Saturday. I didn't have to be on duty until Monday morning. I woke Boner up and we went for a morning run on the beach, then it was another hour in my weight room, followed by a swim in the surf. Ali went to town with Consuela to do some shopping, so we relied on my cooking for breakfast.

"You ready for a tour of the base?" I offered.

"Affirmative on that one," he told me as we walked into the garage.

"Hey I see you finally got your 280-Z down here," he observed as we got in.

"Ayep, I had my father ship her down here about six months ago."

"When did you get THAT thing?" he pointed at my dune buggy next to us in the garage.

"Right after you left last year," I explained as we cruised along the narrow road listening to the Cuban music from the stereo.

Coming into the base I pulled out my Military ID and Boner had to show his green Military ID before we were allowed through the gate. The armed guards wrote down our names in their gate log. I slowly drove along the main road and parked next to the hanger. Once inside the hanger we walked around. I pointed out my personal Mig-21and Boner climbed up the orange ladder into the cockpit.

"I remember the first time I saw you in one of these things, I couldn't believe my eyes," he remarked.

"Yeah, that was a weird experience, seeing you flying next to me in an F-18 while I was flying in a Russian MIG, disguised as a Cuban fighter."

"Well maybe I'll get lucky and I'll be able to be your wing man again."

"If Antonio has anything to say about it, it's as good as done," I assured him. He climbed out and we walked around the fighter, as I pointed out the modifications that Antonio's company had made to the MIG. The modifications included modern avionics, modern on board computers, and a helmet-guided weapons system. Carbon fiber panels covered the exterior further reducing the radar cross section of the fighter, plus greater engine performance that extended the fighter's range. The idea was to rebuild these old fighters into something that could hold its own in an air combat situation with the newest machines. It was more cost effective to modernize an existing fleet of fighters than to purchase new fighters at a higher cost. For some countries it was the only way they could financially afford a modern type air force. The modernized MIG 21s were not what the modern American fighters were, but they could hold their own and made excellent air to air missile launching platforms.

"I'll bet she's a monster to fly," he said.

"She's a beast aright, a lot different than flying the F-18. C'mon, I'll give you a tour of the factory," I offered. We climbed into the Z, and drove to the other side of the base where Antonio had built the huge company complex. I put my right thumb into the receptacle that was part of the security system for employees at the front door. I ran my company ID card through the scanner to gain access. I had to sign Boner in as a visitor and he got a yellow visitor's badge.

Once inside a wave of noise hit our ears. Fighters from different countries were in various stages of dis-assembly inside the huge hanger. Two A-4 Sky hawks, three French Mirage, two Mig-21s, and a Mig-23 were surrounded by techs in their white overalls working on the different fighters. Boner's head was on a swivel as I walked him around the floor. We walked within the two white lines that formed a pathway around the inside of building. Armed guards with automatic weapons dressed in black uniforms patrolled the building. I wore my company ID on my shirt so they would know who I was. Most of them recognized me and nodded as we walked by.

"Man this is amazing, I never dreamed Antonio had anything this big here," Boner said in awe as we walked, his head looking up.

"Yeah, this is the company headquarters, lemme show ya my toy," I told him as we exited the building and walked around the rear of the building.

"Antonio lets me store her back here," I told him as we rounded the corner. His mouth dropped open as the silver Mig-15 came into view.

"This is YOURS?" he asked.

"Oh yeah."

"She fly?" he asked, putting his hand on the polished aluminum.

"Like a bat outta hell, completely restored, fully functional," I told him as he looked at the Cuban flag painted on the tail. I opened the canopy and showed him the modernized cockpit with the electronic multi functional display flight panel.

"I've had her updated, and the canopy has been modified for better visibility."

"The cannons still work?" he asked, squatting down, running his hand over the gun barrels protruding under the front fuselage.

"Sighted in perfectly," I promised him.

"Damn Grey, you gotta let me fly her sometime."

"You bet, I'll check you out in her. You'll love flying her. Although it's almost like letting another man make love to your wife," I explained.

"Man she's a beaut. How did you come across this?"

"When the modernization of the air force began, I found her abandoned and in disrepair. I paid Antonio's techs to strip her down to the airframe and completely rebuild her, adding a few new parts to her. She is a true crotch rocket."

"I've never even seen one of these before. Here you have one of your very own to play with. Man, I'm jealous," he told me.

"Well if you decide to move down here, there's no telling what you can pick up. Once you get established here, I'm sure Antonio will come up with ways for you to make a little extra money on the side," I explained.

"Yeah like you did. I'd LOVE to earn a quarter million dollars," He teased me good naturedly, referring to the money I had earned for my part in the mission that helped Cuba emerge from an oppressive Communist government.

"C'mon, I'll buy you lunch, I know this great place right across from the beach," I offered. We left the base, cruising down the boulevard, Boner tapping his hand on the doorjamb to the stereo. The place we ate was one of several outdoor cafes along the boardwalk. We sat there watching the tourists walk the beach and the locals on their way to who knows where. Almost everyone had cell phones and pagers hanging on their belts. Cell phones had become the newest status symbol in Cuba. Anyone who was anybody had a cell phone. Cell phone towers had sprung up all over the island's highest points. New cell phone companies generating jobs were helping keep the population in contact with each other.

"What ever happened to that base we bombed in Bejucal?" Boner asked between mouthfuls of fiery hot rice.

"The US took it over, it's now a jungle training school for Cuban and US Special Forces," I answered.

"I'll bet the Chinese were pissed about losing it," he grinned.

"The new Cuban Government told them that the days of electronic spying on the US were over, the Chinese packed up and left. I'm sure that's one reason they are trying so hard to help create a Communist government in Guatemala now," I explained.

"They want to replace what they lost when the Communist government here collapsed," he offered.

"Precisely, a lot of people here are very worried about what's going on west of here. We recently arrested three Chinese restaurant workers for spying for the Chinese government. They were caught trying to take photographs inside one of our airbases."

"It just proves how determined the Chinese are about keeping a presence here in this part of the world," I told him.

"I wish our new president would get his head outta his ass and do something to prevent it from happening. The last thing we need is a Communist government in Guatemala who's allied with the damned Chinese." He remarked.

"Well there is an upside here. The Cuban Government signed an amended 100-year lease with the US concerning their base at Guantanamo. Plus we do joint war games here at least twice a year with the US, Britain, Mexico and Chile. British warships dock here twice a year. We have war games with these countries. We fly our MIGs against their fighters; it helps us stay sharp by flying against dissimilar fighters using different tactics." I told him.

"That's a smart way to keep your pilots trained." he admitted.

"Ayep, helps us stay on our toes, and it gives the US another tropical training ground to play in. Both sides benefit from it. It's great having the US as an ally. Economically, things have improved dramatically here. Cruise ships dock here every week, tourists from around the world visit here to spend their money. The four casinos have generated millions for the island. There are six new construction companies from Miami working round the clock here putting up new buildings all over the island. Three new car dealerships from the US have opened offices here. The big three rental agencies have cars to rent for the tourists. Medical care is free for every Cuban resident. Banks from all around the world have opened offices here. There have been at least four movies shot here. The television and radio stations have modernized. It's wonderful to watch the transformation. People are happy here. We've become the economic center for the Caribbean. So if you're really serious about starting a new life here, this is the time to do it. Get in on the ground floor now," I advised.

"Sounds like good advice. I'd love to be making good money and living the good life."

We watched as two liberty boats arrived unloading Sailors from a U.S. Navy Aircraft carrier at anchor offshore. We both looked at each other remembering when we both did the same thing when we were stationed aboard the U.S.S. Grant. We spent the afternoon at an outdoor bar trying to see who could drink frosted schooners of ice cold beer the fastest, the loser paying as the cold beer burned our throats. We reminisced about our days together in the Navy. We staggered out to the beach across the street and sat in the shade of a palm tree. When I had sobered up somewhat, I slowly drove us back to the house.

It took me three times to get the code punched in correctly to get the security gate to swing open.

When Ali and Consuelo got home, they found us swimming in the ocean. She waved at me as the two of us staggered out of the water both buck-naked. She started laughing at us as we tried to pretend we were sober. We made it to the patio and wrapped towels around our waists, sitting at the big round table under the umbrella. Consuela clucked her tongue at us and shook her head as she disappeared into the house.

"Looks like you two had fun today," Ali said, kissing me warmly. I reached out and pulled her onto my lap.

"Down boy," she told me.

"When is dinner?" I called out.

"In a couple of hours, why?" she asked.

"Wanna drive the dune buggy?" I looked at Boner.

"Hell yeah," he said, standing up grabbing his towel.

"Boys and their toys," Ali responded. Ten minutes later with Boner driving, we hit the stretch of beach in front of the house. The rear tires of my Volkswagen powered rail buggy throwing rooster tails of sand behind us as we raced along the edge of the water. It felt great to be able to relieve some of the stress that had been building inside of me for the past few weeks.

We returned to the house, somewhat sober and ready to eat. After dinner on the patio, Ali and I went to bed. Our lovemaking that night left us exhausted in each others arms. There was no nightmare that night. The next morning Boner and I enjoyed one of the many sport-fishing boats for hire. We spent all day on the water.

Monday morning I was in uniform. I kissed Ali as she and Boner got into her jeep for the ride to the company building. Boner had an appointment with Antonio to discuss his future employment as a pilot for the company. My driver arrived on time. Anna greeted me with my usual morning coffee. She told me Raul was on the phone for me.

"Sean, we have a meeting in 15 minutes," he told me.

"I'll be there," I carried my coffee across the road to the other building that housed Raul's office. One of the many perks of being in Cuba was the excellent Cuban coffee grown here. Raul nodded as I entered. We both walked to the conference room where our superior was waiting for us.

General Roberto Rodriguez sat at the head of the table and nodded as we both entered. He was a tall thin veteran fighter pilot, from the old air force, twice decorated for bravery in Angola. He was in his fifties, no longer flying fighters. He had just returned from Mexico, with orders from our superiors to assemble a team of pilots for a joint Mexican Cuban flight exercise. We were to act as an aggressor squadron against the Mexican pilots to help assess their combat readiness. Then diplomatically as possible help up-date their training system.

Sitting there next to Raul drinking my coffee I listened to the plan he shared with us. It called for us to approach the Mexican coast from the south, attacking their air base. Reading between the lines, it didn't take a rocket scientist to understand the motivation behind this exercise. The Mexican government was concerned about a possible threat to their south. They wanted to increase their intercept readiness abilities. Intelligence reports of the Chinese Navy increasing their flight training with their newest carrier prompted the Mexican government to escalate their readiness status. The same information Antonio had given us the night before.

By flying their pilots against us, the Mexican Air Force would receive a higher level of training. This was the first indication that a real shooting war was anticipated involving the Chinese. It was no longer if but when. This information was considered classified and not to be discussed with any unauthorized entities. Raul and I looked at each other reading each others minds. Antonio had known about this for weeks, and had already shared this info with us. I was convinced that he knew about this training exercise before we did.

Raul and I were assigned the task of coordinating the attack plans of our two units. Raul and I had eight pilots each under our commands. That meant 18 MIG-21s from our command would be flying the mission. We were grinning at each other, glad for the chance to get away from behind our desks and get some air combat time in again, even if it was only a training exercise.

The charts on the wall indicated the location of Mexican Air Force base we were to simulate attacks against. We would fly from Cuba to a designated base we were authorized to operate from, and then later simulate aerial attacks against it. The Mexicans were hoping to kill two birds with one stone. They were hoping our mission would sharpen the skills of their fighter pilots as well as sending a message they were ready for any incursion into their air space.

"What's our position going to be if a shooting war does erupt south of us?" I inquired.

"We are to remain neutral, to take no hostile action," The Colonel answered. I inwardly cringed at those words. Raul looked at me and grinned remembering my orders while I was flying Navy F-18s between Florida and Cuba. Boner and I were given these same orders, the same orders that I disobeyed after witnessing two American civilian aircraft shot down by a Cuban MIG-21. The same orders I ignored while pursuing and shooting down that Cuban Mig pilot and his wingman in a fit of rage.

"I wonder if that will be possible," I replied.

"Those orders WILL be followed to the letter, do you understand me?" the General asked glaring at me.

"Yes sir," I answered. I caught Raul shaking his head at me out of the corner of my eye.

"The Mexican government has decided on an upgrade program for their A-4 Sky hawks, along with the upgraded Mig-21 program that is underway," the general continued. I glanced over at Raul, our minds thinking as one again. Antonio again had already informed us of this.

Wisely we both remained silent. We were getting better intelligence and earlier from him than from our superiors. Better we remain silent and not ruffle the feathers of the higher ups by bragging. Besides, there were still several old timers who resented an American being a part of their air force modern or not.

"We'll do our best on this assignment Colonel," Raul told him.

"These orders come down from the top," he told us. Which explained why we had been chosen. Someone up the chain of command decided since Raul and I were veterans of actual air combat, they knew we could deliver. Raul's flying experience in Angola and my flight training from the US Navy made an excellent training combination.

"One week from now your two wings will be flying to Mexico to act as advisers and fly simulated attacks against their fighters and air bases." he went on.

"How long will we be gone?" I asked.

"One month. Then we will rotate another two wings there. We plan to rotate wings for at least the next six months. It will help their pilots and their anti-aircraft crews increase their skill level,"

We walked to the mess hall discussing the upcoming mission. I was grateful that one of the modernization jobs was a gleaming new mess hall here at the base Different types of food was available three times a day. Good food was a morale booster no matter which military you were in. Raul and I chose steak while General Rodriguez chose fish.

"Old habits are hard to break," he explained, eating his fish." The Mexican Air Force is really depending on us to help train their new pilots," he went on. "Ever since the new American president had taken office six months ago, his cutbacks in military spending included the end of training foreign troops. The new President being more concerned with funding his domestic social programs,"

"Since Mexico traditionally has been one of our closest allies, our superiors have decided to fill the vacuum created by the United States military cutbacks. By assisting the Mexicans military modernization program, our superiors hope to stay out of the Communist problems developing west of us. With the recent change of the United States administration, we stand alone," he went on.

As usual I was sitting there with a déjà vu feeling, wondering what I had gotten myself into again. My life was stable now, I had two good jobs, a great wife, a nice house on the beach in a modernized Cuba. I could resign my position with the Cuban Air Force any time I chose, keeping my position as a test pilot for Antonio's company. I had money in the bank, and a few good investments that were finally starting to pay off.

"If Mexico falls to the communists, we could be next," Raul observed out loud.

"Precisely. So it is in our best interest to assist Mexico in any way possible to prevent that from happening,"

"A Communist government in Mexico would refocus U.S. concerns away from Taiwan," I added.

"How did you know about that? That's classified information," the General's eyes burned into mine.

"Just idle gossip," I replied.

"Well you are correct, it would turn US interests away from Taiwan. This new U.S. administration is very concerned with improving the economy in America. Part of this includes less interest in Taiwan and increased interest in low cost Chinese labor," he said. I sat quietly pondering the future we were discussing. It was like being on the beach on a warm sunny day, looking at huge black rapidly approaching storm clouds on the horizon. Once again I was being thrust into world events.

One part of me was glad to be involved in something that would put me back in the air, another part of me was sad because I knew the consequences of a Communist Central America. The future of another country rested partly in my ability as a fighter pilot and my ability to pass on what I knew to others.

"I guess play time's over," I remarked.

"Truly," Raul agreed.

CHAPTER FOUR

That night at dinner Boner shared with us his meeting with Antonio.

"I'll be given an apartment at the complex rent free, free medical, and I'll be test flying shit hot fighters for a living, man it doesn't get any better than that," he said excitement in his voice. We were sitting on the patio drinking beers watching the sun go down.

"When Antonio made his sales pitch to me years ago, I felt like he was throwing me a life preserver," I told him.

"Well hell it sounds like a great way to live,"

"Just be careful, I'm sure he has an ulterior motive up his sleeve concerning hiring you. He sure did with me,"

"We would never have met if he hadn't," Ali said looking at me with a smirk.

"Well I'm too young for the ole ball and chain. I can't wait to come down here and play the field. When I go back I'll set the paperwork in motion. I'm sure I'll stay in the Naval Reserves. Extra money and I'll still get to fly,"

"I wouldn't tell anyone about your new position here, I'm sure it won't interfere with being in the Reserves, but why take any chances. Once you are a citizen here, there isn't much they can do. Long as you make your reserve dates, you should be OK," I warned.

"Yeah sounds like good advice," Consuela brought out the food and we ate under the stars with a warm ocean breeze blowing.

The next four days Raul and I prepared attack plans on the Mexican air base. We were to operate from the newly renovated air base at Tuxtla Gutierrez. The Mexicans had built an Air Wing there of newly upgraded Mig-21s. Very soon the air over that base would be thick with Mig-21s buzzing each other in mock air combat. I looked forward to the chance to pit my skills against the Mexican pilots. The only down side to this would be living without Ali. I would miss her.

Friday our preparations were complete. Each pilot had his personal interests taken care of. The fighters had been gone over with a fine tooth comb. Raul and I had completed our attack plans. Saturday morning I took Boner to the airport for his flight back to the states.

"When I get back from Mexico we can have dinner," I told him. Hopefully by then he would be out of the Navy and a test pilot for the company.

"Won't be long we'll be tearing up the sky together again," he said with a grin.

"Ill be looking forward to that, have a safe trip," I said shaking his hand. I watched him board the yellow 727 that flew several times a week between Miami and Havana. People here had nicknamed it the Havana Banana because of its bright yellow paint scheme. That night Ali and Consuelo cooked a special meal for us. Antonio came to share the feast.

"The Chinese have completed sea trials of their carrier. Their J-11s will be practicing flight ops soon." he revealed.

"Won't be long now," I replied as we sat out on the patio looking at the stars. "I can't believe the United States is going to sit back and do nothing about this. It's crazy. Doesn't the administration realize what will happen if China gets a foothold in Central America?"

"They didn't believe their own intelligence reports about Iraq until Kuwait was invaded," he pointed out.

"How solid is this information?"

"It's been confirmed, by three different sources. The Americans also have good intelligence on the situation there. Problem is the President is trying diplomacy to deal with it,"

"They talk while China prepares for war, when man does not study history he is doomed to repeat it," I remarked taking a sip of my beer." Once the Chinese control Central America, they can shut down the Panama Canal, or at least control who uses it. That would have a major impact on the American economy. You'd think they would understand that,"

"Well the Chinese are their economic partners. They wouldn't do that," Antonio said with disgust in his voice.

"That's what Stalin thought right up to the day the Nazis invaded Russia,"

"Well there are plans in the works to deal with that situation if it comes down to that," He revealed.

"Why doesn't that surprise me," I said with a smirk.

"Are you two still trying to save the world again?" Ali asked as she came out onto the patio.

"Somebody has to" Antonio answered. "Is your group ready for the training operation in Mexico?"

"Yes, it's all complete. I'm sure we'll give them a run for their money,"

"You do realize how critical this is for them," It wasn't a question.

"Absolutely. If the Chinese ever decide to move against them, we want them flying into a meat grinder,"

"The harder you push them the better it will be for them in the long run,"

"You're preaching to the choir Antonio, I know the possible future of Cuba if China gets a grip on Central America,"

"We can't allow that to happen to Cuba again," He said with a tight voice. He did not want Cuba returning to a Communist island, and he would lose millions he had invested in his company.

"We train like we fight Antonio, as if our lives depend on it, because it does, that was drummed into our heads in flight school back in the states. I train my pilots the same way. I don't cut any corners. I push them hard. I pat em on the back when they do well. Then kick em in the ass when they screw up,"

"I know, I've read the reports on how you train your pilots," he revealed. That came to no big surprise to me. There wasn't much that happened on this island nation he didn't know about.

"I guess I'm just worried about our future. I never want to see Cuba return to the nightmare it was under the communist government,"

"We'll do our job Antonio, don't worry," I assured him." What's the level of technology the Chinese have compared to what the Mexicans have?" I asked wanting to change the subject.

"Their J-11 is the Chinese version of the Russian SU-27,"

"That good?" He had my attention. I knew all the details concerning the capabilities of the Russian SU-27 fighter.

"Yes, now you can understand why I'm worried. What we are supplying to the Mexicans is very good, but the Chinese J-11 is tactically superior. They will have their hands full if it ever comes to a war." He explained. I nodded quietly, knowing how sophisticated the J-11s were. They were better than the Mig-29 in many ways. The Chinese J-11 was the home grown version of the Russian SU-27, which was an extremely dangerous fighter in its own right.

"It'll take em time to work all the bugs out of the system," I told him." It's not an easy feat to fly off a carrier. I'm sure their naval J-11s have been modified to land on their carrier, stronger landing gear, beefed up airframe, folding wings, among other things," I said.

"The longer it takes them to perfect their naval fighters, the better prepared they will be when they decide to use them. Our intelligence sources tell us the Chinese are preparing for war. It's only a matter of time Sean. It's a race against time for us," He explained in a tense voice." When the time comes, we better be ready, Cuba's future depends on that,"

"You really believe that the Chinese will try to make a move against us?" I asked sitting up.

"Yes, I've heard many things from my friends in Singapore. The Chinese plan is to help the rebels in Guatemala gain control of that country, then use it as a spring board to attack Mexico, then Cuba next. They plan to secure a presence in Central America, which they hope will tie up American assets here, then they can attack Taiwan at their leisure," He told me repeating what he had explained earlier. I knew his information could be depended on. His sources of information came from his many contacts around the world. It was a necessity for him to know what was happening behind the scenes of different countries. It helped him stay in business. Ali looked at us with sad eyes, understanding the danger of the situation. She also knew as I did, that if it came to a shooting war, I'd be part of it.

"We'll just have to prepare a few unexpected surprises for them," I said with a grin, hoping to lighten the mood.

CHAPTER FIVE

Monday morning my driver arrived early. Ali rode with me to the base to see me off.

"I miss you already," I told her. She leaned against me in the back of the Humvee as we rolled along.

"I'll miss you to Hon," she replied. The guards at the gate verified who we were, and then we were rolling out to the hanger.18 Mig-21s were gleaming under the Cuban sun. Maintenance had gone over every bird to make sure they were ready for the flight to Mexico. My driver carried my bags behind us as I looked at the Cuban flags on the tails of the birds. I remembered when seeing that on the tail of a Mig-21 gave me chills down my spine. Now it was the flag I flew under, the flag of a country I had sworn to protect when I accepted the rank of colonel.

"Kinda reminds me of India, you being here, me flying off again," I told her.

"We do live an unusual life," she agreed.

"You keep Antonio in line now ya here?" I teased her.

"Don't go falling for any Mexican senoritas while you're over there," She told me half joking. Raul was waving at us. Like me he was in his flight suit.

"I'll be back soon," I told her, kissing her goodbye. I watched as the Humvee drove away in the morning sun. Raul and I walked into the pilot's ready room. Inside the 16 other pilots that made up our two squadrons were sitting in the briefing room, cutting up as usual. They stood up to attention as we entered.

"Take seats," Raul called out. Even though we were the same rank, he was my superior. He began the pref light briefing, reviewing the information everyone had been studying all week. Once the briefing was completed, Raul and I walked to the ready room, got into our inflatable G-suits, grabbed our

29

helmets and then walked out to the flight line. I walked to my Mig-21, doing the external inspection, taking my time. The tires looked in good shape, the brake lines weren't leaking, the intake was clear of any obstructions. I walked around running my hand over the surface of the fighter, like running my hand over the skin of a beautiful woman. I ducked underneath and looked at the belly tank, it wasn't leaking. I tried to move it with my hands it was secured. I slowly ran my hand over the surface of the Copperhead missiles under the wing. Below the fuselage the old cannon had been replaced with a modern Gatling gun. Anytime we flew outside of the Island we always flew armed.

The ground tech handed me the clipboard and I signed my name accepting the fighter as flight ready. I climbed up the orange metal ladder to the cockpit, and settled in. I fastened my knee board around my thigh and the ground tech helped me strap in. Oxygen line, G-suit pressure line, the cable that ran to the electronic helmet that displayed multiple information images on the inside visor. I moved the multi-function stick side-to-side and front to back making sure it was free and clear. I hooked the tiny cables to the back of my flight boots that were attached to the front of the ejection seat. I pulled on the multi-function helmet moved it around until it felt right. The ground tech pulled the safety switches arming the ejection seat, holding them up for me to see.

I gave him thumbs up and he climbed down removing the ladder. I hit the power switches and watched the instrument panel come to life. The two square electronic displays came up. Engine start switch came next, fuel pump toggle was up, hydraulic pressure booster was on, and parking brake was set.

Double-checking the throttle was in the idle position; I spun my finger in a small circle so the ground tech was warned I was starting the engine, and mashed the engine start button. The turbine on the big Turmansky jet engine started to whine as it slowly started to spool up. The fighter began to vibrate from the engine as the fighter came alive around me. I wondered whether I was becoming part of the fighter or the fighter was becoming a part of me.

The engine instruments all showed normal, engine temp was acceptable, generator switch was on, ADF and marker were on. I punched the coordinates into the nav computer telling the fighter where we were. GPS was functioning normally. The fuel tanks and oxygen gauges both showed full, altimeter was set at the proper altitude, I looked at the gyro and verified it was properly aligned. The multi function display verified there were four live Copperhead missiles hanging off our wings. There were 500 rounds of ammo for the cannon. We never flew outside the country without being able to defend ourselves.

The ground tech verified all my flight surfaces were moving correctly as I moved the stick and the rudder back and forth. I set the flaps at 24 degrees, and the elevator and aileron trim to neutral. The ground tech disconnected the shoreline from the side of the fighter. I held up both hands so he could see I wasn't touching any switches as he removed the red-tagged pins from my missiles arming the warheads. I closed the canopy and hit the lock with my left hand. I connected my oxygen mask, calling the tower getting clearance for takeoff. I looked over and the canopies of the other fighters were closed. One by one over my headphones the other fighters were calling the tower. I released the brake and pulled onto the ramp leading to the runway waiting my turn to takeoff. I was number three in line. My turn came and I taxied to the end of the runway. I locked brakes, did a quick cockpit check. All the indicator lights were green.

When I was satisfied, I sat back, right hand on the stick, left hand on the oval shaped throttle moving it forward. I let off the brakes, put afterburner on maximum, and was thrown back into the seat as the fighter roared down the runway. Rotation came at 230 kilometers an hour. I pulled back on the stick and I was airborne, angled up aiming at the sky. I moved the gear lever and felt the gear come up and lock with a thunk. The gear lights showed green, verifying they were up and locked. I pulled in the flaps, and adjusted my engine speed for maximum fuel performance.

I joined up with my wing man, at 32,000 feet we turned west. I engaged autopilot then rechecked the flight map on my knee pad. There were 18 Mig-21s flying in formation, two by two heading west towards Mexico. We were flying two groups of nine MIG-21s each in a vee formation. I looked over my left shoulder at the green and blue Mig flying slightly behind me. Flying at 32,000 feet the blue green Gulf below us looked flat. It felt great to be flying. The powerful Turmansky engine was putting out over 20,000 pounds of thrust, there was clear blue sky above us and the light blue green ocean below. It was a thrill to be away from a desk again. The information displayed on the inside of my helmet visor was telling me the Mig was functioning perfectly. Our helmets designed in Israel, had green images on the inside of the visor. It was identical to the heads up display in the clear lens atop the instrument panel. This design allowed us to look away from the instrument panel, and still see fuel levels, compass heading, speed, altitude, range and other important information. When I looked down at the MFDs the numerical images on the inside of my helmet visor vanished so I could read the information being projected on the two screens.

Raul was leading his wing; I was leading mine on the roughly 900-mile flight to the modern Mexican Air base at Tuxtla Gutierrez. I heard Raul call their tower when we were halfway there, alerting them of our ETA. Two Cuban transports had already landed with our techs and equipment. Here I was a former US Navy fighter pilot, who learned how to fly a Russian MIG-21 in India, who had been instrumental in eliminating the Communist Government of Cuba, now a Colonel in the Cuban Air force, flying a modernized Russian Mig-21 to help train Mexican fighter pilots. What a crazy way to earn a living.

"Feet dry," I heard Raul's voice in my headphones as we approached the Mexican coast. I could see several tiny white specs that were boats, and their small wakes behind them. Checking the flight map on my knee board, we were right on course and on time. As the blue green waters of the gulf drifted to our rear, I could see mountains and green jungle below us.

"I wouldn't want to bail out over that," my wing man told me over the radio.

"Let's hope we never have to," I replied through my oxygen mask mic. I couldn't imagine surviving in that tropical forest below.

Minutes before the base came into view, Raul again called the airbase and I could hear the ground controller in the tower give us landing clearance. He spoke in English, the international language of aviation.

I was thankful my Spanish had improved considerably in the past two years. People who did not know me took me for a Cuban with my tanned skin and my wider knowledge of Spanish. It would come in handy in Mexico.

I could see the runway of the base come into view as we crossed over the mountains of Tuxtla Gutierrez. Raul's flight was ahead of mine and began their approach.

"By the numbers," I heard his command to his flight as they began to land. I kept my flight circling as his Migs landed.

"Make me proud gentleman," I called out over the radio to the pilots as I made our turn to descend.

I was on final, moved the lever and heard my gear come down with a whine. Gear lights showed green, all three were down and locked. I adjusted the flaps, moved the throttle with my left hand to 80 per cent. Watching my airspeed at 450 kilometers an hour. At a thousand feet out I adjusted flaps again, lined up perfectly with the center of the runway, and flared just before touching down. When all three wheels touched down I hit the brakes and deployed the air brakes then drag chute as I gradually began slowing down. I looked to my left where Raul's Migs were lining up in one row. A white jeep came out onto the ramp with a big red FOLLOW ME sign on its rear. I pulled up behind him and followed him, steering the nose of the Mig towards the other Migs. I watched a ground tech with white orange overalls and two long red sticks pointing to my parking slot. I slowly turned the nose watching him. He kept moving the sticks one over each shoulder as I followed him. He then used his sticks to make an X and I tapped the brakes stopping the Mig. He used one of the red sticks to make a slashing motion across his throat and I shut my engine down. I locked my brakes, secured the stick in place, and shut down the panel. I used my left hand and unlocked the canopy as a ground tech moved a white metal ladder to the left side of the fighter and opened my canopy. I disconnected my lines and harness. He reached over putting the safety pins into my ejection seat, and then climbed down. I slowly slipped off my helmet. I took my time getting out, putting my sunglasses on when I stood on the tarmac.

I stood watching the rest of the Migs land one by one. Raul and I had both decided not to make a dramatic fly over before landing here. Latin machismo being what it was we didn't want to offend anyone. We were here to assist their pilots, not show them up. We wanted to put our best foot forward, ease into the situation. I could see the others had gathered in front of the hanger. Raul was talking with a Mexican officer in uniform. When all the Migs had landed, we stood in formation inside the hanger to listen to a welcome speech and the sounds of the Mexican Air Force band butcher the Cuban national anthem. Afterward we were shown to our quarters. Since Raul and I were commanders we would bunk together. Our room had two beds, a modern bathroom, a desk with chair, and two large lockers and boasted a color TV set. The walls smelled of fresh paint. The other pilots were assigned quarters with four bunks to a room. After we had stowed our gear, we were taken on a tour of the base. The fact this was a newly constructed base was everywhere. I saw new buildings, green lawns, and fresh paint on the asphalt. All the hangers were new. This was a modern base. The Mexican flag flying in front of the main building that was surrounded by heavy-duty chain fencing with razor wire on top, and guard shacks at each gate with uniformed guards with automatic weapons and guard dogs. Other than the fact that we were in Mexico, it looked like any US Air Force Base in the states. Raul and I exchanged glances in the back seat of the jeep as we were driven around. We had the same thought; the Mexicans were serious about the security of this area of their country.

We pulled up in front of a hanger and were guided through the rear doors. Inside ground techs were working on a Mexican Mig-21. Outside on the other side of the hanger, were 25 Mig-21s lined up wearing the Mexican flag on their tails. Antonio's company had been very busy indeed. This was where the birds that I had been flight-testing for the company the past two years had gone.

"I'm impressed," I said quietly to Raul. He nodded his head in agreement, as the Mexican Colonel was talking in rapid fire Spanish.

He was explaining that a briefing had been scheduled in the auditorium tomorrow. There we would meet the Mexican pilots we were to help train. Their pilots were proficient in flying their Migs but had only received the basics of air combat. It would be our job to sharpen their skills as well as fly mock air attacks against this base. It was a mission I was looking forward to.

That evening in the mess hall, we sat with our pilots eating, watching the Mexican pilots. Their boots were polished, their hair was cut military, and their uniforms were new.

"They look professional," I remarked to Raul.

"True, but can they fly?" He replied.

After eating I walked to the flight line in front of the hanger we had been allowed to use for our aircraft maintenance. Inside it was bright and our Cuban ground techs that had flown here earlier were unpacking their equipment and setting up their workstations. I walked back to our quarters, inside Raul was unpacking. Our quarters were typical military, clean, modern, two beds with two large metal lockers and a desk with a chair. The TV was on; it looked like some type of Mexican game show was being played.

"Background noise," He explained.

"This is going to be interesting," I told him sitting down on my bed.

"I just hope they will be ready when the time comes. Lord knows it won't be easy for them,"

"The Chinese will be well trained, and ruthless." I remarked.

"We have to push these guys hard, so they will be ready. Maybe not right away, but when we are done, they need to be the best there is here," He said.

"We'll make it happen," I told him." They are an important part of what stands between us and a Chinese Communist Cuba,"

"I have a feeling that once it starts we'll all be involved in it, regardless of what the brass are telling us now," he lamented.

"I've had the same feeling myself ever since this started, its crazy"

"When is war ever sane Sean?" He said closing his locker. I nodded sadly not having a reply. I peeled off my sweaty flight suit and took a long shower. Standing under the water I felt depressed. Knowing what was coming to this part of the world, it was frustrating not having the power to do anything to stop it. It deepened my resolve to do my part no matter what the outcome. It took a long time to fall asleep on the new bed. I missed holding Ali. Finally I drifted off.

After a light breakfast the next morning we gathered in the auditorium that still smelled of fresh paint. Raul and I stood on the raised stage and introduced ourselves and he gave a short simple speech. As I looked down at the young eager faces, I couldn't help wonder how many of them would not be coming back once the war started.

Using a slide projector Raul and I verbally explained the basics of air combat using slides we had prepared in Cuba. One of our pilots handed out instruction books we had brought with us. The information was similar to what they already knew. I passed out information booklets that explained the basics of an air attack on their base. Raul and I spent the morning discussing this subject. We knew their senior flight officers had already gone over the information prior to our arrival. When the class was finished I stood in front of them.

"This afternoon there will be a mock attack against your base here," I explained to them." You may want to prepare and plan to deal with this attack. I suggest you plan well gentlemen," I warned them.

I left the stage and we went to eat at the mess hall.

The atmosphere in the ranks was one of excitement and anticipation. The Mexican pilots were full of optimistic fantasies of how they were going to successfully wipe us from the sky. Raul and I just looked at each other as we ate a light lunch.

We gathered in our ready room after eating, getting into our suits and reviewing our attack plans with our pilots. We planned to keep it simple, to give the base anti-aircraft gunners and missile crews a chance to get a feel for what it would be like. As Raul and I were going over the plan with our pilots we could hear the Mexican Migs taking off.

"Lambs to the slaughter," One of my lieutenants remarked.

"Don't underestimate them," I cautioned. He just gave me a grin. I just shook my head at Raul, He just smiled. We filed out and climbed up into our cockpits. One by one we started up our engines, closing our canopies. I knew their tower would be giving the Mexican pilots updates on our position using their ground radar once we were in the air. Our plan was to use this against them. Raul's flight would fly high cover; my flight would attack the airfield. Raul's wing would attack any Mexican Migs that attempted to intercept my wing.

I lined up on the runway, released the brakes and rocketed into the air. Once all of my pilots were in the air we circled once and headed east. Marco joined up on my right wing, his MIG at my 4 o'clock. Raul took his wing north. We didn't use our radios, knowing the tower would be monitoring our frequency, ready to transmit any of our transmissions to their pilots. I lifted my left wing and turned to the south, Marco was right behind me. The rest of the flight following. We reached our mark and the flight split. My four fighters headed west and the other five turning north. The plan was for us to hit the base in two waves from two different directions. My flight would hit first from the southwest crossing over the base heading northeast, five seconds later the second flight would attack from the southeast and cross over heading northwest. Raul would be flying at a higher altitude over us, ready to dive on any unsuspecting Mexican Migs hoping to catch us in their sights.

Raul had split his two flights up to circle east and west of the base at a higher altitude keeping the tower's radar screens busy and to get the anti-aircraft gunners aiming in the wrong direction, thus missing us as we attacked. On paper it seemed to be a simple plan, but in reality it relied on split second timing.

I turned and then dove to the deck my left hand moving the throttle to military power. We were flying at 50 feet, staying below their radar sweeps. My compass showed my heading as northeast. We had shut down our radar to avoid giving the tower anything to receive. We didn't want to give the tower a chance to pick up our radar giving away our direction of attack. The jungle was flashing below me in a green blur as I approached the base. I came in over the base making my turn to avoid the tower blasting past it. Marco was glued to my 4 o'clock as we screamed over the runway and back over the jungle. Right behind us the other two MIGs roared past the tower behind us. I turned right and looked over my shoulder to see the other Migs make their run over the runway flying left of the tower, coming from the southeast. My RWR was going off in my headphones telling me the base radar was trying to track us, but I was hoping we had hit them too low and too fast for them to get a lock on us. I turned and led my flight away from the base, to regroup with Raul's flight.

"Tiger two Tiger one," I called out over our frequency.

"Tiger one, go," I heard his voice reply.

"Mission complete, ready to recover," I told him.

"Acknowledged, regroup," He ordered. I came up to 5000 feet and circled waiting for his flight to join us. It wasn't long before his flight joined up with ours and we turned to land.

"Tower this is Tiger flight requesting landing clearance," I heard Raul's voice over the radio.

"Tiger flight is clear to land runway 12 east," Came the reply. I could almost swear I heard the tower operator grinding his teeth. I grinned under my oxygen mask as we began to line up for landing. One by one we came in, landing and taxiing to our holding area. We lined our fighters up in perfect alignment. We waited until all our fighters were in perfect position, and then we opened our canopies all at once as we shut down our engines. I looked over my shoulder watching the Mexican Migs landing, as I climbed out of the cockpit. The other pilots of my wing were backslapping each other and grinning. I felt proud of my pilots; they had followed the plan, right to the second. Back in our ready room as we were taking off our gear it was very loud. I didn't say anything, wanting them to enjoy the moment.

I located Raul in the back.

"They never saw you coming. Their tower radar picked up our flights, their Migs split coming up at us, and we circled around and got their six. It was great," he said with a big grin.

"It was a great plan wasn't it," I grinned back." Well, we better go debrief them,"

"Yes, let's not appear too smug, we want to teach them a lesson not take all their steam away," He told me as we walked to the auditorium. As we entered, there were two Mexican Colonels talking in low tones near the front. Their pilots were sitting, very quiet, with long faces.

"If looks could kill," Raul whispered as we looked at the faces of the pilots. We had just made them look ineffective in front of their superiors; in front of the whole base. I knew they had been swaggering around the base full of Latin machismo. There was none of that here now. The two colonels talked with us, reviewing the attack. Their checklists revealed the base had been totally destroyed; their side lost ten Migs, with four damaged. We had lost one with one damaged.

Their missile launchers never got a lock on us, so they could only launch after we had made our attacks. Their anti-aircraft gunners had been facing the wrong way, getting info from the tower on where Raul's flight was, instead of detecting us approaching their base. All in all it was a humiliating experience for their team. When the two colonels finished, they walked out the door leaving us with the Mexican pilots.

"Defeat is a bitter experience," Raul began talking to the pilots." The trick is to learn from it and not allow it to happen again. This is an example of what can happen here if an experienced enemy ever attacks you. This is why we are here, to help you prevent this from happening in a real life scenario. I know you are all good pilots; otherwise you wouldn't be sitting here in this room. Our job is to make you better pilots. Tomorrow we will do this again. In time after more training, you will be able to not only successfully defend your base, but shoot down several of the enemy as well. That is all," He finished.

It was a totally different atmosphere in the mess hall that night. There was a chill in the air between our side of the room and the Mexican pilots. I hated their pilots feeling so low, but I knew it was necessary. We had done this on purpose as a way to break through their Latin machismo. We needed to get their attention. Better they get their pride hurt than lose their lives and the lives of the people on their base that depended on them when the balloon really went up. The trick now was to let them know when they acted correctly as well as when they made mistakes.

We had to help build them back up one step at a time. That night before turning in I wrote a quick letter to Ali, turned out the desk lamp and went to sleep.

CHAPTER SIX

Next morning after our calisthenics and morning chow, Raul and I with our pilots gathered in the ready room to review the day's attack plan on the base. I dropped my pen onto the floor and reached over to pick it up. Looking under the table we were using I saw a tiny black box. I climbed down and looked at it. It was a tiny mic, attached to the wood. I grinned to myself as I stood up. It seemed the Mexican pilots had decided to employ clandestine intelligence gathering methods to intercept our attack plans.

Before leaving Cuba Raul and I had drawn up several different attack scenarios. I knew that the attack plan he was discussing now could easily be changed. I waited until he had finished speaking and made a chopping motion across my throat. To a pilot that meant engine shutdown. Raul nodded with a strange look on his face. I kneeled down and pointed to the mic under the table. At first he had an angry scowl on his face, but then I saw the smile creep across his face watching him come to the same conclusion I had. He nodded his head with a grin. We knew we were going to slam them again today, with their help even.

We walked out into the bright morning sunshine with evil grins. Raul gathered everyone into a circle away from our fighters and more importantly out of hearing range of their ground techs. He outlined a new attack plan for us. It would be dangerous for us, but it was guaranteed to work. When he finished talking we were backslapping each other with smiles and grins at the prospect of surprising them with our new plan.

I had a big grin on my face during my external pref light walk around. I climbed up into the cockpit and got settled in. When I was strapped in secure, I hit the power switch watching the instrument panel come alive. The ground tech pulled out the ejection seat safeties and climbed down. I spun my finger in a circle warning him of my start up. I hit the start switch and the big engine started to come to life. The whine was increasing to a thunder that shook the fighter. I loved the initial start up of the engine. It reminded me every time how much power I was sitting on.

I closed my canopy and locked it in place with me left hand. I punched in the coordinates into my nav computer telling the fighter where we were. Fuel was full; hydraulic pressure was good, I moved the stick back and forth, then my feet on the pedals verified the rudder was clear. The chronometer showed the correct time, fuel boost pressure gauge was at 100 percent. I called the tower testing my radio. Their reply was crisp.

Raul's voice came over the headphones to all of us. We were ready.

I let out the brakes and slowly taxied in line with the other Migs on our way to the end of the runway. I was in a giddy mood, knowing we were going to beat them at their own game again. At the beginning of our first attack of their base I had a sad feeling inside, knowing we would catch them off guard and what it would do to their egos. Today was something different. I had no sympathy for them now. If they had never tried to eavesdrop on our plans with their mic, I would have given them a 50 50 chance against us, but today I felt no mercy for them. They had tried to change the rules of the game, and luckily for us I had spotted their mic. Now that the game was up, it was their own fault for the upcoming successful attack of their base a second day in a row. I'm sure the rest of our pilots were feeling the same way, smiling behind their oxygen masks.

My turn came and I sat at the end of the runway, locked my brakes and double-checked everything.

"Rolling," I called out to the tower in my mask, let out the brakes, moved the throttle forward with my left hand and hit the afterburner. I was slammed back into my seat as I rocketed down the runway. The front gear came off the tarmac and the wings lifted me into the air. I raised the gear, they locked into place then I raised flaps and started my turn to link up with my wing man Marco. When we slid into the groove I looked over and saw him giving my thumbs up. I returned it nodding my head up and down. I could hear him chuckling over the radio. I just shook my head side to side.

According to Raul's change in the attack plan, there would not be two separate flights today like there was the day before. Instead everyone would be attacking the base; there would be no overhead flight to protect us as we hit them. Raul led us north of the base, and then we came down to fifty feet and flew south. I knew their team would be at a higher altitude looking for us and expecting us to attack from a higher altitude, as our original plan had called for. Instead today would be completely different. There was a mountain range north of the base. It had several deep canyons and narrow walls inside it. We would use this to our advantage, as they would not anticipate anyone in their right minds to use the twisting and turning of the mountain range to hit the base. It was an incredibly dangerous thing to do. Raul and I had enough faith in our pilots that we knew they could pull it off.

With a waggle of his wings we followed him into the narrow canyons. One by one we threaded the needle, turning our fighters almost completely sideways to navigate the canyon openings. I looked up through the top of my canopy at the canyon walls rushing past me, knowing one wrong move would change a highly sophisticated deadly fighter into a smear on the rock walls. I loved it. The adrenalin rush was incredible.

We flew out of the mountain range like a flock of hungry eagles looking for prey. One by one we came screaming down on the runway, some crossing over the missile launchers, others hitting the four barreled GSU gunners. The rest of us hit their hangers, their headquarters, even the mess hall. Lastly came the runs over the tarmac, simulating bombing runs destroying the long runway.

"Free to engage," I heard Raul's voice over my headphones. I turned on my radar and armed my electronic missiles. Suddenly the sky was alive with Cuban Migs attacking Mexican Migs. Marco stayed with me as I climbed under a target. I aimed at his fuselage with my helmet moving the green little box inside the larger box in my helmet visor. When I got good tones I squeezed the stick button launching an electronic missile at the underside of a Mexican Mig. Then I lifted my left wing in search of another target. I kept turning and burning not wanting to give one of their pilots an easy target.

I heard the RWR tone, there was a Mexican MIG locking onto my fighter with his missile radar. I kicked left rudder and moved the stick, hitting afterburner and climbed like a rocket hoping to ruin his lock on. Then I inverted pulling the stick into my stomach I completed the loop feeling my G-suit inflate on the way down. My head was on a swivel hoping to get a visual. With a quick glance over my right shoulder to see Marco there,

I looked down and caught site of two Mexican Migs that were a second slower than I was. Getting a good lock on the leader I squeezed the stick again, watching them split, hoping to confuse me. I knew I had a good lock on the leader, the computer simulated a missile launch, which meant I had electronically shot him out of the sky.

"Take him," I called over to Marco. He accelerated forward, I could see his orange tail as he engaged his afterburner, going after my target's wing man. I pulled in on his left wing following him; taking a position at his 8 o'clock I looked over my shoulder then double checked the radar screen to make sure we were clear to the rear, while Marco concentrated on his kill. Even though this was just an exercise, my heart was pounding and my adrenalin was dumping into my system by the gallon. It was what a fighter pilot lived for. Close air combat against another fighter pilot, our skills against theirs, and our technology against theirs.

Marco's target pulled into a climb with Marco right on his tail. He wasn't going to let him get away. I stayed right on his wing. When Marco pulled away, I knew he had taken his shot at the other Mig.

"Tiger flight join up," I heard Raul's voice again. We climbed up to 22,000 feet over the base. Raul requested landing clearance from the tower and we lined up for landing. I could hear the frustration in the controller's voice when he replied. I had to smile at that. When my came, I lined up with the runway, adjusted flaps, and lowered my gear. All three indicator lights showed green, I adjusted the throttle and slid her down as smooth as silk, holding her tightly, just barely touching the tires down. I hit the brakes and released my drag chute slowing the fighter. I knew people on the base were watching us, I wanted to perform as perfect a landing as I could. It would be like the frosting on a cake.

I taxied to our holding area and lined up next to the other fighters. I heard Raul click his mic three times as a signal after we had stopped and locked brakes. Every one of us shut down our engines and opened our canopies at the same time. It was precision. It was sending a message saying 'Hey look at us, we're hot shit'. I loosened my helmet and slowly pried it off my sweaty head. I looked over at Marco and could see him grinning. I grinned back. Yeah, this was a great feeling.

Our ground techs were moving the orange ladders against the sides of our fighters one at a time. I disconnected myself from my fighter and climbed out. On the ground we were slapping each other on the back and whooping it up. We watched as the Mexican Migs started to land.

"Poor bastards," Marco remarked.

"Better them than us," I replied. I joined up with Raul, who had a huge grin on his face.

"Almost like ole times aye?" he asked quietly to me.

We walked into our ready room and took off our equipment. The guys were loud and in a happy mood. I didn't do a thing to diminish their enthusiasm. They had done well and deserved to let off steam. I followed Raul into the auditorium and again the same two Colonels were there with the observer's results. This time their anger was evident. They didn't try to hide it. I didn't care and I was sure Raul felt the same way. The report showed the base was completely destroyed; none of the missile launchers had a chance to fire at us let alone lock on. The runway was cratered and would be out of action for at least three days, almost every building had been destroyed, seven of the eight missile launchers had been destroyed and all six of the ZSU anti-aircraft guns had been destroyed. When the observer had finished talking the two Mexican colonels stood up without a word and walked out slamming the door behind them, the sound echoing throughout the auditorium. I looked over at the Mexican pilots seeing disgust and defeat on their faces. Some had angry hatred in their eyes looking at us. I knew something had to be done.

"Tomorrow we will start training flights," Raul said to the Mexican pilots as he stood up.

"We'll have classroom time in the mornings and flight time each afternoon. Each one of you will be flying on the wing of one of our pilots. You men might have had a 50 50 chance against us today except for one thing," He said as he pulled out the little black mic from his flight suit. "We found this under our table this morning, so we used it against you," I saw several heads look down at the floor in defeat.

"Although I must commend you on your ingenuity, unfortunately it backfired on you. Nice try gentlemen. Remember, this has only been an exercise, part of your training. Imagine how many dead bodies would be lying out there right now if this had been the real thing. You're superiors know you are good pilots. Otherwise as I've already said before you wouldn't be here. Please don't let their reaction to what happened today diminish your own self worth. We need to sit down with them and go over their base defense plans to help improve this base's survivability during an enemy attack. Thank you for your efforts today gentlemen. Please understand that in time all of you will become skilled heart breakers and life takers," he finished smiling at them. He walked over and lifted the phone making a call.

"We have a meeting," He told me. I knew he meant we had a meeting with the base commander and his staff. I gathered up my notes and followed him out. There was a jeep there waiting for us with a driver. He took off with a lurch towards the headquarters building. The jeep stopped in front of the building and we climbed out, the guard at the door saluting us as we entered. Returning the salute we were shown into a conference room where the Base commander was standing talking with officers at the end of a table. We both saluted him, and then stood at attention. He nodded at us.

"Please gentleman sit down," He said holding his hand out at the chairs. Raul and I sat down; I placed my notes in front of me.

"Seems you have done an excellent job of making us all look like fools," he said with undisguised disgust in his voice.

"No sir, not at all. Your men are very good pilots, and it's obvious even to the most casual observer that a lot of effort has been put into this base. There is however a big difference between peace time flying and combat flying. That's the reason you're government in Mexico City has asked us to assist you in sharpening the edge of your pilots here so to speak," Raul said quietly. "It's very difficult if not impossible sometimes to see the weaknesses of any military base when you are responsible for its security. One has to learn to look at each installation from the view of an enemy attacker. That is where we come in. We haven't been the ones to put blood sweat and tears into constructing this modern facility here, so it gives us an unfair advantage in our mission," He finished. I could tell by the expression of the General's face that Raul's words were having their intended effect.

"I have to give someone an A for effort for their creative thinking this morning," He continued taking out the little black mic and laying it on the table.

"If we hadn't been so careful in our security sweep before our briefing this morning we might have been caught unprepared in our attack on your base. It was only at the last minute that we changed our attack strategy to counter your intelligence gathering attempt," The General's face let out a tiny grin. I had to put my hand over my mouth in a casual manner to hide my own smile. At least Raul was giving them something to be proud of.

"If I may sir, I'd like to make a few suggestions to help you improve on the fine job everyone here has done in building your base security systems," he said quietly.

"Please Colonel continue," The General replied.

"Well for one thing, today we were able to exploit the close proximity of the mountain range that borders the north side of the base here by flying very dangerously through the canyons. This prevented your anti-aircraft gunners from hitting us as well as your SAM missile launchers from getting a radar lock on us. Part of the problem lies in the fact that we were able to fly under the radar sweep at fifty feet above the ground," The General's face registered surprise when he heard we had flown so low to the ground. You could have heard a pin drop it was so quiet.

"I'd advise the construction of another radar installation on one of the mountain tops above the base to be able to detect possible intruders at a greater distance. You would also need to install SAM missiles nearby to help protect the site. It would be the first target an enemy would hit in their attack on this base. Next, if an attack is expected you might want to keep two fighters flying a fighter sweep on an outer perimeter of the base as an additional security measure. These building here are well constructed, but you need a bomb hardened control center that can remain operational during an air attack, as well as hardened shelters for your alert fighters. Alert fighters are two or four fighters that are on the ground with their pilots in them ready to take off and engage an approaching enemy in a matter of minutes, as a backup to the two fighters you have up flying a perimeter. You'll also need to train your ground crews to reload and refuel fighters at the same time. True it's a dangerous procedure, but during wartime operations it truly can make the difference between life and death."

"Next you may want to invest in a triple redundant communication system with other bases in this area so that in the case of an attack you can still communicate, ground lines, radio transmission and then possibly satellite communication systems. You can construct a communication grid that will effectively enhance your ability to respond to an aerial attack. Make it expensive for an enemy to attack any of your bases. If one base is destroyed in an attack, then with this comm system you can send out the word so that other bases can put up their birds and knock down the attacking force, which by then will be out of weapons and low on fuel. This makes it easier on your forces to eliminate the attackers and makes the enemy think twice before making another attack when they lose all their birds," Raul stopped taking a long drink from his bottled water.

"Your base fire crews need to be practicing and drilling on possible fires, crash handling procedures, the correct ways to extricate wounded pilots from their birds when they crash land, as well as how to safely handle the weapons these birds carry."

"Your medical staff I'm sure are very well trained, but they need to drill on mass casualty procedures. As I've said earlier, there is a difference between peacetime military and wartime military. That's where we come in. We can help you reach that level. Once you understand all the ramifications of a wartime situation, only then can you modify your procedures to be able to successfully counter an attack here. General I have to compliment your men on their skills and abilities. Their level of competency reveals the professionalism of their commanding officers above them and to you sir for your excellent ability to lead and command."

"To further enhance the results of an attack here we have brought some visual aids with us," he said nodding to me. I stood up and passed around color photographs of various air bases that had been destroyed from aerial attacks. Some of them were extremely detailed and gruesome, showing dismembered burned bodies, shattered aircraft caught on the ground, burning hangers and destroyed headquarters. Runways that had been cratered, refueling facilities that were burned, communication towers toppled, and aircraft that had crashed onto the runway.

"I'll display these tomorrow to your pilots to further motivate them and push home what can happen if they fail. Do to the skill of your pilots and the modern facilities you have built here, I truly believe it will be but a short time before this base can successfully repel an attack from an enemy. Once everyone understands how to create a wartime mentality here, you'll see that swagger return to your pilots sir," He finished. We sat there in silence watching the looks of horror on their faces as they imagined this base looking like the bases in the photos. It was obvious Raul had gotten his point across to them. When the General looked up at us there was renewed respect on his face.

"I must compliment you on how you presented this information to us Colonel. I can understand why your superiors chose you for this mission. Not only are you an experienced pilot, but you are an excellent diplomat as well. I truly thank you for your efforts," He told Raul. The conversation seemed to change as the other officers there began to ask questions almost all at once. We were no longer intruders, the bad guys. Now we were an accepted part of the team. The meeting lasted late into the night.

CHAPTER SEVEN

We were standing again in front of the Mexican pilots. I set up the slide projector, as Raul began talking to them. He didn't talk down to them. He talked to them as equals. He nodded to me and I hit the start button. The images flashed up on the screen in the darkened auditorium. The pilots were silent as Raul described in detail each photograph being flashed up on the screen. When it was over, he began to describe in great detail different flight maneuvers used in air combat. Raul did the talking. I ran the slide projector. He used two small fighters on sticks to visually demonstrate the maneuvers. It may not have been a very high tech way to explain each maneuver, but it was successful.

"Colonel Murphy will lead a flight of pilots defending the base, with some of you flying with our pilots; I will lead a flight of pilots attacking the base also with some of you flying with us. Tomorrow we will reverse roles and the rest of you will be able to participate. We will be doing this for the next two weeks. Then we will move on to the next section of your training. With this type of training, accidents may occur. Sometimes when the heat is on, pilots make tiny errors, errors that can be fatal. It is expected during air combat training. Our goal is to prevent these accidents. Well gentlemen, to your aircraft," He ordered.

Raul and I worked from a plan conceived in Cuba before we had left. The plan called for the Mexican pilots to fly farther away from us than normal during these exercises as an added safety measure. We also extended our timing during the attack plans of the base. During these initial attack exercises, the Mexican pilots were just along for the ride. Later as their skill increased, their participation would increase.

On the flight line I spent a few minutes speaking with the Mexican pilot assigned to fly as my wing man. I went over what I expected from him.

"Today your job is to be an observer. Later your turn will come to be a participant. So for now, just try and keep up," I explained. He snapped a salute and we walked to our birds. My flight consisted of 2 groups of 4 fighters. Raul's flight had doubled as well. Soon there would be many Migs flying over the base. Heaven help us.

I took my time examining the exterior of my fighter. Once I was satisfied, I climbed up the ladder and into the cockpit. Once I was settled in I slipped on my helmet, while the ground tech helped connect me. He pulled out the safeties from the ejection seat and I hit the battery switch watching the panel light up. I hit the starter switch and felt the engine come alive.

The fighter began to vibrate as the turbine spooled up. The ground tech disengaged the umbilical. I lowered the helmet visor and studied the information being displayed on the inside. Everything looked good. I called the tower and got clearance for takeoff. One by one we lined up waiting our turn to take off.

My Mexican wing man for this exercise had a number 97 on the side of his fighter. I'd join up with him once I got into the air. When I got clearance for takeoff, I locked my brakes, checked all the gauges and electronic readouts, and checked the readouts being projected on the inside of my helmet. Everything was green. I leaned back, my left hand on the throttle, my right hand gripping the stick. I moved the throttle forward and punched the afterburner. I was pressed back into my seat from the thrust and the world outside my cockpit began racing by as I roared down the runway. The whole fighter vibrated around me, then my front wheel came up and I eased the stick back, the wings gaining lift. The ground vibration ceased as I lifted off and climbed for altitude. I brought the wheels up and adjusted flaps. Once I reached altitude I began a racetrack pattern around the airfield, waiting for the Mexican pilots who had taken off before us.

Once the pilots from my wing had taken off and joined up with me, we climbed higher looking for our students. We found them and joined up one by one. I looked over and saw the number 97 on the side of the silver Mexican Mig as it slid into position. The pilot gave me a wave. I returned it. My plan to protect the base included splitting my flight up into two groups, one group of four that flew a racetrack pattern circling the base at low altitude and the second group of four to fly at an extremely high altitude giving us the ability to dive on the attackers. I lead the attack group. I looked over verifying my

Mexican wing man was keeping the agreed upon distance, then glanced back checking my radar screen. Knowing Raul, he would make it as difficult as possible to detect his flight. The scan and track radar in my MIG was the most up to date version available, but there were tricks a pilot could do to evade detection. Raul knew this and would have a plan to defeat it.

Our fighters were equally matched technology wise, the only difference being the skill level of each pilot. An exceptional pilot in an older fighter could kill a lesser pilot in a more advanced fighter. That had been the rule since the first time pilots had ventured into the sky to battle each other.

My RWR detected a flight of fighters coming at the base at 32,000 feet from the south.

"Fights on," I called over the radio as I lifted my left wing and began to dive. Soon info formed on the inside visor of my helmet and I was able to detect the attacking flight. I dove at the attacking Migs from their rear and chose a target. When I had a positive lock on tone I squeezed the button on my stick and an electronic missile on my screen launched, then impacted on my target. The attackers then split up into two plane formations then climbed higher to engage us. At this time a second attacking flight of Migs came screaming in from the west, being pursued by the second team of my defense plan. The air over the base was thick with Migs turning and slashing each other in air combat.

Suddenly a Mig from the attack group flew in front of me so close my fighter was rocked by his exhaust as he turned to avoid me, in the process colliding with my wing man. I wrenched the stick over savagely turning away hoping to avoid sucking any debris into my engine. There was an orange fireball behind me as I turned away.

"ALL FLIGHTS ABORT ABORT!!!" I heard Raul's voice calling through my headphones. My heart was pounding and my mind racing as I tried to regain control over my emotions. I climbed and flew west of the base. As I turned I could see two separate columns of smoke from the field below me. My head was on a swivel trying to look for parachutes hoping that the two pilots had been able to eject. There were none. Two lives had been snuffed out in a heartbeat.

"Alpha flight form on me, Bravo flight RTB," I called over the mic to my two flight wings. My heart was pounding in my chest and my mouth was dry.

One by one the Migs came down and landed, I was still shaken when it was my turn to land. I sucked in a deep lungful of air as I made my approach double checking everything. I had a green board. I took my time came in smoothly and touched down. I deployed my air brakes released my chute and when my MIG slowed turned at the end of the runway past the fiery wreckage of what had been a gleaming silver fighter only a short time before. I pulled up into my slot, locked my brakes and shut down the engine. I opened my canopy, slid off my helmet letting the cool breeze wash over my face. I just wanted to sit there a few minutes before I climbed out. I knew there would be a long drawn out investigation with tons of paperwork. This was a part of air combat training. I just hadn't expected it to happen so soon.

I looked over my shoulder at the column of smoke rising into the blue sky. Yellow fire trucks were racing there; I knew the futility of the ambulance following behind them. There hadn't been any chutes. It had happened too quickly.

I slowly disconnected myself from the fighter climbing down the yellow ladder to the ground.

I slowly walked around my fighter checking to see if any damage had occurred from the collision. I ran my hand over the skin, kneeled down to check underneath. I looked at the intake and the belly. I walked to the rear looking up at the tail and checking the ailerons then looking into the rear exhaust. Everything looked normal. Walking into the hanger I wondered if it had been just dumb luck or if something of a greater power had protected me. It could have been me in that smoking pile of twisted metal at the end of the runway.

Inside the coolness of the breeze helped dry the sweat on my face as I walked into the locker room and took off my inflatable G-suit and survival vest. I placed my helmet on the holder with my name painted on it. I went to the bathroom and stood under the shower, the image of the two Migs colliding and the explosion kept replaying over and over in my mind. Later in the ready room I wrote the incident report while it was all still fresh in my mind. Even though it was an event that occurred in the blink of an eye, the paperwork was always mountainous and took forever to complete.

"You all right?" Raul asked me taking a seat next to me.

"Yeah no problem," I lied to him trying to hide the pen that was shaking in my hand as I tried to write.

"What happened?" He asked.

"I guess the oncoming MIG misjudged the distance and came between my wing man and me when he tried to correct he took out the other MIG," I explained.

"Ok, well put it all in your report. Then we'll debrief," He told me getting up leaving me to my writing. I nodded. It took me 30 minutes to complete the report. I knew I had to prepare a letter of condolence to both families of the crash. That would come later. When the paperwork was completed, I sat back and drank a cup of coffee trying to settle my nerves. The debriefing was a solemn affair. The two Mexican Colonels listened quietly as I recounted what happened. Training accidents were an unfortunate occurrence during air combat exercises, but not something you ever got used to. I handed in my report and the Colonel slipped it into his folder. They had been watching the exercise on the radar screens from the tower. Raul listened as we discussed what happened and how to prevent something similar from happening in the future.

"Sounds like our pilot had a little too much of the tiger in him," one of the Colonels commented.

"It's common for young pilots to take risks. You want them to be out there on the edge taking risks. The trick is to know when and where you can take the risk," I explained." You don't want weak pilots flying these machines. You want aggressive life takers and heart breakers in those cockpits."

"It's our job to teach them when and how to stretch the envelope up there. I believe they are coming along fine. Have faith in them, they'll be hotshit pilots in a short time, you'll see," Raul told them.

"Thank you gentlemen," The other Colonel said as he stood up indicating the meeting was over.

Upstairs in our quarters Raul handed me a bottle of beer from our little icebox as I tried to write the letters to the families of the two dead pilots.

"It's never easy writing one of those," he said quietly.

"Have you written many?" I asked setting back.

"When I was in Angola I had to write a couple yes. I hated it, you never get used to it, and it's a necessary evil of command,"

"Well hopefully there won't be any more to write," I lamented. I took a long swallow from my beer.

"We're a good team you and me. We'll teach these young studs what it's all about. It'll take some time sure. We'll get it done," he went on.

"Damned straight we will. Too much is at stake here not to. I wonder if those guys understand that," I replied.

"Once the Chinese make their move in Guatemala, they'll figure it out real quick. Sad part about it is I believe we'll wind up right in the middle of it no matter what our superiors tell us. It's just too big for them here. Once it starts, they'll be screaming for help. I'm not sure the U.S. will be of much help, so that means we'll be the ones to step in, we are the only ones in this region who can help,"

"You really think the U.S. will stand by while their neighbor is attacked? There is a lot of U.S. manufacturing that goes on in Mexico. They are an important economic partner for them," I said.

"I dunno, this new administration has been stripping their military to bare bones. I'm concerned by the time the Chinese make their move; the U.S. won't have a lot to spare. Think about it, two of the United States most important economic manufacturing partners fighting each other, I'll bet their diplomats will be busy,"

"Diplomacy," I snorted with disgust. "Since when did diplomacy ever work when two countries wanted to go to war?" I scoffed.

"Amen to that," He grinned back at me. I returned to my task and within an hour I had both letters completed. I began a letter to Ali leaving out the details of the mid air. Four pages later it was done.

The next day was a holiday. We wouldn't be flying. Raul received an invitation for us to accompany a group of pilots into town. We dressed casually and boarded the blue bus. It was a dusty 28-kilometer ride into town. Once there we were dropped off in the Zocala, the town's main square, which was called Plaza Civica.

One of the Mexican pilots volunteered to be the groups guide and off we went, 20 young Latins trying not to feel out of place. The people were both modern and traditionally dressed, many of them Indians in their colorful wraps and shirts. Some of the men wore large machetes, some with large belt buckles. The hotel we would stay at was located on a high hill that overlooked the town with large fountains in the front. The pretty receptionist gave us our hotel keys after confirming our reservations. After dropping off our luggage, Christo, our unofficial tour guide, lead us to a little open-air cafe he promised served excellent food. I was pleasantly surprised to see it was a cyber cafe with computers at every table. The price was around 15 pesos per hour.

Raul and I sat at the same table and ordered the local beer with burritos. I was surprised to see fried insects on the menu. While we waited for our food I typed an e-mail to Ali. True to his word, the food was very good. The burritos were large and filled with spiced meat, cheese and vegetables. The local beer wasn't as good as the green label beer I usually drank but it was cold.

We sat there eating and watching the people stroll by. Later we strolled around the town, stopping in front of the 16th century San Marcos Cathedral. There were 12 dolls that were supposed to represent Christ and the 12 disciples. Every hour the 48 bells would sound and the 12 dolls would march on their pedestals as the bells chimed songs.

Raul and I stopped in a silver shop and I bought a necklace for Ali. Christo lead us to the zoo, a large modern facility. There was no entrance fee but contributions were accepted. We all gave something. Inside we were treated to an amazing exhibition of the types of animals that populated the jungles of Mexico. There were Eagles and different types of colorful birds. The serpentarium had both poisonous and non-poisonous snakes.

"I'd hate to meet one of those muthas out there." I told Raul.

"No wonder the locals carry those machetes," he replied.

There was a large collection of Jaguars and other types of cats that were indigenous to the jungle. When the tour was over we climbed into a rickety city bus and rode to a restaurant that Christo guaranteed served the best steaks in town.

We got out in front of a modern looking restaurant with a statue of a large black bull in front of it. I was glad to see they had my green label beer on the menu.

The steaks came with large salads and plenty of garlic bread. It felt good to relax and be away from the base. We were joking with each other and laughing as we ate. The waitresses were hustling trying to keep up with the requests for all the beers everyone was drinking. After we were done, 20 half drunk pilots followed Christo back to the hotel in the semidarkness. We went to our rooms and changed into our trunks for a refreshing swim in the hotel pool. I leaned back on the side of the pool looking up at the stars in the cool water drinking a beer. Some of the pilots were roughhousing around in the water. Raul and I were mellowed out. I was rather young to be a Colonel, yet I felt years older than these pilots my own age. It reminded me of a saying I'd heard years ago. Those who row the boat are less likely to rock it. It was the responsibility of command that made an old man of you fast. Later it was nice to sleep in a large comfortable bed instead of the small military bunk at base. I stretched out my legs enjoying the room and fell asleep.

The next morning we all ordered room service, ate a huge breakfast then took a dip in the pool.

"This is the life," Marco told me as we enjoyed the water.

"Oh yeah," I replied.

"So meho, tell me how a U.S. Navy pilot who shoots down two of our MIGs winds up being a Colonel in our air force," He said.

"Just lucky I guess," I told him with a grin.

"Naaa c'mon, you can tell me meho," He grinned at me. I glanced quickly at Raul for help. He just smiled back at me enjoying my discomfort. The other pilots started to gather round to listen in on the conversation.

"Some one had to bring civilization to the natives," I replied with a grin.

"HO HO so we are ignorant peasants now," Marco said with mock anger.

"How many bandits have you shot out of the sky Marco?" Raul asked him.

"None, YET, Colonel," he replied enthusiastically.

"Colonel Murphy has four confirmed kills to his credit," Raul explained. He didn't add the MIGs I had shot down during our secret mission to eliminate the leaders of the prior Cuban government.

"He also is an honary Colonel in the Indian Air Force," he added. An uncomfortable silence permiated the air.

"I need another beer," I told them getting out of the water. I made my way to the outdoor bar dripping water. I ordered another beer from the well-endowed white shirted barmaid behind the bar and charged it to my room. Her nipples were showing through the thin white material of the low cut blouse. I watched as a bead of sweat rolled slowly between her breasts. I turned away looking at the pool, wishing Ali was here.

I sat on the stool in the shade of the bar, enjoying my beer, remembering the dangerous mission Raul, Manual, Alexi and I had volunteered to fly. We had trained for months prior to that mission, wringing out the MIG-21s to the extreme. Then the long flight to Andros Island off the coast of Florida in Antonio's customized Lockheed Constellation. We flew our mission from a deserted airstrip on Andros Island.

"Uno Cervasa porfavor," Raul interrupted my memory as he came up behind me, and ordering a beer. The barmaid gave him a big smile as she pulled one from the cooler, taking the top off and handing it to him.

"You okay?" He asked me taking a seat next to me.

"Betcha," I told him.

"Don't let them get your goat," he said.

"Naaaaa, can't blame them for asking and wondering. I'd be wondering the same thing if the roles were reversed, besides once the war starts it won't matter anymore. We'll all be fighting for our lives,"

"Unfortunately I believe you are right, Nueva Cuba," He said with a grin raising his beer bottle.

"Nueva Cuba," I replied back with a grin at our personal joke tapping the neck of my beer bottle with his. We sat there grinning at each other.

"That was the mission of a lifetime," I said quietly.

"Best one in my life as well. You ever regret flying it?" he asked me seriously.

"Never, not for a second. We helped bring freedom to Cuba; I'll never regret that,"

"I keep remembering that poor officer on Grand Cayman after we landed and asked for asylum; poor man didn't know what to do,"

"Yeah, and when we went to that hotel, the look on that poor girls face when we plopped down those Cuban Identity books as passports, I'll never forget her face, that look of horror she had," I said taking a drink of my cold beer.

"I remember Perry and his damned Marine Corp morning exercises,"

"That first morning there we were, hung over, and trying to run together on that beach at Andros, Gawd. I was so miserable that day," I laughed.

"I'm hungry," He said. We looked at the menu on the wall and both ordered lunch. We sat there at the bar eating and watching the other pilots as they strutted around the pool for the benefit of the few bikini clad women working on their tans. Marco was sitting next to a young blonde clad in a tiny string bikini. He flashed his best smile at her.

"It never changes," I remarked.

"Fighter pilots and women?" Raul asked around a mouthful of rice.

"Ayep, no matter what country I'm in, it's always the same. It's almost as if we are all created from the same mold. Fighter pilots are the same the world over,"

"Except Alexi,"

"Yeah, he lives only to fly it seems,"

That evening we gathered in the hotel bar and I watched the pilots, some with their dates on the dance floor. I missed Ali, missed holding her body in my arms. I ate a good meal, finished off my beer and went to bed.

The next morning found us aboard the blue bus again for the dusty ride back to base. The Mexican Air Force had begun constructing a fortified radar facility atop the highest peak of the mountain range overlooking the base. The SAM missile launchers were positioned to protect the facility as well as the base below. It was a relief to know they were accepting our suggestions.

That afternoon there was a memorial service for the two pilots who died in the training accident. It was a moving experience for us all. There were speeches made and the Military band played the Mexican national anthem. Three Mexican Migs flew in formation over the base.

Then it was back to work. The seriousness of the training accident was evident on the faces of the Mexican pilots. Death had visited their ranks for the first time. It showed in their flying. There was a seriousness lacking just a few days before. They listened intently to the classroom training, and when we were in the air flying against them, there was none of the jovial banter over their radio frequency.

Slowly they were getting their act together, they were developing their edge. This was an important skill that would keep them alive in the air against an airborne enemy. Raul and I continued to switch between being the aggressor and the defender. By the end of the month their radar installation atop the mountain was completed. Their base defense system had been improved with enhanced radar firing coordination, and communication.

There were practice bombing missions, as well as ground strafing missions. Thankfully our team would not be involved in night combat training. This would come later with another team.

Their pilots were working as a team, and the base was successful in their efforts to enhance their war footing attitude. We had done our job; it was time to return home. There was a ceremony for us followed by a dinner.

Each of our Cuban pilots received a certificate for their participation in the training exercise. Our maintenance crew worked hard at getting our birds ready for the flight to Cuba. Raul and I were given awards for our input and efforts.

The morning of our departure we said our goodbyes and climbed into our birds. I connected the Lines into my helmet, hit the starter switch and felt the MIG come alive around me as the turbine began to spool up. I locked the canopy, requesting takeoff clearance from the tower. I let out the brakes and turned towards the runway waiting my turn. I watched Raul lift off the runway with his flight. When our turn came, Marco pulled up beside me and waited as I lined up at the end of the runway. I went through my usual pre takeoff checklist. When I was satisfied, I released the brakes, moved the throttle forward with my left hand, hit the afterburner and was pushed back into my seat from the force of the thrust. I had no bad feelings about this place, but like the rest of my men, I was eager to get home.

The front gear lifted off the runway and I moved the stick back and was airborne. The rumbling of the wheels on the runway ceased as I lifted off and gained altitude. I raised the gear, adjusted the flaps, and when I got to altitude, cut the afterburner. I looked over my shoulder to see Marco in his usual position to my right and slightly to my rear.

I rechecked the map on my thigh board and sat back enjoying the flight. I looked out the canopy at the clouds as we passed through them, so close I felt like I could touch them. I thought back to the first time I had soloed in a Mig back in India. The joy I felt after successfully completing the training course and soloing the MIG for the first time. The feeling of power and freedom I held in my hand as I gripped the stick. The happiness that came with returning to the sky flying a combat fighter. The Mig was roaring along in this blue sky with green blue sea below us.

"Sure is a beautiful day for flying," Marco interrupted my thoughts.

"Roger that," I replied.

"You think they will ever become as good as we are?"

"They will, given enough time, if they train hard. Besides our team isn't the only one helping to train their pilots. Another Cuban team will be going to another one of their bases very soon. The plan is to help them train and modernize their air force, to help them become used to being on a war footing. We can talk about this another time Marco, you never know who may be listening in on our traffic," I cautioned him. I didn't know if there really was anyone listening in on our radio traffic, but I wasn't going to take any chances. I looked at the water below us noting the white wake of a ship wondering what type it was and where it was going.

The green sea beneath me, the blue sky around me, and the steady hum of the jet engine streaking me through the sky. The sheer joy of flying, there was nothing like it.

Off to my right I could barely make out the shape of land. Cuba, green and brown on the horizon. My heart beat sped up slightly as I requested landing clearance for my flight from our base. I could Hear Raul's voice doing the same. I wasn't the only one eager to get home it seemed. I rechecked the code on my IFF to verify it was functioning correctly. Then as the green island that was Cuba became more distinct, I heard Raul's voice again over my headphones.

"By the numbers," Raul called out to us. I smiled to myself under my oxygen mask, remembering those exact words a lifetime ago.

"Alpha flights clear to land, runway 7 left, and welcome home." I heard our base tower in my earphones. Raul's flight would be landing first.

"Thank you tower," his voice replied. His flight started their turn from the north losing altitude; they were landing two at a time.

"Bravo flight is clear to land, runway 7 left," our tower called out to us indicating Raul's flight had landed.

"Copy that tower,"

"Welcome home," I heard him reply.

"Thank you, it's great to be back," I turned the fighter and made my approach for final. I had the runway in sight, I lowered my gear, adjusted my flaps, moved the throttle, made sure my straps were tight, the cone was in its proper position for landing. Everything on the instrument panel and on my helmet visor looked good. I lined up perfectly with the runway and began my descent.

At around 1000 feet, flaps were down full, throttle was at 80 percent, nose was up slightly. Slowly almost in slow motion I flared slightly then touched down, the wheels screeching as the Rubber made contact with the runway. I tapped the brakes, opened the speed brake, and released my drag chute. I was home. The base around me slowed as I came to the end of the runway, turning onto the tarmac.

It felt great to look out and recognize my base. I turned her nose to the ramp and slowly taxied to the line of Migs to my left. I pulled into my slot, locked my brakes, raised the flaps, shut down my external lights, and shut down the engine. I unlocked the canopy and a ground tech moved a yellow ladder against the left side of the fighter. He climbed up and opened the canopy. I slowly disconnected my oxygen mask, unhooked the connections, and slid off my helmet.

Once I was disconnected, and the tech slipped the ejection seat safety pins in place, I released my straps and climbed out.

I breathed in a breath of warm Cuban air, looking around as the other fighters moved into their slots. I walked to the ready room, and heard the other pilots of my flight joking and laughing and carrying on. They too it seemed were glad to be back. Raul found me and we went to the General's office. He greeted us with a big warm smile. I was relieved to see he was in a good mood.

"I've received good reports from our Mexican allies. Seems they were very pleased with your efforts while you two were there," He told us. We debriefed him giving him our written report we had completed before leaving Mexico.

"What are your opinions concerning their level of readiness?" He asked.

"Much more intense since the accident," Raul told him. He looked at him with a quizzical look on his face.

"Accident?" He asked. "I wasn't aware there had been any accident,"

"There was a training accident early on between two Mexican Migs. They collided with each other, almost took out Colonel Murphy here, his Mexican wing man was hit by another pilot. It killed both pilots," Raul explained.

"I never received any information about this incident," The General informed us, a concerned look on his face. "I'm relieved you were not injured or killed Colonel Murphy," He said with genuine warmth in his voice.

"Thank you sir. They have modernized their radar and SAM missile systems, as well as their communications systems. The attitude of their pilots has changed to a more serious level. I'm sure the training accident helped bring home the seriousness of air combat." I explained trying to change the subject.

"Our first two simulated base attacks helped to reveal their air defense weaknesses. I believe we provided them with a real life experience when we exploited their weaknesses. Colonel Murphy discovered a hidden microphone they had planted in our ready room. We changed our attack tactics and caught them with their pants down on our second attack mission. I'm sure it insulted their Latin egos, but it definitely helped bring home the element of surprise," Raul continued.

"When we met with their base command staff, the Colonel here masterfully explained what their weaknesses were, but more importantly he was able to give them advice in a positive manner that assisted them in bringing their base air defense systems up to date," I added.

"I understand now why the report I received from their Commanding Officer was so positive. Seems you two worked well together in this mission. I'm glad to see that. I must admit Colonel Murphy, when I heard you were going to become a part of our new air force I had many reservations. I must say, you have earned your place here among us," he revealed.

"Thank you sir," I replied.

"Well I'm sure you two have other places to be now," He said standing up indicating the meeting was over. We stood up and walked out of the room.

"Talk to you later," Raul told me as we split up. He gave me a salute that I returned, grinning as I walked out into the sunshine and to my office.

"Welcome home Colonel Murphy," Anna greeted me as I walked in hanging my hat on its hook. She handed me a cup of coffee with a warm smile. "There is a stack of paperwork on your desk waiting for you sir," I groaned and she grinned wickedly at my discomfort, knowing how much I hated paperwork.

"Would you get my wife on the phone please Anna?" I asked her as I walked into my office.

"Well sir," I heard as I saw Ali sitting behind my desk, already waiting for me. Ali jumped up launching herself into my arms with a squeal.

"Whoa easy there girl," I said smiling. "This is a nice surprise," I said as she reached up and kissed me. I heard Anna close the door behind us.

"I have missed you so much," Ali told me hugging me. I looked into her eyes and smiling face.

"I've missed you too Hon," I told her. The sound of fighter jets taking off shook the building as we stood there holding each other. It felt good to hold her in my arms. To my surprise there were no paper on my desk. Anna had thoughtfully stashed them away for another day.

"Ready to head home?" I asked her.

"So early in the day?" She asked with a huge smile.

"Well I AM a Colonel, rank DOES have its privileges," I joked with her.

"Let's go flyboy, you have a lot of work at home to catch up on," she grinned up at me.

"Anna can you get my driver here," I called to her knowing she could hear my voice through the thin walls. A minute later there was a knock on the door.

"Your driver will be here in a few minutes Colonel," She told me opening the door.

"So how was Mexico, tell me all about it," She said as we sat down. I pulled out the necklace I had bought for her, I watched her eyes light up as she put it around her neck. I gave her a quick rundown as we waited. The phone rang and Anna's voice was telling me the driver was out front.

"Time to go," I told her.

"What about my jeep?" She asked me.

"We can get it later, c'mon," I said as we walked out.

"See you tomorrow Anna," I said as we left. The drive home was filled with her telling me all the local news and non-classified tidbits. The driver pulled the Humvee up in front of the house and opened the door for us. We were barely inside the door when Ali began tearing off her clothes pulling me into the bedroom. Seconds later we were both naked on the bed. She climbed on top of me running her hands down my chest.

"I've missed you so much," She whispered. Her long hair was hanging down, and her breasts were moving in tune with our bodies. Later we lay holding each other and talking. Then she jumped up and walked outside, still naked, pulling me along.

"Ready for a swim?" She asked. We both plunged into the ocean enjoying the warm water. I then filled her in on most of the details of Mexico, leaving out the training accident. I didn't want to cause her any more worry than necessary.

"Antonio will be coming by for dinner tonight. He wants to hear all about your time there," she told me as we held each other in the warm water.

"Our fist night together?" I moaned.

"Oh don't worry, I have plans for you later," She warned me. I smiled at the thought.

The doorbell rang and Consuelo answered it. Boner and Antonio came in followed by his bodyguard.

"Welcome home Sean," Antonio greeted me as I walked into the room.

"Hey there, Boner this is a surprise," I said to them. "When did you get here?"

"I've been here for almost two weeks," he told me.

"You are looking at the company's newest A-4 test pilot here in Cuba," Antonio said with pride.

"Well shit congrats mate, that's great news. That was quick," I said.

"Yeah buddy, I've already been working on my tan," Boner told me.

"That's not all he's been working on, he has my secretary in a tizzy already," Antonio informed me.

"You dawg you," I joked.

We walked out onto the patio and found seats. Again the doorbell rang I looked up.

"I've taken the liberty to invite everyone here tonight for a quiet briefing," Antonio told me. I gritted my teeth not replying. This was not what I had hoped for, my first night back from Mexico. I looked up to see Raul, Manuel, Alexi and Perry all walk in. I was happy to see them, but tonight?

We all said our hellos and walked out onto the patio. I watched as Antonio's bodyguard walked out onto the beach and circled the house. I knew he took his job very seriously. Consuelo took everyone's drink orders and we made small talk until she returned with a tray. She then went back into the house closing the door behind her. Ali came out and sat on the arm of my chair.

"What are your opinions concerning their pilot's abilities?" He asked looking at Raul and then me.

"I think they get the idea," I began. "It's gonna take em awhile to get up to where they need to be. Their pilots aren't as good as ours, but they have the courage of lions, typical fighter pilots. By the time we left they had the basics down cold. They improved their radar systems and SAM missile systems. They built a radar facility on the highest peak of the mountain range covering the base to better detect incoming aircraft, one of the suggestions Raul gave them. It took awhile for them to upgrade to a wartime mentality," I began.

"Everything changed after the training accident," Raul added.

"Training accident?" Antonio asked. Every face looked at Raul then.

"Oh yes, Grey here was flying with one of their pilots as wing man. Another of their pilots got a bit too aggressive and climbed up at them. Somehow he misjudged the distance and maneuvered to avoid hitting Grey here and slammed into his wing man instead," Raul went on. "It was a massive fireball, there weren't any chutes,"

I took a drink of my beer trying to appear nonchalant. I could feel Ali's eyes burning into me. She didn't say anything but I knew I'd get it from her later for not telling her earlier.

"I was lucky," I explained not wanting to talk about it further. I could see Ali glaring at me out of the corner of my eye.

"How will they stack up against the Chinese when the time comes?" Antonio went on.

"How long do they have?" Raul asked.

"From what I hear about six months," Antonio replied.

"That long," I said trying to sound sarcastic. It didn't help. It got very quiet as we all pondered that fact.

"The Chinese have already made two supply deliveries off the west coast of Guatemala at Puerto Quetzal. Many more are to follow. They also offloaded two groups of their special forces. With this last delivery a sub accompanied their supply ship. It was a military supply ship disguised to look commercial,"

"How the hell did they refuel their sub," I asked.

"They refueled at sea from the supply ship," Antonio answered. I looked up at Antonio's bodyguard as he walked past the patio nodding at Antonio, letting him know quietly the area was secure.

"I have spoken with some friends in Chile concerning the Chinese submarine situation. We will be getting some assistance in that department very soon," He went on. He didn't continue further on that subject, which meant we weren't privileged to know what he had worked out.

"We were hoping it would be longer, but it seems the Chinese have stepped up their timetable," Antonio went on.

"That'll surely interfere with our planned training rotation then," Raul added referring to the planned Cuban flight teams to Mexico assisting them with their modernization program.

"Talk about on the job training," Manual threw in.

"The leadership of Mexico has requested our company put together a rapid response team that can travel to Mexico once hostilities commence there. This is why I asked all of you to come here tonight. It'll be a strictly volunteer operation," Antonio informed us.

"What about our commitments here?" Raul asked.

"Anyone who wants to go will be listed as TDY," He answered.

"How much?" Alexi asked.

"Well we can discuss the details at a later date, but the figure offered was 10,000 a month per pilot. Lesser amounts of course for other personnel, but it will still be a lucrative amount,"

"What happen to the plan the Cuban government came up with to send our pilots to help fight alongside the Mexican pilots?" I asked.

"The idea now is to keep that plan as a last resort. They like the idea of a small group of volunteers to spearhead the task of assisting the Mexicans first," Antonio explained." That way there can still be a formidable air force here to protect Cuba."

"Politicians are the same the world over," Perry threw in.

"I don't expect any answers right now. I am however seeking volunteers to form a flight group to assist the Mexican Air Force when the time comes, "Antonio continued. I drank the rest of my beer and listened. I knew that Ali would be against me joining this group, but I didn't want them to go into combat without me. I had great respect for the Mexican pilots and didn't want to see them slaughtered. I knew that Raul and Alexi would volunteer, as well as Boner. I wasn't sure about Manuel; he was going to be a new father soon. Perry would go without question. I was curious how many others would volunteer.

"You can't let them go without you," Ali surprised me, reading my mind.

"Are you sure?" I looked at her.

"Yes. Just promise me you'll come back," She said in a soft voice. My head was spinning inside.

"You got yourself a volunteer," I said before she could change her mind.

"I'll go," Raul threw in.

"I will go as well," Alexi said.

"Can't let my favorite wing man fly without me," Boner said with a grin.

"Marie is going to kill me, shit. I'm in too," Manual added.

"I'll be just like old times," Perry threw in.

"Gawd we better get into shape before we leave," Manual moaned.

"Don't worry boys, if you're not in shape when we get there, you will be after I'm done with you," Perry said with a sadistic laugh. This brought groans all around.

"We'll need an edge against those Chinese J-11s," I told Antonio.

"What kind of edge?" Antonio looked at me.

"Jamming," Alexi answered for me.

"Those J-11s are nothing to play with. Jamming can give us an edge when they attack the bases," Raul continued.

"I'll look into it," He promised nodding his head up and down.

"We'll need aerial photos of their bases they plan to fly from in Guatemala," I added.

"Some type of early warning system would be great to," Manual put in. We were starting to come together as a team once again.

"I can put together a crack maintenance crew," Perry told us.

"You'll have to with Alexi and Raul flying MIG-29s and Boner flying an A-4 and the rest flying 21s," Antonio told him.

"Not a problem boss, can do," he shot back with a grin.

"Damn jar heads," Manual joked.

"I'll remember that once your morning workouts begin," Perry told him with a smile. I shook my head.

"Here we go again, "I looked at Antonio.

"We'll need more pilots than we have here," Raul said.

"Do you have anyone in mind?"

"Marco," I said quickly.

"Jesus," Manual said.

"Yes, I have a few ideas," Raul answered.

"As do I," Alexi said. Antonio was making notes into a palm pilot.

"Then there is training, "Alexi reminded us.

"Training? I'd think everyone here is well trained," Antonio said.

"When you put different pilots together that haven't flown with each other, it creates problems," Raul reminded him.

"Ahh yes, you're right, I'd forgotten," Antonio admitted." I'll make some phone calls,"

"Then there is command and control," I said. Then everyone started talking at once. It was a long night. It was after midnight when everyone left.

"You'd better come back to me," She told me as we sat there holding each other under the stars. "If you promise me you'll come back I know you will,"

"Thanks for your confidence in me,"

"I'll be right back," she told me jumping up and running back to the house. She returned with a large beach towel, and spread it out on the sand. She lay down on it and slowly removed her blouse, her breasts reflecting the moonlight, then she stripped off her pants and lace panties. She lay back down on the towel and beckoned me with her moving finger.

"Show me how much you missed me," She whispered in the darkness. I stripped off my clothes and joined her on the towel, the sea breeze blowing over our naked bodies. It was wonderful to feel her body in my arms. I thought back to the night in Mexico, at the bar watching all the other pilots dancing with their dates. I felt so lucky to hold this beautiful woman in my arms. Later we swam naked in the warm ocean.

CHAPTER EIGHT

When I arrived at the base Anna had a stack of paperwork for me to complete. Then there were meetings and phone calls concerning the flight team's actions in Mexico.

I was going through the pile of paperwork when Anna opened my door and pointed to the television set in the corner of my office.

"You might want to see this Colonel," She said in a soft voice. I turned on the set with the TV remote I kept on my desk it was already on the cable news channel. The voice of the on the spot reporter was giving a verbal blow by blow from Guatemala City. Guerrillas had attacked the city and the main military headquarters as well as the air force base there. The guerrillas had already taken control of the international airport and the main TV. And radio stations. This reporter was using one of those modern portable video cameras able to transmit to a satellite. Tanks were in the streets fighting other tanks it was pandemonium on the screen. The reporter was explaining the guerrillas had staged a coordinated attack all over the country. I didn't need anyone to explain what that meant to me.

"Get me the Colonel on the phone please Anna," I told her.

"Right away sir," A moment later the phone rang and Raul was on the other end.

"Are you watching this shit?" I asked him.

"Watching what?"

"Turn on the cable news channel," I waited for him to come back to the phone.

"OK I'm watching, where is this?" He asked.

"Guatemala," I told him. He didn't say anything. We both sat there with our phones in one ear, while listening to the TV with the other.

"Antonio DID say six months, didn't he," I said.

"Yes, he did," I heard him sigh." OK, thanks, I have some phone calls to make. I'll get back to you,"

"Copy that," I hung up the phone, watching as a Guatemalan APC exploded after being hit with an RPG. The camera shook from the detonation wave. I sat there quietly contemplating the ramifications of what I was seeing. The second training flight of Migs had not left yet for Mexico, it was too late for us to send a flight to help the Guatemalan government during this battle. From the looks of this situation the Guatemalan forces were on their own. If the guerrillas were successful with their coordinated attacks across the country, Guatemala could go the way Cuba had gone. A Communist country would be created in Central America again. Knowing Antonio's reliable history for gathering correct intelligence from around the world, a six-month estimate was probably right on.

"Anna could you get my wife on the phone for me please," I said over the intercom.

"Are you watching this?" I asked her when she answered.

"Yes, we all are, Antonio is on the phone now talking with the president in Guatemala City. He says it doesn't look good. The whole country is being attacked, Antonio is ready to send a plane to fly out the Guatemalan president as we speak." her worried voice replied.

"We just lost contact with them," She told me sadly as the Presidential Palace was hit with mortar shells on the screen. The T.V. Screen suddenly went blank as the anchorman returned onto the screen, telling us what we already knew. I felt helpless just sitting there not wanting to accept what was happening. I hated that Antonio was right, I hated that Guatemala would soon be Communist, I hated knowing we would be dragged into it. I really hated the United States for having the same intelligence we had, and doing nothing to help prevent this from happening. What could that air headed liberal president be thinking right now? Oops we goofed? There was nothing positive about any of this.

"Anna, could you get me all the information you can about the Chinese Air Force and any technical data we have about the J-11s? I'm sure it will take you awhile," I told her over the intercom. I'd have to rely on Antonio to supply the rest of the information I would need.

"Ali is Boner around?" I asked her over the phone.

"Sure hang on a minute,"

"Hey mate, aint this some shit, just like Antonio predicted," I heard Boner's voice over the phone.

"Yeah, look, get with Antonio, see what info he can dig up about their air combat tactics, also see if he will allow you to fly as an aggressor using an A-4 against us," I told him, my mind going a mile a minute. "He'll have to find a way to clear it with our higher ups here. It looks like we'll be flying against the Chinese soon and I want every edge we can get,"

"You got it, I'll see what I can do, ain't this some shit though?"

"Yeah, shit is exactly what it is, thanks Boner," I said hanging up. The screen on the TV showed a map of Guatemala, and the locations of where fighting was taking place. Puerto Barrios, Coban, Jalapa, San Marcos, Mazatenango, Amatitlan, Quezaltenango, and Cotzumalguapa were being attacked as well as Guatemala City. The four Major Air Force Bases were also being overrun. Several Military bases were being attacked.

From everything Antonio had told us earlier, it wasn't hard to figure out ex-Cuban Communist and Chinese antagonists had taken leadership roles in this endeavor. A well coordinated simultaneous serious of attacks across the country could not have been organized by a few narco guerrillas. This took a great deal of planning, and it required a secure logistics program. I wondered how many Chinese troops were involved in the fighting.

The anchorman on the screen was talking about the countrywide shutdown of all radio and television stations. That was normal in situations like this. Secure the airwaves, and you control the flow of information to the masses. I wondered if any of the Guatemalan military leaders were a part of this behind the scenes, as sometimes happened in takeovers like this. I thought back to the report I had read about Guatemala being a so-called developing country. I wondered now how far it would develop under a communist Government, probably not much under a communist government if history was any indication.

All the airports had been shut down, no flights in or out of the country were being allowed. I cringed at the thought of tourists being caught in the middle of all this. I had to give them credit; the cable news channel was doing an excellent blow-by-blow report of the demise of this country.

Just then another camera from high atop some building in Guatemala City came to life. Fighting was visible from this camera angle. People running around trying to escape the shooting, cars burning, and the hulks of burning tanks were visible throughout the city. A few buildings were on fire, victims of direct hits from the shelling going on. A military helicopter making what looked like a strafing run on a guerrilla position was hit by ground fire. It exploded, smoke pouring from it as the pilot courageously turned away trying to avoid crashing amongst the buildings in the center of the city. The screen shook from an explosion violent enough to rock the building the camera was located in. I watched an aircraft come in and a missile fired from the ground rise up into the air, and follow the aircraft as it twisted and turned trying to escape it. The missile followed the aircraft and impacted creating an orange explosion. The fact that the missile was ground launched by the guerrillas, and followed the aircraft to impact told me the type of weapon it was. The guerrillas were carrying shoulder-fired wire guided anti aircraft missiles. Not something easily obtained by narco guerrillas. The Chinese must have supplied the missile. Either that or Chinese troops were actively fighting and were carrying these missiles.

Three smaller explosions in rapid sequence followed next, probably from mortars. The anchorman was explaining how the city's hospital was being swamped with victims of the fighting. What a nightmare it must be there I kept thinking.

I thought back to the black and white newsreels of the Second World War of the fighting in different cities. Now I was sitting here in the comfort of my own office watching the same thing in living color. It felt surrealistic. Like this really was not happening, that it was just another bad Hollywood movie.

What a horrible thing it was to watch a country die on television, especially knowing what the future held for those people there.

That evening Ali and I were on the couch together watching the play by play of the actions in Guatemala. The government forces were still fighting the guerrillas all over the country. That gave me hope. I fell asleep on the couch. Ali woke me the next morning so I could go to the base on time. The news on the television was bleak. During the night, the guerrillas had made gains all across the country. At the base, I finished the paperwork from the day before. Raul and I had lunch at the base mess hall, and talked about Guatemala. The mess hall was alive with chatter as everyone was talking about the war. That was the subject of the day all over the base. By evening the news reported that the guerrillas had control of 70 per cent of the country. Some government leaders had escaped the country, many had made their way to Cuba, others had been killed during the fighting. A few had already been executed. Antonio was able to slip a private jet into a rural airfield to help rescue the president and his family.

Ali and I watched the first televised message from the new leaders of Guatemala, now called The People's Republic of Guatemala. The new flag served as a backdrop during the message. The woman reading notes spoke to the camera in a no nonsense monotone voice. She informed the world that the previous corrupt government no longer existed. The Guatemalan People's Army had liberated the people of Guatemala. All nonresident aliens would be allowed to leave the country the next day. The new government would be a New Communist Guatemalan leadership. The new leaders were grateful for the assistance of their Chinese allies.

A chill ran up my spine listening to her cold hard voice. This was the future of Guatemala. Soon they would request recognition by the U.N. North Korea and Iran had agreed to the membership, big surprise there. Beijing had already recognized the new nation.

"What's next Mao and Stalin return from the dead and have a reunion?" I said to the television screen.

"Are you all right?" Ali asked next to me.

"No I'm not, I'm pissed. I'm pissed that Antonio was right, "I said angrily.

"You're mad he was right?" She asked in bewilderment.

"It's hard to explain, I'm not angry with him, I'm angry that it happened,"

"I understand, I've felt the same thing many times since I worked for him," she said.

"I just wish the U.S. had stepped in and helped avert this mess, and then we wouldn't have to go in and deal with it," I complained.

"You think that the U.S. could have stepped in and prevented this from happening? How?"

"Buy putting in CIA operatives, by giving Guatemala military assistance, training, by economic assistance, medical assistance to the people in the rural areas, things like that. Education programs that help the people learn how to read, they can afford to provide things like that," I told her.

"Maybe, it's possible they could have done all that and this still would have happened,"

"Yeah, maybe. Guess I'm just venting," I explained. We talked late into the night under the stars on the beach.

The next two days I flight-tested an upgraded Mig-21 that was newly completed by the company. It looked factory fresh as I walked around the fighter during my external pre-flight check. Antonio had completed the promised contract of Mig-21s that India had requested. These Migs were on their way to the Mexican Air Force as part of the ongoing upgrade of their air force.

I walked around checking the tires, hydraulic lines, and intake, external lights, tail surface, Aileron movement. I climbed up the yellow ladder and lowered myself into the cockpit. Perry whacked me on the top of my head in greeting, he helped strap me in and connect the lines. He climbed down after I plugged in the helmet fittings. I hit the power switch watching the instrument panel come alive. The two flat screens came on, panel lights came on, I checked to see that the throttle was all the way back, gear were locked, battery switch was on. I moved my feet on the rudder pedals moving them making sure they weren't jammed. The parking brake was set, the stick was free and clear, foot pedals moved, air brakes were in, flaps were set, elevator trim was set to neutral,

I looked out the left at Perry and spun my finger in a circle warning him I was starting the engine. He nodded. I hit the starter switch and the turbine started to spool up slowly. I checked the drop tank fuel levels. They were full. The internals were all full of fuel as well. Generator showed green, hydraulics good, pressure booster was within limits. External lights were on. Turbine temp was within limits. I moved around a little to settle myself in for the flight. Perry climbed up and closed the canopy for me. I locked it in place.

"Greywolf 1 requesting clearance," I called over the radio to the tower.

"Greywolf 1clear for takeoff, runway 7 west. Wind is at 4, humidity is at 32, pattern is clear," the voice came over my headphones. The bright green images being projected on the inside of my helmet visor were accurate.

I punched in the coordinates telling the nav computer where I was. The fighter was trembling, all this power being held back. She was alive and ready to fly. I gave Perry thumbs up and he pulled away the ladder then the landing gear chocks. I let out the brake and gave her enough power to taxi down the ramp to the end of the runway.

Once there I again locked the brakes, went through a thorough panel check. Everything looked green. Fuel was full, generator was on line, radio was on the correct freqs, IFF was working, pressure was within limits, I was ready. I let out the brakes, moved the throttle forward with my left hand, hit the afterburner and felt the familiar rush of acceleration as almost 20,000 pounds of thrust rocketed me down the runway. The base raced past me, the front wheel lifted off the runway. I gained lift, pulled back on the stick, and left the runway. Gear came up. I gained altitude, and brought the flaps up. Afterburner was shut down and the steady hum of the engine vibrated the fighter around me.

I circled the field and dropped my gear, then retracted them. I manipulated the flaps, then the ailerons. They functioned normally. I did a series of maneuvers to test the maneuverability of the fighter.

I made a series of slow gentle turns. I pulled the stick to the right and rotated the fighter around, watching the horizon spin. I engaged the afterburner and pulled back on the stick climbing straight up. The Turmansky turbine functioned flawlessly. I pulled back on the stick and grunted to deal with the g forces. The blue green ocean was below me as I pulled the nose of the fighter towards the horizon and level flight again completing the roll. I pushed the stick forward and dove the fighter within it's safety limits before pulling back on the stick, several hundred feet closer to the surface of the ocean. Off in the distance I could see the wake of a large ship as it made it's way towards Cuba. It had a dark blue hull and a white superstructure. Giving the appearance of some type of cruise ship. I flew lower to get a closer look at this ship and as I flew past its starboard side bow to stern, I was surprised at the lack of people above deck. Most cruise ships I had seen were heavily populated on deck. This one looked desolate of any tourists. It was showing a Panamanian flag. My RWR went off telling me she had some type of military type aircraft detection radar on board, a curious thing for a cruise ship to have. I made note of her name amongst the notes on my leg board and turned away. I'd pass this on after landing. I circled around the rear of the ship, and then turned west.

The helmet projection system was working normally, displaying speed, direction, altitude, fuel levels, and compass heading. I used the selector switch to change the different images being projected onto the interior of the visor. It was an amazing system that was designed to assist pilots during air combat to keep eyes outside the cockpit during the various maneuvers. It was vital for survival.

I gained altitude and made a turn back towards the island and the base. I radioed the tower receiving landing clearance, adjusted the flaps, and trimmed her for landing. Flying my approach I went through the checks, adjusted throttle, and cone was in the correct position, gear came down with a secure clunk. About 1100 feet out I adjusted flaps again, lined up perfectly with the runway, adjusted throttle. The air brakes were out. I flared slightly just before the rear wheels touched down. The front landing gear came down and I hit the brakes deploying the drag chute.

At the end of the runway, I dropped the chute, brought the flaps up, pulled in the air brakes, turned her onto the side ramp and taxied back to the front of the hanger. I set the brake. The throttle was back full. I went through the shutdown procedure hitting various switches putting the fighter back to sleep.

This was the first of several flights I would make in this fighter before I signed her off as airworthy and ready for delivery. I was happy that this fighter had performed flawlessly on its first flight. Perry came up with the yellow ladder and gently placed it up against the side of the fighter, climbing up and opening the canopy after I had hit the unlock lever. He reached in and slipped in the safety pins to the ejection seat, then helped me disconnect from the fighter.

"How'd she fly?" he asked me as I climbed out.

"4 O," I told him using the Navy slang for perfect.

"Antonio will be happy to hear that," he smiled at me.

"I'll bet, he's moving right on schedule with this contract so far," I told him.

"Its good business, keeps us in beer," He joked. Later inside the building, still in my flight suit I wrote up the first flight report. When I finished it I knocked on Ali's office door. As usual she had a phone stuck to her ear. Her face brightened as she smiled at me. I sat down across from her waiting.

"Hey sailor," she greeted me as she got up and came around the desk. I stood up and kissed her, wrapping my arms around her.

"You're all sweaty," she giggled. "I'm jealous, I thought I was the only thing that got you all hot and bothered,"

"Well you're my favorite way to get all hot and sweaty," I told her.

"Ya sure, I'll bet you say that to all the girls," She said looking up into my eyes. She let go as the phone began to ring. I sat back down rereading my report as she talked with a far away supplier about engine parts. I was always amazed such a beautiful woman could discuss the finer points of Russian engine parts with the best of them.

"How did this flight test go?" she was all business again hanging up the phone.

"Fine, no problems today. Everything functioned perfectly," I said handing her my report.

"I'll let Antonio know," She smiled. It was a weird life I lived. On one hand I was her husband, on the other hand as a test pilot for the company she was technically my boss. Then outside the company, I was a Colonel in the new Cuban Air Force. It was amazing how we blended everything together to function as well as we did. Company manager and test pilot, husband and wife, Colonel and military wife. Nothing about my life was normal after I had left the U.S. Navy. I wouldn't have traded it for anything.

"I did see something unusual today tho, I intercepted a blue cruise ship, Panamanian flag, yet I didn't see any tourists above decks and she was emitting military type surface radar, might want to let Antonio know about this. It's probably nothing, but ya never know," I told her.

"Ok I will," She replied seriously, writing this down on her yellow pad.

"I'll pass this on Monday too, might be nothing but it might be important," I told her. She had her TV on the cable news channel. The Guatemalan change of government was on. China was setting up an economic assistance program for the newly created nation. I still felt angry about the way the communists had taken over the country.

"Hot Damn!" I yelled jumping to my feet. "Hon where is Antonio now? Is it possible to speak with him?" I asked her. I had just gotten an idea and wanted to talk with Antonio about it.

"I'll find out," she said reaching for the phone. "He's in his office, you can go talk to him now," she said after a minute.

"Thanks Hon, I'll talk at ya later," I told her as I breezed out of her office, still in my flight suit fresh with sweat from my flight. I Banged on Antonio's office door and heard his voice telling me to come.

"What seems to be on your mind Sean?" He asked putting down a folder he had in his hands. He slowly closed it keeping me from seeing it.

"I've got an idea I want to pass by you. We can use guerrilla warfare in the air to fight the Chinese if they attack Mexico,' I said.

He sat back and folded his hands across his stomach waiting to hear the rest of my idea.

"Okay, we know they'll be flying J-11s, and they are nasty fighters. We use hit and run tactics against them, but with a twist. First we need to figure out what type of flying platform to mount these systems aboard, then we use that aircraft to draw them out in a certain direction, while we use our fighters to come at them from really low altitude, launch our missiles, then run like hell," I continued on. He sat forward and placed both hands on his desk, I really had his attention now.

"We fly an aircraft at a certain altitude they can't miss picking up. It emits such a strong radar sweep it'll be impossible to ignore. When our plane picks them up on their radar, it transmits their location to us, waiting down in the weeds so to speak. We'll be hiding within the various mountain ranges and once we know where they are, we pop up, hit em hard and run. They'll never see us comin. We use different types of radar every time, like from an F-15, or a MIG-29, or a Mirage, each time that plane goes up. They will think it's a different aircraft each time," I explained.

"Making it harder for them to believe it will be one single aircraft each time it goes up, our own little version of an AWACs." He finished for me.

"You got it, makes it easier to protect our asset, our one plane will have to have different types of radar systems installed in it,"

"It'll help them think there are many different types of fighters every time, helping to protect it," He read my mind further, sitting back in his chair. I watched a smile cross his face as he pondered it.

"Those J-11s are a bitch, and what we will be flying against them can't touch their technology, But like England did to the Germans in the Second World War, we use guile against them. We'll need a couple of escort fighters to fly security for the radar platform. We take out their fighters one by one, an air war of attrition. The more of them we knock out in the air, the less of them will be available to attack Mexico." I went on.

"You are a sneaky sonofabitch, I'm glad you're on our side," He said with an evil grin.

"We'll have to come up with a plane fast enough and big enough for the job," I thought aloud.

"There is fuel consumption to consider," he added.

"I figure if anyone can come up with an aircraft that can do the job you can," I told him with a grin. "We can do this Antonio, we can make it work, this will give us the edge we need to defeat them in the air enroute to attacking Mexican Air Bases," Excitement in my voice.

"I've been wracking my brain trying to come up with a way to defeat them in the air and here you come waltzing into my office with the answer," He said with a laugh. "Did you have an idea what type of plane we could use?" he asked me.

"How bout a modified Lear Jet, they are fast, maneuverable, and can be easily re configured inside to accommodate what we need," I told him quickly.

"You think fast on your feet," He told me, impressed. "I like it, I think we can do this Sean,"

"Will the brass allow us to train together as a team?" I asked him.

"Yes, I think they will, if it means sending over one team of pilots to fight the Chinese instead of half of the Cuban Air Force, hell yes they will. Question is, can you guys really pull this off?" He asked seriously looking into my eyes.

"Fuckin aye we can, we'll need to practice together. Come up with different attack plans, but hell yes we can do this Antonio. Damned straight we can," I assured him.

"It came to me while I was watching the news on Ali's TV, they were talking about how they used guerrilla warfare to defeat the Guatemalan Military, that's when it hit me. We can do the same thing to them before they decide to attack Mexico's air bases," I told him.

"Awright, you put a report together on paper, something I can pass along to the right people, don't put your name on it just yet. When the time comes I'll see you get recognition for this idea. I'll make some phone calls, and then I'll set up a meeting. You come up with some pilots you think will be good enough for this mission. Get back to me with this plan on paper and a list of pilots. I'll do the talking," He told me.

"Also I saw a blue cruise ship off the east coast, it had a Panamanian flag on it, but no passengers on deck. When I buzzed it I picked up a military type radar, kind of unusual for a cruise ship with no passengers," I added.

"Forget you ever saw it, that ship doesn't exist. Don't speak with anyone about this, understand?" He ordered with a stern look on his face.

"Yes sir." I told him. I had learned that Antonio always knew more than the rest of us about things, and it always worked out to follow his orders. I wore a big grin as I left his office. I felt a lot better inside. Now we had a way to beat those Chinese fighters. I knew we could make this work. He didn't have to tell me to keep quiet about this. I already knew not to share this with anyone. He had my curiosity peaked concerning that unusual blue cruise ship. I still had a great deal of energy left, I went to my flight locker and retrieved my G-suit, then walked out of the hanger and around back. There were several fighters out there, some in various levels of repair. I walked outside behind the hanger.

My Mig-15 was sitting there, shiny as a new car. I unlocked the canopy and opened it, reaching in and taking out the helmet. I did a walk around checking to make sure there was nothing unusual. Everything looked secure. I climbed up on the wing and lowered myself inside.

I strapped myself in and hit the power switch watching the panel come alive. Another switch and the modernized self-starting engine came to life. Two drop tanks were full of fuel, as was the internal tank. I sat there enjoying the feeling of power as the little fighter vibrated around me. I did a quick check of all the instruments, and secured the helmet onto my head.

"GreyWolf is requesting clearance for takeoff in zero 5," I called the tower.

"GreyWolf is cleared for takeoff, runway 7 west, wind is at 5, humidity is at 62, pattern is clear, have a nice flight sir," The tower replied. I lowered the canopy, let out the brakes and moved the throttle slightly. The Mig rolled slowly towards the ramp and out to the end of the runway. I locked the brakes, and did a slow thorough pre-takeoff checklist. IFF was functioning, fuel was full, hydraulics good, pressure was within limits, and radio was set properly. I was satisfied, I replaced my written checklist, and let out the brakes. I moved the throttle forward with my left hand, engaged the afterburner and the thrust rocketed me down the runway. The little fighter lifted off in a shorter distance than the Mig-21. I lifted the gear, and then the flaps. Soon I was out over the blue green ocean and heading east.

Below me I could see the blue cruise ship docking at an industrial dock. That was very unusual for a cruise ship, most of them docked in Havana, close to the shopping section of the city. That made it easier for all the tourists to spend all those American greenbacks. Most curious indeed.

My RWR went off and I scanned the area with my radar, looking for the source.

"TALLYHO!" I heard in my headphones as a white and blue A-4 flashed past my left wing. I had been so busy looking at that cruise ship I hadn't seen the fighter approaching. There was only one voice in the world that sounded like that.

"You up for some fun amigo?" Boner called out to me.

"Betcha, lets go," I called back turning into his six. I scanned the radar screen to verify there were no other commercial aircraft in this area.

"Might as well have some fun while I'm flight testing this one," He told me over the radio.

"You're mine meho," I told him. I watched him engage his afterburner and climb straight up into the sun, then pull back on the stick into an inverted roll. I stayed with him on his six, grunting and feeling my G-suit inflate around my legs and abdomen as I followed him down the backside of the loop. He turned into a tight right turn; I stayed right with him as he raised his right wing and reversed the turn. He dove to the deck and then pulled up about 1000 feet from the surface of the ocean. I anticipated him to turn to the left when he pulled up, so I raised my right wing and cut the corner watching him fly right past my illuminated gunsight being projected onto the inside of the canopy in front of me as he climbed.

"Bad move meho, fox one," I called to him letting him know I had him in my sights, close enough to shoot him down with my cannons.

"Sheeit," He called back. I grinned at his discomfort. "My turn," I told him. He turned to my left as I pulled to the right. He was trying to work his way onto my six for a shot. I Turned left quickly, and split essed. He did manage to get onto my tail. I lifted my left wing and rolled the little Mig, cutting my throttle slightly. I watched him out of the top of my canopy slide past me and I increased throttle, pulled up under him for another imaginary kill shot.

"Your slipping meho, you're outta practice," I mocked him as I came up behind him.

"Yo mama," He joked back. I pulled up on his left wing looking over at him in the gleaming A-4. He threw me a wave, which I returned.

"To the moon Alice," He called over to me as he suddenly pulled back on his stick and climbed, his afterburner pushing him straight up. I pulled back on my stick and engaged my own afterburner. We used to play these games years before when we were both lieutenants in the U.S. Navy aboard the USS Grant flying F-18s. We were climbing for the sun together, one A-4 Sky Hawk and one MIG-15.

"Upstairs," I called out to him as I pulled back on the stick and watching as he did the same coming at me head on at the bottom. By calling upstairs I was letting him know I would pass over him as we passed each other at the bottom of the loop. He flashed below me and I snap rolled to the left as I knew he would snap roll to his right. We had perfected this aerial dance many years ago. It was sheer pleasure doing it again. This was the heart pounding adrenalin pumping exhilarating type of flying. Looking over my shoulder I could see the designs our contrails were leaving in the blue sky. I could imagine what it looked like from below.

"Corkscrew," He called out to me. We again climbed for the sun, this time we spun around each other as we climbed creating a corkscrew effect with our contrails. This was flying for the express pleasure of blasting through the sky together.

"Bingo fuel," I heard him call out to me as we reached the top indicating he was getting low on fuel. I was having so much fun I hadn't even looked at my fuel gauges.

"Copy that," I replied taking position off his right wing. Boner requested landing clearance from the tower and we came in together almost touching wings as we landed at the same time. It was like we were welded together as we both touched down simultaneously. I followed him back to the hanger and parked next to his A-4, locking my brakes and cutting my engine. I slowly unlocked the canopy and opened it. I peeled off my helmet shaking the sweat away from my face.

"HOOYAAH," I heard him call over to me. I smiled back at him as I slowly disconnected my harness. I stood up and carefully climbed out.

I saw Ali approaching us from the hanger door.

"Boys and their toys," She called to me across the tarmac.

"Were you watching?" I asked her.

"The whole base was stud," She teased as she hugged me. "My phone rang telling me an air-show was going on and for me to look outside if I didn't want to miss it, how did it fly Boner?" She was all business again.

"Great, no problems ma'am," He joked taking off his flight gloves. Antonio had been standing against the side of the hanger with a crowd of techs.

"Quite a show guys," He called to us with a grin. "I made a few calls, looks like your idea flies as well as you do with the brass. You need to share your ideas with the rest of the team,"

"When?"

"How about tomorrow? Can you put it all together by then on paper?"

"Can do. I'll have it put together, no problem," I assured him.

CHAPTER NINE

That night I sat at the computer putting together the plan. We had successfully flown a sneak attack during our raid on Cuba two years before, so I had no doubt similar tactics would work. Question was, could it be transmitted miles away to our fighters. The distance was the question, there would have to be some type of booster to send the signal, to us miles away, as well as encoded so it couldn't be intercepted. It was late into the night before I was able to crawl into bed with Ali and hold her soft warm body in my arms.

The next morning Ali and I climbed into the Humvee for the ride to the base. I was in uniform with three tiny sets of gold wings on my left chest. We pulled into the base in front of the auditorium. When we walked in I was surprised at the amount of people that were there waiting. Antonio, Raul, Alexi, Manuel, Boner, and General Rodriguez. Several other Colonels were there as well. What I did not expect to see was the most powerful man on the island, the General who was in charge of the government.

"Did you expect all this?" Ali whispered to me as we walked in.

"Hell no," I replied.

"Welcome," Antonio greeted us. "Ready?" He asked looking at me.

"Sure," I lied putting down my briefcase on the table. Ali took her seat next to Antonio with her own set of my notes in her folder. The room was quiet as I took off my hat placing it next to my briefcase. I opened it taking out my notes.

"Good morning," I started after taking a deep breath.

"I have devised a plan I believe can help our team deal with the advanced Chinese J-11s in the event they attack our allies' bases," I began. "We can use a Trojan horse of sorts to divert their attention in one direction and attack them from another. We do this by using a jet aircraft emitting a military type of radar, which sweeps an area, then transmits their position to our fighters flying inside a mountain range at very low altitude. We'll fly too low for them to detect on their radar screens. After we receive their location, we attack them from below, fire our missiles, then dive and escape before they know what hit them. Every time they launch their fighters to attack, we use a different type of radar, to confuse them into thinking it is a different type of fighter every time. It will convince them we are using different fighters at different altitudes. It will enhance survivability of our Trojan horse aircraft. I propose we use a highly modified Learjet, with at least four different types of military radar aboard with a booster to send the signal to our team. It has to be transmitted encoded to our fighters avoid any unauthorized interception by the Chinese,"

"The Israelis used a similar trick years ago. Except they launched unmanned aircraft transmitting an IFF that was identical to their fighters. Enemy fighters and SAM missiles intercepted these decoys. The Israelis came in behind the decoys and eliminated the dangerous SAM sites, which gave them the edge to successfully complete their bombing runs. By the time the Israeli fighters made their runs, the enemy fighters were already low on fuel,"

"Won't the Chinese catch on after being hit like this a couple of times?" General Rodriguez asked me.

"Not if we attack them in two waves from two different directions. They will never catch on to how we are intercepting them prior to their bombing runs." I explained.

"Hot damn," Boner exclaimed with a grin. Raul was smiling. Alexi was nodding his head up and down at the idea.

"We'll kick ass," Manuel threw in.

"The Chinese J-11s are very nasty fighters. Not to mention the radar sites I'm sure they are building right now on the border with Mexico. We may not be able to beat their technology right now, but we can beat them using guerrilla war tactics in the air. Anticipate their plans, and then sucker punch them," I went on.

"How do you propose to predict their plans?" General Rodriguez asked.

"By planning missions against the Mexican targets ourselves. We put together an attack plan based on the defenses of each base, and the terrain surrounding each base. Decide how WE would attack these targets. The Chinese after all have to operate within these same parameters. So we explore the boundaries they have to operate by and exploit their weaknesses. Then we use knife edge tactics that give us the advantage,"

"How dangerous will this be?" The General finally spoke.

"Extremely dangerous sir. Our team will need to study Chinese tactics, apply them to an attack plan we devise, and then devise a strategy to deal with their tactics. It will require split second knife edge coordinated flying on our part," I answered.

"What do you anticipate the training accident rate will be?" he asked.

"Well, I believe we can accomplish our training routine with very few losses Sir. During the Second World War there was a group of American volunteers that were sanctioned by President Roosevelt to help the Chinese fight the Japanese Air Force, before the United States entered the war. They used older P-40 War hawks, that were inferior to Japanese Zeros. The general assigned to lead this unit, General Chenault, devised an early warning system that was very primitive. Yet it worked very well, giving the American pilots prior warning to the Japanese bombing raids. General Chenault devised a series of simple air tactics that exploited the weaknesses of the Japanese tactics. Every time the Japanese flew bombing raids, not only were they intercepted early, they lost aircraft during every raid. The P-40s would fly at a higher altitude then the approaching Jap bombers, and then dive on them out of the sun. We can devise tactics to intercept their fighter, and then use hit and run tactics to shoot them down," I explained.

"Won't they be able to predict your direction?" he asked.

"Not if we hit them from two or three different angles. If we hit them two or three times and always from a different direction, we'll whittle them down to nothing before they can arrive at their target. It'll be a war of attrition. Over time well just wipe the skies clear of them. If every time their fighters take off to attack a Mexican target, their fighters never return, it won't be long before they rethink their goals, like every pre invasion plan, control of the air is the first step. If the Chinese gain air superiority, then their next step is to send in ground troops. We deny them air superiority and they can't send in ground troops. We learn from history. The British defeated the German s in the Battle of Britain. By denying the Germans control of the air over England, it prevented the Germans from invading." I added.

"Do you believe you can really do this?" General Rodriguez asked me.

"Yes sir I do. Our people are that good sir. We'll need more than what we have right now to form our team. I'm convinced that once we have our team assembled, and trained, we'll be able to eliminate anything the Chinese throw up at us," I told him confidently.

"Can you provide this Trojan Horse Antonio?" The General asked looking at Antonio.

"Yes, we can. We can provide what is necessary. First we'll need to purchase the aircraft, and then we can install the systems," He answered confidently. "I have the financial figures already together," he added handing him a folder. We all watched the General open it and read through it. I looked at Alexi, then Raul. They both were watching the General's face. Boner was sitting there relaxed and calm as ever.

"Colonel my people have been trying to create some type of plan to deal with the possible Chinese attacks on Mexico. It seems you have come up with one. From what I can see here, it sounds like a good one. I authorize you people to put together this team in the eventuality we may need you to help our Mexican ally defend their airfields. You may have whatever you need, within reason to form this team. Please contact me personally if you need anything. My door is always open to you Colonel." He said looking at me. "Antonio, you may begin work on this project right away. I'll have the economics ministry deposit the funds into your company account in the usual manner. Don't let us down gentlemen. The future of Cuba could very well rest on your shoulders. "He stood up and we all stood up snapping to attention. He nodded his head once and walked out of the room. The rest of the Colonels followed him out.

"You really think we can pull this off?" Manuel asked when they had left the building.

"Da, yes. We can do this," Alexi told him.

"Well, we'll need to put our heads together and figure out all the details," Raul added.

"Do we get to choose our wing man?" Boner asked with a grin.

"Yes you do. I guess you just enlisted in the Cuban Air Force," Antonio told him with a smile.

"Hot Damn, together again, the dynamic duo, HOO YEAH!" Boner yelled out. I grinned at him.

"What is this country coming to," Generall Rodriguez said shaking his head, with a grin.

"Awright. First we'll need to make a list of possible recruits for our little band of outlaws here. Raul and I can do that, with a little help from the other base commanders around the island. Alexi, once again we'll be depending on your instructor skills to help push us to our limits. Antonio, we'll need any intelligence you can provide us about the Chinese air combat tactics, as well as the operating abilities of their J-11s. I'll talk with Perry I'm sure he'll be glad to volunteer as our drill instructor again," I told them.

"Aw shit," Manuel exclaimed.

"Damn," Raul added. I heard Alexi moan cursing in Russian. Antonio shook his head smiling.

"Again?" General Rodriguez asked with a perplexed look on his face.

"Inside joke sir." Antonio said quickly. Boner looked at me with but kept quiet.

"Where do we operate from?" Manuel asked.

"I will find us a home, don't worry. You heard the General. He said we could have whatever we need within reason. If you are going to train together then you'll need your own section of the base to operate from," Antonio told him.

"I can help you there, I know of an unused maintenance hangar on the other side of this base you can use, it may need some work though," General Rodriguez volunteered.

"Good, that will be a start," Antonio told him.

"Who is the leader of this band of outlaws?" Boner asked. Every eye looked at Raul.

"Raul has my vote," I said quickly.

"Here here," Boner put in.

"I'll drink to that," Manual said.

"Mine as well," Alexi added.

"Once more into the breach," Raul told us." I'll need an exec tho," he said looking at me.

"Lead on oh fearless leader," I joked. Colonel Rodriguez sat there listening.

"May I ask a question?" All our heads turned in his direction. "Is this the group that bombed the Bejucal installation?" We all stopped cold. Ali's face went white. We all looked at Antonio.

"It's as I suspected. There have been rumors here for a long time about you people,"

"General, if that was ever to be thought of as the truth, we could all wind up in an alley somewhere with our throats slit," Raul told him.

"You have nothing to fear. I've suspected for some time. I've never said anything about this. Besides I never believe in rumors," He said with a smile." I will do whatever I can to assist you. I do not wish to see any young Cuban pilots killed uselessly in a war with the Chinese any more than anyone else does. This team you propose could be a firewall of sorts that keeps us safe here. I too understand the consequences of a Chinese victory over Mexico. I for one do not wish to see Cuba return to the old ways. You spoke of slit throats in alley ways Colonel," He said looking at Raul. "I have no illusions about how long I would live if I should ever speak out of turn," He said looking at Antonio.

"I do protect my people," Antonio said with a voice as cold as ice, His eyes dark. Alexi stood up wordlessly staring at Rodriguez. Antonio put his hand out and Alexi sat back down. It was more of a show of strength than anything else. It was well known within our group that Alexi could snap a man's neck with his bare hands. We all were very loyal to Antonio, Alexi more so. Antonio had given Alexi a job as a flight instructor for the company when the Soviet Union collapsed leaving Alexi abandoned in India. He had been there training Indian Air Force pilots flying the Russian MIG-21. When the Soviet Union collapsed, Alexi was left without a job, and penniless. Alexi would do anything for Antonio, including making people disappear if necessary.

"I'm an honorable man, a man of my word. Confidentially I was glad to see the old regime fall away. Cuba is a happy country once again. I do not wish to see this end," he told us.

"From this point on, all of you may call me Roberto. No one else dare call me that. You sit here thinking I hold your lives in my hands. I do not forget that all of you hold my life in your hands. I love my family and do not wish to prematurely leave them. You have my word I will never reveal what I've suspected to anyone. If ever you need anything, please ask, I will do what I can to help. I too wish to volunteer to join your little band of outlaws as you call yourselves, that is if you'll have me," He said, looking at us one by one. We all looked at Antonio.

"Welcome to the family, Roberto," Antonio said getting up and reaching with his hand. Roberto shook it. One by one we reached over and shook his hand. I was hoping Antonio knew what he was doing. He was betting all our lives on this decision.

"We'll need a liaison officer for this unit Roberto, so I guess you're elected," Raul told him." We will be very busy soon, by helping to streamline the red tape and paperwork between us and the government, that will free us up to concentrate on the rest of the mission." Antonio told him.

"I would be honored, I am too old to fly, but there are many other things I can contribute to the unit," He assured us. "How will it be possible to be reassigned to this new unit?"

"You heard the General, he said whatever we needed, within reason," I reminded him.

"I'll speak with the General Roberto. I'm sure he'll arrange it," Antonio told him. We spent the next two hours planning, talking, and taking notes. We had a new mission. It felt good to be part of something active again. Something more than just training young pilots to fly. What a crazy idea, guerrilla fighter pilots. What the hell, There were crazier ideas out there.

The next day instead of test flying the Mig a second time, I went with everyone to inspect a hanger on the far side of the base. It was old, and unused, but would suit our purposes. It was large enough to do maintenance on our fighters; there was a small room we could convert into a conference room, as well as two offices. There was a large bathroom with showers, and a kitchen.

We spent the next two weeks doing our own repairs on the building and modernizing the interior. Phones were installed, computers hooked up, plumbing was replaced, furniture was brought in, an air conditioning system was installed, a weight room was also added. We built bunk beds and moved in lockers for sleeping quarters. There was a small TV lounge next to the living quarters. Manuel and I designed a logo for the team. It was a wolf howling at the full moon under a sky of stars.

It was green and black inside a circle. We hung the large wooden emblem on the inside hanger wall. It was the first thing visible when you entered. Out in front of the hanger we put up a flagpole with a large Cuban flag at the top. Fourteen days later we moved in and held our first team meeting.

"I've got some detailed information concerning the Chinese J-11s," Antonio told us. We were seated around the huge old round oak table Perry had scrounged. The giant window air conditioner was humming in the wall behind us that Roberto had acquired for us.

"It is a fly by wire fighter. These aircraft have two Lyulka turbofans with afterburners that put out 55,000 pounds of thrust. Top speed is around Mach 2 plus, max ceiling is 60,000 feet, with a range of 1000 miles. They are armed with a 30-millimeter cannon, and can carry up to 10 missiles. There are eight under wing hard points plus two wingtip rails. There is a helmet mounted sight system slaved to the missile guidance system. They can carry up to ten radar homing and infrared missiles. These include the Aphid, Archer, and Alamo. Their radar includes Infrared track and search with look down shoot down capability using a Doppler Pulse system. They carry a rear facing radar emitter that illuminates targets to their rear. This gives them rear target firing capability. It is an all weather capability fighter. They do not have in-flight refueling capability. Supposedly the autopilot contains the ability to return to level flight from any position at the push of a button. They can carry external ECM pods. Their naval variant has folding wings, and was developed from the Russian SU-27K naval version. They have completed flight testing on their new carrier, which is now fully operational." He revealed. There was silence around the table as we sat there ingesting the info. This was one badass fighter. The only thing we had that was even close in capability was the Mig-29.

"The Chinese have 150 of these fighters, 25 being the naval variant. The Chinese have spent years purchasing decommissioned carriers from other countries and reverse engineering the designs. Their carrier is the former Soviet Navy Kuznetsov class Varyag. It was rebuilt at the Dalian shipyard in Northeast China. She has an elevated flight deck at the bow." He sat back closing the folder. I looked around the table wondering if we had bitten off more than we could chew.

"I'd like to add this, the Chinese think long term. They are experts at reverse engineering. If they can't copy a weapons system, they dismantle it and discover how it works. If they can't produce a similar system, they work on creating counter systems that they sell to other countries."

"They then use that money to purchase state of the art military systems from around the world. This makes them dangerous adversaries," He finished. We sat there digesting his words.

"Can you handle the maintenance without any trouble?" He asked Perry. He would have to do system maintenance on Alexi' and Raul's MIG-29s, Boner's A-4 and the MIG-21s that Manuel and I would be flying. It would be a logistics nightmare.

"My team can handle it boss no problem," He said confidently.

"Here is a list of pilots we have come up with to add to the team," I said handing him the folder. I had talked with the pilots on the list earlier, and they had enthusiastically agreed to join the team. He opened it and scanned the names. He nodded his head.

"I'll pass these along," He said." Perry, can we use the same transport we used for the last mission? Will you need more than one? You have three different types of aircraft to keep flying,"

"No, one will not be enough. We'll need at least four."

"OK Ill see what I can arrange. The Cuban Government is footing the bill for this one, so I want to keep this mission as affordable as possible," Antonio went on.

"Ok, from now on every morning 0800, calisthenics and hand to hand fighting classes will be given here, we don't want any pussies on this team," Perry grinned wickedly. This brought groans from everyone. Antonio smiled at us. Ali shook her head looking at the floor.

"We will have a shooting class at the base range. If any of us survive ejection, it will help to keep us alive," Alexi told us with a serious look on his face.

"Yes, very good idea Alexi thank you," Raul answered him.

"We'll be rootin tootin Chinese shootin beer drinkin nightmares from hell," Boner said with enthusiasm.

"That's what I like to hear. A positive mental attitude," I said grinning.

"I took the liberty of designing team patches for everyone," Roberto said opening a yellow envelope spilling the green and black circular patches on the table. The design was identical to the emblem hanging above our heads.

"Wow check this out," Manuel said grabbing one. We each reached in and took one.

"I can paint this onto the tail of each fighter pretty easily," Perry told us looking at the patch in his hand.

"On a more serious note, concerning getting shot down," I said, as it got silent around the big table. "Is there any way we can go through the jungle survival course being run at Bejucal by the U.S. Military? I think it would go a long way in helping us get back in the event we do have to eject over the jungle. I know none of us want to think about it, but it would be a good idea. Also right before we deploy we might want to practice some parachute jumps as well," I finished.

"I'll make some phone calls, see if that can be arranged, good idea Sean," Antonio told me. Ali was writing furiously on her notepad. She had a serious look on her face. She was trying to keep up with us as we were coming up with ideas.

"As economics go, those of you that are in the Air Force will continue to receive your usual military pay, but there will be something extra in your company check. Perry, Boner, you'll receive additional compensation for your part in this," Antonio explained. "As far as the Cuban Government is concerned those of you in uniform are officially listed as attached to this unit, with Raul as the Commanding Officer, Sean as the exec and Roberto as our liaison officer, Alexi as the training officer. Perry here will put together a joint company and Cuban Air Force maintenance team that will be traveling with you. Ali will handle any supply needs. Get with her as usual Perry," Antonio went on. Perry nodded at him.

"You are already familiar with the setup at the Tuxtla Gutierrez base you were TDY at in Mexico, the team will be stationed there. I've been told there have been some major modifications all over the base since you left. They have purchased a lot of new weapon systems, from our company as well as from other companies. They are taking this threat very seriously. Seems your suggestions hit home with them," Antonio said looking at Raul.

"They'll need them," Raul said.

"You think we still have a six month window?" I looked at Antonio.

"At least that long yes. They need time to organize. The Chinese are not supermen. They are good pilots yes, but not invincible. They are weak at night flying, as well as during bad weather. They have poor low altitude combat tactics. Their interceptions are tightly controlled from the ground. They have their weaknesses. You should be able to exploit these weaknesses to your advantage," He tried encouraging us.

"The Chinese built indigenous WS-10A turbofan engines for their J-11s. From the intelligence reports I've received these engines have numerous technical problems and it has less thrust than the original Russian AL-31F engines."

"This means the Chinese J-11s have less maneuverability than the Russian SU-27s. The Chinese J-11s lack the Russian thrust vectoring abilities. The Chinese J-11 has a heads up display with their helmet system. It lacks a hands on throttle and stick system. Their Phazon Pulse Doppler radar system is not top of the line. It is plagued with false alarms. I've heard it is a bit complicated to use and it does have certain blind spots. Chinese J-11s have KNIRTI SPS-171/L005 Sorbtsi phased array RCM pods located on the wingtips. These internal jammers came from the design used in the Russian backfire bombers."

"We are in the process of acquiring the frequencies their missiles use, so you'll be able to jam them," He went on. "That will give you an advantage," His look told me I didn't want to inquire about the means being used to get this information.

"I'll do everything I can to supply you with whatever you need to succeed. I've also spoken with the General about a plan to create an early warning system to alert you when the Chinese fighters lift off from their bases. If it succeeds, it will give you the warning you were asking for." He finished. With that the meeting ended.

The next morning I drove to our hanger and walked inside away the early morning sun. I punched in my code that opened the heavy steel security door. There were six fighters inside being worked on. I walked up to the closest Mig-21 and saw Perry upside down in the cockpit, his feet hanging out.

"SUNOVABITCH!" His voice echoed inside the hanger. A wrench came sailing out and landed on the concrete floor with a clang. He slowly extricated himself from the cockpit and sat down on the yellow metal work platform next to the fighter.

"Mornin Marine,' I called to him.

"Fuck you," He returned my greeting with a red face.

"You're not my type, too hairy," I grinned up at him.

"Funnee, damn squids," He replied.

"What can I do to help?" I offered.

"You got rubber fingers?"

"No but I am double jointed if that helps,"

"Well sheeit come on up and lend a hand," He grinned at me. I climbed up the ladder and moved next to him on the yellow metal platform.

He explained what he was trying to install and between the both of us we were able to finish the job. I climbed down walking into the office we all shared. The air conditioner was humming along. Since I had arrived before everyone else I did the honors and started the coffee maker. When the pot was full I poured some into a stained cup. I grabbed my white coffee cup from the hook with my call sign painted on the side under the USS Grant emblem and filled it. I walked back out into the hanger.

"Coffee?" I asked handing the cup to Perry.

"Bless you, I take back what I said about squids," He said sipping the hot black liquid.

"Ahhh fuck you, damn jar head," I replied with a grin. We both laughed. Alexi and Raul walked in together then stopped as Manuel came in behind them.

"Boner should be here soon. There's fresh coffee in the office," I offered just as he entered carrying a cardboard box.

"Breakfast has arrived," He called out. We all followed him into the office as he placed the box on the old wooden table. Inside were two dozen donuts. Hands flew as we all reached in. One by one the others came in, one by one going for the coffee and donuts.

"Breakfast of champions," I joked as we ate and drank coffee. When we had stuffed ourselves, Perry led us outside to the back of the hanger. I was surprised to see a primitive obstacle course.

"You've been busy," I commented.

"Gotta whip you pussies into shape," Perry said with an evil shark-like grin.

"Oh God, not again," Manuel said hanging his head.

"OK girls line up lets go," He called out to us. We lined up and followed him as he jumped up grabbing the bars and swinging one to the other of the overhead ladder, his muscles straining as he swung like a monkey. One by one we followed behind him as we all went through the obstacles.

"Jumping jacks, one an two an one..." He called out to us as we tried to keep up. I could hear Manuel swearing as he tried to keep up. Perry ran us through different exercises for an hour. We were sweating trying to keep up with him. Perry seemed immune to the strain, his muscular body moving like a machine.

"Doesn't he ever get tired?" Boner asked as we switched to pushups.

"No, he doesn't," Manuel answered in between breaths.

"OK Ladies let's take a leisurely jog around the runway, c'mon keep up now," Perry called out as he began to jog. We fell in behind him gasping for breath, our bodies sweating under the hot sun.

"When I was young and in my prime..." He sang.

"Shit not this again, tells me he's not singing," Manuel said.

"He's not singing," I told him breathing heavily.

"God, I hate when he sings," He replied beside me.

"I used to do it all the time. But now I'm older n have more sense; I use a knothole in the fence. C'mon ladies keep up sing along," He called out.

"When I was young and in my prime," Our voices blending together as we ran, panting under the morning sun.

Later we all piled into the back of an ancient faded green military truck that looked like it was left over from the Second World War. Perry shifted gears and the transmission groaned in pain and the tired engine smoked as the truck shook and rattled along the road to where Alexi had set up the shooting range. The brakes squealed in protest and we climbed out. There were six black and white human shaped targets set up in a line on a hill of sand as a backdrop behind them. We unloaded the two wooden boxes and Alexi opened them with a crowbar. One box contained six A-47 assault rifles, 12 thirty round magazines, and three thousand rounds of ammo. The other box contained six 45 caliber 1911 pistols with spare magazines and boxes of ammo. Alexi picked up an AK and held it in his hands.

"This AK-47 is a shoulder fired recoil operated open sight air-cooled magazine fed Russian designed assault weapon capable of firing a 7.62

by 39 caliber full metal jacket military round at 1800 feet per second at a range of 1500 feet with accuracy at three hundred rounds per minute" He barked out in one breath.". It weighs in at 6 pounds unloaded, eight pounds fully loaded. It has been chosen by several countries as a primary military weapon because of its ease of operation, simplicity of design and it's history of reliability during wartime operations. It is an excellent weapon when used within its design limitations. You can drop this weapon, get mud inside the chamber, pick it up, urinate into it to clean it out, and it will fire reliably. Should you find yourself behind enemy lines after a successful ejection, this is the weapon you will encounter. Here you will learn to become proficient with this weapon," He finished. We each lifted one out of the box and he handed out the magazines.

We started to load them. He taught us how to properly seat the magazine inside the opening in the bottom front first and then snap it in place. One by one he showed us how to fire the weapons and how to control the burst of fire when firing it on automatic.

"Short bursts, use fire control," He explained as he fired at a target, holes appearing in the center chest area." If you have to fire from the hip, place the weapon securely against the hip as you fire. Use your body as a firing platform. Otherwise fire the weapon from your shoulder in short fast bursts, maintain trigger control. Remember to conserve ammo as well, you may not have much," He went on. He quickly ejected the empty magazine and replaced it with a full one.

"Always put the empty magazine inside your shirt so you don't lose it," He said as he brought the weapon to his shoulder and fired at the target, alternating between the chest and head filling the paper target with holes.

It took me awhile to get used to mastering the short burst trigger control. I was able to hit the target but my groups were all over the target. There was a satisfying feeling shooting the AK. It fit well in my hands, and the recoil was very manageable. It was a pleasure to shoot. It was a simple straight-forward rifle. The only trouble I had was getting used to the short stock. This weapon was designed for men with shorter arms than I had. By the time the ammo boxes lay empty on the ground we were sweating. Alexi explained how to disassemble the AK and how to clean it. We broke down our weapons and cleaned them.

Next came the 45s. One by one we fired at the targets, learning how to control the heavy recoil of the big handgun. My accuracy had improved by the time we ran out of ammo. We broke these down and cleaned them as well. We policed up our brass and took down our individual targets comparing them to each other. As expected Alexi had the best score, with Perry a close second.

"You have fired these before?" Alexi asked Perry pointing to his AK.

"Oh yeah, in the Corps, many times. I have a healthy respect for the AK, it's a good weapon, it takes practice though like anything else," Perry explained smiling, holding up his paper target with the holes in the center as proof. Looking at my target, holes peppered the target, but not in the center. I knew it would take a lot of practice to become proficient with the weapon. We repacked the weapons into the boxes and loaded them back into the truck.

We climbed up into the back of the truck and rattled our way back to the building with Perry driving. Manuel looked at me with a grin. It reminded me of when we were on Andros Island preparing for our raid on Cuba two years ago. The same feeling was in the air, men working together. I wondered this time how many of us might not be coming back. I had great respect for the Chinese pilots and the capabilities of their fighters. This wasn't going to be a onetime mission like before. This time it would be a campaign.

A constant series of battles until it was over. It was a sobering thought. The others were cutting up and cracking jokes as we rumbled our way back to the hanger.

At the hanger, we climbed out of the old truck and carried the wooden crates inside, locking them up in lockers in the hanger. We walked over to the chow hall and ate lunch. Later we walked back to the hanger and gathered in the meeting room with the huge oak table. The window air conditioner was running as we went over aerial tactics to help us against the Chinese when the time came. The radio was on in the background softly playing a love song from a famous female Cuban singer who now lived in Miami. I was a big fan of her music from her very first song. She now owned a popular restaurant in South Beach.

That night Ali and I sat under the stars holding each other the waves tickling our bare feet. Off to our right the Havana Banana was climbing into the night sky on its last nightly run to Miami.

The next morning the list of pilots that would join our unit arrived. It had been approved by higher ups. As planned we joined Perry out back for our morning workout, sweating and swearing as we jogged around the tarmac. At the end we gathered in the comforting air-conditioned hanger. We looked up as Antonio entered with a folder in his hand.

"This is a list of pilots authorized to join the unit. I hope they are as good as you believe they are. It seems you've stripped the best pilots from around the island and their Commanding Officers are pissed." He told us with an evil grin. We looked over the orders with the official stamp of the Cuban Air Force at the top. Every pilot we had requested was on the list.

"Hot damn, the best of the best. You must have really called in a few favors for this one," I remarked. He just sat there with a smile. I turned the page and looked at another set of orders, all our names were listed. We were to report to the Jungle Warfare Training center at Bejucal run by the U.S. Army. We had two days to report.

"You are a miracle worker." I told him looking at the orders. I passed it around for everyone to read.

"Seven days of fun in the sun," Antonio replied.

"We get to jump, AWRIGHT!" Perry exclaimed with a big smile as he read.

"Oh joy, just what I wanted," Manuel remarked.

"We get to jump out of a perfectly good aircraft, what fun," Boner said sarcastically.

"You awright Alexi?" I asked him looking at his face. It had paled after reading the order.

"I do not like parachuting," He admitted quietly.

"Why Alexi, I believe we have found a chink in your armor," I joked. He remained silent.

"You get to jump into their training facility as a way of beginning your training." Antonio informed us.

"Its not just a job…" I said.

"Its an adventure," Boner finished.

"More American humor?" Raul asked.

"It was a Navy recruiting slogan," Boner explained.

"AH yes, your navy had to advertise for recruits," He grinned. Our attention was diverted by the sound of truck engines outside.

"Your pilots have arrived it seems," Antonio remarked. We got up and walked out into the morning sunshine. Two large deuce an a halves had pulled up in front of the building their diesel engines idling as pilots in green Cuban Air Force uniforms climbed out. I recognized a few right away from seeing their faces in the mess hall. A few looked up at the emblem on the front of the hanger. Some were smiling and joking as they got out. I opened the hanger door and they strolled in looking around as they entered. The truck engines grew loud in our ears as they drove off.

"Gentlemen, form into ranks, stand at attention" Raul barked out taking charge. Twenty pilots formed up into four ranks at attention. The rest of us stood around quietly watching.

"Welcome to Wolf Squadron. You men have been chosen because you are the best. WE will make you better. Believe that. While you are part of this squadron you will follow the rules, obey our orders. I am your CO, Colonel Murphy is your XO." He pointed at me.

"If you follow my rules, we will all get along. If you do not, you'll be the sorriest sonsofbitches in the whole Cuban Air Force. You will report here everyday at 0800 for physical training. After that there will be classroom time, in the afternoons there will be flight training. You will be able to do things with your fighters that even the manufacturers couldn't imagine. Two weeks from now we will report to the Jungle Survival School at Bejucal. Right now you'll be in the capable hands of our physical training instructor. That is all. "He nodded to Perry.

"Gentleman, if you will follow me to the rear of the building. We have designed a wonderful playground for your entertainment." Perry barked out. I didn't envy these guys. We had the luck of doing our exercise program earlier in the morning before the temperature was up.

We watched them follow Perry out into the hot sun.

"Gentlemen, I wish you luck in your endeavors." Antonio told us as he left his huge personal bodyguard in tow. We spent the rest of the morning reading the files on our newest arrivals. After chow we again loaded into the rusted troop carrier and spent the afternoon on the firing range. Many of the new pilots were very skilled with the weapons.

That night Ali and I drove the Z into the city and had dinner. Afterwords we walked hand in hand along the beach. We carried our shoes and our bare feet left impressions in the sand as we walked along the waterline. The stars twinkled above our heads and a warm breeze blew through her long black hair.

"I'm really scared Sean, I'm really worried about you. I don't want you to disappear over some foreign land." She told me.

"I know hon. It'll be all right. I'm flying with the best-trained pilots in the whole Cuban Air Force. You'll see. I'll come back to you. Don't worry, please." I assured her putting my arm around her. She laid her head against my shoulder. I could feel her warm body though the tight dress she wore. I glanced over at her and saw the moonlight reflecting off her cleavage. She looked up at me and grinned at me, digging her elbow into my side.

"Pervert." She told me.

"Ayep, that's why you married me,." I joked back. Later as we drove home we held hands and enjoyed the ride. It was a perfect Caribbean evening. The stereo was playing; the night sky peeked in through the open moon roof as the warm breeze came in. I felt very lucky indeed. My thoughts traveled back to the days when I was imprisoned awaiting my court-martial for shooting down two Cuban MIG 21s against orders. I remembered the deep depressing despair I had felt inside the white concrete walls of my cell, and the kindness of the guards that did their best to sneak me little gifts. Back then all I could see was the ever-widening blackness engulfing me. I felt the U.S. Navy had abandoned me and wanted to make me a scapegoat for political reasons.

Then the generous offer of employment by Antonio after being discharged from the Navy. He hired me to be a test pilot for his company. I went through flight training in India. Alexi a MIG instructor from the old Soviet Union had joined the Indian Air Force as a flight instructor when the Communist Government there collapsed. Later he joined the company. Then the fateful day while flight demonstrating the new weapons systems in the upgraded MIG-21 for the Indian Air Force two Pakistani F-16s jumped me. During the ensuing dogfight, I shot them both down.

This enabled the company to win the contract for the modernization of their fleet of MIG-21s.

Later I was offered a chance to take part in an aerial raid of the Chinese electronic gathering station located at Bejucal south of Havana. The leaders of the Cuban Communist government were holding a secret meeting there with the Chinese representatives. Raul, Alexi, Manuel and I flew three modernized MIG-21s painted in the colors of the Cuban Air Force. We sneaked in, bombed the building, and shot our way out of Cuban airspace landing in the Cayman Islands with empty fuel tanks.

After the demise of the Communist government in Cuba I joined their Air Force and was awarded the rank of Colonel, thanks to Antonio. Now I was going to embark on another adventure. My life seemed full of unexpected twists and turns. Driving along in the Caribbean night with the stars above me and Ali next to me I felt like the luckiest man alive.

When we got home Ali dragged a big towel out on the sand under the stars. She slowly slipped off her dress. She stripped off her lace panties and beckoned me. Together we exhausted ourselves over and over again.

The next morning after our daily workout, Raul, Alexi, Boner, Manuel and I sat around the table finishing paperwork, and preparing everything for our seven day training course in the jungle. We brought in our survival vests and examined each item. What was old or worn we replaced. My flight boots were old but worn in. I knew that if I replaced them with new ones, blisters would form during the next week if we had to do any long distance walking. I had two magazines in my vest and one in my 45. Extra rounds were stored in my vest pockets. In the outside of my right boot I carried a long knife the backside was serrated.

Our survival vests were the best on the market. They were heavy and bulged all over with pouches full of items we might need if we ever ejected. It gave me some comfort to know we had them.

"Better to have these and not need them…" Perry started.

"Than need them and not have them." I finished.

"You have been through this before I assume." Raul asked us.

"Oh yes." I answered back.

"It was a required course during our Navy flight training." Boner added.

"We had a similar class as well." Raul told us.

"I remember very big mosquitoes." Alexi added.

"Well let's hope we won't need these. Besides I hate being anywhere without female companionship," Manuel threw in with a grin. I smiled to myself as I ejected the magazine from my 45 and began field stripping it.

I cleaned it thoroughly and then cycled the slide several times after I put it together. The barrel was clean as was the rest of the weapon. The magazine slid into the handle and seated with a click.

Later we had the new pilots to our team do the same with their survival vests. We supervised their efforts.

CHAPTER TEN

We were in high spirits in the chow hall. We ate at our own table as usual. The other pilots found their own seats together.

"You ready for this Meho?" Boner asked me.

"No, but I'll git it done." I assured him. After chow we were to practice jumping out of a perfectly good aircraft, something most pilots hated. Boner and Perry were two of the few who really enjoyed it.

Later all twenty five of us boarded a green four engine transport and took our seats, our backsides heavy with our parachutes. The ancient Russian transport had that old aircraft smell inside. We sat there thinking our own thoughts as the racket from the huge engines shook the aircraft as we lifted off. I mentally crossed my fingers hoping we would make it into the air. I was glad I had a parachute strapped to my back. If nothing else, at least I was getting out of this flight alive. I wasn't to sure about the pilots. It was too noisy for conversation. I had butterflies in my stomach as it had been years since I had done this. I glanced over at Alexi and saw his face was white. He had a serious look on his face. I nudged Boner next to me and nodded at Alexi. Boner grinned at me nodding his head. This was the first time since Id met him, that Alexi showed any sign of fear. I could see the sun changing sides through the portholes as the aircraft turned. This one was one of the old Soviet troop carriers that all four engines still ran. I looked around me at the faces of the other pilots. Most of them had serious looks on their faces. Boner was grinning like an idiot. He was looking forward to the jump.

The warning buzzer went off, loud above the roar of the engines and the red light came on near the jump door. We all stood up and turned. I checked my helmet to make sure the straps were tight. Boner whacked me on the back of my head and I held up my tightly clenched fist thumb pointing up. The Cuban sergeant opened the hatch and latched it. Sunlight streamed in.

I could hear the change in pitch of the engines as they changed speed. We were flying straight and level.

The light changed from red to green and the klaxon sounded three times telling us it was time to jump. As our leader Raul was the first out the door.

I followed. I braced my legs as I stood at the door, looked straight out, then jumped. The noise of the transport grew less in my ears replaced by the sound of the rushing air. I reached over with my hand and pulled the metal handle and felt the chute release and then the jerk as the canopy filled with air. I looked up and saw it was full.

Raul and I had requisitioned modern canopy style parachutes, the type you could steer as you descended. They were identical to the type we wore while flying our MIGs.

Below me and to my right I could see Manuel. He was drifting farther away from our group. It looked to me like he was going to land a lot farther away from the rest of us. Over my left shoulder slightly above me Boner was floating down. I looked straight out at the horizon at the blue green ocean, then down below me at the green grass at the end of our airfield. The harness was tight around my body and my legs hung down as I floated down. It was a peaceful feeling. For a few seconds I could just enjoy the ride.

I began to make out details below me. I watched as Raul touched down to my right. He hit and rolled, then stood up. I concentrated, picked my spot, and bent my knees ready for impact. There was no wind. I saw the ground rushing up at me. When I landed my feet were together, knees bent, as I rolled to my right, then stood up. I hit the quick disconnect clips so I wouldn't get dragged and watched the chute fold in on itself as it hit the green grass. I looked over and watched Boner do a perfect standing touchdown. He was grinning from ear to ear. I undid the straps of my helmet and slid it off. I turned and started to roll up my chute. The rest of the squadron was landing one by one around me. I was relieved to see everyone land safely. No injuries.

Alexi had a look of great relief on his face as he rolled up his chute.

"Survived another one ay Alexi?" I said with a grin. He only nodded. We jumped two more times. I was amazed that the clunky Russian transport still flew.

That night Ali and I cooked a whole pig under the stars on the beach behind our home. We sat there drinking wine and stuffing ourselves, listening to the waves wash up on the shore. Later we made love under the stars. Her body felt wonderful on the blanket under the stars as the warm Cuban wind washed over our bodies. It was a perfect way to spend the night together knowing we would be apart for seven days.

The next morning as was our custom when I went on trips, Ali rode with me to the base in the Humvee. She held my hand as the scenery flashed by us. We were both quiet. I peeked at her white blouse as we rolled along.

She was looking out the window on her side as I looked at her cleavage. She turned back and saw me peeking and nudged me in the ribs with a grin.

"Gonna be awhile," I said smiling. In front of the hanger on the base she gave me a goodbye kiss that made steam come out of my ears. The others there started yelling and clapping at our antics.

"You are a lucky man." Alexi told me with a smile.

"Yes indeed." I replied waving to Ali as the Humvee drove away.

"Good morning gentlemen." Raul started as the whole unit stood at attention under the morning sun." Since we will be jumping out of a perfectly good aircraft this morning on our way to seven fun filled days in the jungle, we will kindly forgo our daily exercises." There was a cheer from the pilots. "Get inside and retrieve your chutes for our morning jump." We all filed inside the hanger and picked up our chutes. One by one we climbed into the back of the waiting transport trucks waiting to take us to the other side of the airfield. The trucks started off and we held on bouncing down the road. There was too much noise for conversation. The trucks rumbled along the outer road finally stopping in a cloud of dust with a squealing of brakes next to the same worn out transport we had leaped out of the day before. There we climbed out and got into our chutes. One by one we double-checked everyone's chutes and survival vests. Whatever we were wearing was all we would have for the next seven days.

"We are all gonna smell pretty ripe by next week buddy." Boner remarked to me as we finished, climbing into the transport.

"Yeah, I remember. We smelled worse than a skunk last time we did this." I said with a grin thinking years back when we had taken a similar class during our Navy flight school. We took our seats and strapped in. The engines in the old Soviet transport rumbled into life and the plane rattled and shook, as the pilots got ready for takeoff. Soon I felt the plane lurch forward and we rolled out onto the runway. We sat at the end of the runway as the pilots ran up the engines to full power; the aircraft shaking like it was coming apart. The noise was deafening making conversation impossible. The plane lurched forward and we were rattling down the runway feeling the massive transport lift off. The gear came up with a whine and a clunk locking in place. The plane started to turn and the sun changed sides through the small window in the fuselage. We circled four times as the plane climbed to a higher altitude for us to jump. The same Cuban sergeant was sitting at the door belted in with a bored expression on his face watching us. I silently wondered how many times he had done this; thankful my career choice wasn't as boring as his seemed to be.

Finally the tired old transport leveled out and the red light over the door came on. The sergeant unbuckled standing up and opened the hatch. We stood up and turned forward. I reached up checking the strap on my helmet. Raul stood at the door, first to jump as usual. I glanced over at Alexi, his face white with sweat. A grim but determined look on his face. As many times as the rest of us teased him about his intense dislike of jumping out a perfectly good aircraft, we held him in high regards knowing the self discipline it took for him to do this. I nudged Boner and looked at Alexi. He nodded his head and grinned, his teeth showing. His anticipation to the jump showed on his face.

The light above the door changed to blinking green. Raul was the first out the door. One by one we shuffled to the door. When it was my turn I gripped both sides of the door, checked my footing, looked out at the horizon and stepped out into the sky. The transport grew smaller above me as I reached over yanking the handle. The chute came out clean yanking my free fall to a silent steady stop.

Above my head was the green chute of nylon. I looked down at the field using the toggles above my head to steer with. I made slow lazy turns aiming for the center of the field. The ground was rushing up at me. I brought my feet together, bent my knees and landed rolling to my right hitting the ground. I sat up and hit the disconnect fitting watching my chute collapse onto the ground. One by one everyone landed. Boner of course landed standing up, his face lit up with a big smile. Relief showed on Alexi's face as he was gathering his chute. I stood up and began to gather my own chute up.

"It's not just a job..." Boner called out to me.

"It's an adventure." I finished for him. We were both grinning at each other like idiots.

Suddenly from the bushes around us armed troopers in green fatigues came out surrounding us. Their AKs were pointed at us as we dropped our chute harnesses. They gestured with their rifle barrels toward a road. They walked on both sides of the road preventing us from running into the jungle.

Boner and I instinctively paired up together as we walked. Once under the canopy of the trees we could see there was a camp. There were cages made of thick branches with dirt floors. One by one we were searched our survival vests taken from us. We were forced to remove our boots and socks. Four at a time we were shoved inside and a guard was stationed in front of each cage. Our guard looked to be in his mid twenties, athletic looking dressed in green tiger stripes with LBE gear on. His AK never left his hands as he stood facing us with a serious look on his face.

"As captured enemy POWs you are now at the mercy of the People's republic of Guatemala." This came from a large man dressed in green fatigues with the flag of Guatemala on his shoulder and colonel patches on his collar. His round officer's cap displayed the gold metal emblem on the front. His black boots were mirror polished and his uniform was creased. He stood at parade rest with his hands folded behind his back. I was curious to see how realistic this was going to be. I looked around for Manuel but he wasn't in sight. He must have drifted away from us as we came down. Confusion showed on most of the faces of the team, as we stood barefoot in the dirt inside our primitive cages. Marco and Rico were to my left Boner was to my right. The sun rose higher and the heat was starting to come out of the jungle. My body started sweating from the humidity.

"I wonder how much weight we'll lose this trip." Boner whispered to me. I shrugged my shoulders in reply. Thankfully no one else in our team spoke. The last thing anyone in this situation needed was undue attention from our tormentors.

"You will not find much mercy here". The colonel continued with a smile. I scanned the cages filled with our men. They had grim looks on their faces. I was glad to see they were taking this serious.

"Why are they doing this to us?" Marco asked in a hushed voice.

"Training is training." I answered quietly.

"Take it as it comes" Boner added. I nodded slowly when Marco looked at me. I scanned the guards; they were well-fed, fit and paying attention to their job. I knew this wouldn't be easy on any of us.

I thought back to the incident before the mission against the Chinese electronic intelligence gathering station in Bejucal. I was kidnapped and hustled away in the dark. I was interrogated and physically beaten trying to soften me up to reveal information about the mission. It wasn't serious, but it was scary and painful. I was surprised to see Antonio walk in while I was tied to a chair. He ordered me to be released then helped me up. It was all very confusing. He explained to me later that since I had never been captured and tortured, this incident was a part of my training. He wanted me to experience a small taste of what I was in for if I was shot down and captured by the Cuban military. It helped motivate me to take the mission seriously, and gave me a better perspective of what we were up against.

"No one knows you are here. No one is going to come for you. Your government has forgotten you."

"Your stay here will be more comfortable if you cooperate with us." He smiled again. I knew none of the men believed this, but it added a sense of realism to the situation. The colonel removed a canteen from his belt and took a long drink. It made us aware of our own thirst. He replaced the canteen and pointed at our cage and snapped his fingers. Five guards appeared in front of the cage door and they piled in grabbing Marco and dragged him out. It happened so fast we didn't have time to react to it. They pulled him away and out of sight into a large green tent. the colonel still smiling walked into the tent. I looked around and sat down in the dirt. Boner followed suit.

"Sit down Rico. Take it easy, they won't kill him" I told him. Rico sat down with a look of fury on his young Latin face. I looked across the camp at Raul. He had the same look of confusion on his face as the rest of us, so I knew this was as unexpected for him as it was for the rest of us. I looked up at the cage and noticed it was constructed of thick branches tied with heavy rope.

I settled back against the branch bars a bit more relaxed knowing Boner and I were thinking alike. Neither one of us wanted to spend any more time in here than was absolutely necessary. Just then a piercing scream filled the camp. The sound came from the green tent. Even the guard was taken by surprise. He turned his head for a moment looking at the green tent then back at us. I looked around at the other cages. In front of each cage was an identical attentive guard.

Marco was brought back to our cage as another pilot was taken from the cage next to us. Marco sat on the ground breathing heavily. We gathered around him checking him.

"I'm fine really" he told us.

"What happened?" Rico asked him.

"They roughed me up a bit." Marco replied. "But I told them nothing." He smiled. I felt around his body with my hands finding nothing broken. We sat down on the ground again. One by one a man was taken from each cage into the green tent for the rest of the day. As the sun started to set three guards brought canteens of water to each cage. We drank from the canteens slowly, savoring the water. There was no food.

Another guard walked up to our cage and the first one walked away. I watched as this event took place throughout the camp. The clouds had moved in front of the moon.

Just then the guard at the front of our cage collapsed. Manuel was behind him dragging the unconscious guard away. I joined Boner at the rear of the cage as Manuel appeared using his knife to cut away the ropes holding the thick branches together. We slowly crawled out of the cage on our bellies like silent snakes in the darkness.

We stopped at the back of the tent kneeling. There was an armed guard at the front of the tent. We could hear snoring inside. I slowly moved on my hands and knees in the darkness along the side of the tent. The smell of canvas came to me in the heat as I moved carefully along the side. I moved slowly not making any noise. I knew that Boner was doing the same on the other side of the tent. My heart was pounding and sweat was rolling off my face in the heat. When I came to the front I slowly peeked around the side and looked up at the guard. He was staring off into the darkness completely unaware I was on the ground. I saw Boner poke his face around the other side of the tent and nod. I stood up quickly catching the guard by surprise. He turned towards me and Boner's arm came from behind around the guard's neck, his Adam's apple in the crook of Boners arm. I grabbed the AK before the guard dropped it and slowly the guard sagged down to the ground. Boner's arm had stopped the blood flow to the guard's brain putting him to sleep. I reached over and felt for a pulse. it was strong and steady. Boner pulled the sleeping guard back away from the front of the tent and laid him on the ground. With the AK in my hands Boner and I opened the flap and we walked in.

There was a small kerosene lantern on a small table; its orange glow illuminated the room. We could see the colonel asleep in a cot, snoring peacefully. Boner grinned wickedly at me. I watched out the front of the tent while he went to work. He slowly took out the laces from the colonel's boots on the ground and wrapped one around the sleeping man's feet. I was grinning like an idiot. Boner took the other long lace and carefully tied it around the right wrist, then pulling it underneath the cot and tied the other wrist tight. The sleeping colonel was now tightly tied to his cot, still snoring away peacefully. Outside Marco tied the guard using his bootlaces, hands behind his back and ankles together. Now we had two AKs.

We went back inside the tent and gathered around in a circle. There were four cages with four guards out in front of each one. We were all whispering ideas at each other all at once in the heat. Marco was watching out the front of the tent while we whispered. I pulled out the magazine from the AK and looked at the cartridges inside it. They were blanks. We were grinning like idiots in the orange light looking at the plugged brass rounds. It meant that the guards in front of the cages were also carrying blanks in their weapons. We didn't have a clue as what to do next. Looking around the inside of the tent I saw a long knife hanging off the colonel's pistol belt.

I glanced around again and looked at the kerosene lantern. Slowly a plan began to form in my mind. I motioned to Marco and explained my idea to them. I took out the long bladed knife and cut the back wall of the tent from top to bottom. Marco and Boner slowly lifted the cot with the sleeping colonel and carried him out the newly made opening. They kept slow and quiet and carried the cot away from the tent.

Slowly they carried the sleeping colonel to the rear of our cage and pried open the branches. Then they carried the cot into the cage and set it down in the dirt. They carefully replaced the branch bars back into place and crept back to the tent. I opened the cap of the lantern and poured the kerosene onto the inside of the wall of the tent. I looked out the back of the tent to make sure I could get out safely then turned and opened the glass blowing the flame with my breath onto the wall of the tent. It erupted in flame instantly. I ran out the back with the colonel's pistol belt in my hands.

One by one the four other guards started running to the burning tent, all with the same thought that their colonel was still inside. One by one an arm reached out from the darkness taking them down. We tied them with their bootlaces, and carried them into the same cell as their still sleeping colonel. Marco ran and released the rest of the pilots from the cells. Raul assigned three guards to watch over the cell with our former captors. We put out the fire of the burning tent.

Marco found the mess tent, and Rico, a chef before joining the Cuban Air force started the outside grill and began cooking food. Soon we were all feasting on steak and eggs and fish steaks. Someone had found two coolers of cold beer, which was passed around. This was a welcome addition to our meal. I had my flight suit tied down around my waist enjoying the cool morning breeze. Raul and Boner were sitting next to me at what had been formerly the colonel's table eating. The orange rays of the rising sun began to peek over the horizon as the sound of a rapidly approaching jeep came to us. Much to our surprise Perry was in the front seat.

"What the?" We heard Perry's surprised voice as he got out of the front seat of the jeep. Just then four of our pilots armed with the guard's AKs sprang from the jungle and fired off their magazines of blank ammo causing Perry to hit the dirt face first.

"Welcome to the party jar head." I called out to him as he stood up cursing. I tossed him a cold beer from the cooler. Rico came up to him with a plate of food grinning. He looked at the cell of tied up guards, then slowly sat at the table next to me. No one said anything to him. We were to busy eating. Just then a shout came from the cell with our tied up guards, followed by loud cursing.

"Colonel's awake." Boner said to no one shoving a piece of egg in his mouth.

"Ayep." I replied.

"Colonel picked out some great steaks, have to thank him later." Raul said. I burped in reply. Perry just sat there taking it all in.

"Excellent breakfast, dig in Perry." Boner told him.

"How the fuck...?" Perry asked.

"Ahhh it was easy, really." Boner answered.

"Piece of cake." I added stuffing steak in my mouth followed by cold beer.

"You didn't really expect us to stay in those cages did you Perry?" Raul asked him.

"Not with all this great food out here just waiting for us to tear into? Damn this is what I call a breakfast. Steak, eggs, grilled fish steaks and ice cold beer. Survival training doesn't get any better than this ole buddy." I added turning the knife a little bit more. He looked at me with daggers in his eyes. I just smiled back at him taking another drink of beer, draining it.

"Incoming." Boner called out as he tossed me another beer from the cooler. Perry sat there looking around at the rest of the pilots eating and back at the cell with three pilots guarding it.

"Don't worry, they already ate." Boner told him. Perry sat there shaking his head at our cavalier attitudes.

"What the hell..." He said shaking his head as he started eating. "I came out here to check on you guys and see how everything was going and this is what I find. Man the instructors are going to be pissed."

That morning our survival training started in earnest. An American Air Force Major was our instructor. We were in an outdoor classroom, sitting at primitive tables on benches cut from trees. We were given handouts with drawings and photographs as visual references.

"Good morning gentlemen." He said as he walked under the roof out of the morning sun.

"I'm glad to hear you were able to enjoy a good meal, it may be your last for awhile." He told us with a grin. His last statement was greeted with a few catcalls as we grinned back at him.

"In all my years as an instructor your group is the first to ever pull this type of stunt. We will have to adjust our training system to avoid anything like this in the future." He looked straight at me. I was beginning to like this guy.

"All right. So you have ejected out of your aircraft, and landed safely. Unfortunately you have landed behind enemy lines. First thing you should do is save your parachute. You may be able to use it as a shelter. The trick is to camouflage it as much as possible when you do. If you land in an open area, seek cover as soon as possible. When it is safe, take inventory of what you have with you. Try to identify your location, and then decide upon direction of travel."

"Always remember survival is thirty percent skill level and seventy percent attitude. If you make the decision to survive, then you will find a way to do it. Your brain is like a computer. You will be amazed at all the things you will remember during a survival situation. Once you decide to survive, your brain will switch gears and start coming up with solutions to your problems."

"The jungle is an alien environment. Being in an unusual environment will increase your stress level and cause disorientation. This class will help you become familiar with the Jungle environment and help reduce your stress level and any sense of panic. Remember almost everything you need to survive is here in the jungle just waiting for you to use."

Since water was so important to survival in the jungle, we were taught how to find water, how to catch rainwater, and how to store it. We learned which vines contained water, and how to cut them just right to suck out the fluid inside.

We learned that the jungle is a living entity that will literally eat you alive if you stand still too long. We were taught what plants were poisonous and what plants you could eat raw and cooked.

I never realized just how much food really existed in the jungle. During the following week we steamed wild carrots, fried Taro root, cooked and ate Yucca plants like potatoes, These plants could be boiled, fried or baked. We ate smoked snake meat, smoked monkey meat and learned which reptiles were edible. We looked for Plantains, Guava, Mangos, and bananas.

We built fish traps, learned which tree held the sap that could stun fish, and then cooked the fish in palm leaves in a fire roasted over hot coals. Salt tablets would help with any nausea we might feel. I knew I would run out in a short period of time taking four every hour.

We learned it is much more comfortable to get wet from the rain and air dry rather than to use ponchos and sweat out all our internal water supply. The trick is to work with the jungle and not against it. Better to walk around an obstacle using less energy, than to try and climb over it.

Even though it was uncomfortable, it was better to wear long sleeves to keep the mosquitoes and other insects at bay. In the jungle the insects will eat you alive nonstop.

For those seven days we stank, sweated, and thirsted our way through the training. My face itched from not being able to shave. My underarms grew raw from constant sweating, as did other parts of my body. My flight suit was constantly wet and felt like sand paper. I changed my socks three times a day, trying to keep my feet dry to avoid trench foot. My whole body ached, and my bowels complained from the unusual food I was eating. We built hammocks from our parachutes and slept during the hottest part of the day to conserve energy. The heat got so heavy it was difficult to breathe sometimes. We learned though. We learned everything they taught us. The seriousness of what we were doing was ever present on our minds. As fighter pilots we did not enjoy the thought of being shot down behind enemy lines.

Night comes quickly in the jungle. We learned to build our remain over night positions quickly. I knew that no matter how uncomfortable I was, it was only training in a controlled situation. If I were ever shot down for real, it would be a nightmare. I started thinking about the changes I would need to make to my survival vest.

When the class came to an end we were all awarded our certificates. We boarded an old gray bus for the long trip back to our base. The Cuban Air Force like air forces everywhere was always trying to keep their operating expenses low. This fact explained the return trip in the old bus rather than by helicopter.

After our time in the hot jungle, the first blast of air-conditioning hit us like an arctic wind as we entered our hanger after piling out of the bus. Like everyone else, all I wanted was a shower and a cold beer. The water felt like heaven as it washed away all the dirt and grime from my body. Afterwords I changed into a clean flight suit. I learned it was easier to get used to living primitive than it was to try to get used to civilization.

That night Ali and Consuela made a feast. We had Lobster and Grouper with assorted fruits and vegetables. I drank ice-cold green-labeled beer out under the stars making love until we were exhausted.

The next morning General Rodriguez was already at our hanger. He was reading a report on our activities at the Jungle Survival School.

"I can't send you guys anywhere can I?" He asked us with a grin as Raul and I walked in.

"It was good for moral." Raul explained. "Needed to show them what we are made of."

"Well they won't be caught like that again I can assure you. The General sends his regards. Says he is proud of your efforts there. He was tickled pink to show the Americans what his men are capable of." The general said closing the folder in his hands. I grabbed a cup of coffee from the pot and took a seat at the table. We sat there discussing the changes we needed to make to our vests. Then it was out to the obstacle course and our exercises followed by the usual run around the runway. Later after our workout Antonio visited us at the hanger.

"I heard about your little incident at the training facility. Seems your actions there embarrassed the American instructors. They have made a few changes there to prevent anything like that from happening again." He told us with a grin. "I can't send you outlaws anywhere can I?"

"They hid the beer." Boner told him smiling.

"They wouldnt share either." Manuel added with mock seriousness.

"They were very impolite." Alexi added stern faced.

"I'm glad you boys are on our side. Seriously tho, you did surprise them with your actions. The general was very pleased. Did you learn anything?"

"Once things settled down we learned a great deal about how to survive in the jungle if we are shot down. It was an excellent course and well worth the time there." Raul assured him.

"Yes grilled monkey can be very tasty." Alexi said.

"Don't forget the snake." Manuel added. Antonio shook his head as he grinned. Since we were officially snake eaters there was talk of adding a dead snake in the jaws of our wolf emblem.

As the weeks went by we did our workouts each morning, and every afternoon we flew against each other. Alexi and Raul flew Mig-29s against us as aggressors. Antonio was cranking out updated fighters, I was flying training sorties during the week and test flying Antonio's MIGs on my weekends. Boner was test flying the A-4s on his weekends when he wasn't flying his A-4 with us as an aggressor. Flying was as familiar to us as breathing.

The information coming out of Guatemala from Antonio's informants revealed the Chinese were training Guatemalan pilots. The Guatemalan Air Force was mostly made up of Chinese PLAAF pilots and former Cuban pilots flying for money with former Guatemalan fighter pilots learning to fly the Chinese J-11s. The Guatemalan government was getting stronger with help from their alliance with China, North Korea and Iran. It was nothing but bad news for us.

One morning Antonio greeted us in the hanger after our morning workout.

"I have a few photos that have been smuggled out of Guatemala you boys might be interested in." He told us as we took our seats around the big old wooden table. The air-conditioning felt wonderful helping to dry the sweat off my skin from our run. He opened up the yellow manila envelope and passed the photos around the table to us. The first photo showed a Chinese J-11 being worked on in a hanger by green suited Chinese technicians. The nose was folded upward and two of the techs were working on the antenna. Another photo showed J-11s lined up on a ramp with techs wearing blue overalls arming and fueling these fighters. I sat there looking at another photo showing a two place J-11 rolling on a ramp. The white helmets of the flight instructor in the rear and the student pilot up front could be clearly seen. It reminded me of my own training in India learning to fly the MIG-21. Sitting there looking at the photos brought home a realism that was lacking before. It was one thing to know they were building an air force, but it was quite another thing to see color photos of it happening. I think that was Antonio's reason for showing us the photos, to help bring home the seriousness of what we would be facing. Something about Antonio's demeanor caught my attention.

"What else is there?" I asked him looking into his eyes across the table.

"I've been in contact with certain individuals in the Mexican Government. They are deploying troops along the border with Guatemala. There is a lot of jungle there, so they cannot put their troops along every mile, but they are adding troops to the region. They are setting up bases along the border."

"We all understand that successful ground campaigns require air superiority. The Chinese know this as well as we do. Any first strike would begin with an air attack against Mexico's air bases in that region. The Mexican Air Force has begun flying air patrols along their border." He explained.

"The Chinese have to be aware of this." Manuel stated.

"Of course. When they make their move, they will know when and where to hit." Antonio pointed out." I do have some good news tho, we were successful in acquiring the frequency used by the Chinese J-11 missile systems."

"So we will be able to jam their missiles?" Raul asked.

"Oh yes. We will program the info into the anti missile systems of your fighters. It should help prevent their missiles from locking on to your fighters." Antonio revealed.

"I'm all for that." I told him.

"Amen to that. Anything to give us the edge." Boner added.

"Finally some good news." Raul commented.

"This is their newest carrier. Now they have finished their flight trials I expect them to deploy it to the region soon." Antonio said picking out photos of the new Chinese aircraft carrier. We grabbed the photos like they were cold beer on a hot day. This carrier looked like it was of Russian design, the hull of a destroyer with a flight deck on top. The bow was angled upward. It was massive. There were anti aircraft missile launchers on both sides on the ship. The flag of China was on the fantail.

"She has a complement of 30 naval J-11s, a Russian version of an AWACS plus ASW helos. She has a ski-jump style bow to aid their fighters to take off from the deck without using a catapult system." He went on." She is powered by steam turbines, can steam at 30 knots, weighs in at 70,000 tons."

"She looks like the Kuznetsov." Alexi commented." They have copied our design."

"It's the former Russian Vayarg. She was purchased from the Former Soviet Union for 20 million dollars, stripped of course. The Chinese have been rebuilding her and now she is ready for open sea duty."

"Yes, we design and build and the Chinese buy or steal what they need." Alexi said with disgust. It was well known within our little group that although the Soviet Union no longer existed, and Alexi was turned loose when that country collapsed, he was still very loyal to the old Soviet

Union. We were always very careful never to insult his origin or make jokes about Russia.

"How do they take off without a catapult?" Manuel asked.

"They use a blast shield behind the fighter, The brakes are on, the engines are run up to full speed, then the brakes are released and the fighter rockets forward and up the ramp into the sky." Alexi explained.

"A slingshot system." I said.

"Very similar. The answer to your next question is yes their fighters can take off with full armament." Antonio read what I was thinking.

"Mid air refueling capability?" I asked.

"No they haven't added that ability yet. But they do have drop tanks, two located under the belly." Antonio explained meaning the J-11s could extend their range by carrying extra fuel in tanks under the fighter's belly that could be dropped when empty.

"I have to go, just remember this info is classified." Antonio told us as he stood up. We sat there going over the photos and discussing what we had learned.

"This just gets better and better." Manuel remarked shaking his head looking through the photos. He was voicing what we were all thinking. The possibility of a Chinese carrier off the West coast of Mexico with Chinese fighters only added to our stress level.

"My instructor flew the MIG-21 over Vietnam against the Americans during the war." Alexi told us. "He shared many stories with us. I remember he explained that when they were able to force the American fighters to drop their bomb loads to engage the MIGs in combat it was considered a success."

"That's all we have to do. Stay invisible on their radar, employ hit and run tactics forcing the J-11s to drop their bombs to engage us." Raul told us.

"We know the terrain around the Mexican air base. We can use it to our advantage." I added. Soon everyone was throwing ideas out. Raul grabbed the aerial photos we took of the Mexican air base from the file cabinet.

"There is a mountain range here that is very similar to the one surrounding this air base. We can train there. It will help us counter their air attacks." Raul explained to us laying the photos on the table. We examined the photos drawing flight paths on them with markers.

Later we practiced nap of the earth flying the rest of the day with Alexi and Raul flying MIG-29s acting as aggressors. We flew between the mountains hidden from their radar. Again and again we climbed out of the valleys in pairs to attack them. We decided that training our team using two man teams was the best idea.

Boner and I switched positions as flight leader. Air combat is a complicated environment. The wing man has to be able to switch roles and assume the position of flight leader at any second as the tactical situation changes. We were given their flight direction, altitude and speed information from the tower via a data link system. We appeared from nowhere surprising them repeatedly. Flying between the mountains at high speed took total concentration. One mistake and we would be a paint smear on the side of a mountain. My heart was pounding in my chest, the adrenalin was pumping through my body by the gallon. It was the type of flying I liked best. Total concentration on flying shutting the rest of the world out.

"Bingo fuel." I called out to Boner. My fuel level was low, it was time to return to the base.

"Copy that." he replied. Together we left the mountain range and turned towards the base. Later I took a shower in the locker room washing the sweat away. I slept a lot better that night knowing we had a workable plan to deal with any air attacks against the Mexican air base we would be defending.

The next month was a blur. It was day after day of flying nap of the earth between the mountain tops. We rotated each flight team through the course Raul had set up for us to fly. Each morning after our physical workout, Raul acted as our Information officer giving us briefings on the mission using aerial terrain photos and charts on the wall as we sat there taking notes. Although we flew the area daily, each mission was different.

We were training our pilots to fly nap of the earth. We attacked Raul and Alexi using two flight teams approaching from different directions seconds behind each other. Again and again our fighters would appear from between the mountains to quickly lock onto their fighters, simulate a missile launch, then rocket away while the second team would pop up from another direction seconds later thwarting their attempts to attack. We flew these missions every day. Some times when we popped up the aggressors were within visual range enabling us to use our helmet guided radar systems to launch our electronic missiles. Other times we popped up and the aggressors were beyond visual range forcing us to coordinate with the data link information from the tower radar.

Again and again we flew low and fast screaming out from between the mountains to attack. Flying nap of the earth amongst all the ground clutter with the element of surprise was our best plan. This type of flying would be our best defense against the J-11s look down shoot down radar. We would use the ground clutter to help hide us. If they got a radar lock on one of our fighters their missiles would kill us. Their missiles were that good. There would be very little we could do to counter them. I had no illusions concerning our ability to counter the J-11s. We would have a slim chance against them. That thought weighed heavy upon us all.

I was sitting in my office filling out reports one morning.

"Colonel there is someone here to see you." Anna's voice came over my intercom. What now I thought as I put my pen down on the desk. She opened the door for me and Antonio's bodyguard walked in looking around. He nodded at me as he left. Antonio walked in and sat down.

"We have some great news Sean." He said greeting me." I have brokered a deal between the Mexican government and the Indian government. The Indians have agreed to lease an A-50 Mainstay AWACs to them."

"Hot damn!" I stood up. This was a great bit of news. "This will really improve our chances now. This sure beats the hell out of the Lear jet idea."

"Well you truly are full of good news today." I felt as if a giant weight had been lifted from my shoulders. "We can have a data-link with the A-50 that will help give us improved early warning than from their radar on top of the mountain, and we can remain passive." I was grinning like an idiot. I knew the advantage of having an AWACs available to us from my time flying F-18s off the carrier. We had an AWACs and used it to our full advantage.

"Shit Antonio how the hell did you work this deal?" I asked.

"Well I worked some magic." He smiled.

"Ill say so. Well hell that's wonderful news."

"I know you guys have been really worried about your chances against those J-11s. Of course if the Chinese get wind of this it will affect their plans." He warned me.

"I understand. I'm sure they will find out about it soon though. Thank you for telling me. This is a hell of a morale booster for me."

"Yeah I figured you needed some good news. Only the five of you know right now. The rest of the team will find out when they get to the base in Mexico." His face serious now. This was a great piece of news knowing we would have an AWACs sending us data about any J-11s attack.

"You are a miracle worker. This dramatically increases our chance of success now." I told him.

"Well you guys have put together quite a team. Ive kept up with your progress. You will need every break you can get for this mission."

"Aint that the truth. Some of us wont be coming back Im afraid."

"I have a lot of faith in your abilities. If your team does as well in Mexico as you did here in Cuba those J-11s wont have a chance. I'll see you later Sean." He told me standing up.

"Thanks Antonio." After he left I went to my computer and looked up the A-50 for a quick look. There was a lot of general information along with the usual photos. Anna knocked on my door and her face appeared interrupting my thoughts. Raul had come in.

"Has Antonio been here yet?" He asked me rushing in as Anna closed the door.

"Yeah he just gave me the good news." I answered excitedly.

"This really will give us an edge." He grinned at me sitting down.

"We'll kick their asses. They wont know what hit them." I added.

"I feel better than I have in weeks Sean. We really have a chance now."

"Yeah. I've had this lead ball in my stomach for weeks now. Man this is great." I told him.

"By the time our team arrives at the base, they will have the necessary guidelines for us to coordinate with the AWACs worked out. The AWACs will be in control of all air activities We'll have to adjust to their system once we are there." He warned me.

"We can do that, no problem. I flew using the AWACs system off the carrier when I was in the Navy. The U.S.S. Grant had a great AWACs system. I'm familiar with how to use it." I assured him.

"We could have used one flying over Bejucal." He told me as he sat down.

"Yeah it would have helped a lot. We did ok back then. We caught them by surprise."

"Yeah, we were lucky. They were slow to respond and by the time they sent up their fighters we were ready for them. We will do the same thing in Mexico" He said.

"Oh yeah. We'll kick their ass. They'll never see us coming, by the time they do it will be too late for them." I grinned.

That afternoon I flew with a renewed sense of security. Sitting in the cockpit I maneuvered between the mountains pushing my self and the fighter to the limit. Boner and I began flying tighter and faster popping up on Raul and Alexi faster than we had before. Again and again we screamed out of the valleys at them seconds ahead of the second attack team before they could respond to us. I didn't envy their position trying to maintain steady flight with two sets of MIGs coming at them with simulated missile and cannon fire. Raul had decided to include tactics using simulated canons against them as well. It was a favorite tactic used by the North Vietnamese pilots. They would Scream up at the American F-4s, slash them with their canon fire passes, then rocket away.

Boner and I flew together, Raul and Alexi flew as a team, Manuel and Julio were another. Manuel and Julio did well together. In all there were twelve teams training between the mountains of central Cuba. We practiced using our guns at targets towed behind other slower aircraft. Our radar slaved to our guns showed us where the rounds would impact instead of where we thought they would. It enhanced our shooting abilities. Ground control would give us the enemy position via data-link, we would get them on or radar, pop up, attack, then escape. Month after month we trained together, flying low and fast maneuvering between the mountains.

The key to our success was SA, or situational awareness. The ability of a pilot to keep track of everything happening around him. In ACM the loser usually never sees the other fighter that kills him. Our plan revolved around knowing the position of the enemy, flying low to hide from them, sneaking in behind them, and launching missiles at them before they even knew we were there. After which we would scream away before any survivors could retaliate. The idea was to fight on our terms as much as possible.

Training together month after month we became very sharp using these tactics. Flying nap of the earth takes extreme concentration. There is no room for mistakes or miscalculations. Flying together with the same wing man helped sharpen our skills as a two ship team. It was basically guerrilla warfare in the air. Practicing tactics in the air that helped you gain the advantage over the enemy and ambushing him. The Cuban government was paying for the fuel and we flew as many hours as possible.

Unfortunately as it happens in training accidents due occur. We lost two pilots flying nap of the earth. One young Cuban pilot hit the side of a mountain in an orange ball of flame. Another pilot flew to close to the ground and crashed. Both times we had military funerals. Followed by drinking parties to celebrate the fact these men died doing what they wanted to do. Flying for their country.

CHAPTER ELEVEN

The day we got our orders to deploy to Mexico caught me by surprise. I knew we couldn't keep flying training sorties forever. Antonio and the General had met with Raul and they had decided on a date. Antonio was informed the Guatemalan government was ready to make a small incursion into southern Mexico. That meant they would have to neutralize the Mexican air assets in the southern province first. We had two weeks to get ready. Raul came to my office to tell me in person. We never spoke on the phone concerning sensitive subjects. We never knew how secure the system was.

That night Ali and I walked barefoot holding hands on the sand on our beach as a full moon hung above us. She carried her sandals in her hand as we walked, the water covering our feet as the tide came in. I wanted to capture every second of it.

"I wish I could take this night and put it in a bottle to take out any time I wanted to." I told her. She put her head against my shoulder as we walked. I looked down at her and saw tears silver from the moonlight run down her face. I stopped and held her tight to my chest as the breeze caught her long hair. She started to cry, her body shaking as she sobbed. When she finally stopped I took her face in my hands and kissed her. When she calmed down we walked back to the house. It reminded me of the night before I left on the mission to Andros Island. The four of us had flown on Antonio's restored Lockheed Constellation from India to Israel then stopped in Spain to refuel before making the ocean crossing over to the island. Ali was deathly afraid I wouldn't be coming back from that mission.

This time Ali knew more detailed information about what we were facing. She knew what our chances were. Now Antonio had neglected to tell her about the AWACs deal he had arranged. I was under orders not to reveal that information to anyone, not even her. I felt like hell inside not telling her, knowing it would help ease her pain. Like it or not I was in the Military and I had orders. That night like many other nights we took a blanket out on the sand and made love as the ocean breeze and the light of the moon washed over our bodies. She sat above me her breasts reflecting the dim light as she arched her body and moved to a silent rhythm all our own. She called out into the night as her body exploded with the orgasm. She lay on me breathing heavily our hearts pounding, her nipples hard against my chest. I held her tightly looking at the stars above us, the stress fading along with our spent passion.

When I wasn't at the base, or flying, we spent every minute together. It felt like we were trying to store up a million memories squeezed into a small time frame.

The morning our team was to leave she rode with me to the base. Ali always rode with me to the base whenever I left the island. We didn't speak much, everything that we wanted to say to each other had already been said. We came through the gate after the guards checked our ids and parked at the hanger. Everyone was there standing around talking. The General arrived with his convoy of guards, Antonio was there with his bodyguard. Manuel's wife was there. There was a somber feeling in the air as the general and Antonio walked around talking to each pilot. I kissed Ali one last time and then we all entered the hanger to walk through to the flight line. Our jets were there lined up ready for us. There were twenty one blue and green MIG-21s with the flag of Cuba on their tails lined up in a row. Painted on each tail was the green and black emblem of the wolf, the team emblem. The same emblem that was on our flight suit shoulder patch. The sight made me stop a minute. It was the first time any of us had seen this many MIGs together at one time.

We walked to our fighters and performed our walk around checks. Boner was checking his A-4, Alexi and Raul their MIG-29s. I took my time checking mine, running my fingers along the skin, shaking the drop tank verifying it was secure. The four missiles under each wing were secure. I took the checklist on the clipboard from the ground chief who was in charge of maintenance on my fighter and signed my name.

"Bring her back to me." He said with a grin.

"Yeah well what about me?" I joked.

"Well you got to fly her back I guess." He grinned slapping me on the back.

I climbed up the metal ladder and climbed into the cockpit adjusting my helmet to my head. The tech pulled out the safety pins of my ejection seat and helped strap me in, hooking my connections to the fighter. I hit the panel switch and the instrument panel came on, I spun my finger in the usual circle warning the ground tech I was starting the engine. I jammed the switch on the panel and the engine started to spool up, the fighter coming alive around me. The noise and vibration around me as she began to live again.

Brakes were set, instrument panel was operating normally, engine temp was in the green, generator was on, ADF and marker were on. The nav computer was already set with the proper coordinates telling the fighter's GPS system where it was. Fuel and oxygen tanks were full, the gryo was properly aligned. There were four CopperHead missiles under the wings along with the drop tank and five hundred rounds of ammo in the hopper. I ran through the different screens on my two head up display panels, checking radar and armament configuration information. I moved the stick back and forth and moved my feet on the pedals watching as the ground tech gave me the thumbs up. I set the flaps to 24 degrees, the elevator and aileron to neutral. I closed the polished bulging canopy locking it with my left hand and sealed my helmet. Information was being properly displayed on the inside of my helmet visor. The ground tech saluted me after I gave him a thumbs up and I returned his salute.

We already had clearance from the tower to take off. One by one the techs yanked the wheel chocks away and we released our brakes inching forward off the tarmac onto the ramp lining up two by two ready for takeoff. I was sure most of the base was watching us. Boner was right behind me as I pulled out. Two by two the MIGs rolled up to the runway, did their takeoff checks and roared into the sky.

When it was our turn we rolled up, locked brakes, did a quick cockpit check. Everything was in order. I looked forward out the clear one piece bulletproof screen ahead of me and let out my brakes shoving the throttle forward. The MIG shot forward gathering speed, pushing me back into the seat. The base rushing past my canopy as I lifted off, the noise of the runway ceased. I hit the lever and lifted the gear. They came up and locked with a clunk. When I reached altitude I pulled in the flaps and we joined up with the rest of the flight with Boner at my four o'clock position. We turned west and left Cuban airspace.

"Feet Wet." Boner called out to me over my headphones.

"Copy that." I replied. smiling behind my oxygen mask.

"Once more into the breech." He replied.

I looked out the canopy at the ocean below us and then at the billowing white clouds around us. The MIG was humming along with a slight vibration from the engine. I looked at my thigh board with all the flight info. It felt good to be flying just for the sake of flying. So many times I strapped myself into a fighter ready to battle an enemy in the sky. Flying along peacefully was a welcome change. It was a rare treat. Some pilots thought it was boring, but I enjoyed it. The feeling of being in control of this fast deadly flying beast that she was never ceased to thrill me. The right radar screen showed twenty MIGs in four ship formations. There was no turbulence, just the steady sensation of flight. The top of the ejection seat had supports on either sides of the top preventing me from seeing left or right without having to lean forward. They were there to help prevent injury to my head during extreme maneuvers. I leaned forward looking over my right shoulder at Boner riding along at my four o'clock position. He raised his hand and waved I waved back. I scanned the instrument panel then ahead out the front of the one piece windshield. There was blue sky and white clouds ahead.

Down below us the green ocean was flat, above us the clouds were white and all around us was blue sky. The view was magnificent. Soon the dark line of land was ahead of us. The east coast of Mexico was coming into view.

I heard Raul over my headphones asking for clearance from the tower for us to land. We were swinging wide and coming in north of Villahermosa. I could look down and see the wakes of small boats below us as the coast came into view. I thought back to the last time we were here and wondered how many of us would not be coming back. Such dark thoughts on such a beautiful sunny day.

"Feet dry." Boner called out to me. I smiled remembering how we used to call the ship every time we were coming over land using those same words when we flew off the carrier. The tower called back giving us wind direction and landing instructions. My RWR lit up like a Christmas tree from the different types of radar reaching out to us. I could see the mountain range just north of Tuxtla Gutierrez. The air base was located ten miles southeast of the city at the base of a mountain. Two by two the MIGs began their descent and began to line up for their approach on the sixty six hundred foot runway. We circled above as each team landed. When it was my turn, I lifted the wing and turned lining up on final. My flaps were down, my gear came down and locked, all three gear lights showing green. Boner stayed clear as my landing speed was faster than his was. I came in and touched down, the tires hitting the tarmac easily. I deployed the air brakes, tapped the brakes and then released the landing chute and felt a slight tug as it caught air. The fighter finally slowed.

I taxied behind the rest of the group off to the left following the white truck with the big FOLLOW ME sign behind it. One by one we pulled in front of the hanger at an angle. I raised the flaps, locked the brakes, shut the engine down. I hit the switch and the instrument panel went blank. I opened the canopy and disconnected my helmet opening my visor and feeling the warm air hit my face. A ground tech slipped an orange ladder up to the left side of the MIG and crawled up. He swiftly slipped the safety pins into the ejection seat and helped disconnect me.

"Hola, Beinevididos a Mexico." He greeted me grinning.

"Muchas gracias." I replied climbing down the ladder. I set my helmet inside and waited as Boner's A-4 pulled in next to us. He shut his engine down and threw open his canopy. He slowly climbed out and we both walked together into the hanger. This time there was no band to greet us as before. This time we were greeted by the base commander and a few other Mexican officers. I recognized two or three from my last visit. We shook hands and then we were led into a small auditorium. We sat down and I slipped off my thigh board.

"Greetings gentlemen and welcome to Mexico." The commander started. "You will see there have been many changes since your last visit. Thanks to your suggestions, we have made many new changes that will help defend our base against any attack." He turned the meeting over to a colonel who showed us aerial photos of the new SAM sites. There was an inner ring that surrounded the base, and an outer ring that surrounded the mountain. There were two new radar stations on the tops of the mountain ranges north and south of the base. The room thundered from the sound of jet engines as two Mexican MIGs took off.

"We have two MIGs in the air 24 hours a day on patrol around the area. Our radars constantly sweep outside the mountain ranges looking for any intruders. We feel confidant that with your assistance we will be able to defeat any intruders." He smiled. He went on to explain about the AWACs Mexico was leasing from India, and how that would enhance our chances should there be any unwanted visitors from the south. There was a loud applause from our pilots. I could see them smiling and nodding in relief. He went on to explain the AWACs was at a different base, under tight security, away from any prying eyes. Naturally it was a secret they wanted to keep as long as possible. I was sure the intelligence arm of the Guatemalan government knew we had just landed here, but I hoped the AWACs would catch them by surprise. Sooner or later they would find out about it. More later than sooner I hoped. Boner and I sat quietly as the colonel continued.

The briefing included general information concerning how we would interact with the AWACs aircraft. The Mexican Air Force had several Russian Hind helicopters available to be used for SAR purposes for anyone having to eject. We all carried miniature radios, able to communicate with aircraft coming to extract us. The Mexican government had constructed several radar installations along the border with Guatemala to monitor the area. They had also started patrolling along the border.

"Maybe we wont be needed here after all." Boner whispered to me.

"That would be great. I've never known Antonio's information to be wrong though" I answered. He nodded silently. After the briefing, we were assigned our quarters. We were in the same building I had stayed in before. Raul and I shared quarters as before. We collected our gear from the hanger where it had been shipped aboard the two transports from Cuba. Perry was there to greet us as we collected our gear. He was in the process of setting up the maintenance facility in a hanger he would be using to work on our fighters.

"Tomorrow we start our usual workout boys." He told us with an evil grin.

"Aw crap." I said hoping to be away from all of that. I knew how important it was to be in shape but hated the process.

"Yeah I get to torture you guys as usual." He smiled.

"You're sadistic Perry." Raul told him.

"He's a Marine." I reminded him. Raul just shook his head while Perry and I grinned at each other.

Good as his word Perry woke us up at our quarters the next morning and informed us we were to line up in front of the hanger for our workout after chow. We made our way to the mess hall for breakfast. later the whole squadron gathered in front of the hanger in our workout suits and started by jogging around the runway. Later inside the hanger we did our usual workout routine. After our mid day meal, we were ushered into the same auditorium Raul and I had been in the last time we were there.

We received an in depth briefing about radio call signs, radar information, and how to work with the AWACs A-50. We were issued maps for our thigh clipboards. The SAM sight locations were shown on the screen on the wall using a slide projector. We marked down these locations along the Mexican border with Guatemala. Photographs of the four major Guatemalan Air Force bases were shown detailing the position of J-11s and the hangers, refueling tanks, support vehicles, and communication buildings. These bases had undergone a massive upgrade to accommodate their new fighters. The bases were surrounded by SAM missile launchers. This was the first of many detailed in depth briefings.

At the chow hall that night we mingled with Mexican pilots to discuss the situation. We talked until they threw us out to clean up. Later we gathered at the hanger and talked late into the night. The next morning after our workout, I flew my first fighter sweep of the area. Boner and I were teamed up with two Mexican pilots to sweep the southern border areas. It was to identify landmarks and become familiar with the area.

We took off behind the two Mexican MIGs and formed up into a diamond formation heading south. We kept to our way points pre programed into our flight computors. It was an odd combination, two Mexican MIGs, one Cuban Mig, and one A-4 with Cuban markings flying in formation together.

The Sierra Madre mountains below us looked foreboding I looked below at the green jungle thinking back to the survival class we took. I felt secure inside that I was prepared to survive there in the event I got shot down, but hoping I didn't need to use any of the training.

"Nasty looking down there meho." Boner's voice interrupted my thoughts.

"Yeah buddy, you got that right." I answered back.

The flight took us out over the gulf west of the base and south over

Tapachula near the border. My RWR sang out telling me we were being scanned by strong military radar to our south. The Guatemalans had installed radar installations along their border. During the briefing earlier we were shown photos of the Guatemalan base at Retalhuleu which was located directly south of our flight path. Their base was located west of a large mountain range and their runway had been lengthened to seven thousand feet from it's original forty nine hundred feet to accommodate large military transports. There was a massive Chinese radar station atop the mountain range west of the base. The distance between our two bases was one hundred and sixty six nautical miles. It was only about a fifteen minute flight time from their base to ours. Even with the AWACs giving us warning of any flights leaving that base, it wouldn't give us much time to respond to their fighters.

Our flight path kept us well clear of the border. We were not their to antagonize, only familiarize. Our mission was two fold. We were to become familiar with this area as well as send a message to the neighbors to the south we were up there and ready. We flew in formation south and west out over the gulf, then turned north back to the base.

As we pulled up to the hanger, Raul was there waiting standing next to a jeep. I climbed down from my fighter and he waved.

"Hop in." He told me as I walked over to him. I climbed in and he drove to the briefing room. Inside the air conditioning hit me like a wall of water cooling the sweat off my face.

"What does it look like?" He asked me as we walked in.

"Very mountainous, lots of jungle, wouldn't want to have to bail out there. Their radar reaches over the border, so they can track us flying long before we ever get there. I picked up three different radar sights not to mention the radar from their base at Retalhuleu." I explained. I pointed out where the radar sweeps hit us on the huge wall map of the border. The giant topo map had pins and writing on it denoting altitudes of mountain peaks as well as areas of known SAM sites. Raul marked radar beams on the map from notes off my thigh pad. Next to the map were aerial photos of the area including detailed photos of the four Guatemalan Air Force Bases. The photos were so detailed I could clearly see ground personnel and pilots next to aircraft on the tarmac. Newly constructed SAM sites surrounded the bases, easily distinguishable by their star shape emplacements.

"Interesting photos." I commented.

"Antonio supplied them for us." he explained with a grin.

"He is amazing." I replied.

"They had four J-11s up flying while your flight was up." He informed me. It made my blood run cold.

"We never detected their radar." I said.

"They were passive." He explained they had turned off their offensive radar when we came within range, switching to their passive system to pick up our individual radar beams. We never knew they were there.

"Where were they?" I asked looking at the giant map on the wall.

"Right here flying very low over the Inter American Highway south of Guatemala City." He explained pointing with his finger. The fact we never detected them really bothered me.

"Didn't the AWACs pick them up?" I asked him.

"Yes with their passive systems. They shut down their offensive radar the same time the J-11s shut theirs down so as not to alert them they were in the air. Security reasons." He explained. The Mexican government wanting to keep the AWACs a secret for as long as possible. By shutting down their radar, the AWACs prevented the Guatemalans from detecting the AWACs.

"The J-11s detect the AWACs?" I asked.

"I don't think so. Time will tell." He said with a grim face.

That evening after chow we had a meeting with all the pilots. Raul, Alexi, Boner and I along with the leading Mexican pilots sat down together with the maps and aerial photos discussing tactics. Boner's experience while flying at Miramars Top Gun school was of great help to us. His input helped our ambush plans greatly. It was one thing to discuss tactics on paper, it was another to make them work in real life. He had flown hundreds of hours in his little A-4 fighter attacking larger fighters as an instructor. Our numerical superiority was the only edge we had over their technically superior fighters. The more fighters we could put up when they attacked us meant more missiles we could launch at them.

We assigned teams combining Cuban and Mexican pilots that would fly together in four ship diamond formations. There would be twenty four teams of forty eight fighters flying together. There were enough teams to stagger the flying team schedule.

"Remember, anything we can do to convince the J-11 pilots to drop their loads and abort any attacks is the same as shooting them down, it is still a victory for our side. By coordinating our ground launched missile attacks with our fighter attacks against them we make it too expensive for them to bomb us. Their less experienced pilots will be easier to frighten and will be the first to panic and jettison their bomb loads aborting their bomb run." Raul explained.

"Each four ship flight team will have one MIG with an external ECM pod on a launch rail. It will go a long way in helping to blind any enemy air to air missiles. The frequencies of the enemy missile seeker heads have been programmed into these ECM pods. Along with each MIG's own internal countermeasure system, this should help in keeping you guys alive." Perry added.

"We are all in agreement of that." Alexi remarked.

"Amen there." Manuel added. With that the briefing was over.

The next day I stood in the control room with Raul watching a screen on the wall displaying the first two flight teams. The Top Mexican team leader stood next to us as the flight split and flew different directions. Team Alpha flew just north of the border in between the mountain ranges, while Team Bravo flew west low over the ocean. using data link info from the AWACs radar, Team Alpha would intercept Team Bravo flying in from the west. Team Alpha would stay low until team Bravo came into range. Team Alpha popped up undetected and made electronic missile attacks from the rear of Team Bravo's flight path. The next scenario consisted of team Alpha coming in from the east being attacked by Team Bravo coming up from between the mountain ranges.

The next day more sorties were flown using the same attack plans. Raul and I watched from the control room as the fighters flew their ambush flights again and again. We made notes, and discussed minor adjustments fine tuning the attack plan using the AWACs data link info. The J-11s would know where the Mexican SAM sites were located along the border. They would avoid them on their flight path coming north. Predicting their flight path would aid us in our ambush plans.

The Hind helos were up every time our fighters flew, ready to extract any pilot having to bail out. The helo pilots needed to know the area as intimately as they knew their own back yard to be able to rescue any downed fliers. Every team flew the same mission, we rotated each team to fly as many hours as possible.

The Chinese had delivered another shipment of J-11s to Puerto San Jose. Antonio had sent a message to us detailing the delivery. The Guatemalan Air Force now had 24 J-11s flying, and the last shipment included another twelve. It was sobering news. They had six J-11s assigned to each of their four bases. I knew there would be more soon.

The next Monday was our turn again to fly. Boner and I again took off behind the two Mexican MIGs and headed south. This time while we were close to the border I aimed my radar south and adjusted the beam, narrowing it to increase it's power. I was able to pick out four aircraft flying far south of us this time. We were over Tapachula flying east. That little town had been transformed overnight into a large Mexican Military base. It's location being so close to the border made it a key location in the defense of southern Mexico.

"We got an audience Boner." I called over to him.

"Whats that?" I heard him reply.

"They are at our sierra, about one hundred miles. I narrowed the beam to pick em up." I explained.

"Well now, there they are." He told me. I could hear him chuckle over the headphones. "They don't wanna come out and play." he remarked.

"Soon." I warned him.

"Copy that." He answered. As we changed altitude to avoid the mountain tops ahead of us. Looking down at the jagged peaks as we flew over them, I kept an eye on the multi function radar screen at the four white triangles that represented the four aircraft flying south of us. They must have known I was hitting them with my narrowed radar beam. Suddenly my RWR alarm sounded telling me they had reciprocated by turning on their radar and painting me with theirs. The computer identified the type of radar as Zhuk-10PD, the type of radar used by Chinese J-11s. There was no doubt now who was out there.

"Hot damn Grey seems you woke em up." Boner observed.

"Roger that." I replied. Suddenly the multi function screen showed the four white triangles changing direction heading north towards us.

"Arm em up asap." I ordered Boner. I hit the switches arming the four

Copperhead missiles under my wings. The MFD showed me the stores display confirming the four Copperhead missiles under my two wings were live and ready for launch.

"Greywolf to Control are you watching this?" I called back to Raul.

"Affirmative Grey wolf. Don t start anything, repeat, do not start anything."

"Copy that Control." I replied. I checked our position on the other screen to verify we were not to close to the border. We were twenty miles north of the Mexican Guatemalan border. The radar screen showed the four white triangles heading north at a high rate of speed.

"Our missiles are live as well Grey wolf. We are ready if they become aggressive or attack." The Lead Mexican pilot assured me.

"Copy that." I answered. I didn't believe the J-11s would become aggressive, more likely they were just playing a game of chicken with us.

"Adjust our position further north." I ordered as I kicked left rudder a bit. As one our four fighters turned slightly north together as we flew east over the mountains. I knew we could launch our missiles without having to change our direction to the south. Our helmet visors would give us accurate radar info enabling us the ability to launch at a target while flying away from it.

"No use pouring gasoline on the flames." I added.

"Well if they feel froggy..." Boner called back.

"Not today Boner. We aren't here to start an international incident." I replied. Watching the screen ahead of me. They four J-11s were coming at us from our three o'clock position. My heart was pounding in my chest as they got closer.

"They're really comin at us Grey. Wonder if they'll stop at the border." Boner wondered aloud.

"They will, they aren't ready to start anything yet. They're just playin chicken." I answered. My heart was pounding and my mouth was dry. I slowed my breathing down trying to calm my heartbeats. I was wondering just how close they would come before turning back.

"Ill bet ya fifty bucks they don't turn back before ten miles." Boner taunted me.

"You got it meho, I say twenty." I called back thinking of all the beer fifty bucks would buy.

"I want in on this action as well, Ill bet five miles." The Mexican pilot called to me.

"All bets are in." I answered. I could hear Boner chuckling over the headphones.

I watched as the four white triangles on the radar screen suddenly turned east matching our direction, speed and altitude.

"You win Grey." Boner called out as we all saw they had changed direction at eighteen miles. Close enough for me to win the bet. We were still painting each other with our radars as we flew east along the border. Looking down below I could see thin wisps of smoke from the ground. There were several refugee camps on the Mexican side of the border, people were already fleeing the communist government in Guatemala.

We stayed in formation flying west to east adjusting our flight path slightly to stay north of the border. The four triangles on the radar screen did the same shadowing us from their side of the border. I was ready to attack them if they changed course and painted us with their missile radar. At the same time starting an incident would only give the Guatemalan government a propaganda coup and an excuse they were looking for to start hostilities. Something we wanted to avoid.

We turned north away from their border, but our flight path remained at the twenty mile mark on our side of the border. I was sure there were people sweating bullets in the control room back at base. My hand was steady on the stick and I was relaxed hoping the situation would remain stable.

"Situation seems stable Control." I called back to base wanting to help calm their fears.

"Copy Tiger one." Raul's voice came back. I could hear the stress in his voice non the less.

"He sounds worried Grey." Boner called over to me.

"Ill bet he's not the only one there that's worried." I replied.

"If they were going to do anything they would have already done it by now" He radioed.

"That's my thinking too." I answered. The four triangles on my radar screen maintained a twenty mile distance on their side of the border as we did. Just far enough to avoid any misunderstandings yet close enough to be able to fire their missiles accurately if they felt threatened. I could not see them visually so my helmet system was of no use to me, but the powerful radar sensors in the nose and along the sides and rear of my fighter were working perfectly keeping track of their position. I knew I could launch one or two missiles at this range if need be. I checked my fuel status and saw it was getting low.

"We need to RTB." I called out to the other fighters. I waggled my wings and turned back toward base. As we changed course I kept an eye on our counterparts to the south. They flew a racetrack pattern to our six staying in their area behind us as we flew northwest towards base.

"Tiger One RTB." I called back to the tower. We got landing instructions and landed without incident. The debriefing of our flight was held in the control room, with our flight path shown on the huge map. We had not deviated from our assigned flight path. Our radar contacts were highlighted on the map every step of our flight.

"Did they initiate aggressive actions?" Raul asked us.

"I narrowed my radar beam and pointed it south, I picked them up immediately and that's what spooked them. I think they thought they could stay invisible like that last time, when I hit them with my radar beam it may have agitated them. They changed direction, turned their radar to active and started north towards us. They changed course at the twenty mile mark south of the border and shadowed us as we flew east." I explained.

"They were sending a message it seems." Boner offered.

"It seems you are correct." Raul observed looking at the map. The base commander was there listening to our conversation.

"Maybe I injured their Latin Machismo." I said.

"Could be. Good thing you didn't push them any further." Raul observed.

"I know what you are thinking Raul, I had no plans to initiate any kind of incident with them, I was merely curious to see if they were out there this time. I understand what is at stake here and what the consequences are. I'm not going to go off half cocked and start my own little war." I explained.

"Okay Grey. I believe you." He accepted my reasoning.

"Now me on the other hand..." Boner offered with a grin. Raul just looked at him shaking his head. After the debriefing was over I went back to my quarters and took a long shower. I ran through every aspect of the flight and wondered what I would have done had the J-11s had become hostile. Would I have fired? Would I have tried to escape? It had been two years since I had fired a missile in anger. I knew I had changed inside since then.

Thinking about it under the water I finally concluded I would have resorted to my training and fought like hell. I was the flight leader and I would have defended myself and my pilots if they had switched to a hostile posture. I put the matter out of my mind. Later I wrote a letter to Ali and went to the mess hall to eat.

I looked up as Raul sat down next to me with a tray of food.

"I trust you up there Grey, I know you wouldn't have done anything stupid. As Commander of this team I have to look at all aspects and try to be ready for anything. I'm responsible." He told me using his hands as he spoke.

"I know Raul, the burden of command and all that." I replied." I wouldn't do anything stupid up there. I've learned the hard way years ago what my temper can do if I don't keep it disciplined." I reminded him.

"Yes, I believe you do." He smiled. I grinned back.

"I don't regret what I did shooting down those two MIGs, but on the other hand I did learn from it. If it wasn't for Antonio I might be a helicopter pilot for a radio station in Miami or some crap like that instead of flying hot shit jet fighters ready to go to war. I owe him a debt I can never repay." I explained.

"Yes, it seems Antonio has given us all a second chance." He offered.

The next morning I was in the control room early with Raul. I had coffee in my mug with the USS Grant emblem on the side. It got quite a few comments, and I was asked to share a few stories of carrier life. We were quiet as the days fighter sweep took off. This flight was led by Marco and Julio. Everyone was curious to see how the J-11s would react today. The air was thick with anticipation. These fighter sweeps were necessary, but at the same time they could be the catylist if the Guatemalans wanted to start an incident.

"I wonder if we should put another flight on alert today." I suggested to Raul. He looked at me hard for a minute trying to see inside me. I knew what he was thinking, it was all over his face. He was concerned I was going to volunteer to be on the alert flight waiting on the runway, looking for an excuse to get into a fight.

"Maybe Alexi might be the right choice." I offered. I watched his face relax with relief.

"Yes, good idea, set it up will you?" He asked.

"Right away." I reached for the phone and called the flight quarters. My next call was to Perry at the hanger asking for two fighters to be put on alert ready to fly. I nodded at Raul as the base commander was talking to him. Seemed like people were very curious about this flight. I couldn't shake the dark feeling I had deep down inside. It wouldn't go away. I wondered if I was the only one in the room with a feeling of impending doom. The minutes ticked by, the clock on the wall seemed to freeze as we waited.

"There are four J-11s south of the border Colonel." The radar tech called out to Raul.

"What is their position?" He asked looking at the map.

"Sixty miles south of Tapachula." Raul marked it on the map along with the time, speed, direction and altitude.

"I've got a bad feeling about this Raul." I warned him.

"I think we all do Grey." He replied. We waited as Marco's flight came east over Tapachula twenty miles north of the border.

"Enemy radar has them." The radar tech called out." Tiger flight has been painted now sir." Both fighter groups had their radar on each other.

"Tiger flight, maintain flight way points." Raul called out over his throat mike to Marco's flight.

"Copy that control." Marco's voice replied over the ceiling speakers. I felt a wave of anxiety was over me.

"We need to launch Alexi." I warned Raul. He just looked at me waiting.

"Tiger flight has been locked on colonel." The tech called out. The J-11s had painted Marco's flight with their missile's radar.

"Launch now!" Raul called to me. I had the phone in my hand calling the tower.

"Launch them now!" I ordered. The tower acknowledged my order and we heard Alexi's voice talking to the tower. Minutes later Alexi's MIG-29 was in the air heading south at high speed, his radar was on and his missiles hot. His wingman right behind him.

Marco's flight locked their missile radar on the J-11s who now were streaking north.

"Range on the J-11s?" Raul asked.

"Thirty miles and closing sir." Raul shook his head looking at the map. The base commander reached for the telephone speaking rapid fire Spanish.

He was calling his superior in Mexico City hoping they would be able to contact his counterpart in Guatemala City to cool things down.

"Launch sir, the J-11s have launched colonel. Two missiles, twenty five miles and closing."

"Tiger flight you are cleared to engage. I repeat you are cleared to engage. Alert fighter two, engage, engage!" Raul called over his throat mike.

"Acknowledged Control." Alexi replied. We knew Marco's flight would be too busy trying to evade the two incoming missiles to reply.

"Meade" The base commander called out. Raul kept his cool. There was nothing we could do except wait. Marco's team turned south, fired off four missiles, then disappeared from radar. We knew what they were doing. They were following our training protocols. They went to the deck after firing their missiles to avoid the enemy radar, hoping to disappear.

"J-11s have fired again, two missiles." The radar tech called out.

"ETA of Tiger flight two?" Raul called out.

"Four minutes sir." Raul just nodded watching the map. We were all seeing the fighters on the map, the action unfolding in our minds.

"Targets locked on, engaging." Alexi's voice came over the overhead speaker.

"Tiger flight two has fired four missiles sir, now six have been fired by Tiger flight two." There were now a total of ten missiles headed south and four missiles headed north. It would all be over in seconds.

"Tiger flight one has lost two fighters sir." My heart spasmed wondering who had been hit. Alexi and his wingman had changed course and also disappeared from radar.

"Three J-11s have disappeared from the scope sir." This brought shouts and cheers from the other officers in the room.

"SILENCIO" The base commander yelled out. The clock was still ticking on the wall.

"Can you verify that?" Raul asked.

"Two of Tiger flights missiles and three of Tiger flight two have made contact sir. One J-11 is heading south at high speed sir."

"Acknowledged." Raul replied.

"All Tiger flights maintain fighter sweep, report in." Raul ordered over his mic. Marco called in, as did one other Mexican pilot. That meant we lost

Julio and one Mexican pilot. Alexi and his wingman both called in. They were both safe.

"Please have helos look for any survivors." Raul ordered.

"Yes sir." I grabbed the phone calling the tower. They had already called the two Hind helicopters flying SAR and gave them the grid locations to look for survivors.

"We lost two, they lost three." The base commander commented.

"Yes sir." Raul replied.

"Excellent work gentlemen." He nodded to me. "I must call Mexico City and report now."

"Thank you sir." Raul told him. He shook our hands and left.

"Good job Grey, thank you." The commander told me.

"Maybe they will settle down now." I offered.

"Maybe, though at what price. We lost two good pilots today." He said with a heavy voice.

"Yes we did, but we proved we can fight and our tactics work. Maybe this will make them think twice before they try something like this again. They have tested us and we have proved ourselves worthy." I said. Raul only nodded. The phone rang, Raul picked it up.

"Thank you." He spoke into the phone. He had a big smile as he replaced the receiver.

"Good news, Julio's survival radio signal has been picked up, the Hinds are on their way to pick him up now."

"Hot damn. Wonderful news. I sure hope he isnt injured." I told him.

"There will be a hell of a party tonight."

Raul and I rode out to the tarmac waiting for the fighters to return. Marco's MIG landed first with the Mexican MIG landing behind him. Alexi's flight came in behind them, they pulled up to the front of the hanger and shut down their engines. Black smoke stains on the bottom of their wings from the missile exhaust and empty pylons testified to everyone present the MIGs had drawn blood. One by one the pilots climbed out of their fighters, sweaty faces greeting us.

"I saw Julio's chute open after he ejected." Marco told us excitedly.

"The Hinds are on their way to pick him up now Marco. You guys did great, good work." Raul told them shaking their hands.

"Well we really showed them didn't we." Marco told us. His adrenalin was still pumping through his veins.

"How many did we shoot down?" Alexi asked as he walked up.

"They lost three." I answered. He grinned broadly.

"What the hell did you do to my fighters?" Perry yelled out as he walked up to our little group grinning like a maniac. "You drew blood ay?" he whacked Marco on the back and shook Alexi's hand. We were all laughing.

Later in the auditorium, we held a short debriefing. Marco's flight had dove to fifty feet right after launching their missiles. Marco and the lead Mexican pilot were the first to launch and head for the deck. The time lapse of the other two MIGs not diving fast enough had given the J-11s missiles a chance to lock onto their fighters. All six fighters had launched counter measures, and performed anti-missile maneuvers. Alexi and his wingman had launched as soon as they had a positive lock on the enemy fighters. They were not targeted by the J-11s missiles. Of the ten missiles launched by our fighters, there was no way to know which missile hit which fighter.

We were all gathered inside the hanger when the sounds of the Hinds rotors grew louder. We ran outside watching the two helos make their approach and touch down on the tarmac. We ran up to the choppers as the side hatch of the closest one opened and Julio climbed out wearing a huge smile carrying his helmet in his hands.

He had ejected cleanly after his MIG was hit in the rear by the missile. He separated from the ejection seat and landed in the jungle. He made his way to a clearing turning on his survival radio. He got a clear signal calling in the Hind helos. The other Mexican MIG exploded before the pilot was able to eject.

Later Raul made a call to Havana describing in detail the event. He typed up a report and e-mailed it to the General. We had lost one MIG and the Mexicans lost one MIG and a pilot, the Guatemalans lost three SU-11s. It was unknown if any of their pilots were able to eject.

Our training worked, our fighters were capable, and the avionics and weapons systems functioned perfectly. We were attacked by modern up to date highly maneuverable jet fighters, and we had come out the victor. Beyond visual range air combat was reduced to having the right weapons systems slaved to a modern radar system guiding a dependable and accurate missile. We had just showed the world it was not only possible, but profitable to use older fighters with modern avionics and upgraded weapons systems. The air battle would be won by the proper use of the missile weapons systems as well as the experience and training of our pilots. I wondered if the Guatemalans would make the same mistake again, or if they would change their tactics and engage our fighters in eye to eye dog fighting next time. We had trained hard using within visual range dog fighting tactics in Cuba. I knew we were very capable using that type of tactic. If they used that style of fighting against us, they were in for another surprise.

That evening everyone gathered at the bar on base to celebrate the victory. Marco and Julio shared their story in great detail. Alexi was quiet as usual. The party went late into the night. I lost count of how many beers I drank. I staggered back to my quarters, climbed into my bunk still dressed. The bed began to spin in circles so I held onto both side of the bed so I wouldn't fall out from the spinning.

The next morning everyone was in high spirits at the mess hall. Raul and I had a long detailed debriefing with all the pilots of the attack. Marco had detected the J11s missile launch first and had fired two missiles in response. He then dove for the deck and flew gut wrenching maneuvers to avoid the incoming missiles. Julio and his wingman had fired one missile each before diving low, seconds after Marco did. It was enough time to give the incoming missiles a chance to lock onto their fighters before they dove low. Mere seconds was all it took to make the difference between the J-11s missiles losing their lock and hitting the MIG-21s.

Alexi and his wingman had arrived at the scene after the J-11s missiles were launched, so they were never targeted.

We dissected the attack over and over again, threshing out each move and all the details. If the MIG-21s had been flying nap of the earth the whole flight, there was no way the J-11s would have acquired a missile lock on them. That meant our theory and training concerning flying nap of the earth would be successful when they came across the border. Our MIGs would be too low amid the ground clutter for the J-11s to detect us. The trick would be to dive low fast enough before the J-11s would be able to acquire missile lock onto us after we launched our missiles at them. We were gambling that by using our counter measures and diving low quickly after our missile launch it would be enough to deny them the time they required to lock onto us with their missile radar.

The cable news was full of the shoot down details. It was replayed every hour. The whole world now knew of the attack and all the details. Only one of the J-11 pilots had ejected.

"This will really bruise their egos." Raul commented. "They wont let this pass. They will be looking for payback." He warned.

"I'm sure you're right. Lets not give them the chance." I offered.

"I'm sure they will be trying to instigate more situations again soon." He lamented.

"Maybe, not right away though. They will study us, look for patterns, search out our weaknesses first." I told him.

"Lets not give them any. We cant afford to lose any more pilots, or give them the excuse they want to start something." He told me.

Technically firing missiles across a border at another country's aircraft was considered an act of war. The Politicians in Mexico City had decided to ignore this fact, especially since the opposing force had come out on the shitty end of the stick. There was a very large state military funeral for the Mexican pilot killed in the exchange. There were many kind words describing the heroic actions of the dead pilot fighting to protect Mexico from evil communists south of the border. The politicians were playing it up for all it was worth.

There was the usual complaint filed in the U. N. which we knew would go nowhere and achieve nothing. The U.N. had proven many times in the past it was willing to do nothing concerning actions of communist countries. The United States sided with Mexico, as did Israel and India, France and England. Other South American countries parroted the same anger about the attack. Of course the usual response came from China and Iran and North Korea as well as Venezuela. Their attitude revolved around the fact that Guatemala was within it's rights to protect itself from what was perceived as a threat from the Mexican Air Force and their Cuban lackeys.

I had to laugh at the Cuban Lackeys comments. What a crock. That meant at least publicly anyway they had no idea of our skill level. They believed the Mexican Air Force was the main thrust behind the response to the attack and we were there just to provide moral support. That was fine with us. The less they knew the better for us.

Antonio sent a message to Raul congratulating our team for the great job we did. The Guatemalans still had no idea we had an AWACs at our disposal. He heard the Guatemalan Air Force leaders were very angry at losing three modern J-11s to old outdated MIG-21s. Raul was correct on his assessment of bruised egos.

The morning after the military funeral Raul and I held a briefing with all the pilots. We adjusted the flight paths of our fighter sweeps to thirty miles north of the border, and reminded all the pilots to keep their cool up their and not launch first as it would give the Guatemalans all the excuse they wanted to start attacking Mexico. We stressed discipline and communications and avoiding any threatening gestures that could start something. I could hear the murmuring among the pilots in front of us in the auditorium remembering similar orders given to Raul and I not to long ago. Every pilot in the room wanted a crack at the J-11s. Enthusiasm wasn't enough to shrink the technological differences between our two forces, tactics would be. The tactics we had trained on would give us the edge we needed, along with the AWACs.

Raul and I were once again in the control room watching the map on the wall as our fighters made their sweeps north of the border. The J-11s were up along their side as well, they matched our fighters actions flying west to east but kept to twenty miles south of their border. Thankfully nothing happened. They kept our fighters on their radar but never locked them up with their missiles.

"Things look peaceful enough." Raul told me as I grabbed a cup of coffee.

"For now anyway." I grinned.

"Yes thankfully." The base commander agreed. "Their first test of our air defenses bloodied their noses. Im sure it was an unpleasant surprise, thanks to your help."

"Well it's not over yet colonel." Raul told him. "We will be here for some time I'm sure."

"Yes, the worst is yet to come I'm afraid." He answered.

The next two days four of us went into town for some well earned R and R. We took rooms in the classiest hotel, ordered room service, swam in the pool, ate out at restaurants, and drank too much beer. Boner and I went with Marco and Julio. We hired a taxi and toured the city the first night just for fun. I had been there before so I knew all the hotspots and the best places to eat. We stumbled to our rooms and passed out in the big beds.

The next day after a huge breakfast Marco and Julio were in the pool playing water polo with two long haired dark skinned local women wearing string bikinis. Boner and I were at the bar. Boner was making eyes at the barmaid.

"They sure grow em nice down here." Boner commented his eyes drawn to the low cut white blouse of the well endowed barmaid.

"Oh yeah they do." I answered drinking my beer facing the pool watching the action in the water. Boner turned around watching the four polo players in the water.

"They seem no worse for wear." He observed.

"Yeah, amazing what a little fun an sun can do."

"I remember back to our little field trip over Cuba. Man that was an adrenalin rush to say the least. We sure kicked some ass that day."

"Ayep, it was indeed. We were lucky to have survived." I observed.

"Luck had nothing to do with it, we were the dynamic duo together again." He laughed.

"Yeah we had surprise on our side, they didn't know what hit them." I smiled at the memory. I could remember the roller coaster adrenalin rush as we out flew the SAMs and then fought off the Cuban MIGs.

"Now here we are sitting under the sun by the pool drinking cold ones, flying Russian fighters for the Cubans protecting the Mexicans against the Guatemalans who are flying Chinese fighters built by the Russians. Christ what a screwed up world we live in." He said shaking his head.

"Ayep, I'm an American, in the Cuban Air Force, flying Russian fighters for a former enemy I helped eliminate. You're working for a company as a test pilot, now flying for money as a mercenary. It doesn't get any weirder." I replied.

"GAWD I love it." He grinned at me.

"Doesn't get any better." I assured him emptying my beer.

"Senorita, cervesa tambien por favor." I looked at the barmaid. Her eyes looked into mine and she smiled warmly as she opened another cold beer, condensation sliding down the side in the heat. Yeah, the only thing missing is Ali I thought to myself as I watched Boner stumble as he practiced his Spanish on the barmaid. She was giggling at him.

"I think she likes me." He said hopefully.

"You and every other good looking guy here. She probably is married with six kids at home." I warned him.

"Naaaaaaa, she is a slave to my charm, you'll see. Ill be sleeping with her tonight, you watch." His eyes looking over her body. I just shook my head and headed for the pool jumping into the water holding my beer high so it wouldn't go under the water. The water was warm but refreshing never the less. It helped with the hot Mexican sun.

Later that night true to his word the barmaid went to the restaurant with us. He left with her in a cab together. I went back to my hotel room and placed a call to Ali. It was great to hear her voice, even if it was only over the telephone. I rented a movie on the hotel room TV and fell asleep halfway through it.

The next day we took a cab to the huge zoo and wandered around. The barmaid, whose name was Cecilia, was on Boner's arm the whole time. She hung onto him like he was a life preserver. She had to work that evening, so we went to a local steakhouse later without her.

"So how is she" Marco asked Boner.

"She is like a wild animal. We cant get enough of each other." He explained.

"She speak any English?" I asked.

"Not much, and my Spanish is weak, but we communicate really well." He grinned.

"Yeah there doesn't appear to be any problem there." I grinned at him. Later we gathered at the pool under the stars with the pool lights on splashing around, getting drunk, Boner glued to the bar with Cecilia. He spent the night with her after she got off work.

When it was time to return to base, I waited out front with Marco and Julio. I had Boner's duffel bag already packed. We were waiting for the big blue bus to arrive to take us back to base. We stood and watched as an old Chevy cab approached the hotel. It pulled up in front and Boner climbed out of the back, handing the driver some bills. Behind Boner was Cecilia climbing out. He turned around and she wrapped her arms around his neck giving him a long kiss that melted his ears. She smiled at him and returned to the cab.

"Have a good time?" I asked him as the cab pulled away.

"Betchur ass I did, man that woman is an animal" He grinned at us. Marco just shook his head.

"Marco and I did real well." Julio bragged.

"The girls in the pool?" Boner asked picking up his bag.

"Oh yeah. Ole Grey here had to sleep alone." He teased.

"Yeah I did, but man wait until we get home. It'll be worth it." I smiled at them.

"Yeah, that's for sure meho." Boner told me. The big blue bus finally pulled up and we climbed inside, the morning heat already turning it into an oven inside. The bus pulled away and we sat there looking out the open windows as we rode back. It felt good to get away from the base for awhile.

When I got back to my quarters, Raul pulled me outside to talk. I guess he was worried about our room being bugged or something. I knew it would be difficult to get someone into our base, then into our quarters, as there were always armed guards inside and out of our building.

"I just got a message from Antonio, he says there will be a C-130 aircraft at our disposal. It is filled with jamming equipment." He revealed. I stood there looking at him in wonder.

"How the hell did he manage that?" I asked.

"Who knows. I think he has a few friends in the American government that are willing to help us out on the sly. They are painting it now with Mexican colors to hide the fact it came from America."

"An AWACs AND an aerial jamming aircraft? Wow that really does even the odds in our favor." I told him getting excited.

"It sure does."

"My my he HAS been a busy boy hasn't he?" I smirked.

"Seems so." Raul answered smiling.

"He never ceases to amaze me. He sure is full of surprises." I said shaking my head. By using the AWACs and a jammer together, we would be able to identity the locations of the J-11s and jam their radar along with their ground control radar and radio traffic. They would be unable to communicate with their ground control, and it would hamper their ability to launch their air to air missiles.

"The sun sure looks a lot brighter today." I told him grinning.

"Yes it does." He agreed. "They have been repositioning our mobile SAM launchers near the border. It will make the other side work harder trying to locate them again."

"Well glad to hear that. Anything to give our side an edge." I told him.

"Exactly. The more they reposition them, the harder it will be for the J-11s to keep track and attack them." He commented.

"Has Antonio heard anything about when they might attack us?" I inquired.

"No, nothing yet. Just that he has high suspicions they will when they feel they are strong enough."

"I hope that is a long time from now."

"Me too." He said." The AWACs has been up, they were able to record the attack without being detected. I've been reviewing the tapes Seems there was a hotshot flight leader that was eager for his first kill. He jumped the gun, acted on his own without orders. His orders were to just patrol the border, not to become aggressive or engage."

"Was he one of the pilots that was shot down?" I hoped.

"No, seems he initiated the attack, but the other three pilots paid for his mistake with their lives. He was the only one to escape." He answered.

"Figures. Isnt that always the way it works" I shook my head in disgust. "Course their government is busy trying to cover his screw up with the usual communist propaganda."

"Yes, that's how they operate." He said "Antonio has received intelligence their government has decided he is too much of a hothead to fly the border flights, so he is now chained to a desk. If they start a war with us he will probably be flying then." He explained.

"Everyone will be flying then." I said.

The next few weeks were quiet, the Guatemalans flew daily border sweeps as did our pilots. Every day and night we put up two fighters to sweep the border.

The other side didn't have many pilots with good night flying capabilities. Night flying was a whole different animal. Disorientation was quite common. Having flown the F-18 off my carrier in the navy I was well aware of the dangers. There was nothing more terrifying than landing an F-18 at night onto a carrier in the middle of a thunderstorm.

The Mexican pilots we were flying with were improving their flying skills. Flying the border sweeps were monotonous. We rotated their pilots through our ACM classes when they weren't flying along the border. We began rotating our pilots back to Cuba for R and R. When it was time for my unit to rotate back, we were more than ready.

CHAPTER TWELVE

Boner and I were thrilled when our turn came to take off from the base. Flying East towards Cuba I was excited and happy. Flying along looking at the clouds around us and the flat ocean below I couldn't help thinking about how lucky I was. The MIG was flying perfectly, it's engine humming the fighter vibrating from the power. I double checked the info on my thigh pad and verified my IFF was turned on and emitting the correct signal. I didn't want to be mistaken for an unidentified aircraft approaching Cuba. The island was ringed with modern upgraded SAM sites able to shoot down any hostile aircraft. I leaned forward looking back at Boner's fighter off my starboard wing. We were flying along in a perfect sky. I called Havana tower for landing clearance and made my turn. I lined up with the runway, flared at the last minute and landed perfectly. Boner came in right behind me. We pulled up in front of our hanger with the unit emblem on the side. I shut down the engine and slowly opened my canopy. There was a thunk to my left as the ground tech slid the orange metal ladder into place. I slowly disengaged from the fighter and climbed down. Boner was right behind me as I walked to the hanger door. One by one our pilots landed their MIGs.

Once inside the cool hanger we headed for the locker room to strip off our inflatable G suits and hang up our helmets.

"Who buys the beer tonight?" Boner asked me as he slid off his G suit.

"Knowing Antonio, he will be at the house as soon as I get home wanting a personal debriefing." I warned him.

"Yeah, well okay, maybe later then. I have some phone calls to make anyway, see who is available tonight." He told me grinning. I shook my head at him. I picked up the phone and made a call to the company office.

"Oh my God I cant wait to see you!" Alis voice greeted me.

"Well I cant wait to see you either, but anticipate Antonio wanting to talk to me first." I reminded her.

"Yes, Ill tell him you have arrived, maybe you can talk with him first before we go home, that way we can be undisturbed." She laughed wickedly into my ear.

"I love a woman who thinks ahead." I told her.

Later I rode over to the company hanger. I ran my id card through the slot and punched in my numerical code watching as the thick steel door opened electrically. A wall of noise assaulted me as I entered the hanger walking in the white lined walkway. All around me were mechanics working feverishly on different fighters.

"War is good for business I gather." I told Ali opening the door to her office. She jumped from behind her desk and ran into my arms almost knocking me over.

"Whoa easy there girl." I teased holding her body tightly in my arms, she felt like heaven.

"I have missed you so much." She whispered into my ear, her arms around my neck. My heart was pounding like a jackhammer.

"Welcome home Sean." Antonio's voice interrupted us as he entered the office.

"Hello Antonio, nice to see you too." I told him letting go of Ali. We shook hands warmly. We spent the next hour in his office reviewing the attack along the border. The air conditioner in his window hummed as we discussed the details. Antonio had a habit of discussing an event with each individual involved hoping to get one or two details missed by each participant. By the end he would have a completely detailed picture of the event. He never relied only on paperwork information.

"They have completed flight testing their newest J-11s. I've heard from my contacts inside Guatemala City there may be an attack soon. They believe the technology of their newest J-11s will overcome the numerical superiority of our MIGs in southern Mexico. I've sent word to the military in Mexico City so they are aware. The base has been on full alert, four MIGs are in the air at all times, the SAM sites along the border have been moved again to make it harder to detect them. There are Mexican Navy gun boats patrolling the coast and we have an early warning detection system in place near their two northern most air bases. We will know the moment they launch their fighters and Mexican radar will be able to detect their direction of travel whenever they decide to head north." He explained.

"I knew some of this, I didn't know they were this close to attacking." I replied.

"That's not something many people know. No reason they should." He went on.

"Then why was our unit allowed to return here now, shouldn't we be there ready and waiting?" I asked.

"They keep track of our flight patterns. They know we just allowed a team of MIGs to return here on R & R."

"So you want them to think we are unaware of their plans by allowing us to return, because after all no one in their right mind would weaken their forces prior to being attacked." I finished.

"Exactly." He smiled at me. I smiled shaking my head.

"Do you ever sleep Antonio?" I asked him smiling.

"When I can." He replied. I sat there looking at him my mind working.

"Whats on your mind Sean?" He asked.

"By allowing our unit to return you create an oppurtunity for them to attack." I answered.

"And?" He asked with a slight grin.

"You try to get them to attack on your time table as well, which means we are ready for them." I continued.

"You always were a smart one." He grinned. "We have teams of special forces in the mountains with shoulder launched surface to air missiles." He explained further.

"MANPADS?" I asked.

"Yes, we hope they will fly low to avoid the radar and fly under the SAM's radar....."

"Giving the shoulder fired SAMs a chance to hit them because shoulder fired SAMs are impossible to detect from a jet fighter until after they are launched." I finished his thought again.

"Right again Sean, good job."

"Pray I never have to play chess with you."

154

"I used to play while I was in Prison here while Castro was alive." He explained.

"I really wanted to take part in the defense of the airbase." I told him.

"You will take part in the retaliatory strike. You have experience doing that type of mission." He grinned at me. I knew he was referring to the strike mission I flew against Bejucal years ago." Go home, enjoy yourself. You've earned it." He smiled getting up.

"I will, thank you." I told him as I stood up.

"Ill be in my office catching up on paperwork, Ill see you tonight." I told Ali sticking my head inside her office.

"Oh no you dont!" She told me coming around her desk. She wrapped her arms around my neck kissing me taking my breath away making my heart pound. "You don't get away that easy." She whispered into my ear as she raked my crotch with her fingernails. "I told Antonio if he bothered us tonight Id scratch his eyes out."

"I'm a lucky man." I told her.

I spent the rest of the day doing paperwork in my office.

Later that night we feasted on rock lobster. Ali sat in my lap stuffing lobster into my mouth.

"I cant eat anymore I'm stuffed." I told her. She got up and pulled me out the door after her snagging a blanket on our way out to the beach. We spread it out onto the warm sand. The stars twinkled above us as we made love to the sound of the ocean.

I spent the rest of the week dealing with paperwork, and test flying a new MIG. At night Ali filled my arms as we slept. Antonio woke us up on Sunday morning. He had news from our base in Mexico. The J-11s had raided our base the day before. The AWACs had detected them as they lifted off from their base in Flores. Two were shot down by SAMs as they crossed the border, four were shot down flying NOE through the mountains by shoulder fired MANPADs. The J-11s were forced to drop their bombs as they dealt with the SAMs and MIGs from the base. Three more were shot down as they recrossed the border returning to their base. The base was untouched due to the J-11s aborting their mission, but we lost three MIGs to their missiles. My unit was to return to Mexico at once. I took a quick shower as Ali got my flight suit ready. I ate a small breakfast as I laced up my flight boot. Ali's face was tense as she realized I was flying into a shooting war. Our unit was to take part in the first of two retaliatory strikes into Guatemala. Ali rode with me in the Hummer to the base. Antonio was there in the hanger as we arrived. Boner arrived as we pulled up. I could hear the MIGs engines on the other side of our hanger. Our fighters were already being warmed up waiting for us.

"Best of luck to you Sean, come back to us." Antonio told me. He stepped forward and hugged me. He turned quickly and shook Boner's hand. Ali gave Boner a quick hug.

"Bring him back to me Boner." She told him.

"Count on it" He smiled at her.

"Come back to me." She whispered into my ear as we held each other.

Boner and I walked into the locker room together to put on our inflatable G suits and strap on our survival vests. Helmets in hand we walked side by side out into the sunlight and climbed into our fighters. Our birds had been armed and fueled and preflighted by the ground techs for us. I did a complete cockpit check and closed the canopy locking it into place. We got clearance from the tower, lined our fighters up and took off. Once in the air I turned on the autopilot and looked over the notes on my thigh pad. It was a silent tense flight to the base. I was wondering who we lost to the J-11s.

I called the tower and got landing clearance. We got our information, my radar warning indicator lit up letting me know we were on their radar and SAMs were lighting us up. I made the turn, dropped my gear, adjusted my flaps, lined up with the runway and flared just before touching down. I tapped the brakes and let out the drag chute slowing the fighter down. At the end of the runway I turned and rolled up the side ramp towards our hanger. One by one our fighters landed. This time there were concrete revetments for us to park in. I locked the brakes, shut down the engine and power to the instrument panel. I unlocked the canopy and removed my helmet. I climbed down the orange metal ladder my helmet under my arm. I saw Raul waiting for me at the front of the hanger. Boner and I walked together to the door.

"Welcome back guys." He greeted us.

"Who did we lose?" I asked him.

"Julio, and two Mexican pilots." He replied. My heart sank. Julio was Marco's wingman.

"Anyone eject?" Boner asked him. Raul just shook his head. We followed him into the office and sat down grateful for the airconditioning. Raul took his time detailing the attack, the direction of travel, altitude, locations of each shootdown, and areas of MIG interceptions. It took about two hours, but by the time he was finished we had a complete understanding of the attack details.

"There will be a strike on their airfield at Flores two days from now. We will hit them early in the morning just as the sun is coming up. Intelligence supplied to us from Antonio reveals thats their weakest time of the day. Some of our fighters will carry bombs, some will fly cover for the bombers. The fighters will take off in the dark, and approach the base from the east out of the sun to make their bombing runs, covered by the attack fighters. Hitting them on the ground and shooting down any fighters they try to put up will give them a bloody nose they wont forget for a long time. There will also be another attack on their base south at Retalhuleu. The goal is to eliminate as many of their aircraft as possible, denying them control of the air, which hopefully will convince them to abandon their goal of marching into southern Mexico." We spent the rest of the day creating a working attack plan. Perry was working his people overtime to get the fighters ready for the attack.

"Perry has come up with an addition to our MIGs. he has constructed dual missile rails for our launchers. This will double the amount of air to air missiles we will be able to carry." Raul explained. Boner and I grinned in anticipation. This would double the number of targets we could fire at. We poured over the maps of the Flores airfield. There were SAM launchers around the field as well as ZSU anti aircraft radar guided guns. It was a formidable defense network surrounding the base. The first fighters in would bomb their radar center that would be firing the SAMs. We would attack any airborne fighters flying aircap over the base. I went to bed that night both excited and scared about the coming attack.

The next morning we performed our exercise routine. Then after morning chow we all gathered into the auditorium for the pre attack briefing. A combination of maps, drawings and satellite photos were on the wall. We reviewed the attack plan, assigned flight positions, and went over escape paths. We all had the emergency frequencies programed into our escape radios in our vests. The Hind rescue pilots listened quietly keeping track of our flight paths in and out.

I would be flying with Marco as my wingman, we would be carrying missiles flying cover for the fighters carrying bombs. Boner would be flying with another A-4 piloted by a Mexican pilot. Raul and Alexi would be flying their MIG-29s with two other MIG-29s also piloted by Mexican pilots. I didnt like flying without Boner as my wingman, but flying with dissimiliar aircraft wouldnt work out well. There would be twelve MIG 21s, four A-4s bombers and four MIG-29s flying cover for 18 MIG 21s carrying bombs. A total of thirty eight fighters would be attacking the airbase in Flores. Eight MIGs would be flying cover over our base, and eight more MIGs would be waiting to cover our retreat if any of the J-11s attempted to follow us across the border.

That night I wrote a letter to be delivered to Ali in case I was shot down and didn't make it back. I put it in with my gear that would be returned. It took forever for me to get to sleep. I tossed and turned in my bunk until Raul entered and we talked late into the night about our attack in the morning.

"We survived with a lot less attacking Bejucal, we will survive this one as well Grey. We have a lot more going for us this time." He told me.

"Yeah we didn't have any rescue helicopters then either. We were really on our own then weren't we." I remembered.

"Yeah it could have been really bad if any of us had been shot down trying to survive the aftermath of our mission. Running around the Cuban mountains waiting for the government to change and someone friendly locating us would have been a bitch." It helped to have someone to talk to in the darkness lying there in our bunks. Eventually I fell asleep and the alarm clock ringing was a surprise to me. It took a bit to wake up. I took a shower and slipped into my flight suit waiting for Raul to take his shower. Together we walked to the chow hall for breakfast. Then it was to the auditorium for a short quick review of the attack plan. I met Boner in the ready room and we spoke for a few minutes as we adjusted our G suits and slipped on our survival vests. One by one we walked to our fighters in the dark. When I closed my canopy I was again alone in my own little world. I was ready.

The fighter came alive around me as I checked every system There were eight Copperhead missiles under my wings and a modified elongated drop tank hanging below me with additional fuel. These new drop tanks had been modified into a different shape and enlarged to carry more fuel than before giving us longer range. There was no radio traffic between the fighters and the tower. This was to avoid giving any radio signals to potential listeners across the border. Instead there were coded light signals from the tower, instructing each flight when to take off. The instrument panel in front of me was aglow with red, green and blue lights along with the two multi function diplays. Information was displayed in green on the inside of my helmet visor. I had adjusted the helmet to eliminate any displays when I lowered my head to look at the muli function displays. When I turned my head away the display returned inside my visor.

My heart was pounding in my chest when it was my turn to pull onto the runway. The tower flashed a coded signal using a red signal light. Marco and I pulled up together side by side. I locked my brakes, rechecked the instrument panel, looked over my shoulder at Marco. He gave a wave with his gloved hand. I let out the brakes, pushed the throttle wide open and was thrown back into my seat as the fighter rocketed forward into the darkness. I pulled back with the stick in my right hand and lifted off the runway aiming up into the dark sky. I reached over raising the gear. They came up smoothly with a clunk and all three lights were green. Marco was right behind me at the four oclock position.

Our waypoints had been programed into the flight computers slaved to the autopilot. Our computers would direct the autopilot to fly our fighters the route to the point of attack. Then we would take over manually. Our fuel settings were set to peak to avoid wasting any fuel. I double checked the info on my thigh pad as the fighter flew the course east. Flying nap of the earth in the dark we were all alone inside our fighters. Unable to talk to each other until the attack only magnified the feeling. I had confidence in my abilities and those of the men around me. There always was the unexpected or unplanned element in any attack no matter how much time was spent in the planning stage. The rest would be up to the Lord above. I was sure many of the other pilots were praying silently, I know I was. I looked up at the stars above me remembering the last night Ali and I were together on the beach behind our house under these same stars. I knew she would be sleeping alone in our bed while we were flying along getting ready to attack and kill what we all hoped would also be a sleeping enemy. Antonio's intelligence information had never failed us before. I had faith it wouldnt fail us now.

The fighter began its turn at another waypoint as the computer made an adjustment in the flight path. I looked over my right shoulder at Marco's

MIG his helmet reflecting light from his instrument panel and his wing lights glowing in the darkness. The AWACs was up and sending us the position data of the enemy fighters flying over their base. Altitude, direction and speed were displayed with four white triangles depicting the enemy fighters, along with type of radar being emitted. This was it, no holds barred now. I grabbed the stick and manuevered the fighter heading north then west. I punched loose my drop tank and it dropped away cleanly.

The computer decided which of the J-11s were an imediate threat and I aligned the aiming recticle on the box and heard good tones in my headphones. I squeezed the trigger on my stick and closed my eyes briefly to avoid being blinded by the white hot exhaust of my first missile as it dropped from my wing and roared away at its BVR target. The computer acquired a second target and again I closed my eyes for a fraction of a second as my second missile launched. Soon the air was full of launched missiles as the sun began to come up into the sky behind us turning the sky orange and pink and blue.

The four MIG-21s I was protecting began their bomb run and one by one their bombs fell from beneath their wings impacting into the hangers below. Building after building disintegrated into balls of flame and heat as the MIGs angled away and roared off towards the west.

The radio came alive with calls and yells as the other attack fighters began their bombing runs on the base. Long white trails sprouted from the ground as SAMs came up at us. Tracer rounds were criss crossing over the field from the anti aircraft guns. There were explosions in the morning sky as fighters from both sides fell from the sky. The airfield was ablaze in orange fire as flames leaped from hangers, fuel tanks and ammo storage buildings. Four J-11s had made it into the air right before the attack. Marco fired off two of his missiles at targets, their long white exhaust trails reaching out into the distance finding their targets and exploding them almost side by side.

My RWR was beeping constantly as the ground radar mixed with the radar from the J-11s reached out sweeping my fighter. I turned and maneuvered again and again pushing the little fighter to its limit to defeat any missile lock ons. The automatic computer controlled anti missile system was functioning perfectly, alternating between releasing chaff and flres. The electronic missile jammer was changing frequencies to confuse any independantly radar guided missiles coming my way. Marco was right there like glue as I searched for targets in the sky as our MIGs found their targets dropping their bombs. Smoke and orange fire blanketed the air base from one end to the other. There were at least four fires on the ground where J-11s had crashed.

My headphones were alive with calls of fighter locations and yells from one pilot to another. I looked to my right just in time to see a SAM heading my direction with an orange glow at the bottom white smoke trailed behind as it tried to reach out to me. I turned violently and changed altitude to get below it just as a stream of tracer fire flashed past my canopy from a radar guided ZSU. The computer ejected countermeasures automatically as I changed direction and altitude again rocketing over a building and through thick black smoke.

My RWR was going off as a J-11 launched a missile at me. Again the computer ejected countermeasures as I completed another extreme maneuver to defeat the missile's lock on me. Another SAM flashed past me on its run up ito the sky and a violent explosion rocked me from the left as a fighter exploded in an orange and white ball of flame.

"You awright Marco?" I called over to him.

"Still here boss." he replied. I glanced above me in time to recognize a J-11 flashing by. My missile radar growled at me informing me it had a lock on. I moved my helmet at it moving the aiming recticle inside the box and again squeezed the trigger on my stick launching a Copperhead missile at it. My missile dropped cleanly from below my right wing and with a long thin white exhaust streaked upward and into the belly of the J-11 causing it to explode as pieces of it continued along until gravity won pulling them earthward.

I turned the fighter looking down at the field at a massive Russian built transport just sitting at the end of the runway all four of it's engines running. I aimed the helmet sight at it, got a good missile lock on it and squeezed the trigger. I watched as my missile dropped from under my wing again and turned rocketing down impacting the huge white transport in the center. I kept the little box in my visor on the transport. Seconds later there here was a massive explosion with orange flame and white heat rising from the crater where the transport had been.

Bombs exploded in the center of the long runway creating craters, another hanger exploded throwing debris into the air and pieces of burning metal into parked J-11s creating secondary explosions.

To my right two fighters collided creating a massive fireball and shockwave as I turned my fighter away to avoid injesting any pieces into my intake. To my left were two J-11s far behind a MIG-29 trying to manuever away. I heard good tones from my next missile and squeezed the trigger. The missile dropped off it's rail and with a flash took off after the rear of one of the two J-11s. Marco launched two of his missiles at the same time. They imeadeatly turned away trying to avoid the Copperhead missile. I kept my helmet sight on the rear of my targeted J-11 and was rewarded as my missile flew right up it's tailpipe blowing the fighter to pieces. Marcos missile flew straight and true the first one detonating under the J-11 breaking it's back destoying it completly.

Below me to the left on the side of the runway sat a silver gleaming Russian Bear bomber its eight counter rotating propellor glinting in the morning sun. None of our intelligence reports had indicated they had any Bears. I knew this aircraft could fly amazing distances and could launch cruise missiles as well as drop bombs. I climbed for altitude then turned and manuevered again to defeat any possible missile locked onto my fighter. I wanted that bomber. I wanted it destroyed so it wouldnt be used in a cruise missile attack on our base. I turned changing direction again locking onto it with my helmet sight and squeezed the trigger. A missile lept off the rail and flew down hitting the Bear right between the wings. It detonated and the bomber exploded with a massive explosion. The fuel tanks must have been full as the shock wave reached up hitting my fighter and I fought to keep control.

"Good hit boss." Marco called out.

The abort signal came over my headphones alerting us it was time to leave.

"Lets head for home Marco." I called out to him as I changed direction heading for the deck streaking west.

"Im right with you boss." He replied.

My heart was pounding in my chest and adrenalin was pouring through my body as I double checked the displays to verify my fighter was undamaged. Everything looked normal. The green jungle was flashing below me. I still had two missiles under my wings with plenty of fuel to make it back.

"Roll call." I heard Raul's voice as we left the smoking burning airfield behind us. One by one each pilot called out his call sign. Boner made it, Alexi made it, Marco and I called out, We had lost two pilots from our team and there were three missing Mexican pilots. A heavy price to pay to destroy the airfield. But destroy it we did. Heading west I recieved radio calls from our base as well as the reaction team of MIGs ahead of us circling waiting to pick off any J-11s foolsih enough to try to catch us from behind. As we passed over the mountain peaks my RWR warned me of handheld MANPAD missile radar beneath us. Teams of Mexican special forces were on guard scanning the sky around us ready to launch their missiles at any following J-11s. Above us eight MIG 21s flying in two four ship diamond formations circled around behind us. The AWACs was transmitting data to our displays but there were no J-11s behind us.

I called ahead to the tower and was told to circle the field as there were two MIGs ahead of me trailing smoke from their damaged birds. I pulled up to a higher altitude and Marco and I circled the base as the two fighters landed. When we were cleared to land I made the turn, dropped my gear adjusted flaps, moved the throttle with my left hand and came in on my approach. I adjusted the flaps again and lined up perfectly with the center of the field. I flared just before touching down, dropped the speed brake, tapped the brakes and released my drag chute cutting power to the engine. At the end of the runway I turned off and rolled to the front of the hanger. One by one our birds came in. I parked the MIG in front of the hanger, cut power to the engine and shut down the instrument panel. I unlocked my canopy and there was a thunk as the ground tech moved the ladder to my left side. I took off my helmet and sat there as the breeze washed across my sweaty face. I breathed deeply savoring the smells and glad to be alive.

The ground tech helped disconnect me and I slowly climbed down to the ramp. I walked around my fighter looking at the black blast marks under the wings from the missile exhaust. The outside of the fighter was gray and black from the smoke and burning fuel I had flown through. This fighter had been blooded by the residue of warfare. She had fought well and gotten me home. Looking up at the blue morning sky the sun wasnt even halfway above me. This was a morning I would remember for a lifetime. I walked to the ready room Marco came up behind me excited and laughing slapping me on the back. One by one our pilots walked in laughing and yelling, excited and relieved to be alive. We were more than just pilots flying practice missions, we were now warriors. We had taken war to the enemy and lived to tell about it. I had tasted the flavor of war in the air three times before. I knew it would take time for the adrenalin rush to fade, then I would be ravenously hungry and ready for sleep.

"Hey meho we surviived after all." Boner said as he slapped me on the back grinning.

"Amen to that. Id kill for an ice cold beer right now, man that airfield must be a hell of a mess right now." I told him.

"Yeah maybe this will teach the bastards not to screw with us anymore."

"I dunno, time will tell. We caught em with their pants down thats for sure."

One by one we were debriefed by a group of Mexican Air Force Generals and Colonels. One by one we gathered in the chow hall, tired and sweaty. There was a wall of noise in there from everyone talking at once. Raul and Alexi sat next to Boner and I. Marco pulled up a chair next to us. Our Cuban group of pilots gathered together talking loudly and eating. One by one we shared our experiences with people cutting in with their observations. The building shook as More of our MIGs took off flying an aircap over our base in case there was any retaliation from our attack.

"I dont think there will be anything to worry about today from them." I remarked.

"Not after what we did to them, hell no." Marco replied.

"I already sent a short report to Antonio giving him the highlights." Raul told us. I nodded as I ate. The base had been on a communication blackout for the past two days. No one was allowed to leave or enter, and all communications with the outside had been cut with the exception of traffic to and from the Mexican high command in Mexico City. Now that the mission was complete the ban was lifted. Looking around the interior of the chow hall at the laughing happy pilots I felt we had done our duty training these pilots. They were a good bunch.

I stood under the shower for what seemed like an eternity, the morning's events replaying over and over in my mind. Later Raul and I replayed the film from the fighters of the attack. Combined with radar info we were able to construct an accurate chain of events of the attack. I was credited with shooting down three J-11s, and destroying two aircraft on the ground. Raul,

Alexi and Boner were credited with one kill each, Marco was credited with one kill. Total kills for our side was eight. Total aircraft destroyed on the ground was six.

I sat at my desk and wrote the required letters to the families of the men from our team we lost. It was never an easy thing to do trying to explain to grieving families why their sons died. I felt inadequate to the task. That night there was a massive celebration at the club. I dont remember making it back to my bunk.

Two days later it was my turn to fly aircap over the base. Boner flew as my wingman. There were four MIG-21s and four A-4s flying two figure eight patterns around the base. Our SAM operators were on constant alert, the radar station on the mountain that overlooked the base changed operators every four hours.

"Meho check your data." Boner called over to me. The AWACs had been sending us data. I turned my head and saw eight white triangles on the multifunction display. I had turned off my helemet display not expecting any trouble this morning. I quickly switched it on and the computor identified eight J-11s streaking toward our base in two four ship diamond formations from the south.

"Tiger flight you are free to engage!" The voice came over my earphones from the operations center. I could imagine the flurry of activity that was taking place below us. I knew Raul and the base commander would be running to get to the center.

"Light em up guys." I called to the other pilots. I turned on my missile radar and with Boner in tow dove for the deck maneuvering between the mountain ranges.

We screamed south flying NOE towards the incoming fighters. At the right moment we popped up above the mountain range and my missile radar growled at me. The computor chose the closest J-11 that it considered a threat. I squeezed the trigger and a missile dropped off my right wing and with a flash raced off towards it's target. Again the computor chose another target, the missile growled over my headphones and I fired again. I saw two missiles streak past me from Boner's A-4. We both dove for the deck not waiting to confirm any hits. I wanted to get below their radar and confuse them in the ground clutter.

We twisted and turned fifty feet off the deck. I looked up at the mountain wall as we roared along the rock face maneuvering in and out. Above us missile trails criss crossed the sky as the J-11s launched their missiles in hope of hitting our fighters. I lead my flight up again out of the valleys and turned north coming behind the J-11s. I was rewarded with another growl from my missile radar telling me a target was already locked on. Again my gloved hand squeezed the trigger sending a Copperhead missile away. This time I watched it all the way as it followed the twisting turning J-11 until it impacted with the rear of the enemy fighter creating a massive orange and white explosion against the blue sky. I didnt have time to savor the victory. I again dove for the deck, changeing course and popping up again on the right side of three J-11s. This time Boner beat me to the punch launching his missiles first. The three J-11s split up and dove lower trying to confuse the missile radar. One J-11 exploded from being hit from a SAM launched from the base. Boner's missile exploded over the top of one of the enemy fighters shredding the top of the fighter killing the pilot instantly. The J-11 flew along for a few seconds before it slowly dove and flew straight into the ground.

The other pilots of our group were launching missiles at the remaining J-11s then diving for the deck dissapearing from radar. I heard a man screaming as one of our MIGs exploded in a ball of flame the victim of a J-11s missile. The J-11 turned south quickly and roared south away from us. My first instinct was to give chase, but after looking at my fuel level I knew I lacked the amount of fuel required to give chase. I would run out at the border. It was just as well as above me three more J-11s were heading south away from us.

I turned north towards home and leveled out, keeping an eye on my radar display for any straggling enemy fighters. There were none. Four MIGs lifted off the runway from the base to replace us in the air. One by one we lined up with the runway and landed. Our training had paid off and we had fought off an attack on the base. Again we had lost one of our own, but we had hurt the enemy worse. Our tactics were eliminating the technical edge the J-11s had over our older fighters, that and the poor fighting skills of the Guatemalan pilots. We had better training methods. Our pilots were defending their base and their country, they were better motivated.

I rolled up to the hanger and shut down the engine. I sat there for a few seconds trying to slow my heartbeats and control my breathing. Everything had happened so fast. I unlocked my canopy and slowly opened it locking it in place. I slid off my helmet and looked over at Boner's fighter. He was already climbing out. I got up turned around and climbed down the orange metal ladder.

"Man we kicked ass did you see that bastard explode, one minute it was an expensive fighter, then boom the next it was just junk. Gawd I love this job." He was grinning from ear to ear.

"Ayep, beats settin behind a desk anyday." I replied. We walked over to the operations center together after putting everything away in the ready room. Raul was there with the base commander looking at the huge map on the wall and moving little red pins around.

"We need to hit them again but this time at Retalhuleh." Raul stated.

"Hell yeah lets go Im ready." Boner called out. Raul and the base commander both looked up at Boner, then Raul looked over at me. I shrugged my shoulders and looked at the floor. I understood Boner's enthusiasim.

"Looks like there is no shortage of volunteers." The commander said.

"Betchur ass, ah sir." Boner replied. He was starting to calm down from the adrenalin rush.

"We lost a pilot sir. Im sorry to report." I told them. Raul nodded silently. He was already aware from watching the radar screen.

"They lost another fighter to a SAM site at the border." Raul told us. That made me feel better inside.

"Hot damn, we keep this up and they wont have any more fighters to fly against us." Boner remarked.

"It does appear that way." The commander replied.

"Reminds me of the Battle of Britain." I threw in.

"It does indeed." Raul commented.

"The Chinese will be sending more fighters soon Ill bet. I bet they will change their training system as well. They wont hit us the same way again next time. They will keep changing their tactics to confuse us." I added.

"If we have one more large raid at Retalhuleh, it should slow them down for awhile. They cant attack us if their fighters are burning hulks in their hangers." The commander told us.

"We'll be ready sir." I told him.

"You have already proven that son." He replied with a grin. I went to my quarters and took a shower washing off the grit and sweat. I wrote Ali a letter and put it in the base mail. Boner met me at the chow hall and we sat there eating and drinking coffee. Boner was still pumped from the fight. I sat there patiantly listening to him rant on.

"You dont seem as pumped up lately whats up?" he asked.

"Well Ive done this a few times. There was the shooting down those Cuban MIGs, then I shot down Two Pakistani fighters, then there was the mission over Bejucal. The attack on Flores, and now this fight. Guess Im adapting to it." I explained.

"Yeah I hear ya. You have a couple on me." he observed.

"I guess I look at it differently. This is a job, ya know, Im part of the air force. Im in the military again. Plus Im married." I told him.

"Oh yeah being married definitly can change your perspective on things. I guess I look at it differently, it is like an adventure to me. I get to test fly A-4s for the company, but right now Im part of the Cuban Air Force. Who knows what the future will bring."

"People handle things differently." I said. He nodded in understanding as he drank his coffee. We both looked up as Raul came up to our table with a tray of food.

"There will be a briefing this afternoon. We will be attacking Retalhuleh tomorrow." He told us.

"Hot damn, we'll bomb em back to the stone age." Boner said with a grin. Raul looked at Boner and smiled.

"Glad you are so enthusiastic." Raul told him.

That afternoon in the auditorium Raul gave the briefing complete with aerial photos and maps with diagrams. We recieved new radio frequencies for the Hind rescue helicopters. The satilite photos were detailed and showed the airfield from southwest to northeast. The airfield was located southwest of the city of Retalhuleh with an oval dirt racetrack north of the strip. This was a modern air base bristling with sophisticated air defense systems. SAMs, ZSUs, and radar guided flak guns were placed strategically around the long runway. There were several newly constructed hangers and buildings and sandbagged revetments with J-11s parked in them.

The large swimming pool below the dirt race track was clearly visible. It was a perfect landmark for locating the airbase. I could see SAM launchers clearly visible around the base. There was a long railroad track next to the base that traveled all the way to the coast.

There would be two attack flights. One would come in low over the ocean, the second attack would come through the mountain range and attack from the northeast. Studying the detailed color photos gave us all an idea what everything looked like. It would be easy to recognize.

Champerico was a small coastal fishing village located west of Retalhuleh. The Chinese had rebuilt the southern part of the town into a major deep water industrial port on the coast where oil tankers and supply ships unloaded. The long railroad track was used to ferry the fighters and fuel to the airfield. There were several SAM sites and ZSU anti aircraft guns located around the harbor. It was to be hit after attacking the airfield. My flight would fly NOE through the mountains, hit the airbase, and hit the port on the way out. It would prove to be an exciting mission. Hopefully it would put a crimp in their air war against Mexico. The idea was to force them to run out of fighters before we did.

Everyone gathered in the hanger after the chow hall closed. The base watering hole was closed so as not to tempt pilots into drinking the night before a mission. Perry and his crew were fine tuning each fighter for the mission tomorrow.

"Sure is a lot simpler working in here than it was on Andros Island." Perry whispered to me.

"Yeah, it seems like such a long time ago." I told him looking at the Cuban flag painted on the tail of my fighter.

"Give em hell tomorrow buddy. Kick em in the ass." He was grinning.

"You know it." I assured him.

"It's just a shame we have to leave it to an ole burned out squid to do the job, now if we had some Harriers flown by Marines...." he jabbed me in the ribs.

"Damn jarhead, if you had it your way you would be down there kicking ass all by yourself."

"Well Id call a few buddies of mine to go along, just for fun ya understand. You'll do awright I guess. Im gittin a little old to be playin in the jungle anymore." He grinned again.

"Age catches up with all of us eventually." I agreed.

CHAPTER THIRTEEN

I got up early the next morning before the sun rose. As usual I beat Raul to the shower. I turned on the little coffee maker waiting for the water to heat up.

"Morning already?" Raul asked sleepily.

"Coffee is ready." I offered.

"Bless you. It takes forever for me to wake up." He sat up yawning. He sat there his bare feet on the tile floor. I handed him a cup of hot black coffee. he just nodded accepting the cup. I finished lacing up my boots.

"Perry was joking last night about how he was getting older." I told him.

"Perry will outlive us all, he will be lifting weights along with Alexi when you and I are in our wheelchairs dribbling oatmeal on ourselves." He said sipping his coffee.

"Yeah but imagine all the stories we'll have to share."

"Boner will be chasing all the nurses in the nursing home."

"That he will, now that they have a pill for old men, he will never quit." I joked. Together we walked to the chow hall for breakfast. As usual before a mission the noise inside the chow hall was thunderous. You could feel the excitement in the air.

Later Boner walked up to me in the ready room and stuck out his hand.

"Good luck today meho, kick ass." He said grinning.

"Thanks, you too." I told him.

I walked out into the morning sunshine and Manuel was already checking his fighter. he gave me a wave as I put my helmet in the cockpit of my bird. I slowly walked around the MIG, checking the front landing gear and the tires. There were no leaks, I ran my hand inside the front intake to make sure there were no foriegn objects inside. The rear of the fighter was clear. I ran my hand along the skin feeling the carbon fiber panels that hid anti missile jammers and other electronic equipment. I checked the two rear flare ejectors, they were secure. There were eight Copperhead missiles hanging from both wings. The fighter had been modified to carry the extra weight. The enlarged airodynamic drop tank was full and tight, it didnt wiggle when I shook it. I signed the form and handed the clipboard back to the ground tech and climbed up the metal orange ladder into the cockpit. Once inside I wiggled around until I was comfortable. I slipped the helmet on and the ground tech yanked the safety pins from my ejection seat. He climbed down and removed the ladder. I hit the power switch and the instrument panel came alive, the electronic multi function displays were working. I spun my finger in a circle warning the ground tech I was starting the engine, he gave me a thumbs up. I hit the switch and the engine started to whine as it spooled up. I closed the canopy and locked it with my left hand. I could feel the fighter start to vibrate around me as the engine powered up.

As usual there would be no radio traffic from us to the tower. Everything on the panels looked good. I sat there waiting my turn to taxi to the end of the runway. Looking over my shoulder I saw Manuel, he gave me a thumbs up sign with his gloved hand. I returned it. He was my wingman today for this mission. Our flight would consist of four MIG-21s carrying missiles as escort for six MIG-21s carrying bombs. Raul and Alexi were part of a four ship formation of MIG-29s. Boner would be flight leader for four A-4s covering six MIG-21s carrying bombs. Boners flight would be attacking from the ocean, My flight would be attacking from the north coming out of the mountains. Raul with Alexi were part of a four ship MIG-29 team. They would be acting as a quick reaction force to cover both attacking flights over the base, then to follow us as we hit the port.

When the colored signal light came from the tower ordering me to take off, I released the brakes and taxied to the end of the runway. I locked the brakes, double checked the instrument panel, everything looked good. I slowly released my brakes, increased throttle with my left hand and was thrown back into my seat from the force. I pulled back on the stick and the fighter lifted off the runway. I brought the gear up and they locked into place with a clunk. I adjusted flaps and with Manuel on my four o'clock position joined up with the other two MIG s. We flew a four ship diamond formation leading six MIGs behind us with bombs hanging under their wings. Our computors steered our fighters by our autopilot, flying NOE at fifty feet twisting and turning in between the mountain peaks. We followed the Sierra Madre Mountians all the way south. We passed the border and my RWR told me enemy ground radar was looking for us. I doubted they knew we were coming, they were just watching the skies.

Boners flight would be attacking first. That meant they would be warned and already striking back as we came down on them from between the mountains. Our fighters would be flying low, then pop up to a higher altitude to avoid being damaged from explosions from their bombs. Then we would be flying low again on our way west to attack the port hoping to stay below their radar. The damage from our one two punch attack on their base and damaging their port would hamper their ability to re arm their airforce quickly.

We popped up from between the mountains, the AWACs was sending us data of J-11s flying defensivly around their base. I could see the fight unfolding on my screen. Raul's flight was ahead of us keeping the J-11s busy as our bombers were hitting the base, with Boners flight flying cover for them. The bombers from his group had already dropped their loads. We came screaming west, smoke in front of us from fires on the ground. SAMs were in the air and tracers were reaching up from the ground trying to shoot us down. I lifted my right wing and circled around giving the bombers room to drop the first of their bombs. They would drop half their bomb load on the base, and the other half on Champerico. My missile radar growled at me telling me that the radar had a target painted. I squeezed the trigger and a missile dropped off my right wing rocketing off towards a J-11. I turned away, with Manuel on my wing trying to prevent the enemy from locking onto my fighter.

Again as over Flores, it was a free for all. Fighters on fire falling from the sky, SAM s lifting off climbing towards us, green tracer rounds from the ZSUs, the radio was alive with voices and calls for help and pilots calling out targets as explosions rocked the base with orange flames sending smoke columns up into the sky. I was twisting and turning trying to keep up with our six MIGs as they dropped their bombs and turned west towards the ocean. Manuel and I turned west following our MIGs, diving down following the railroad tracks away from the base. I could hear Raul and Alexi as they were chasing two J-11s coming up behind us, my computor ejecting counter measures from my fighter as we twisted and turned. Seconds later the two J-11s dissappeared from my display as missiles from the MIG-29s destroyed them.

I climbed higher over our bomb ladden MIGs covering them with Rauls flight right behind us covering our six. Off in the distance I could see a locomotive pulling a long line of tank cars full of fuel. I smiled behind my oxygen mask. I came down in front of the other MIGs, Manuel covering my wing and sighted the aiming recticle on the locomotive. I switched to guns and the squeezed the trigger briefly. My canon thundered below me rounds spitting out hitting the black monster exploding it with a cloud of smoke. Manuel behind me aimed and fired hitting tank cars creating one explosiuon after another as each burning tank car caused the next one in line to blow up. We pulled up over the black smoke with multiple explosions behind us. We screamed westward quickly approaching the town of Champerico, the green ocean in the distance. We pulled up again and circled around. I saw a SAM missile lift off and I was able to turn and fire off a Missile at the large radar dish on the ground. It exploded and the SAM flew west out over the ocean away from us. The MIGs behind us started dropping their bombs on their targets. Three huge round fuel tanks exploded in massive orange balls of flame, I watched as one of our MIGs approached the long red tanker with a, Chinese flag on it's stern. The MIG dropped a bomb dead center on it's deck. The massive force from the explosion split the ship in half lifting the two broken halves up out of the water before it disappeared in a circle of flame. Out of the corner of my eye I watched another ship in the bay explode. The concussion slammed into my fighter almost moving it sideways. What looked like fire works were shooting out from it, telling me it must have been an ammunition transport. Raul and Alexi were chasing another J-11 that must have followed us from our attack on their base.

The huge dock was a blazing inferno as was the tank the fuel from the tanker had been pumping fuel into. Our mission was a success, it was time to RTB.

My RWR was going wild and suddenly there was a massive explosion in the rear of the fighter. Instantly a sharp stabbing pain hit my left shoulder and warning lights appeared all over my instrument panel and my stick was usless. It felt like my fighter had been kicked in the rear by a giant hammer. I knew I had been hit but by what? There wasnt time to think about it as the eject warning horn sounded in the cockpit and the canopy blew off. My boots were pulled into the front of the ejection seat by the cables attached to the back of them. It was a safety feature to protect my feet during the forceful ejection. Just as I was thinking oh shit the rocket beneath my seat fired and I was rocketing up and out into the sky above my fighter. The seat seperated and the parachute released and I was suddenly hanging under my chute floating above the action below me. The sudden jolt was like fire on my injured shoulder.

It took me a few seconds to realize what happened. Our fighters were installed with an automatic ejection system. If the MIG was damaged criticaly or certain malfunctions occured and the pilot's life was in danger, the ejection process automatically initiated. Shit, one second I was flying a MIG fighter and the next I was hanging from a parachute with my ass over enemy terrirtory.

I looked over to the right just in time to watch my MIG trailing a long black plume of smoke with flames coming from the rear crash into the ground. There were fighters flying all around me, tracer rounds were coming up from the ground, secondary explosions were going off, I could clearly see the remains of the two ships on fire in the harbor. Manuel's MIG circled me he was waving.

I had an overwhelming feeling of nakedness and helplessness hanging there in the sky. I could see the air attack all around me but couldnt take part in it. I was at the mercy of gravity and the wind. I looked around between my legs and began picking out my landing spot. To the north of the town was a large green jungle. Perfect place to land and hide. The ground was coming up fast. I Bent my legs, remembering the class back in Cuba jumping out of the old Russian transport. I could see the detailed tops of trees beneath me. Suddenly I was in the trees branches ripping at my chest and face as I crashed through and hit the ground hard. I screamed in pain when I hit the ground my shoulder on fire. I kept my knees bent, rolled to my left, as I hit the ground and rolled. I lay there mentally doing inventory of my body. I couldnt feel any broken bones. I slowly rolled over and stood up, I slowly unbuckled the parachute harness using my right hand and dropped it to the ground. I slowly started to move my left arm relieved that I still had full use of it, wiggling my fingers. I reached up and unzipped my survival vest and my flight suit. I felt around with my fingers and over the top of my shoulder. There was a painful laceration on the back of my shoulder, my hand came away with blood on it. I quickly broke open the tiny first aid kit from my vest and found a rolled military issue bandage. I painfully removed my vest and my flight suit and felt around with my right hand placing the bandage over the wound. I let out the two fabric rolls and tied the bandage around my shoulder as tight as I could. I slipped back into my flight suit and my survival vest.

I started to roll up the parachute into a ball and looked around. I was in a tiny clearing with trees and branches above me. I slipped off my helmet, remembering the survival class tips. I reached into my escape vest and pulled out my folding knife. I cut the lines to the chute, then rolled up the chute as best as I could. I cut the lines and rolled them up. I dug a hole with my hands burying the harness and covered it with dirt and grass hiding it from view. I dug out my tiny rescue radio turning it on, I was relieved to see the green light telling me it was still operating.

"Greywolf to Tiger One." I called using Raul's call sign.

"Copy Greywolf." I could have shouted I was so glad to hear his voice.

"Greywolf is done, I repeat Greywolf is down."

"Copy Greywolf is down. What is your status?"

"Landed safely, minor laceration to shoulder, nothing serious. Im secure." I called back.

"Follow procedures, You'll be contacted, hang in there buddy, we'll get you out, Tiger one is clear." His voice was gone and I was alone in the jungle surrounded by the enemy with a shrapnel wound in my shoulder. I picked up my helmet and started walking getting away from the clearing. The jungle around me wasnt thick, but there was plenty of vegatation to hide in. I found a little rise and sat under a tree. I took off my survival vest, and went through all the pockets. I knew they would work on a plan to rescue me, but being in the middle of enemy terrirtory would make it complicated. I rechecked my forty five to make sure it was loaded. I pulled the slide halfway back and saw the gold of the shell in the breech. Letting it fall back it made a satisfying sound. I knew I had at least three magazines of ammo I could use, but I was praying I wouldnt need them. I drank the small amount of water in the little bottle in my vest, I was already thirsty for more. I took out the map and studied it, remembering there was a small river that ran north of Champerico that emptyed into the ocean. I slowly started walking north trying to stay as silent as possible. I knew it wouldnt be long before there would be a patrol out looking for me.

I could smell the water before I saw it. I came up a little hill and below me was a slow moving river of water. It was green and muddy, but it was water. One of the improvements to our survival vest had been a small water purification straw. You simply put the straw in the water and sucked. I looked around me to make sure I was alone before lying down on the bank and putting the straw in the water. I greedily sucked on it and sure enough water began to come through it and down my throat. It was warm but it was clean. I drank as much as my belly could hold before rising to my feet and moving away from the river. The first place they would be looking for me would be by the water. I didnt want to make it easy for them. I found a bush I could crawl under and it gave me some protection from the sun, but not the heat or humidity. I lay there trying to relax, I heard monkees calling to each other and a Mcaw as well. I stretched out behind a large bush and fell asleep. I woke up to sounds of men talking in low tones. I couldnt see them but I could hear them. The sounds of their boots in the mud by the river told me where they were walking. I froze, trying to slow my breathing, I couldnt remember if I had left tracks pointing to my hidden bush. I slowly parted the big green leaves and peered out, there were eight men in green camouflage, one who seemed to be the leader was pointing his finger in the face of a smaller soldier and talking in low angry tones. They were carrying AK-47s, with a harness with extra magazines. My blood ran cold as I saw their faces, they were Chinese.

I had no illusions about what kind of treatment I would recieve if they found me. I began praying silently to myself and slowly layed back down on the ground under the bush. I thought back to that night of torture that was part of my training prior to the mission over Cuba. I was yanked out of bed in the dark, blindfolded and driven to a dark room where I was beaten and ice cold water was thrown on me. The exercise was designed to convince me that a group of people had kidnapped me and wanted information about our mission. In the end it turned out to be just an exercise designed to teach me what I could face if I was ever shot down and captured by the enemy. That was nothing compared to what these monkees could do to me.

One of them stopped and refilled his canteen, while the others stood around their weapons at the ready, trying to look through the jungle. The leader took out a map and was looking it over. I suddenly remembered my radio was still turned on. A stupid mistake, not only would it drain the batteries but if someone tried to contact me it would audibly alert anyone within listening distance. The last thing I needed was to recieve a signal and the soldiers hearing it. In slow motion so as not to disturb the leaves around me, I reached into my vest pocket and turned it off. I had been holding my breath the whole time. I lay there under the bush in the mud, sweating, my heart pounding, praying silently they would move on.

To my great relief the leader folded his map and stood up. The patrol resumed their march heading west. I never left the safety of my bush. The light around me started to change and soon the sun quickly set. One minute there was light and the next it was dark. The sun goes down quickly in the jungle. The jungle was alive with the calls and sounds of different animals. The leaves of the bush helped to keep most of the insects away, but my whole body was soaked with sweat from the humidity. I needed water again and I wanted to try and use my radio. I slowly crawled out of the bush and stood up. There was a full moon, which gave everything an erie shape. I was grateful for the dim light as I slowly made my way to the river bank.

As slowly and quietly as I could I made my way to the water again. I whipped out the metal and plastic straw and sucked as fast as I could. This time the water was cool, a refreshing change. When I couldnt hold any more. I jury rigged the straw to the top of my water bottle and plunged the whole thing under the water. I couldnt see under the dark water, so I waited until I felt it stop gurgling before pulling it up. After putting them in my vest pockets I could hear sounds of bodies moving through the grass and bushes. My heart froze, they were walking slowly and carefully but I could hear the leaves brushing against their uniforms as they walked.

I crawled to the base of a tree and lay there hoping they would pass by. One by one they passed not looking down but looking into the jungle around them as they slowly walked on by. My heart was pounding like a jackhammer in my chest as I lay there in the mud. I stayed there for what seemed like forever before standing up. I turned around and right in front of me was the short soldier that had been scolded by the patrol leader earlier in the day. He was standing there with his hands between his legs taking a leak. He was facing away from me and his weapon was leaning against a tree. In a flash I knew what I had to do, instantly my forty five was in my right hand and I used it to smash his skull. I hit him four times as fast and as hard as I could as he sagged to the ground. I stood there panting, my heart racing, the pistol still in my hand looking at him curled up on the ground. I knew that if he had yelled out the patrol would have been on me in a flash. I stood there looking at him on the ground in the moonlight shaking all over. My knees felt weak as I realized it had been him or me and I was faster and luckier than he had been. His blood was on the side of my forty five. I slowly wiped it on his pant leg before slipping it back into the holster on the side of my vest.

I reached down to his throat trying to feel for a pulse. I couldnt find one. In a way I was relieved as what would I do with a prisoner? I rolled him over and felt around his body, I removed the harness with the pouches on it, and the belt around his waist. I pulled his body to the water and dragged it into the water up to my knees. I pushed him into the water and came back to the bank. I hoped they wouldnt notice he wasnt with them in the darkness. The thirst was back again and my stomach was growling. My left shoulder was throbing in pain. Insects were trying to make a meal out of every bit of exposed skin I had. I remembered what the survival school instructor had said about keeping my sleeves down to keep the bugs away from my skin. I couldnt do anything about my face or my hands.

Back on the bank I picked up his harness and his AK, and carefully left. I walked south away from the river, then cut west. I figured the patrol might come back east looking for him, and I wanted to be behind them, not in front of them. I still carried my helmet with me, dont ask me why. I guess it made me feel better to have it. There I was in the jungle in the dark of night still carrying my helmet with me. I walked for a long time wanting to get away from the spot I had killed the young soldier. The further away I got the better I felt inside.

I sat down at the base of a tree in the dark and pulled out my survival radio. The green light came on and I raised the antenna.

"Greywolf here." I called out.

"Greywolf this is Scorpion, what is your status?" A strange voice came back. Somewhere out there in the darkness was another friendly pilot flying near the border.

"Im stable, a patrol is out looking for me, I have plenty of water, I killed a man that was a straggler of the patrol." I replied.

"What is your authorization code?" The voice asked. Every pilot had two codes in his file in case he was shot down to verify his identity. One code was given if the enemy had him prisoner and was forcing him to use his radio, the other code was used to signal he was still safe. It prevented the rescue team from falling into a trap.

"My authorization code is Sammy One, Sammy One." I replied. Sammy was the name of my first dog I had as a child.

"Stay out of sight, tomorrow night there will be a team coming for you. Area is too hot to make an aerial pickup." The male voice came back.

"Copy that." I replied. Shit that meant I was stuck here another twenty four hours minimum.

"Listen for instructions at twenty one hundred tomorrow night."

"Acknowledged, twenty one hundred." I replied.

"Hang in there guy, it wont be long." The voice clicked off and I was alone again. I stood up and walked further west, helmet in one hand and the dead soldeir's AK in the other. I walked until I couldnt go anymore, the humidity had soaked my flight suit, and the air was getting cooler. My flight suit was sticking to the back of my left shoulder from the blood and insects were buzzing all around me like I was the turkey at a Thanksgiving Day dinner. My belly was hungry and I was thirsty again. I found a spot deep in the grass under another bush and rolled up in my parachute that I had cut up. It wasnt a sleeping bag, but it did help keep away some of the hungry insects.

The next morning the sun was up and there was mist above the trees. I listened for about ten minutes before I crawled out of the rolled up parachute. All I heard was the usual jungle racket around me.

I sat up and slowly took off my boots. My socks were soaking wet, and my feet were white. The air would do them good. I rolled the socks up into a ball and squeezed them trying to get the sweat out of them. I hung them on a tiny branch hoping they would dry.

"Wonder whats for breakfast?" I asked myself. I hadnt taken the time to examine the harness from the soldier I had killed. Now seemed a perfect time as any. The harness was well made, almost similiar to the US design. The belt has an AK bayonet in a metal sheath, it was the kind that when the two were connected you could cut wire fencing with it. There was also a full canteen of water, and a small pouch with an odd looking green metal compass in it. There was a pouch next to it containing a first aid kit. A Larger pouch held a bag of rice with bits of fish and vegtables in it. There was some type of bread rolled up. There was just enough there to make one meal. I hungerily gobbled it up using my hands to eat it with. My fingers couldnt scoop the cold rice fast enough into my mouth. I drank the canteen dry. I felt a lot better. I unsipped the flight suit and reached around and slowly pulled off the bandage. I replaced it with one from the dead soldier's first aid kit yanking it tight to prevent more bleeding. I dug a hole and buried the bloody bandage not wanting anyone to come across it in their search for me.

I examined the large chest pouches, there were three of them. There were three loaded magazines for the AK, and the magazine in the AK was loaded. That meant I had almost one hundred and twenty rounds of ammo. If I had to use the AK, at least I had a good amount to use. Firing it on semi auto would make the ammo last. With what I had in my survival vest and now the harness, I felt more confident inside. I packed everything up and sat there glad to be alive, hoping I wouldnt be stranded here much longer. I kept wondering what type of missile had shot me down, how many of our guys had made it back to base. I knew the mission was a success. The two ships were an added bonus, as they werent expected to be there. Attacking the train was like frosting on the cake. A long line of rail cars filled with fuel and a locomotive were now just burnt hulks of metal. I knew we had hurt them bad. It would take them awhile to recover from our two raids on their air bases. Maybe they would reconsider any further attacks into Mexico.

They lost fighters on their first attack of our base, then our attack on Flores. They lost fighters during their second attempt to hit our base, and god only knew how many they lost during the attack at Retalhuleu. The attack at Champerico would diminish their ability to rearm or refuel any remaining fighters they had left. The training we had done back in Cuba had paid off well. The Mexican Pilots had flown well and protected their air base. They had lost men, as we had. But it was their country they were fighting to protect.

My feet felt better and my socks had dried. The boots werent wet, and my belly was full. I was ready to move on and refill my canteen and water bottle. Slowly I pulled on my socks and boots. I rolledup the parachute and secured it to the harness. After standing I adjusted the harness to fit my body and with my helmet in one hand and AK in the other off I went. using the wierd looking compass I carefully made my way back towards the river. I found a place I could lie down behind a tree and bush and watch the river bank for awhile. I didnt want to be surprised again. I watched for an hour until I felt safe, then low crawled to the bank. There I used the straw to fill the canteen and my water bottle.

Crawling back I found a different spot to hide in and went to sleep waiting for darkness.

I awoke from a dream of Ali and I making love on the beach under the stars. The sun was going down, the light was fading. I turned on my radio and was rewarded with the green light again. I still had an hour before I would listen for the next message. I crawled further away from the river and deeper into the jungle. I didnt want to jepordize any chances of rescue by staying to close to the water if that patrol returned. They would have found that dead soldiers body by now and his missing weapon and harness would be all the explanation needed. They would know I was out here somewhere and armed at that. They would send out a larger well armed patrol this time.

At twenty one hundred hours I sat up, extended the antenna and turned on the radio, the green light glowed at me as I depressed the mic button.

"Greywolf here." I called out.

"Greywolf this is Jarhead, how do you copy?" Perry's voice greeted me in the darkness. I couldnt believe my ears, was it really him?

"Loud and clear Jarhead."

"What is your authentification code?" He asked.

"Sammy One." I replied.

"Ali sends regards. We need you to proceed to the bathtub. Please acknowledge." He instructed.

"Copy bathtub." I answered. Ali had once told me the ocean in front of our house was as warm as a bathtub. It was an easy code, one I hoped anyone else listening would have a hard time understanding.

"Two hours. Signing off." His voice faded. They wanted me to make it to the beach in two hours. That meant a lot of walking in the dark, where on the beach? Would there be an enemy patrol there waiting for me? Was there a boat there? All these things ran through my mind as I replaced my radio in the vest pocket. I took a long drink from my canteen, I would be needing every bit of water to get there in this humidity. The compass had green glow in the dark markings, making it easier to see in the dark. I carefully rose from my hiding place and started walking west.

One step at a time I carefully listened and looked, the moonlight behind me acting as a guiding light as I made my way. I stopped every few feet reaching out with my ears trying to hear anyone there. I didnt want to make any mistakes this close to being rescued. Each tree could hide an enemy soldier, each shadow could contain the enemy. My nerves were strung tight like piano wire as I slowly quietly walked through the jungle. I mentally thanked God again for the moonlight. It made the way a bit easier to see. I heard a helicopter above me flying west to east. Great another thing to worry about. Whose helicopter was it? I doubted it was ours. they wouldnt send a Hind here to rescue me there were too many SAMs here that could blow it out of the sky, which meant it was the enemy's. Why were they flying west to east? Did they intercept my last radio transmission? I walked on, trying to sort it all out.

I stooped and smelled, there was salt in the air. I was getting close to the ocean. My heart began beating quicker. I increased my pace, had it been two hours? I glanced at my watch. I was twenty minutes early. The faster I walked the more I could smell the ocean. I could now hear the ocean surf not far ahead. I stopped and knelt down trying to calm myself down. I didnt need any mistakes now this close to being saved. When I had calmed down I stood up again and started walking.

The jungle began to clear out and the trees were thinning out. I could see moonlight ahead of me reflecting off the surface of the ocean between the trees and bushes. I hit the ground and low crawled the rest of the way. I made my way to the beach and stopped at the edge of the jungle. The ocean looked beautiful. I looked out and there to my surprise was a conning tower of a submarine, the moonlight reflecting off the water revealed there was a small rubber boat coming this way. I fought the urge to jump up and wave my arms. I knew there was still a chance there might be a patrol out there and what about that damned helicoptor? I watched the boat coming closer, and then the four men jumped out and into the surf pulling it onto the shore. I slowly stood up and walked out onto the beach.

"The Marines have landed." Perry's voice came to me. He was wearing night vision goggles and a black assault suit. I ran up to the boat at the same time the damned helicopter came roaring out from above the trees and began spraying the beach with gunfire. Ground fire was coming from the jungle to our right. I hit the ground along with the rest of the men forming a semi circle facing the jungle as we began returning fire into the jungle. It was a perfect trap, the Chinese knew which way I was walking and had set up a trap hoping to catch me and the rescue party at the same time. The helicoptor turned and headed for the sub at the same time a flash of light lit up the top of the sub as a shoulder fired missile flew up into the sky impacting the helicoptor. The exploson giving the area an erie orange glow. We were firing again into the jungle as two of the men behind me pulled the rubber boat back into the water. As we were firing at the muzzle flashes my weapon came up empty, I yanked out the empty magazine and grabbed a full one, jamming it into place and again returned fire into the jungle using controlled burts. Perry yanked a hand grenade off his harness and tossed it over his head at the center of the muzzle flashes. After the explosion Perry leaped to his feet yanking on my harness jerking me to my feet.

"Cmon Grey, hot coffee is waiting." Perry called to me as we ran for the boat. He was firing into the jungle covering my retreat as I jumped in. Perry was right behind me firing his weapon One of the men in a black rubber suit started the little motor and we were off zig zagging towards the sub. Rounds were hitting the water all around us and the sound of rounds passing over our heads sounding like the buzzing of bumblebees. Four of us were firing into the jungle as the fifth man was steering the inflatable towards the submarine. There were people on the deck of the sub firing into the jungle over our heads as we rode the waves away from the beach. Someone on the deck of the sub let loose with another shoulder fired missile into the jungle causing another explosion behind us. When the rubber boat came up to the hull of the sub, hands reached down and pulled us up onto the deck and quickly shoved us into a round open hatch lit with red light. I practically fell down the brass ladder going into the sub as men above me jumped after me. Rounds were whistling over our heads, then the last man came down, closed the hatch and spun the wheel.

"Dive" He called out over a round mic on the wall. The compartment became brighter as someone turned on the lights.

"This way!" Perry called out to me, I followed him through a hatch and down a narrow corridor. I felt the floor shift slightly as the sub began to dive.

We passed through another hatch and into what looked like a lunchroom with tables and bench seats secured to the floor and a galley to the rear. Perry sat down on a bench and slipped off his rubber diving hood.

"You sure know how to throw a party Grey." he joked. I sat down across from him trying to take it all in. Three other men in black rubber suits joined us and one by one they began stripping off their suits. Perry pulled his over his head. We were all breathing heavily. I sat there trying to catch my breath. My flight suit was soaked, water was dripping onto the deck in a puddle. A young man in a light blue navy shirt came over to the table with a tray of hot steaming coffee in mugs.

"Bless you son." Perry told him grabbing a cup. I slowly picked one up both my hands were shaking. I carefully took a sip. "Told ya we had hot coffee waitin for ya."

"How the hell did you manage all this?" I asked.

"Well ya know, I was bored. This was Antonio's idea actually, he pulled a few strings, besides they were on their way by here anyways, so what difference is one little stop gonna make ay?" he said toweling his head off.

"Welcome aboard, I'm Captain Menendez." A tall red headed man said as he walked through the hatch. I stood up and reached out my hand.

"Thank you sir, thanks for the rescue." I thanked him.

"You are very welcome, glad to be of service. So you are the famous Colonel Murphy that I have heard so much about. You appear to have been shot." He remarked pointing to my shoulder. Peryy stood up and spun me around looking at the blood on my back.

"Well sir whatever you've heard it's all lies. Im very grateful for all your help. This isnt a bullet wound, it's a piece of shrapnel from when my MIG was hit sir." I replied.

"Shit Grey I didnt know you were wounded, how bad is it?" Perry asked.

"Im fine really, it's not bad at all. I have it bandaged and the bleeding under control. It's great to see you Perry, I was surprised as hell to hear your voice over the radio out there in the jungle."

"Yeah well like I said we were just cruising by. Thought we would stop by." Perry said.

"Actually this man jumped out of an aircraft into the ocean at night to rendevous with us. He swam in the water for almost an hour until we located him." The captain revealed. I looked over at Perry speechless.

"Well ya know, I was bored, besides it was my day off." Perry explained.

"Thanks Perry, guess I owe you one."

"Well, we take care of our own. Raul told me you were shot down and stuck over there. The area was too dangerous to send the Hinds over there looking for you. There was no way we were going to leave you out there. I called Antonio, he called a friend of his in the Chillian Navy, They flew me out here, I got to parachute at night. You know how much I love jumping at night. We were afraid you might shoot someone you didnt know at night trying to rescue your ass. So I volunteered to come join the party, figured you might recognize my voice in the darkness." Perry explained.

"Yes about your weapons, we need to secure them I doubt you will be needing them here." The Captain remarked looking at my AK." You will get them back when we dock." I nodded as another sailor took the AK and put his hand out for my forty five. I slowly pulled it out of my vest and slid off the harness. He picked up the vest and harness and disappeared through the hatch.

"We need to get you to sick bay for a medical examination. Then perhaps a hot shower?"

"Ill take him Captain, leave it to me." Perry stood up. I stood up and followed him through the hatch and down another corridor and down another ladder.

There in a small sickbay I met a doctor who prodded me and cleaned my wound. He pulled out a piece of metal and dropped it with a clang into a metal tray. He stitched it up and slapped a bandage on it. He took my blood and gave me shots and told me to take the pills he gave me every four hours to help kill any bacteria that might have made it's way inside me. Then as promised I was led to a bathroom or head as it is called on a sub and I enjoyed a long hot shower. When I came out there was a set of blue dungarees and a light blue short sleeve shirt waiting for me. Back in the galley Perry and I and the other two sailors from the beach feasted on fish and chicken and lobster.

"How did the mission go?" I asked him.

"We lost two Migs over the air base and one besides you over Champerico. But both targets were totaly destroyed. Manuel is beside himself that you were shot down, Ali was freaking, Antonio was worried. Everyone was glad to hear you were safe on the ground. Thats when the real work to rescue you began.

Seems Antonio got word awhile back the Chinese were sending their carrier over here loaded with fighters. They plan on using some for an attack on our base, then flying them to the base at Retalhuleh, which wont happen now since we demolished it. The captain here has been ordered to sink that

Chinese bastard and send all their fighters to the bottom of the sea. So I guess we will be guests of the Chillian Navy for awhile." Perry explained.

"Anywhere is better than where I just came from." I told him stuffing lobster into my mouth.

"Well you seem to have survived ok, where did you find that AK anyway. That sure didnt come with you in your survival vest." I explained everything to him from beginning to end.

"Damn Grey, guess you can handle yourself out there. I thought you guys were just screwing around during survival school. Im glad some of it rubbed off on you."

"I remembered most of it, and yeah it was a great course. Remind me to send a case of booze to that instructor with a thank you letter. Everything he taught us was right on the money. Everything was just like he said."

"Well that tanker is a hulk right now sitting in shallow water at their loading dock, so even if they could get another tanker there they wouldnt be able to off load the fuel. That other ship that blew up was an ammunition transport, and it is sitting on the bottom. It was filled with bombs and missiles they wont be able to use now.

There is another supply ship with the Chinese task force these guys plan on sinking as well." Perry went on.

"I didnt know Chile had a submarine. Im sure glad they do though." I told him.

"Yeah, Antonio does business with Chile sometimes. Seems he knew the president or something when he was a kid. He asked for help from him."

"I remember now that Antonio mentioned something about a plan in the works to deal with the Chinese carrier, I guess this is what he meant." I told him.

"The man is amazing." Perry admitted.

"Those are my exact words to describe him." I told him. I looked around me, everywhere there were pipes and conduit lines. The deck was the only flat area.

"Well you need to get some sleep, cmon, Ill show you where you can bunk at." He stood up. I slowly sood up me legs a bit wobbly. I followed him through the passageway to a small bunk compartment. There were six bunks that folded up into the bulkhead. He reached down and showed me how to pull one out. Soon I was lying between cool sheets under a navy issue wool blanket asleep.

I opened my eyes and it took a few minutes to remember where I was. I sat up and looked around. My flight suit was on a hanger freshly laundered, my belongings in a plastic bag. My shoulder was stiff and sore but worked. I stood up and got dressed. I pulled on my boots thankfull for the warm dry thick socks. I cleaned up my bunk and folded it up putting it back into place. I worked my way to the galley where I smelled fresh coffee. The cook put out a tray of donuts. I sat there by myself enjoying the fresh donuts and hot coffee. It was a luxery compared to what I had eaten the day before. This submarine was smaller than the other U.S. submarine I had visited years before. It was well layed out and compact with a lot of thought about creature comfort as well as function. The captain entered the galley and I stood up as a sign of mutual military respect, but he just smiled and waved me down with his hand.

"There is no need for that here Colonel. It interferes with the ship's functions. How are the donuts this morning?"

"Excellent, better then what I was eating yesterday at this time. I cant thank you enough for stopping and picking me up. I hope it didnt comprimise your security or mission." I told him.

"No, we left that area right away and we are on course and on time."

"I hear you are hunting that Chinese carrier task force."

"Thats correct. We have orders to sink their carrier and supply ships. We plan to interupt their plans of resupplying Guatemala with their fighters and armament."

He explained.

"This sub seems more than capable to do the job."

"Yes this is the newest Scorpene built by a joint French Spanish corporation. We have Black Shark torpedos aboard as well as a few other surprises that are more than capable of eliminating our targets. This sub has state of the art sonar, electronics and fire control systems. She has an AM-2000 Air Independant Propulsion system capable of keeping us running submerged for almost 245 days. Definitly long enough to execute the mission. We can also resupply at sea from a supply ship extending our sea time." He explained proudly.

"Quite a feat for a diesel submarine." I told him.

"Yes it is."

"Arent you concerned about the Chinese retaliating against Chile for sinking her ships? After all that is an act of war." I asked sipping my coffee.

"You are correct, it is an act of war. We want to prevent what occured in Guatemala from happening in Chile. If we allow China to develop a major presence here in South America, Communism will spread and no one wants that. My superiors are extremely concerned about what develped in Guatemala, and their plans to move north into Mexico. If we can blunt their efforts it is possible they may rethink their objectives. If we sit and do nothing, surely they will prevail." He explained.

"Like Winston Churchill once said....."

"All that evil needs to flourish is for good men to sit and do nothing." He finished smiling.

"Im glad more and more people understand that. We are concerned in Cuba as well, hence the reason we are in Mexico." I explained.

"How are the Mexican pilots?"

"Very proffessional and well trained. They know the score and are well motivated. Many have lost their lives so far. Cuba has been a long time ally with Mexico. If Mexico falls, then we could be next."

"Now that Cuba is free, no one wants to return to the dark days of communism." He observed.

"Exactly. We have come to far to let things slide backward."

"You say we, yet you are an American." he observed.

"Yes I am an American, but Cuba is my home now. I dont want to see Cuba fall." I explained. He nodded.

"How did the Chilean Navy become part of this fight?" I asked.

"My father and Atonio have been friends for years. Antonio was the go between for our two governments. He asked for our assistance on behalf of your government."

"Antonio is full of surprises."

"Yes he is, I remember him and my father fishing together. Antonio has some amazing stories." The captain remarked.

"So your father is the President of Chile?" I asked.

"Thats correct.'

"Im in the presence of royalty it seems." I observed.

"Not at all, I began my naval career years before my father became our president."

"Ill bet it creates a lot of interesting discussions around the dinner table." I ventured.

"We manage. Let me give you a guided tour of this amazing submarine." He offered. I stood up and followed him. The sub was a mixture of modern control systems and a warm simulated paneled interior. Most of the compartments were very brightly lit to help deal with depression from weeks under water away from the sunlight. The sleeping quarters were small with three bunks deck to overhead. Each space was cleverly designed to make the most of storage spaces. Everything gleamed and shined in the bright light. The large open modern galley was the unofficial gathering room for the entire crew. There was a large flat screen TV on the bulkhead for nightly movies. The last stop was the control room. The centrally located square table had a lighted center display with a map overlay across it. Our route and position was marked on it with a grease pencil, a sailor was leaning over it marking figures. There were six large multi function displays along the bulkhead with men sitting in front of them monitoring the screens. There was a leather chair with a small hydraulic wheel that controlled the sub's diving and steering. One man controlled it. The Captain started to explain a few things when he was interupted.

"Captian, passive underwater sonar contact, twenty thousand meters ahead of us to port, depth is one hundred meters!" The radar operator informed him.

"Sound General Quarters, silent running!" the captian called out. Instantly the hatches at both ends of the compartment closed and there was a change in lighting in the compartment. I gathered that the change in lighting was a silent method of communicating to the whole sub the change in conditon. I had noticed these lights throughout the ship. I slowly slid to a corner of the control room to keep out of the way.

"Contact is a Chinese 093 Han class nuclear powered attack submarine. She is running at fourteen knots sir, on a heading of six zero degrees. There is slight transient noise sir."

"Those Hans have nuclear reactors, probably their steam turbines. Our tubes are loaded correct?" The captain called out.

"Afirmative sir, all six tubes." Another sailor replied from in front of a different display.

"Program their position data into the warheads."

"Acknowledged."

"Verify our counter measures are loaded."

"Yes sir all countermeasures are loaded."

"Sir Im detecting several surface contacts behind the Chinese sub, at least six. There are two Hatakaze Class guided missile destroyers forward, two Sovremenyy Class destroyers aft, and two supply ships aft of them. There is a tanker following. Their carrier is in the center."

"Plot them on the board." Instantly the contacts appeared on the lighted table. It displayed our position in relation to the other contacts. The Chinese sub was ahead of the surface contacts. The larger of the six contacts was in the middlle of the other four. The captain moved over to the table and the sailor moved aside to give him a better view.

"Sir they have air cover, two aircraft and one rotary." The captain nodded.

"Is there a thermalcline?" The captian asked.

"Yes sir, right below us."

"Make our depth two hundred eighty meters."

"Two hundred eighty meters aye sir." The deck tilted slightly as the sub slowly changed depth.

"There is a temperature difference line below us. It helps hide us from their sonar." The Captain quietly explained to me. I guess he was trying to calm my fears. Being trapped inside this steel hull wasnt my idea of how to fight a war.

"Our hull is covered with a rubber coating, it also helps to hide us as it masks our hull making their sonar usless. As long as we stay deep below the cold layer and travel slowly, they wont detect us." He explained. I nodded silently. This was a different type of combat, it was a war of nerves, a game of hide and seek with fatal consequences to the losing side.

"We have an advantage over the Chinese sub, this diesel sub is extremely difficult to detect due to our silent propulsion system. The Chinese sub over there has a nuclear reacter with steam powered turbine engines. That makes them easeir to hear underwater." The Captain further explained. "The problem is they have a helo up with a listening system in it. They fly around trying to hear subs, they stop and drop a listening device in the water to listen. If they hear us Im sure they will attack with a torpedo. The Chinese make excellent torpedos." I looked at the ceiling trying to picture what was going on above us. Suddenly the compartment was a very small place to be in with no where to run.

"We are at Two hundred eighty meters sir."

"All stop."

"All stop aye sir."

"Distance to contact?" The captain called out.

"Two thousand two hundred meters sir."

"Acknowledged. Prepare to load the nixies after our first salvo."

"Aye sir."

I looked at the screen and saw the task force with the Chinese sub ahead heading east. We were a little over a mile south of them heading north.

"Our position gives us a head on shot and reduces their ability to detect us. We have torpedo mines, aboard. They are designed to sit in the water and are programed with sonar and sound data to recognize certain ships or submarines by their screw noise. Each ship or sub has a sound signature that is different than any other ship due to their prop cavitation. Something like a fingerprint. We program this information into the torpedo's computor. Once we launch them, they stop at a pre programed location and sit silently in the targets course. The proximity warning in the head of these torpedos wakes them up when their target gets within range. They accellerate out of nowheres and attack their target." The captain explained to me.

"This gives us time to get away to a safe distance from your target before the torpedo attacks." I added.

"Exactly." The Captain smiled and nodded.

"Set up torpedo shots on the Han and the two Sovremenyy destroyers." The Captain called out.

"Aye sir."

"Be prepared to increase speed and head west after we fire." The Captain ordered again.

"Aye sir."

"Hopefully we are catching them asleep up there. After all who would dare to attack a Chinese task force in open waters." The Captain smiled at me.

"Okay gentlemen lets go to work. Fire tubes one and four at the Han, then reload tubes one and four with nixies."

"Aye sir firing tubes two and four at the Han now." There was a slight shudder under the deck as the two torpedos left the sub. There was a different noise as the automatic loader reloaded the tubes with the two nixies. On the torpedo officers screen was an electronic display of the four Black Shark torpedos and the two nixies in their tubes.

"Torpedos one and four running straight on course, nixies are loaded sir."

"Acknowledged. Steer torpedo one at the bow and torpedo four at the stern of the Han."

"Aye sir, torpedo one at the bow and torpedo four at the stern." The tech began tapping keys on the torpedo control computer and the two torpedos appeared on the illuminated table screen. The two wire guided torpedos had split and were heading for the Chinese sub. Torpedo one was ahead and to the right of torpedo number four.

"One thousand yards and closing sir."

"Acknowledged."

"Sir the Han has changed course and speed."

"Torpedo one has acquired the target sir." The Han had moved into range of the first torpedo's sonar and the torpedo began moving towards the sub.

"Cut the wires on torpedo one."

"Aye sir cutting wires."

I began to understand what the Captain's plan was, he was using the first torpedo to turn the Han into the path of the second torpedo. I watched the action on the screen silently urging the torpedo to the Han.

"Sir the two destroyers have changed course, their sonar is active. Their data is being updated to our torpedo warheads."

"Acknowledged." The two Chinese destroyers were turning away from the carrier on the board. The first torpedo was changing direction to match the maneuvers of the Han's attempt to escape. The sub had turned towards the second torpedo.

"Torpedo four has acquired the Han and is aceelerating sir."

"Cut wires on torpedo four."

"Aye sir."

The first torpedo on the screen had increased speed and was closing in on the Han. Seconds later there was a dull boom.

"Sir the second torpedo is attacking". The torpedo on the screen was racing to it's target. A second explosion could be heard as that torpedo found it's mark.

"Sir the Han is breaking up." The sonar operator said. Seconds later there were sounds of metal creaking from outside the hull.

"Fire torpedos one and four, two and five, close all outer doors reload tubes."

"Aye sir firing firing now." The floor shuddered under our feet as the torpedos were launched.

"Change course, head west, make our depth three hundred twenty meters." The Captain ordered. The deck angle increased as the sub changed angle and course.

"Sir another helio has launched, the first helio has launched a torpedo in the water, it has not acquired us."

"Launch the nixies, increase speed to six knots."

"Aye sir six knots." The sub shuddered once more as the two torpedos were launched. These specially designed nixes emitted noises and signals mimicking a submarine. The two nixies split up and went east and north. The idea was for the enemy torpedo to chase one of the nixies as we made our escape.

"By launching at the two destroyers now, we keep them too busy trying to avoid our torpedos instead of trying to hunt for us giving us a chance to escape." The Captain continued. This was one shrewd Captain. I understood why they had chosen him for this mission.

"Sir the enemy torpedo is chasing nixie number one. Nixie number two is still circling." He had done it. Everyone began to smile in the control room. "Sir Torpedo three has acquired target Charlie."

"Acknowledged."

"Sir the helo has launched again, torpedo in the water."

"All ahead full, make your depth six hundred meters."

"All ahead full six hundred meters aye sir." I held my breath waiting and watching the action on the board as the first of the two destroyers was trying to escape the torpedo locked on it's stern and the second torpedo dropped from the helio was circling trying to detect us. Seconds later the first destroyer lost the race with the torpedo. There was a second dull boom in the water. I looked up at the overhead trying to imagine the damaged ship fighting for it's life. I knew there would be one less enemy destroyer up there with ASW equipment trying to sink us.

"Sir the second enemy torpedo has acquired the second nixie." The Captain smiled again. We were home free.

"Maintain plot on the Chinese carrier."

"Aye sir." there was an explosion as the Chinese torpedo from their helo detonated our nixie.

"Now that we have destroyed their sub and one of their destroyers, we can come back later and sink the carrier at our leisure." The Captain revealed.

"Maintain present depth and course."

"Aye sir. Sir the destroyer is breaking up." We could hear metal creaking and other sounds as the torpedoed Chinese destroyer split open and sank. Seconds later there was a far off dull boom as it hit the ocean bottom.

"The Sovremenyy had three hundred seventy men aboard. The Han 75. They will be busy trying to recover sailors in the water. I doubt anyone survived from the Han. We are headed west away from the task force for now. Soon we will turn and again attack." The Captain appeared relaxed and confidant as he reached for his coffee mug. This was a different type of warfare, almost like a video game. Quite different from flying a jet fighter.

"Normally we do not allow visitors in the control room during operations. You seem to have been born under a lucky star." The Captain remarked sipping his coffee.

"Indeed it seems that way. I have led an amazing life so far." I told him. We had increased our distance from the Chinese task force. There was little chance we would be detected. The Captain again turned to the center table. There were two less ships displayed on the screen.

"New course, come east, twelve knots, maintain current depth." The captain called out looking at the clock on the bulhead.

"Aye sir."

"We will circle around and hit them again from north, they will not expect this." He grinned wickedly. A bit later the Captain gave orders to change our course and we headed north, still west of the Chinese task force.

"Task force has changed direction and is now heading south." The sonar operator called out. We turned when the task force was southeast of us.

"Change course, head southeast, same speed and depth."

"Aye sir, southeast." The sub turned.

"Helo is southwest of the carrier dipping sonar." The tech called out.

"Acknowledged." The Captain grinned. "Program data to the torpedoes."

"Aye sir." The controller began typing on the console sending the position, and speed of the Chinese carrier.

"Open all outer doors."

"Aye sir, opening outer doors." The tech hit computor keys and the torpedo doors opened. The Captain studied the table screen.

"Range to target?"

"Two thousand five hundred meters and closing sir."

"All stop."

"All stop aye sir." Watching the screen I could see the task force on the screen as we sat there motionless in the water. We were still below the cold layer of water, our bow pointing at the ships. The Captain glanced at the clock, then back to the screen.

"Range to target?"

"Eighteen hundred meters sir."

"Fire all torpedos."

"Firing all torpedos sir." The ship shuddered as each torpedo was fired.

"Very well. Reload tubes one and two with Exocets." He replied. We stood watching the screen as the torpedos homed in on their targets. Four were heading for the carrier and two were heading for the remaining Sovremenyy destroyer. I stood there against the bulkhead watching the torpedos on the screen.

"Sovremenyy destroyer is changing course increasing speed sir." The destroyer had detected the two torpedos on it's port side and was trying to escape. The operator was steering the wire guided torpedos towards the Soveremeny from his console. He was turning the two torpedos into the destroyer. He wasnt worried about the four torpedos heading for the carrier. It was such a large target, there was no way they could miss.

"Torpedos have acquired the carrier sir."

"Very well cut the wires." Once the wires were cut, the four torpedos increased speed heading for the port side of the huge carrier.

"Destroyer is launching countermeasures sir." But it was too late, seconds later there was an explosion in the water as the two torpedos hit the destroyer. Seconds later we heard four individual explosions as the carrier was hit.

"Periscope depth." The captain called out.

"Periscope depth aye sir" Soon the Captain was looking through the scope, he flicked a switch on the side and the screen on the bulkhead came alive with the image of the Chinese carrier listing to port with a trail of black smoke behind it. Sounds of groaning metal were heard as the destroyer began breaking up. Two smaller Hatakaze destroyers were moving closer to the carrier water from fire hoses were being aimed at the stricken carrier.

"Dive." The Captain called out. "Ive taped this for later." He told me as the periscope came down. "New heading, west at six knots."

"West at six knots aye sir." The deck angled again as the sub increased speed and changed course.

"Anything from those helos?"

"Negative sir, they are on the other side of the carrier."

"Very well." We heard a dull boom as another explosion occured. I was thinking of all the Chinese fighters that would be at the bottom of the ocean instead of in the air over Mexico. This would definitley put a monkey wrench in the Chinese plans for expansion. It was an amazing experience, I was standing in the control room of a Chilean Navy submarine watching as two Chinese destroyers a nuclear attack sub and their only aircraft carrier had been destroyed in just a matter of hours.

"This will certainly put a monkey wrench in the Chinese plans." I smiled.

"Monkey wrench?" The Captain asked looking at me.

"Im sorry, it is an American expression, slang. It means spoil there plans."

"Ahhh I see, yes this will put a monkey wrench as you say into their plans, truly." He grinned broadly.

"Periscope depth."

"Periscope depth aye sir." The deck angled up as we ascended. Soon the tv screen came alive again and the sinking carrier came into view. Helicoptors were flying around and there was a frigate on each side of the stricken ship. Smoke was still pouring from the right side and it was leaning more severely to the port. One of it's massive props could be clearly seen out of the water. Water from fire hoses was pouring onto the carrier from the two frigates. The Captain made an adjustment on the periscope and the image on the screen doubled. The carrier shifted slightly again and two fighters could be seen sliding along the deck and falling into the ocean spilling aviation fuel onto the deck. A huge fireball could be seen on deck from the spilled fuel. Then the screen was filled as a massive orange ball of flame erupted from the carrier and smoke increased. Pieces of metal and debris flew off the deck of the carrier, then with a sound of shrieking metal the carrier's stern lifted slightly as it began to slowly slide deeper into the ocean. One frigate pulled slightly farther away from the carrier. It wasnt everyday a person got to watch a Chinese carrier die at sea. The tip of the periscope was just barely peeking up out of the water to avoid being detected. Occasionally a wave would wash over it clouding the image. We heard another massive screeching metal sound as we watched the carrier start to sink bow first. The image was clear enough to see fighters and other deck vehicles slowly sliding on the angled deck as the ship slowly sank into the water. The stern of the carrier slowly came out of the water all four spinning props were clearly visible. Then the stern slowly slid down into the water with steam surrounding it. The water from the fire hoses stopped and small boats from the two frigates began to circle around pulling survivors from the water.

"Exocets loaded?" The captain asked.

"Affirmative."

"Data on the two Hatakaze in the missile heads?"

"Yes sir."

"Launch Exocets."

"Launching Exocets sir." The tech hit the buttons on the console. There was a slight tremor as the two anti ship French Exocet missiles were launched out of the torpedo tubes.

"Close outer doors, reload tubes one and two with nixies, reload three through six with torpedos. Make our dept three hundred twenty meters, all ahead full!" The captain barked out as he lowered the periscope.

Aye sir." The deck angled down as we dove. The two French Exocet anti-ship missiles were designed to be launched from a sub and once above the water they would shed their launch tubes and their rocket motors would start. They would fly close to the surface of the ocean to avoid detection until they hit their targets programed into the computor guidance systems. I reached above my head for the railing holding tight as we dove turning away from the remaining two destroyers.

"Where are those helos?"

"They are heading for our last firing position sir."

"Launch counter measures."

"Aye sir launching now." The two nixie torpedos were launched from the bow tubes.

"Turn ninety degrees now."

"Aye sir turning ninety degrees now sir." The deck tilted again as the sub made the turn.

"By turning we leave a mass of bubbles giving their helos something to shoot at, our counter measure torpedos will circle emitting signals like a submarine. Hopefully their torpedos will track our countermeasures." The captain explained. I grimly held onto the rail as the sub angled downward.

"Two helos launching torpedos sir." The two torpedos were illuminated on the screen. We all watched as the two torpedos began circling around scanning the ocean for us. I noticed sweat forming on my forhead imagining what those torpedos could do to us. Suddenly a far off dull boom disrupted my thoughts. Seconds later another dull boom echoed the first.

"Exocets have hit their targets sir." The tech called out.

"Torpedos have acquired our nixes sir." The radar tech called out.

"Make our speed ten knots. Level out, change course towards the remaining supply ships."

"Aye sir six knots, changing course now."

"We need to eliminate the supplies on those two freighters. No use letting them get to Guatemala. "The captain grinned wickedly at me. I just smiled and continued to hang onto the rail above my head.

"We have the two freighters sir, fortyfive thousand yards and closing."

"Send the data to the torpedos."

"Already done sir."

"Very well, where are those two helos?"

"They are hovering over our last launch position sir, they are dipping their sonar."

"Acknowledged, maintian course and speed."

"Aye sir same course and speed." I watched the two dots on the screen representing the two freighters, the tanker behind them. We were circling around to the rear of the three ships.

"Range to targets?"

"Eighteen hundred meters sir."

"Launch all tubes, reload with two countermeasures."

"Aye sir launching all tubes now." The deck trembled as three torpedos were launched. The torpedo officer's screen indicated the two nixies were being automatically loaded into the tubes.

"All torpedos running straight and normal sir."

"Acknowledged." We watched the three torpedos on the screen moving torwards their targets.

"Topedos one and two have acquired their targets sir."

"Cut their wires."

"Aye sir cutting their wires now." Instantly the first two torpedos increased speed racing torwards the two Chinese freighters. Seconds later there were two individual booms as the torpedos hit.

"Torpedo three has acquired the tanker sir. Cutting wires now." We watched the last torpedo on the screen increase it's speed hitting the huge tanker on the port side. There was another dull boom followed by a larger boom.

"Speed to four knots, periscope depth."

"Four knots at periscope depth aye sir." The deck angled again as we ascended. A few minutes later the captain raised the periscope and we were able to see the surface on the screen on the bulkhead. The two freighters could be seen, smoke was pouring from them. The captain moved the periscope and the tanker came into view. There was a massive fireball with thick black smoke pouring into the blue sky.

"Where are those helios?"

"Three thousand yards to starboard sir."

"Acknowledged." Off in the distance a helicopter came into view aft of the burning tanker. Another explosion occured from the tanker causing peices of metal to fly into the sky. The captain moved the periscope back to the two freighters. The first freighter was sinking bow first, the second freighter was already sliding down into the ocean stern first. The captain swung the periscope back to the tanker in time for us to witness yet another explosion. The ship was hidden behind another giant orange ball of flame pouring thick black smoke into the blue sky.

"Dive, make your depth three hundred meters, course one eight zero degrees, speed six knots." The captain called out snapping the handles up and lowering the periscope.

"Three hundred meters at one eight zero degrees at six knots aye sir." The deck angled down and a slight vibration could be felt.

"Are there any helios close?"

"Negaive sir, they are on the other side of the tanker chasing our countermeasure torpedos."

"Acknowledged." The captain grinned grabbing his coffee cup again. "Excellent work gentlemen, excellent. Seems the Chinese are suddenly missing their task force." The captain said. There was a slight snicker from the techs. The sounds of the two freighters breaking up as they sank could be heard. The sound of groaning metal reverberated through the hull. I thought about those helicopter pilots out there flying over an empty ocean with no place to land. If they located us it would take only one of their torpedos to kill all of us. I thought of the two J-11 pilots flying around without a carrier to land on. Another dull boom echoed through the compartment and a groan of metal signaled another explosion on the tanker.

"The Chinese will pull out all the stops to find out who sank their carrier task force." I said.

"Yes Im afraid you are correct. Antonio has convinced me you and your associate are able to keep secrets." He looked at me.

"No problem there captain. Now that things have gotten this expensive, maybe the Chinese will reconsider their actions in our hemisphere."

"We can only hope." He grinned again sipping his coffee. "We can secure from General Quarters, keep a sharp lookout for any unwelcome visitors." He told the sonar tech.

"Aye sir, Secure from General Quarters."

"Forgive me. Ill have to postpone the rest of the tour until later, I must put all this into a report." The captain apologized. The light on the bulkhead changed from red to yellow back to green. I turned and a sailor spun the wheel on the hatch opening it for me. I made my way down the passageway to the galley. It seemed the only place I felt comfortable. I was a pilot, not a sailor. I didn't have a job here, I felt useless, out of place. The galley represented a comunal gathering area. I helped myself to the chromed coffee urn and found a place at a table. The two cooks were busy in their galley cooking and preparing the next meal for the crew. I marveled at how every piece of equipment was perfectly placed inside this metal tube. Every space was used. There was very little wasted space. This sub was a marvel in design. Sailors were walking back and forth through the galley casting a quick look my way as they did. I got the impression several of them were just making an excuse to walk through to get a look at me. I was relieved when Perry walked through the hatch and sat across from me his ever present cup of coffee in his hand.

"Good news, we will be dropped off soon at of all places Acapulco, can you believe it? Party central. Damn, I guess we get to have some R and R after our little trip." He smiled.

"Maybe Antonio is rewarding you for your bravery in this rescue op." I offered.

"Well lucky us then, lotsa senoritas in Acapulco to play with. "He grinned wickedly.

"Well it has been a grand adventure so far. "I grinned." These guys make the best coffee I've ever had. They can really kick ass with this sub."

"Yeah I heard you got a ringside seat at all the action. You must live a charmed life."

"Well it was impressive thats for sure. But we can't talk about any of this with anyone else. The last thing these guys need is for the Chinese to find out about what they did."

"Amen to that, the Chinese would go apeshit if they knew Chile sank their carrier task force. Course Antonio knows about it, he'll wanna know all the juicy details." Perry remarked.

"Yeah, thats a given."

"Hell our team helped free Cuba from communism. No one has ever found out about that little field trip. This is just another chapter in the book of our lives, and I wouldnt change a page of it. Ive been involved in several little adventures ever since I joined Antonio's little band of pirates. I love it, it's a great life." He smiled again showing teeth. His grin reminded me of a hyena. I could see why Perry and Alexi were such good friends. They had very similiar personalities. Both were short muscular stubborn and tough.

"Yeah I can't think of a better life either, I feel honored to be a part of this team. It's a great life." I agreed. He raised his coffee cup and I did the same in salute.

"Well you have definitely pulled your own weight and done your share of the work. Everyone in this team respects you a lot. It was important to get you back in one piece instead of winding up a Chinese shish-ka-bob. The

Chinese know there is a classified group within this air group here. They dont know much about it, but they hear whispers. It's important we maintain our own internal security to protect everyone. There is still a lot that goes on in our team that isnt shared by everyone. Antonio keeps things pretty tight."

"I can only imagine. Need to know is the only way to stay alive in this type of work." I agreed. We both looked up as the captain entered. He took a cup off the rack filling it with coffee then took a seat on the bench next to Perry.

"I have orders to drop you two off in Acapulco. Im envious of you. Acapulco is a lively place to enjoy." He smiled.

"You got that right." Perry agreed.

"We will surface tonight at twentythree hundred hours and put you in a Zodiac boat for the trip to shore. You will be greeted by the shore team there." He continued." If any of what has happened on this submarine were to get out and be made public every crewmember on this ship would become a target as well as our families." He went on. Perry and I looked at each other.

"We too have our secrets as well captain. We would be targets as well if our secrets were ever revealed." I told him.

"Seems we all live in a world of secrets. "The captain observed.

"Yeah, nothing to worry about sir, if you knew some of the things we have done, you wouldnt worry a bit about us keeping our mouths shut." Perry added.

"Well thank you gentlemen. I must get back to work, Ill see you off this evening." The captain told us as he stood up. Sailors began to enter the galley, the cooks had began putting out the food for the evening meal.

"Shall we?" I said standing up.

"Hey yeah chow time, great idea." He said following me as I got in line.

CHAPTER FOURTEEN

Later the captain met us in the galley.

"It's time gentlemen. It's been an honor to have you aboard. "He ushered us forward to the torpedo room hatch that we had come rushing down under a hail of bullets.

"Captain I cant thank you enough for all your help and the great job you and your crew have done, Id like to give you this as a token of appreciation of my time aboard." I told him handing him my wings from my flight suit.

"Ill say this to you sir, we live in a world of secrets. We are all military men here. We are all used to keeping secrets. You can go to sleep tonight knowing your secrets are now our secrets to be kept until our graves." I finished.

"Thank you colonel." He replied shaking my hand.

"Thanks for the fun sir, it's been a real pleasure." Perry told the captain shaking his hand.

"Take care of yourselves gentlemen." He told us. A sailor brought forward two canvas bags of our gear. Then we were up the brass ladder and again on deck in the dark. We climbed into the Zodiac and once seated we were off towards the brightly lit shore. The trip to the beach was fast and short. The Zodiac crashed up on the sand in the dark and to our surprise Manuel was there to greet us along with Antonio with his ever present bodyguard.

We climbed out of the inflatable onto the wet sand and Antonio reached over and hugged me in a great bear hug. Then he hugged Perry as well.

"Welcome back guys, glad you two are all safe." He said. Antonio's bodyguard picked up our bags as if they were a light load of laundry. I turned and looked behind me but the sub was hidden in the darkness. The Zodiac was already making it's way back to the sub.

"Glad to see you safe again Grey." Manuel said slapping me on the back. I groaned from the pain I my shoulder.

"Cmon guys, we have rooms reserved for you here at the hotel, a little Rand R." Antonio told us as he started to walk. I looked up and for the first time I saw the huge hotel above us all lit up. We followed Antonio up the concrete steps with Manuel in tow the bodyguard following us with our two bags. Antonio led us into a well lit hallway and stopped infront of a room handing me a key.

"Ill see you in the morning for a debriefing, Im sure you want to get some sleep after your journey. Ill give you a wakeup call, sleep well." He smiled as I took the key.

"Talk to you later Grey." Perry told me as he walked away. Manuel just smiled and walked after them. The bodyguard lowered my bag to the floor.

"Good to see you again sir, Im glad you are well."

"Thank you Sebastion." I nodded to him. I put the key in the lock and opened the door. Ali came running at me naked as a jay bird yelling my name catching me as I walked in. She wrapped her arms around me squeling.

"Ow Ow easy, Im wounded here." I warned her.

"Oh my god what happened to you?" She asked backing away. I turned to close the door watching Sebastion smiling as he walked away. I locked the door and turned around.

"I got a piece of shrapnel in my back when my fighter got hit."

"Oh Im so sorry I didnt know. how bad is it?" She asked spinning me around. I slowly unzipped the flight suit and she looked at the bandage.

"Wow Im glad it wasnt any worse. Oh I have missed you so much." She said wrapping her arms around me pressing up against me, her bare breasts rubbing against my chest.

"This is a great surprise. Ive missed you too hon." I told her as she kissed me hard and long.

The next morning the phone woke us up. Antonio was giving us a wakeup call. Lying in that huge soft comfortable bed with Ali next to me, the last thing I wanted to do was get up. I felt the anger building up inside of me.

"Ok Antonio we'll be down in a few minutes." I told him. I slowly sat up My shoulder throbbing like crazy. Ali rolled over a looked at me with one eye looking like a cat that just ate a bowl of cream. After a warm shower we dressed and made our way onto the veranda. Ali and I found them at a table overlooking the beach.

"Morning, have a seat, breakfast is ready." Antonio waved his hand at us. I pulled out the chair for Ali and I took a seat.

"Perry has been filling me in on a few details but I need the rest from you." He told me. There was a cup of hot coffee waiting for me. I reached for it and the waitress walked up ready to take our order. I ordered eggs over easy with sausage and biscuits and gravy. She never betted an eye. I was glad they had that kind of food here. I took my time telling my story not leaving out any detail. I had a captive audience. When I was done Antonio sat there quietly, Ali's face was white as a sheet, Manuel looked at the ground. Perry was the first to speak.

"We got a winner with this guy here boss, he's tough as nails."

"Actually I have to thank Perry here for rescuing my ass, he was there covering my rear as we ran to that Zodiac to escape that beach. He was firing at the Chinese and throwing grenades grabbing my harness throwing me in the boat. Basically all I did was survive. I came back with a piece of a Chinese built SAM missile in my shoulder as a souvenir." I told them tossing the chunk of metal onto the table. All eyes focused on the piece of metal when the food arrived. I attacked it like I hadnt eaten in a year.

"Well you have earned a few days of R and R here Grey, congratulations on your escape. We are all proud of you, it's not every man that has the inner strength to go through what you have. You are a valuble member of the team, an intragal part of our family. This is a war, maybe not a huge war, maybe the rest of the world doesnt care about what is going on here. We do, we are a part of what is going on down here, and the outcome depends on what we do. There are a lot of innocent people who will suffer if we dont win this. We need you in this fight Grey. I know what you just went through must have been hell, but you survived it, you made it out. That shows you have what it takes. I knew that when I offered you a chance to join our little band of outlaws. Welcome home." Antonio told me. I looked around at the faces.

"Thanks Antonio, Im glad to be back. Ill be fine, dont you worry. The quicker I get back into a cockpit the better Ill be." I assured him.

"I never doubted you for a second. Take a few days and have fun with your wife. We can spare her talents for a few days. In fact maybe we all need a few days of R and R. Ive been working way too hard myself. "He grinned. After breakfast we wandered around town taking in the sights. We visited the SanDiego Fort on the hill shaped like a five sided star. Inside is a large museum We went for a swim in the ocean and gathered together for a late dinner. We visited a club and danced and drank the night away. At breakfast the next morning Perry and I both opened our canvas bags at the table overlooking the beach after we ate. I pulled out the AK-47 I had taken from the Chinese soldier along with the harness. I pulled out my flight helmet and set it on the table. Inside the bag was a small cardboard box. Inside the box was a white coffee mug with the emblem and name of the Chilean submarine. Perry had one in his bag as well.

"A little souvinier of our adventure." Perry remarked.

After a swim at the beach Ali and I ate a light lunch in the hotel restuarant overlooking the beach. We enjoyed the jet boats at Puerto Marquez Lagoon. These boats barrel along the surface of the water and then suddenly twist and turn on the surface of the water. That evening Antonio took us out to restaurant that featured cliff divers. These divers perch on the side of a cliff and dive into the water with flaming pieces of wood in each hand.

Four days later we all gathered at the airport and boarded Antonio's private plane. It was a one of a kind renovated Lockheed Constellation Starliner. He had modernized it and turned the interior into a combination aerial office and living quarters. There were two external drop tanks attached to the bottom of the wings giving the Starliner greater range in addition n to the wingtip tanks. The forward section contained four bunk beds, located directly behind the cockpit. Aft was a small but roomy lounge area with a modern office cubicle complete with copier, scanner, fax machine and a very powerful computer. Then aft of that was a modern galley. The rear of the aircraft was Antonio's bedroom complete with a fully functional bathroom with a shower. He ran his company from that plane anywhere he flew in the world. We joked that there was more modern communications inside that plane than Air Force One.

Once airborne, Ali sat at the computer console located behind the co-pilot's seat. This was where the flight engineer formerly sat in the original configuration of the cockpit. The flight engineer would have constantly monitored the four engines performance. The cockpit had been totaly modernized, computors now controlled engine performance leaving an unused space behind the copilot seat. This space had been converted to a space age communications console able to reach anywhere in the world. This was where Ali sat checking on various messages and company info.

The cockpit resembled the space shuttle with a mix of original instruments and the most modern computerized control system available enabling Antonio to fly the massive aircraft alone. The flight controls had been modified with a modern fly by wire system. It was like adding power steering to a dump truck. It aided in maneuvering the large aircraft in the sky. There were a few original instruments, three heads up displays, two computors, electronic counter measures to foil air to air missiles. On each side of the tail were foil and flare ejectors to confuse radar guided or heat seeking missiles. A FLIR unit had been installed under the nose enabling clear images in the darkest nights or the foggiest conditions. A rear unit was installed under the tail to enable rearward viewing. The radio equipment on the Connie enabled him to communicate anywhere in the world. It was an impressive setup.

We sat there on the runway in line behind a row of shiny gleaming modern airliners waiting to take off. I sat in the co-pilot seat looking out the window. Everywhere Antonio flew his plane people would stop and stare. She was a beautiful bird. When he was a child living in Cuba he would often watch the big three tailed Connies land and take off at the airport in Havana. Now that he was a multi-millionaire, he enjoyed owning a one of a kind customized classic from the days of propliners.

When it was our turn to take off, Antonio locked the brakes did a thorough cockpit check. Once satisfied he released the brakes and slowly moved the four ivory white engine controls forward and the big bird rolled down the runway. He pulled back on the stick and the nose came up. We were airborne. I reached over and brought the gear up as we nosed up into the sky.

Sitting there in the cockpit reminded me of the flight we made from India all the way to Andros Island off the coast of Florida in preparation for our attack on Cuba. We each took shifts flying the big bird across the Atlantic. It was a long but enjoyable air trip for us.

I looked out the starboard side window at the set of four huge spinning props the sunlight glinting off them. The eighteen cylinder engines were humming along. Antonio was never happier than when he was flying his plane. It was sheer joy sitting in the co-pilot seat flying the big bird. I marveled at the transformation that had been done to the cockpit. It was like flying a brand new aircraft.

Antonio called for landing clearance as we approached the airbase. He skillfully turned the big bird and aligned with the runway. He brought her down slowly and landed her perfectly on the tarmac. After reversing the four props slowing us down, he taxied to a spot to the side of the runway and parked her, cutting the engines. We were back. The Connie had an internal ladder that electrically unfolded down to the tarmac allowing easy deplanning.

Raul, Alexi and Boner were there to greet us. There were handshakes and back slapping, which didnt do much for my shoulder. I had to relate the whole story again to them and they examined my AK. Ali and I had a few minutes for a private goodbye before Antonio fired up the engines on the Connie and she climbed up the stairs. We stood there watching as the graceful bird took to the air her four engines singing in unison as she climbed into the sky. It was a sad sight watching her leave.

I had to undergo a medical exam by the base doctor. After he was finished he pronounced me fit to fly.

The next morning Raul walked me over to the hanger and showed me my new bird. Someone had painted the correct number of flags on the port side right under the canopy to signify my score of kills. I climbed the ladder and sat in the seat checking everything out. It was one of Antonio's newest birds, straight from Cuba. I looked over the instrument panel, put my feet on the rudder pedals and moved the stick back and forth. Perry had gone over my helmet and tested it. It functioned perfectly. Manuel walked to his bird and climbed in. I climbed the orange metal ladder and settled myself into the cockpit. From then on it was all mechanical. I did everything in order as I had so many times before, brake was set, power switch on, instrument panel came to life, the ground tech helped strap me in. He reached over and pulled the strap with the two pins out of the ejection seat. I spun my finger in a circle as I hit the engine power switch. There was a whine from the turbine as she started rolling and then the familiar roar and vibration as the engine came to power. I closed my canopy locking it in place with my left hand. The bird was on internal power, ready to fly. The two HUDs were functioning showing there were four Copperhead missiles hanging under my wings and a full magazine of rounds for the cannon. All fuel tanks were full. I called the tower and recieved takeoff clearance. The inside visor of my helmet was displaying information in green. The bird was ready, I was ready. I looked over at Boner and he gave me the thumbs up.

I released the brake and started rolling out onto the tarmac, Manuel's MIG followed behind me. At the end of the runway I locked my brakes and went over everything. Once I was satisfied I released the brake shoved the throttle forward, engaged the afterburner and was rewarded with being shoved back into my seat as I accelerated down the runway. I pulled back on the stick and I was airborne. I pulled up my gear and they locked in place with a secure clunk. All three indicator lights verified they were locked. The base descended below as I climbed into the blue sky, Manuel was at my eight oclock. My helmet was functioning perfectly, the information being displayed in green on the inside of my visor verified the fighter was performing flawlessly. The two HUDs were diplaying all the correct information, the MIG handled wonderfully. I was a part of the fighter, it was instantly responding to my touch. I shut down the afterburner and leveled out at altitude. Manuel stayed with me as I practiced manuevers twisting and turning performing rolls, climbing, diving. I was putting the MIG through ever manuever I knew. I was sure she had been flight tested prior to arriving here, but I knew my life depended on how she would fly. I needed to just fly, return to the sky again after being shot down. Sort of like getting onto a horse after being thrown off. My palms began to sweat as I had a flashback of the massive explosion and the brutal ejection. I swear I could feel the piece of shrapnel pierce my shoulder again and the sudden rush of air from being rocketed out of the fighter. My stomach lurched and my heart was pounding like a jackhammer. I was gulping oxygen in my facemask as I felt a wave of panic come over me. I concentrated on flying until it passed.

I gripped the stick with all my strength and concentrated on flying the MIG. I flew the piss out of that MIG until she was low on fuel. I landed by the numbers without a hitch. Back on the ground I pulled her up in front of the hanger and locked the brakes. I shut down the engine and opened the canopy. Yanking off my face mask, I sat there for a few minutes until my heart began to beat normaly. I slowly climbed down the ladder to the ground. I tried to hide the rubbery feeling in both my legs as I got to the ground. Raul met me in the ready room as I stripped off my G suit.

"How did it go, any problems?" He asked.

"Great, no problems. The MIG is is in great shape." I replied.

"I meant you, did you have any problems up there?"

"I know what you meant, and no I didn't have any problems. You can report back to Antonio Im fine and ready for flight status." I told him.

"Well, he was worried about you." Raul said.

"Yeah, I know. Im fine, really, no jitters. No paranoia, I think I was more afraid on the ground in the jungle alone than getting shot down." I assured him.

"Great, Ill finish my report, as of now you are back on flight status. Glad to have you back." He finished. I went to our quarters and took a long shower. My shoulder ached under the hot water. After being so hot and dirty in the jungle, I felt like I would never be clean again. The shower had helped calm me down inside. I walked to the bar on base wondering if this panic attack would happen every time I went up in the MIG. It would interfere with my ability to fly and fight. Lying to Raul was wrong but what else could I do, tell him the truth? Then where would I go? My life would change drastically. At the bar I sat with a few other pilots drinking and talking. I started drinking with a Singapore Sling, then a Tequila Sunrise then a shot of brandy. I ran through three rounds of these until I couldn't feel anything. I slowly made my way back to my quarters, I stumbled around in the dark trying to stay quiet. In my bed I had to grab both sides of the bed to keep from falling out as the bed began to spin in circles. Drinking on an empty stomach wasn't a real smart thing to do, but I hoped it would help me sleep.

The next morning I woke up to sunlight streaming into my eyes, there was a hammering in my head and my mouth tasted like the bottom of a kitty litter box. My stomach felt like a washing machine, and I could feel the floor spinning under my bare feet. Once my dizziness cleared I was able to stand under the shower until my head cleared. I felt stable enough to make my way to the chow hall. Sitting next to Boner and Manuel we ate and talked. I had to retell my story in great detail again.

I guess the difference between what happened to Manuel being shot down and my experience was hiding in the jungle and killing the enemy soldier with Perry saving my ass and our harrowing escape under fire. After chow I had to catch up on all my paperwork. That afternoon I was flight leader for three other MIGs patrolling south of the base. Again I felt the feeling of panic rise inside my chest. We were flying a simple flight pattern but the panic was rising again inside of me. I could feel the explosion all over again, my heart pounding, I was light headed, my palms were wet with sweat, my shoulder was aching and I could hear Manuel's voice in my head screaming at me again to eject. it was so real I actually placed my hand on the round black and yellow rings between my legs to pull to eject.

I closed my eyes and held my breath to slow my breathing down. The panic slowly subsided My flight suit was wet from my sweat, and my face was as wet as if I had experienced a fever. Luckily I was able to maintain a level flight path. I was the last pilot to land, I took my time and double checked everything before I made my approach. I was calm enough by the time the runway came into view to be able to land safely. Maybe it was the fact I felt relief knowing I was landing that helped calm me down.

Sitting there by myself in the ready room I couldn't understand what was happening to me. Was my being shotdown such a traumatic experience that it caused me to panic everytime I went up? Should I seek help? From who? If it got out I was having problems in the air my career would be over and I would be grounded, useless to Antonio. I couldnt let him down, I couldnt let the other members of my team down. After the debriefing of our patrol, I made a call to Ali. It was great to hear her voice. She knew something was wrong but I didnt let on. That night in the chow hall I talked with Manuel about his ejecting,.

"Hell man I couldnt wait to get back into the cockpit and get even with those bastards for shooting me down. It was all I lived for." He explained. I guess everyone has different emotions to the same situations. Somehow I had to find a way to conquer my fears. I kept quiet about my panic attacks. As much as I trusted everyone in the team, I still didnt feel comfortable enough to reveal to anyone what was happening to me. How was I going to solve this problem so it didnt affect my ability to fly and fight? There was a major difference between Manuel's ejection and mine. He was rescued almost immediately.

I buried myself in paperwork and reports. I reviewed Perry's maintanance on all our fighters. I signed requsition orders for spare parts, fuel consumption, missile replacements, the usual paperwork required of a colonel in the Cuban Air Force assigned to a special unit. I had been dodging them for weeks. It gave me an excuse to sit at a desk and not have to face the anxiety of climbing back into the cockpit. Raul and I discussed the flight roster of pilots flying security over our base. I never let on about my anxiety problems and he never said a word about it, tho I was sure he guessed.

Raul had me scheduled to be on the list of alert pilots the next day. It was a two fighter team that would respond to assist the flight team in the air flying security in the event they came under attack. Things had been quiet since our last bombing mission and the loss of the Chinese task force. We assumed the pilots to the south did not have the capacity to form an air attack against us. It never dawned on me that there would be any need for a second flight to fight tomorrow, so I never gave it a second thought. I ate in the chow hall with Boner and Alexi and Raul, after which I wrote a letter to Ali and slept all night without any nightmares.

I awoke the next morning, did my daily workout in the gym, and did a preliminary flight check of my MIG, watching Manuel out of the corner of my eye as he did the same thing to his bird. I signed the book accepting my bird as flight ready, then returned to the ready room to make sure my G suit and helmet was accessable. I looked over at the spot where Boner's equipment usually hung and saw it was empty. He and his wingman were flying their A-4 Skyhawks along the border south of the base this morning. There would be another team ready to take their place soon. I sat down and began to read a three day old paper from Havana while Manuel read an adventure novel.

I was getting bored and had just started to dose off in the comfortable leather recliner when the klaxon went off. My heart seized and I jumped to my feet adrenalin instantly pumping through my body as Manuel and I both put on our G suits, grabbing our helmets and ran out to our fighters. The ground techs had already started the engines on our fighters, the flight information reprogrammed into our nav computors. The little red tags had been pulled from the eight Copperhead missiles beneath our wings. I scrambled up the orange metal ladder and slid into the seat the tech helping me strap in.

"GreyWolf One ready for takeoff." I called to the tower. The necessary information was already being displayed in green on the inside of my visor as I was strapping it on.

"GreyWolf One, runway is clear for takeoff, wind is at eight miles an hour from the west, humidity is at seventy percent, all aircraft are clear overhead, your flight is cleared for immediate takeoff. Alpha flight has detected four J-11s heading north, eta to their position is zero eight minutes. You are weapons free upon contact with bandits, good hunting gentlemen." The tower replied.

"GreyWolf one acknowledged we are rolling now." I called back, I had already released my brakes and returned the hand salute of the ground tech. I didnt stop at the end of the runway, instead I immediatly started rolling, hit my afterburner, was pushed back into my seat as the MIG accelerated down the runway. My heart was still pounding in my chest like a jackhammer and there was still plenty of adrenalin pumping through my veins. Boner, my buddy was up there south of us facing four enemy J-11 fighters who wanted nothing more than to attack and kill him. He needed us to help. I had my missiles armed right after I had my landing gear locked into place and my flaps up. Manuel was glued to my right wing as I turned south, my radar on I adjusted it to search at it's greatest distance. I wanted the J-11s out there to know there were more than just two A-4 SkyHawks to deal with, and I wanted to detect their position, hoping to get in the first shot as soon as possible.

"Hey Grey welcome to the party." Boner called over my headphones.

"Didnt want to let you have all the fun there Alpha One." I replied.

"Well we got two of them headed straight for the base, and the other two are trying to keep us busy so we dont interfere with the two bombers. Why dont you hit them for us while we deal with these two."

"Copy that." I replied. I narrowed my beam and increased the sweep cycle speed hoping to pick up the two approaching J-11s.

"You see them Manuel?" I called over to him.

"Negative, they must be pulling one of our tricks and are flying low through the valleys." He replied. Shit. They had learned from us and were using our tactic of hugging the ground hoping to pop up and hit our base without being detected. There wasnt enough time to launch another set of fighters from our, base. By the time the next team of fighters lifted off the two J-11s would already be dropping their bombs. I pulled back on the stick and climbed up into the sky. I adjusted my look-down-shoot-down radar hoping to locate the two fast moving J-11s as they screamed between the mountains heading toward our base. I felt a sense of fury not felt in a long time as I thought of the damage those two J-11 fighters could do to our base on their hit and run mission. There was no way in hell I was going to let those two bastards kill any of our people, not while I was in the air.

Finally my HUD was able to show the two fast moving dots and the direction of travel. Manuel radioed back to the tower their location and flight path. I moved the stick and dove coming down on them high from their six. They were twisting and turning as they flew through the mountain passes. I could see our base, it would be a matter of seconds and they would be able to release their bombs. My headphones registered a warble indicating my missile had a lock on the second fighter. I squeezed the trigger on my stick, the missile dropped of my wing, ignited and streaked away chasing after my target. Not satisfied I again fired a second missile at the racing J-11. I wanted no mistakes or misses. I could see flares being ejected from the rear of the J-11 as it's pilot tried to confuse the two approaching missiles. I kept the green box being illuminated on my visor right on the enemy fighter watching as the first missile followed the J-11 during it's attempt to evade my missile by twisting and turning. Seconds later the missile hit the rear of the J-11 blowing off the rear of the fighter, the front end of the fighter tumbling over and over until it smashed into the ground.

My second missile having lost it's target automatically began scanning the air in front of it and locked onto the exhaust coming from the rear of the first J-11 and continued streaking faster than the enemy fighter. Seconds later the missile detonated. The explosion covered both sides of the narrow canyon walls with pieces of the fighter as the orange fireball continued forward for a few seconds before joining it's companion impacting into the ground, the wreckage scattering in a giant crater.

"Scratch two, we're heading south towards your position Boner." I called into the mic.

"Hell yeah cmon down ole buddy, we're having a great time here, the more the merrier. We'll lead them right to you. "Boner replied cheerfully. After checking my fuel status I accelerated south Manuel glued to my right wing as we both raced in search of more kills. I could see two J-11s behind Boner and his wingman flying low to the ground twisting and turning trying to prevent the J-11s from getting a missile lock on them. Evidently it did not occur to the enemy pilots to pull up and launch their missiles from a higher altitude. Instead they were locked in a deadly nap of the earth chase between the mountain ranges jinking and turning at full throttle. It would be their last fatal mistake.

Flying higher and approaching the twisting and turning enemy fighters from their front, Manuel and I locked onto the two J-11s with our radar and assigned a missile to each target. Manuel fired first, I fired right afterwards. Our missiles streaked out and down towards the J-11s. Their RWRs must have warned them as the leader suddenly pulled up out of the canyon and changed direction, flares ejecting from both fighters as they climbed and turned south. I kept the enemy fighter in the little green box displayed on my visor. Manuel's missile impacted the first fighter creating an impressive orange fireball of bits and pieces of metal in the blue sky. Seconds later my missile's proximity fuse detonated below the second fighter spliting it in half. I watched as both burning sections tumbled independantly out of the sky into the green jungle below. Boner and his wingman streaked below us as we headed south. By now the base had launched another four MIGs as we made our turn West.

We were getting low on fuel. We had ejected our drop tanks upon sighting the first two J-11s and used our afterburners racing towards the second two J-11s causing our MIGs to guzzle fuel at an alarming rate. We had enough to make it back to base, but no more. My heart was still pounding like a jackhammer but I was feeling elated. I had just achieved three more kills. Gone was the overwhelming feeling of panic. Instead there was a feeling of great joy as I had not only prevented another bombing attack on our base, but I had helped shoot an enemy fighter off my friend's ass for the second time. The first time was during the mission bombing Bejucal, when he was flying an F-18 off the U.S.S. Grant. Boner and his wingman were sent up to investigate our flight of three MIG-21s. As we were approaching the coast of Cuba Boner and his wingman were attacked by a Cuban MIG-29. Boner was being pursued by a MIG-29 and he flew in front of my MIG-21. I fired a missile shooting down the MIG-29.

I knew there would be plenty of celebrating tonight in the bar. There were four MIG-21s flying overhead in a figure eight pattern over our base as we followed Boner and his wingman. We landed minutes after they did. I turned my MIG away from the runway and rolled up next to Manuel's fighter. I unlocked the canopy and the ground tech slid in the ejection seat pins, slapping me on the back as I climbed out. Boner had a huge smile on his face as he walked over to me.

"Guess I owe you again for saving my bacon Meho." He said.

"More like team work, you lead em, we clean em." I replied as we walked to the ready room together.

"They were trying to keep us from stopping the other two bombers." He told me.

"Well we got em. You'd think they would have decided to stop trying to attack us here." Manuel remarked.

"Amen to that. Lord only knows why they havent quit yet." I answered. Later siting together at the bar enjoying ice cold green labeled beer, I was relieved the panic attack was gone. The overwhelming fear was not there while we were dealing with the enemy J-11s. Maybe the fact I was too busy and slightly pissed off replaced the fear and panic. Either way, I was elated, the old feelings of cocky self confidence was back.

CHAPTER FIFTEEN

The next morning we went to a briefing. Raul had recieved information detailing a forthcoming attack on our base. The drawn sober look on Raul's face got our attention before he began speaking. I knew something huge and dangerous was at hand.

"The Chinese have added a new wrinkle to the situation. We have recieved intelligence revealing a planned attack on our base here. They have shipped several CSS-6 surface to surface missiles from China. There have been two flights of IL-76 transports. They shipped the missiles seperatley from the launchers. The IL-76 transports were accompinied by J-11s as security. These aircraft were specially modified with inflight refueling. There are eight Chinese CSS-6 mobile launcher systems in various locations. Three are targeted onto our base here." Raul paused sipping his coffee.

"The Chinese were able to acquire three U.S. made supercomputors out of Japan. It assisted them in designing improved missile guidance systems. These M class missiles are solid fueled, single staged, and highly mobile. They are mounted on specially designed heavy duty German manufactured trucks that act both as a transport system and launching platform. These massive eight wheeled monsters are designed to travel, transport and launch their missiles independant from any type of central command. These missiles are catagorized as MARVs, or Maneuverable Re-entry Vehicles. They can launch and change course and speed several times to survive any type of anti missile defense system. These missiles fly at a speed of mach 6." Raul stopped and drank more coffee. My stomach dropped like I was in an elevator after hearing the last bit of information. this was a worst case scenario, a no win situation.

"We are working like crazy to locate these missiles. Hopefully our intellingence operative working in their government will be able to get this information for us."

There was dead silence in the room. The only way to escape attack by these monsters would be to evacuate this base. It would comprimise our ability to defend the southern part of the country.

"Locating these missiles will result in our attacking them." Common sense told me the Chinese were camouflaging the hell out of these monsters. Raul had photos on the wall using an overhead projector. The photos changed every few seconds detailing the launch vehicles and short stubby missiles. They reminded me of photos of Nazi V-2 rockets mounted on the back of massive eight wheeled Russian trucks.

"Plans are being drawn up now for an airborne attack on military and government targets all over Guatemala as we speak. The high command in Mexico City see no other solution to ending these attacks against this country. There are two factions in the high command. One faction wants to attack, the other believes if we just wait the enemy out, through attrition we will win by outlasting them. I fear the only way to prevent the launch of these missiles is to go on the offensive, if these missiles are launched, there will be only one mission, a ground war."

"The good news is," He carried on. "The high command has contacted the military in the US to see if we can acquire an anti missile system to place near our base."

Well at least that was something. Every time it looked like we had gotten the upper hand, the enemy pulled out another surprise, a new wrinkle that upped the anti against us. I wondered if Antonio would be able to come up with a solution to this problem. I was sure he had the same information we did. The agent in place giving the information about the Chinese missiles had to be one of his people. Soon we would be able to have the locations of those Chinese missiles.

"The bad news is from this point on everyone is restricted to base, and no outgoing communications of any type are allowed until further notice. We must now consider ourselves in a state of war. It has been a long time coming. The high command decided that as long as the enemy attacks were restricted only to air attacks, there would be no war. Since the Chinese have changed the rules so to speak and plan to start launching missiles, the plan is to invade. "If China could not be stopped here now, then they could attack Cuba later. That was obvious. I was wondering what Antonio was planning.

"There have been transport aircraft being readied all over Mexico right now. They have been de centralized so as not to give the enemy any warning of our forthcoming aerial invasion all over Guatamala. Airborne troops are being readied for the attack as we speak. If we cannot acquire the locations of these Chinese missiles by morning, the attacks will begin at 0600. Our job will be to fly security for these transports to protect them from being shot down before they can unload their troops. The transports will return to their takoff points, more troops will be loaded and again there will be more troops being dropped. As soon as key locations have been taken, motorized troops will move down the Inter American Highway. They will positions themselves at locations already captured by the airborne shock troops. Our primary job will be to destroy any airborne threats. Once this has taken place, our next responsibility will be to sweep the air of enemy fighters ptotecting the transports, and attack ground targets in support of the invading forces."

Raul passed out flight maps showing our rendevous locations with the transports. We were to fan out ahead of the transports as soon as the enemy fighters took to the air to shoot them down. Our AWACs would be airborne as soon as the transports took off giving us long range warning of the enemy fighters positions. The date stamped on these maps pre-dated our arrival in Mexico. These battle plans had been worked out on paper long before the Chinese had invaded Guatamala. It gave me a feeling of security knowing the Mexican high command had been ready this early in the game.

"I guess this is really it Meho." Boner whispered to me. I nodded silently in reply.

"Our Hind rescue choppers will be in the air as soon as our fighters cross the border. Our Hinds will be airborne ready to retrieve anyone shot down on the other side of the border. The A-4s will be the primary bombers supporting the airborne troops on the ground, and attacking high profile targets. The 21s will fly air cover. A-4s will have air refueling available from A-4s using buddy packs. Flight teams will be staggered. That will create continious waves of fighters Every ten minutes teams of A-4s and 21s will take off, hit their targets, and return to refuel. "We spent the rest of the day going over our flight plans, reviewing flight paths, codes, call signs, attack targets, and rescue codes to the choppers in case anyone got shot down. The bar was closed that night. Boner and I and Raul were in the hanger with Alexi, Manuel, and Perry. A case of beer magically appeared from Perry's stores and we sat around reminising about our crazy air attack on Bejucal. The beer ran out, and the conversation slowed down. We made our way back to the barracks. I knew that Perry would have his crew up all night getting the fighters ready for the morning. I slept well that night after drinking all that beer. I knew the beer had been brought out to help us sleep.

Morning came early, I crawled out of my bunk, took a quick shower, and made my way to the chow hall. There was a buzz as all the pilots were talking as they ate. I ate lightly. There was a quick pre-flight briefing to review the same material from the day before. Then it was off to the ready room. It was packed, every available pilot was in there slipping into their G suits and checking their survival vests. I was assigned to fly cover for Boner's flight. We walked out to the flight line and again I was surprised by the amount of jet fighters lined up. There were MIG-21s, A-4 s, MIG-29s, A-4s with refueling tanks hanging underneath. The ramp was busy with techs checking fighters, and pilots walking to their fighters. Fuel trucks were going from fighter to fighter, it was a hive of activity. Over head were four MIG-21s flying in a protective figure eight pattern around the base.

"Ill see ya upstairs." I called to Boner as we parted walking towards our fighters. I looked under the wings of my fighter, all eight Copperhead missiles were tight in the launch rails, the drop tank below the belly was tight and not leaking. The landing gear were clean, no fluid was leaking. I checked the cone running my hands inside making sure there were no objects in there. I checked the tail, and the airelons. I ran my hand along the polished skin of the MIG. She was one of Antonio's finest efforts. I had no doubts about her perfomance. I signed the pre-flight checklist and climbed up the ladder. Inside I took my time getting settled in. The ground tech pulled out the ejection pins from the seat and helped strap me in, hooking up the cable to my helmet.

I hit the power switch watching the instrument panel come to life. The two HUDs came on, the left one indicated there were eight Copperhead missiles loaded under the wings, and I had five hundred rounds of cannon rounds available. I adjusted the flight computor telling it where we were located and what altitude we were sitting at. The inner tanks were full of fuel as was the drop tank. I spun my finger in a circle letting the ground tech know I was starting the engines. I hit the starter switch and the turbine began to spin up slowly. Soon the fighter was vibrating from the engine, the ground tech was disconnecting the power cart from the side of the fighter. I closed the canopy and locked it in place. My helmet was projecting the correct information on the inside of my visor.

The tower was flashing coded light signals to each flight team giving them take off clearance. By using flashing colored lights, radio silence was maintained denying the enemy information by eavesdropping on our radio frequencies. Group by group each flight team took off in the darkness to rendeuvous with their assigned transport units. The Mexican high command had been gathering different transports for months. American C-141s, and C-130s as well as Russian built IL-76s and Antonov A-12 Cubs were obtained, repaired and made ready for this battle. Mexican troops combined with Cuban special forces had been training together for months for the day they would be called upon to jump out of a military transport to bring the fight to the enemy.

They also had acquired four C-130 Spectre gunships from the U.S. military for use during the attack. They would be valuable for use to support the troops on the ground. They were equipped with in flight refueling probes allowing them to loiter for hours until called upon. These specially modified transports had been converted into flying tanks able to fire at ground targets in complete darkness. Their weapons included two mini-guns, two twenty millimeter guns, two forty millimeter cannon and a 105 millimeter cannon. These weapons were computer guided and aimed using an infra-red night vision system.

Our flight team recieved the launch order from the tower. The correct light sequence was flashed and we lined up our fighters. Boner's flight team of four fully loaded A-4 Skyhawks took off first. Once they were in the air I lined my MIG up at the end of the runway, put on the brakes and double checked everything. Once I was satisfied, I let out the brakes, hit the afterburner and was rewarded with being pushed back into my seat as my MIG rocketed down the runway with Manuel on my right to the rear. I pulled back on the stick and once airborne folded my landing gear up and my flaps. The other two MIGs of my flight team joined us and we teamed up heading south. Minutes later my HUD revealed a sky full of contacts. The transports and their MIG escorts had joined up and were heading south towards their targets. The AWACs was up and sending us data revealing our position in the giant airborne chess board that would soon begin the long awaited invasion of the war.

The Mexican high command had sent a radio message as we lifted off to the Central command of the communist government of Guatemala informing them that a state of war officially existed between the two countries. A long overdue action that should have been declared after the first attack from them. I never pretended to understand the art of diplomacy. I was a fighter pilot. I was trained to fight and kill the enemy, not talk him to death or try to make deals with empty promises. Our eight plane formation passed over the border and my RWR began sounding in my ears. Suddenly the sky was filled with SAMs. We dove for the deck to get under their radar as Boner's flight of A-4s dropped their bombs on the radar installation controlling the SAM missile sight guarding this section of the border. One by one the A-4s went in low then pulling up sharply tossing their bombs and banking right flying west. Manuel and I were flying behind them but at a different altitude scanning the sky for enemy fighters. There were none in our area. I guessed they had been caught by surprise by our early morning attack. The SAMs without their ground radar to guide them were searching an empty sky above us for targets they would never find.

As Boner's flight turned north towards base to rearm with more bombs, my flight team circled the target area looking at the destroyed SAM sight. Minutes later a flight of four IL 76s flew past on their way to their drop zone. Their target a small but important military base just across the border guarding a paved cross road. By taking this base, our heavy weapons transports would be able to pass by unmolested on their way south.

I watched as troops began to exit the transports, their parachutes reminding me of mushrooms. My RWR went off identifying radar coming from an IZU four barrelled armored anti aircraft weapon. I intsantly kicked left rudder and moved the stick diving on the tracked vehicle. I heard the growl in my headphones telling me the missile had acquired the target. I squeezed the button and the missile left the rail screaming down in a straight line. Seconds later there was an orange ball of flame from the target. One threat had been eliminated.

Just as I was pulling up there were three explosions on the ground from the group of buildings at the crossroads below us. Another flight of A-4s had come in behind us hitting the target, eliminating anti aircraft guns mounted on the roofs of these buildings. Smoke was coming up from the ground as our flight circled around the transports as they started their turn north to return to their bases for more airborne troops. Already below us our troops had landed and were mopping up the remaining resistance. This small but important section of the border would become a lifeline of supplies and troops heading south. It was now under our control. I could see a long line of trucks already moving south on rte 2 heading south.

Suddenly the AWACs was sending data informing us that two J-11s had lifted off from their base at Retalhuleu heading our way. I waggled my wings side to side in silent communication to the other fighters and dove for the deck. I was hoping to hide in the ground clutter, until they came into missile range. We roared between the mountain passes waiting for our prey to appear. We didnt have to wait long. Seconds later my passive radar picked up their radar sweeps and I narrowed my beam. I was rewarded with another growl as my missile radar detected the lead J-11 above us. I squeezed the trigger on the stick and the missile lept off the launcher into the sky. I used my helmet visor guidance system keeping the J-11 in the little green box on the inside of my visor. Sudenly the lead J-11 lifted his left wing and changed direction as he detected my missile coming after him. Keeping track of my position in relation to the ground, I guided my missile right at the target as it tried to shake loose my missile ejecting flares from it's rear, but it was a wasted effort. The missile hit the J-11 between the wings and the enemy fighter exploded. Manuel had launched his missile at the other J-11 right after I launched mine, Sedonds later there was another fireball in the sky as the second J-11 disinegrated. The sky was clear as we saw more transports and MIGs heading south. Our fuel was starting to get low, I radiod back to base informing them our flight would be returning to base for fuel.

Above us there was an orange fireball. What once was a transport full of troops on it's way south was now just random particles falling from the sky hit by an unseen enemy ground missile. Maybe a shoulder launched anti-aircraft missile. Over one hundred men had just died. As we approached our base we recieved orders to fly a pattern until a wounded C-130 could land first. I looked over my lft shoulder and watched as it approached the runway smoke coming from it's right wing in a long stream. It touched down and pulled off the runway and stopped as the crash crews raced across the tarmac spewing white foam from a roof mounted gun covering the engine fire. Instantly the smoke was gone as the white foam choked out the fire. A large tug was already pulling in front of the stricken Hercules to pull it out of the way so other aircraft could land.

We received landing clearance and one by one we lined up for our approach. Upon landing we were directed to sandbagged areas. I pulled in and cut my engine, shutting down the power and opening my canopy. Instantly a fuel truck appeared and began refueling and a smaller tractor with two more Copperhead missiles appeared as men began to attach them to the empty rails. I was out of the fighter long enough to take a piss and drink a cold fruit drink before climbing back into my fighter and closing my canopy. Refueled and re-armed I started her up and joined the other three fighters of my flight awaiting our turn to take off. I could see Boner's flight of A-4s taking off ahead of us, bombs and drop tanks hanging below their wings.

Once in the air again we were flying cover for Boner's team. Their target was a group of heavily protected enemy troops at another road junction further south of the border. Our troops had radiod for assistance. They were under attack and had several casualties. Hind helicopters were already in the air awaiting clearance to land there once the fighting had stopped to evacuate the wounded. Tracer fire rose from the ground as Boner's A-4s made their bombing run on their target. One by one each A-4 successfully dropped their loads onto the target making a giant crater of the enemy position.

"GreyWolf One to command, area has been sanitized, send in the Hinds." I called over our frequency. Seconds later two Hinds came out of the mountains, one Hind was flying circles around the landing sight as wounded troops were being loaded aboard the first Hind already on the ground. When the first Hind had lifted the second landed, the side doors popping open as more wounded troops were loaded aboard. Boner's A-4s had only used half their bomb load on this target. Boner radiod for another target to hit. Once the wounded had been loaded aboard the Hind, and much needed ammunition cases offloaded, the second Hind lifted off streaking north. Above us contrails showed where empty transports were returning to their bases for more troops.

We streaked south looking for a railroad station. Our troops were again under heavy fire from a well dug in enemy. We located the target from the air, and after recieving instructions from the troops on the ground, Boner's A-4s again dove making a bombing run dropping their loads onto the enemy position. After their bombs hit, smoke poured out of the enemy concrete bunkers that were now just blackened craters. Again Hind helicopters landed taking on more wounded, dropping off supplies, heading north with their precious cargo.

I heard a mayday over our fighter frequency. I looked to the south to see another MIG-21 trailing smoke heading north. He was at a higher altitude flying alone.

"I took a hit from ground fire, Im not sure how far this crate will go before she shuts down on me." I listened to the Mexican pilot giving our base his position. Seconds later the canopy popped off and the pilot ejected. The MIG continued on for a few more seconds before becoming an orange fireball. The pilot's chute opened and he was floating down to the jungle below. I radiod base giving our position requesting a chooper to fly to the location to pick up the pilot. Boner's flight had already left the area heading north. We circled as the pilot hit the trees. Once he landed safely our radio crackled with his voice from his survival radio.

Instantly memories flooded back into my mind of my experience. I called to him letting him know the rescue Hind was on it's way. We contiued to circle the area until the Hind appeared and winched a man down into the jungle to help retrieve the pilot. Minutes later we were all heading north again. Manuel and I were making slow wide lazy circles around the Hind as it headed north. The Hind would be a perfect target for any enemy fighter. Landing again we pulled into our sandbagged revetments for refueling. Out again for another piss and more cold fruit juice. I was sweating like a stuck pig, I wondered how many pounds I would lose this time. I had already lost a few pounds from my jungle adventure, now again flying combat I was bound to sweat out more pounds. The specially prepared fruit juice was combined with vitamins and other nutrients. It helped replace some of what I was sweating out, but not all.

Again we lined up ready to take off behind Boner's flight of A-4s. This time our target was the eastern part of Guatemala, an area called Frontereras. There was an important bridge and an electronic communication station

225

there. The eighty five foot tall modern steel and concrete bridge spanned the Rio Dulce. Troops were being transported across that bridge to the northern section of the country. Near it was the old Spanish fortress of San Felipe which had been converted into an electronic communications headquarters for the whole eastern region. Destroying it would help eliminate the enemy's ability to communicate with their force in that region. It was a major target. There were SAM missile launchers protecting the old fortress. This would be no easy target.

We flew east, located highway thirteen from the air and followed it right down to the huge blue lake. The bridge was visible from the air as a thin ribbon. Anti-aircraft tracers were coming up at us. Suddenly two SAMs were launched. Our ECM pods were working jamming the radar frequencies preventing the SAMs from locking onto us. I heard a growl in my headphones and launched two missiles at the closest SAM radar site. I used my helmet sighting system and the missiles rode the signal right down to the target creating a large explosion putting thick black smoke into the air. Boner's A4s made one pass at the long bridge with tracer fire all around them. They dropped their bombs right on target and the bridge disinigrated in a black explosion creating a huge open space between the the spans. There would be no tanks or APCs crossing that bridge. Boner brought his flight in from the opposit position as they pickled off their remaining bombs onto the old stone fortress. Circling the target I could see orange and blue flames creating a mass of thick black smoke.

"GreyWolf Flight returning to base. Both targets eliminated." I radiod base as we changed altitude and turned west. To the north was a black haze from fires from our fighters attacking the airbase at Flores. This was the second time our fighters had attacked that base. Hopefully there would be nothing left of it for the enemy to launch any fighters from. I was exhausted as I landed my fighter and pulled up into the sandbagged revetment. It had been a long day. I dragged myself out of the cockpit and into the debriefing room. Boner and I wrote our reports.

The chow hall was filled as pilots filed in for food. We were all hot, tired and sweaty from hours in the cockpit. There were many key towns and military bases now under our control. The two bases at Flores and Retalhuleu had been attacked so heavily they were of no use to the enemy. Their fuel tanks and hangers destroyed. There were no operational enemy aircraft at either base. The northern part of route two and route one were under our control. More of our troops and armored vehicles would be coming down those two important roads. The Pan American Highway was ours all the way down to Huehuetenango. Our attacks had happened so quickly we had caught the enemy off guard. Four of our MIGs had been lost and three of our transports had been shot out of the sky, one full of troops. Two Hercules Spectre gunships were attacking targets as the sun was going down to keep the enemy from recapturing targets our troops occupied. They would be replaced by the second two Spectres, taking turns hitting targets all night keeping the enemy on the defensive. We had hit them hard and fast preventing them from reacting quickly enough to counterattack our troops. According to intelligence reports they did not have many J-11s left. The ones that were still operational were no longer at their air bases. They had landed on paved roads and were being hidden in makeshift shelters to avoid being destroyed on the ground. I knew they would be up tomorrow trying to shoot down more of our transports resupplying our troops on the ground. Our numerical superiority would overwhelm their technical advantage in the air. Tomorrow we would finally wipe the skies clear of those dreaded Chinese fighters. With air suppiority we would be free to attack enemy ground targets helping our troops.

The US did release four of their ultra modern anti missile systems. They had been set up so their radar could converge covering the whole southern border. Hopefully if those missiles were launched, they would be intercepted in the air and destroyed. I fell asleep in my bunk that night too exhausted to be afraid of being killed by those missiles.

Two hours later the base air raid alarm sounded. I jolted me out of my bunk and I went racing outside clad only in my underwear just in time to see the flames from the rear of a rocket as it dropped from the sky into the main hanger creating a massive violent explosion so powerful it knocked me to the ground. A second missile slammed into the center of our main runway creating an earthquake effect as the concussion rippled across the tarmac shaking the ground. A third missile high above the base exploded in mid air as the US made anti-missile system rocket hit it's target creating an impressive fireball in the black sky. Pieces of burning debris rained down hitting the ground as several parts of the Chinese missile landed. A few minutes later the all clear siren sounded as sirens from the crash trucks began to pierce the night as they responded to the fires around the base. The base was completely dark except for the light from the inferno that used to be our main hanger and the several fires that were formerly the third Chinese missile that had been disintegrated in the air. I ran back inside and threw on jeans and a tee shirt with tennis shoes. I ran down to the sandbagged revetments where our fighters had been, flashlight in hand running for all it was worth. Luckily our Cuban fighters were untouched. Several of the Mexican MIGs were also untouched. Our MIG-29s and A-4s survived the attack. The fireball that formerly was our main hanger was now just an orange burning steel skeleton. Firetrucks were unsuccessfully trying to put out the massive fireball with streams of water. Boner came running up behind me as I stood there gaping at the fire.

"You okay?" He asked.

"Oh yeah, I'm fine. You?" I looked at him.

"Naaa Im fine, just had my beauty sleep disturbed is all. Thank god they didn't get our birds with those missiles."

"Yeah well Ill bet that third missile was targeted for them. Thankfully at least one of those anti missiles hit. We'll still be able to hit them in the morning." I remarked.

"Betchurass we will." He answered.

Perry came driving up in a blue pickup jumping out wearing a US Marine tee shirt and shorts, a bright flashlight in hand.

"Thank god you guys are awright." He told us.

"Amen to that, but it looks like all our bombs and missiles werent so lucky." I observed looking at the flaming steel girders as they collapsed to the ground.

"Naaa I faked the fuckers out. All our munitions and most of our spare parts were already moved out of the hanger yesterday. We anticipated an attack so we moved everything. Bastards didn't get a damn thing except a few spare parts and some cans of oil. I wonder who else didn't make it though." He wondered outloud.

"We'll know soon Im sure." I replied. "Im heading over to the command center." I told them.

"Yeah Ill go with you. "Boner added. We made our way to the command center in the darkness using the beam of my heavy black metal flashlight to light the way. The three guards at the entrance way saluted me and opened the door for us. Inside Raul was on the dedicated phone line to Mexico City informing them of the missile attack. Three other telephones were ringing, and the radar techs were watching their screens for any possible night attack. The four MIG-21s flying air cover over the base had radioed in the sky above us was clear. The radar antenna mounted on the top of the mountain was functionally normally. The command center was operating on the backup generator as the base generator had been knocked out by debris from the missile that slammed into the center of our main runway.

Emergency lights glowed from the windows of the base clinic where the injured were already being treated. I answered one phone, identified myself and was told that the runway damage was being cleared already and temporary steel matting was being laid over gravel and sand to fill in the massive hole in the center of the runway. Another phone rang and I was told that the base generator was totaly destroyed and would need to be replaced. The base tower had their own emergency backup generator and all their systems were functioning normally. All in all considering the intended damage planned by the enemy missiles, the base wasn't hit enough to put it our of action. The crater in the runway would be repaired to the point our fighters could use it for takeoffs.

I called over to the clinic to get a situation report. We had nine dead and twenty injured, most of them security personal and a few ground techs. No one from our team had been injured. I was making notes of the information on a yellow pad of paper as each report came in. I handed the pad of info to Raul and he began to read the information to the person on the other end of the telephone. Boner was answering phones and writing down info of his own. Perry and Alexi were going from fighter to fighter making quick inspections to check their condition, they called into the command center by radio letting me know their results.

"We got off pretty lucky." Raul remarked.

"Id say, thank god that third missile never reached it's target." I replied.

"Well it's business as usual, we have our targets for today and there will be more transports dropping troops. Hopefully we can locate those other Chinese missiles before they launch them."

"Anything from our agent yet?" I asked him.

"No nothing yet, Antonio hasnt contacted us. Hopefully we will hear something very soon before they launch any more at us." Raul replied. Once things had calmed down Boner and I walked out of the command center as the sun was coming up. We made our way to the chow hall which was still in working order. I wondered if next time they could target the chow hall and leave the rest of the base alone, as the food was never the best, just something to fill your stomach. I settled for an omlette, simple to make, hard to screw up. Boner who had a cast iron stomach went for the greasy sausage and eggs with bacon, and weird looking tortillas filled with jalapenos. There was always plenty of coffee. Good coffee. The kind that could peel paint off the wall and give you a caffeine buzz that would last all day.

At our morning briefing we learned we were to escort troop transports to the crossroads of rte nine and rte two. It was a major artery from the port of San Jose where the Chinese were offloading military equipment and supplies. By securing the crossroads, and destroying the railroad tracks, we would prevent material from reaching Guatemala City. The four MIGs in my flight would escort the troops to their drop zone, and provide air cover for Boner's A-4 team as they bombed the rail road junction there. I walked out and checked my fighter and signed for it. I climbed aboard, cranked her up and waited for clearance from the tower. When the correct light sequence was flashed, one by one we lined up our fighters and took off. We joined up with Boner's flight of A-4s and headed south. As we crossed the border my RWR went of telling me we were detected by enemy ground radar from their air base in Guatemala City. Data being fed to us from the AWACs showed a clear sky, no enemy fighters were up. That was fine by me.

Boner's A-4s rolled over and dove at their targets. The A-4s weaved and turned as tracer fire filled the sky from ground fire. Two SAMs lifted off roaring into the sky. They never acquired radar lock on us as they rocketed up above our MIGs. Information projected on my visor indicated the location of the SAM radar site. The great thing about having helmet guided missile technology was having the ability to direct the missile anywhere you wanted. I circled the SAM's radar van with it's massive antenna. I positioned the little green box on the inside of my visor on the antenna and fired my missile. The missile dropped off the wing and turned, diving right down to the target destroying it in an explosion,. There would be no more SAM missiles launched from that site. Two by two the A-4s made their bombing run dropping their ordnance then turned west. With Manuel on my right wing we circled the target watching as smoke began streaming up into the sky. The railroad junction security buildings and SAM site were totally destroyed. I radioed the all clear and minutes later, four transports appeared with troops jumping out, their parachutes filling the sky. Landing they began taking positions. Circling we watched them. There was little resistance after the bombing raid.

The team leader on the ground called up to us informing us the area had been secured. Four Hinds came in, two landed off loading supplies and collecting wounded troops while two circled flying security. When the two Hinds lifted off, the second two landed dropping off supplies and loading more wounded troops. Minutes later after the second two Hinds lifted off, there was a long line of APCs and supply trucks arriving. Troops on the ground began setting up a defensive position. There were no threats in the area. We turned north back to base to refuel for our next mission.

After refueling at base, we lifted off and rendezvoused again with Boner's A-4s and we again headed south. This time our target was the port of San Jose. The Chinese had supply ships there off loading supplies. They were using trucks to transport the supplies as we had destroyed much of their their rail lines. We came screaming in from between the mountains. SAMs lifted off leaving white smoke as they rose up trying to lock onto us. Our MIGs fired missiles at the radar antenna denying the SAM missiles from locking onto our fighters. The A-4s twisted and turned making their bombing runs dropping bombs on the four ships. Two were docked their cranes offloading crates and vehicles, the other two supply ships were waiting in the harbor. Tracer rounds reached up trying to hit us.

The four ships began burning from the bombing attacks. Shoulder fired missiles shot into the sky, our on board system automatically began ejecting flares and chaff. Our jammers found the correct radio frequency being used by the shoulder launched guidance system and the missiles began spinning in spirals losing their lock on us flying off in different directions.

There was a tanker full of fuel docked offloading fuel to a fuel tank. I could clearly see the white metal fuel line connected to the tanker. The tanker was sitting low in the water. That meant it was still full. Boner made another bombing run, the three other fighters coming down right behind him. Bombs hit the tanker in two spots. When the bombs went off the shock wave emitted from the massive explosion in an ever widening circle from the burning ship.

My RWR went off and my visor revealed three Russian made ZSU gun platforms spraying the sky with tracer rounds. These were four barreled radar guided weapon systems. They were deadly to low flying fighters. Enemy forces had a system combining the SAMs with these ZSUs. The SAMs would force our fighters to fly low to get under the SAM's radar giving the ZSUs an oppurtunity to use their low level radar guided cannon to pepper our fighters. It was a deadly combination. The best way to counter this threat was to take out the SAM missile radar antenna, then bomb the ZSU's from a safer altitude. One by one we destroyed the ZSUs using our helmet guided missiles attacking from different directions. I dove on a group of trucks lined up front to back fully loaded with supplies from the ship heading east. I came in low firing my canon hitting the first truck in line. It went up creating a ball of fire and smoke effectively stopping the vehicles behind it. I looked back as I climbed and watched the other fighters behind me raking the line of vehicles with cannon fire. Several trucks in the front of the procession were burning. Some pulled off the road, their drivers abandoning their vehicles, doors left open in their haste to avoid being killed. We made three passes firing controlled cannon fire hitting the line of trucks. That was one convoy of supplies that would never reach the enemy troops.

I made a run at two of the large six fuel storage tanks. Being conservative with my cannon fire I was able to puncture the sides of both tanks. As I pulled up I could see the huge orange ball of flame from my tracer rounds igniting the precious fuel stored in the tanks. There was a shock wave that hit my MIG as the second tank exploded. Boner's A-4s were shooting tracer rounds into the other round fuel tanks two at a time. Soon the sky was filled with columns of black smoke from the burning fuel tanks. The whole area was a scene from Dante's inferno. Burning fuel was everywhere. Burned out hulks of trucks loaded with supplies were either burning, or on their sides from being deserted by their drivers from our attacks. The harbor fuel lines were burning as was the main pumping station. The fuel tanker was burning from bow to stern. The two supply ships that had been offloading supplies were now on the bottom of the harbor right next to the wharf. Their supplies would never be useful.

As I circled around I could see men jumping into the water from the burning ships. They were losing the battle to fight the fires that were raging on their decks filling the sky with thick greasy black smoke. The bombs from our A-4s had penetrated the thin metal of the old freighters and exploded deep in the bowels of these fully loaded vessels setting off fires below decks. One ship was already sinking stern first out in the harbor, her bow rising out of the water flames shooting our of her stack, men were diving off her deck into the water. Again I was a witness to a ship dying as it sank into the depths. The two freighters docked were settling deep into the water where they sat, fire raging from their decks. The third freighter burning, was under way trying to reach the open sea to escape the melee in the harbor. Black smoke leaving a trail in the sky behind the ship. I had to admire that captain and his crew for trying to save their ship. Unfortunately I knew they would find a way to offload their supplies once they successfully stopped the fires.

"You see that ship trying to head out to sea?" I called over to Manuel.

"Affirmative boss. Got him in my sites." He replied.

"He's ours, Ill take the stern, you take the bow." I called out.

"Copy that boss." He answered. I kicked left rudder and moved the stick turning my MIG coming in on the ship's port side. We came screaming in low. I aimed the little green box in my visor at the stern, right at the water line and fired off two missiles. I was hoping the impact and explosions from my missiles would damage the rudder control system and the engine room. Manuel fired two missiles at the bow's waterline. I knew he was hoping his missiles would open up a hole or dent in the bow at the waterline causing water to rush in. The two other pilots in our group fired missiles at the ship's bridge. There were several explosions as our missiles hit. The bridge of the ship was a flaming hole from the missile hits. Circling I looked down watching the ship start to turn in slow circles, the bow lower in the water, as more smoke and fire engulfed the deck. It gave me no pleasure attacking the ship with such a determined crew. I knew the supplies it carried could not be allowed to be offloaded. We all watched as the burning ship slowly began to roll onto it's port side, men trying to jump into the water, It finally stopped rolling lying on it's port side halfway in the shallow harbor still burning. It blocked the entrance to the harbor preventing any other ship from entering the harbor to dock and unload supplies. Fuel getting low I gave the order to return to base and we headed north leaving the chaos behind us. I kept an eye on the data being sent from the AWACs plane north of us, relieved that there were no enemy fighters up to worry about on the way back to base.

After writing up my report, I joined everyone at the chow hall. All of us were in good spirits. We had flown two missions that day with no losses to our side. I was ravenously hungry, even for the chow hall food. They had provided steaks and we gorged ourselves. Later we gathered at the hanger and pilfered Perry's stash of beer from his personal cooler. He would toss a beer to each person as they entered. We sat there going over the days mission critiquing our attacks. Alexi had flown his team of MIG-29s against hard targets further east. Raul joked and laughed at our efforts to disable the burning freighter using our helmet guided missiles.

"I wonder if this is the first time in history that a ship was sunk using helmet guided air to air missiles." He observed.

"Well I'm not sure if we actually sank it using our missiles, but at least we did enough damage to her to disable her. She rolled onto her port side and settled in the shallow end of the harbor effectively blocking it. I'm sure it will take quite a lot of work to remove her." I explained.

"Meanwhile it denies them the ability to offload supplies there." Perry observe.

"Not to mention the loss of another tanker full of fuel." Boner said.

"We hit their fuel storage tanks as well. We made a mess of that site." Manuel grinned.

"We have made significant progress on the ground as well, Our troops hold most of the northern part of the country, important locations anyway." Raul admitted.

"We will make the push for Guatemala City soon. We secure the important outlying towns first before we attack the capital. We will need a lot of air support for the troops as they enter the city. It will be a lot slower going than when the communist forces first attacked the city. The communist troops are aware we are coming and will be prepared. Our plan is to allow as many flights out of their main airport as possible. Many of the Chinese officials have already left."

"Rats escaping a sinking ship." Alexi remarked.

"We hope they do. Better they leave before the conflict is over, they leave behind only the lessor trained troops to act as leaders for the final battles. Makes our efforts easier." Raul explained.

"Anything on the locations of those Chinese missiles?" I asked him.

"No nothing yet." Raul answered." Hopefully we will receive the location of the missiles before they launch them."

"Not that I'm complaining I'm just wondering why they havent fired off more of them." Manuel remarked.

"Copy that." I added finishing my beer."

"It's possible they were damaged en route, technical problems, etc." Raul told us.

"Either way, better for us." Alexi remarked.

"It wont be long before we own the whole country and the threat will be over. Our job will be done and we will all be able to go home." Raul said.

"Hear hear." Boner said raising his beer in the air.

"Everyone in this team has done an outstanding job here so far. Lets keep up the good work. It'll all be over soon. Hang in there guys." Raul told us.

"We have troops on the ground from all over Central America. Cuba, Peru, Argentina, Ecuador, Chile. There are even some former American Marines from Puerto Rico fighting wearing uniforms from different countries. Many of them volunteered and joined the military's of various countries just to get into the fight. It is surprising how many people realize the danger of a Communist Central and South America."

"Everyone except the United States." Alexi observed.

"It seems that way yes. Their president seems more concerned with liberal domestic problems than the security of this hemisphere."

"Thats okay boss, fuckem. We don't need em. We can do the job without em." Manuel remarked.

On that note we all finished our beers and made our way to our bunks. I knew Perry would be working all night with his crew getting our fighters ready for the next days mission. I never understood how he did it, that man must never sleep. I reminded myself to tell Antonio when we got back that Perry deserved something extra for all his hard work and sleepless nights. Raul had been correct, all of us had been doing more than was asked from us during this war. Regardless what the rest of the world thought, being here all of us knew it was a real war. We were but a part of it, an important part nevertheless. I was glad I wasn't on the ground fighting in the heat and humid jungle environment.

The next morning in the briefing we were surprised to find we would be a part of the invasion of Retalhuleu Air Base. We had destroyed it to the level that it was no longer operational to the enemy. The plan was for our troops to capture the base and to rebuild it for our own use. Sitting there taking notes on my thigh pad I understood this was a pivital part of our involvement in this war. The plan was for us to fly cover for the transports as they dropped their paratroopers. At the same time, armored units would be attacking from the north. There were certain hard ground targets that would have to be destroyed during the battle. Again My flight would be flying cover for Boner's A-4 bomber flight. The plan called for a lightning quick attack from the air, supported by the armor units attacking as the paratroopers captured the air base. Our fighters would be bombing hard targets such as the command center which was a concrete building, as well as their communications building, and roads from the south leading to the base to deny the enemy the ability to transport extra troops to the base to support their fighters.

Once we owned the base, we could use it to attack other parts of the country from the air and help support the attack on Guatemala City. It was a bold plan. It would double our time in the air due to halving our range to target. It would cut in half our fuel requirements. Less fuel use meant more time in the air. The plan to attack Guatemala City would require our troops to attack from the east and the north at the same time. It would force the enemy troops to fight two fronts effectively splitting their forces. Anytime you can split your enemy's forces, it weakens their ability to fight a coordinated war. I understood now what Raul had been telling us earlier about a coordinated multi-nation unit. Our side must have a large group of troops to be able to attack the city from two fronts at the same time.

Once again we walked to our fighters early in the morning darkness. The instrument panel came alive with light in the darkness as I hit the ignition button and felt the engine start. The fighter vibrated around me as the engine spooled up. Once my start up was complete, I closed my canopy and locked it in place. It was the silent signal to the tower I was ready to take off. One by one the other pilots closed their canopys. We were given the correct light signal from the tower and I inched forward the throttle and turned my fighter towards the end of the runway. Once in position, I made my takeoff check. I was satisfied and released my brakes and moved the throttle forward. The fighter moved down the dark runway, Manuel was to my right as we both lifted off together into the dark sky.

The four of us joined up with Boner's A-4s and we streaked south.

We approached the target from the southwest. Paratroopers were already dropping from the sky as the sun was coming up. Boner's flight of eight A-4 Skyhawks began their bombing run. They flew in two at a time. They made four runs as we circled overhead watching for enemy fighters. The data sent to us from the AWACs showed a clear sky. Soon the buildings that housed their command center and communications equipment were burning fiercely. The roads from the south leading into the base were cratered making vehicle traffic impossible. Our paratroopers from the five transports were now all on the ground. I could see tanks and APCs arriving from the northwest followed by trucks and supply vehicles. It went as planned. Our paratroopers were securing the smaller buildings and wrecked hangers as the tanks and APCs were circling the field. I could see support fire from the armor hitting targets as our ground troops were running from one building to another. Since a ground attack was not expected, there weren't many enemy ground troops. Most of the personnel were support troops for the now destroyed airbase. It was a short lived battle. There was a large group of tanks supported by ground troops entering the town northwest of the base. There was minor street fighting, but resistance was small with the tanks firing at buildings enemy troops were using to fire from. It wasn't long before the firing stopped. Burning buildings were ignored as our troops took up positions around both the the airbase and the town.

More and more vehicles were pouring into the base. I kept a close watch on the HUDs looking for any potential enemy fighter threats. There were none. We were given the RTB signal. As we headed back to base another flight of our MIGs were coming south to fly air cover for the troops on the ground. As I pulled away I could see construction equipment already being unloaded. The plan was to repair the runway as soon as possible giving our fighters a level landing field. We landed at base and taxied to our revetments to refuel. We had not fired any of our missiles.

Transports loaded with supplies were taking off after we were done refueling. We took off and joined up with them flying cover for them as they flew south. Looking down as we approached the runway at Retalhuleh we could see The construction crews had completed laying metal grating down over the cratered runway. The transports received the signal to land, and we watched as they made their approach and one by one touched down.

A voice on the ground called our frequency giving us clearance to land.

I turned, lowered my flaps and pulled back on the throttle. I lowered my gear and again adjusted my flaps. I kept the fighter level as I came in over the unfamiliar runway. I carefully moved the stick forward and slowly touched down in a cloud of dust. I let out the air brakes, and taped the brakes opening my drag chute. I was glad for the long runway. It had been lengthened to accommodate the large Chinese military transports, which were now burned out blackened hulks from our previous attack on this enemy base. They had been pushed to the side of the runway. It gave me a creepy feeling to be landing here. Even though our troops had secured the base, I still thought of it as an enemy air base.

I dropped my chute and turned off the runway onto the side ramp. The construction crews had done an excellent job of laying down the metal grating so fast. They had filled in the craters and layed the thin metal interlocking strips across the dirt giving our fighters a solid flat landing surface. I followed a green army jeep with a "Follow Me" sign attached to the back. Slowly carefully I inched the throttle forward and taxied the MIG behind the jeep. Manuel had landed right after me and was following behind me. We were led away from the runway to a clear undamaged concrete area. It looked like it had been previously used to park vehicles, as there were yellow lines painted on the concrete the size of automobiles. There was a ground tech already waiting using bright orange wands pointing us to our pre-selected parking spots. He motioned me with his wands and then crossed them. I tapped the brakes and brought the throttle all the way back. He made a cutting motion across his throat and I shut down my engine. I hit the switches and the instrument panel went dark.

To my left another ground tech rolled an orange ladder up to the side of my fighter and released the outer latch. I opened my canopy and he climbed up slipping pins in my ejection seat as I pulled off my helmet. It was a weird feeling as I descended the orange ladder that I'm sure was used not too long ago by enemy pilots to climb down from their fighters. Manuel was looking around as he climbed down from his fighter. The buildings that Boner's A-4s were still burning. No one was even paying attention to the flames and smoke coming from what was earlier two buildings filled with men. Mobile missile launchers were being set up around the base, and the control tower was now manned by our communications people. There was activity everywhere around us as we stood next to our fighters. It was an odd feeling, we had landed and now we were being ignored as troops were setting up equipment all around us. Manuel walked over to me shaking his head.

"Loco mano, this is weird." He told me.

"You got that right. Erie." I replied. Just then a green troop truck came around the corner and stopped in front of us. Perry jumped out with a cigar in his mouth grinning like an idiot. He was dressed in camo toting an AK, wearing a helmet and harness.

"Welcome boys, glad you could make it." He called out. "Just sit tight here for a bit until we can clean up this mess. There are still a few unfriendlies running around here. It'll be awhile before we can get things in order. Our guys have secured the control tower, and their chow hall. We are rounding up their ground techs. Wont be long and you will have a nice place to stay courtesy of the Guatemalan Air Force."

"You look like you have been having fun." I told him.

"You bet, There wasn't much resistance. Once we landed and our tanks started showing up, they quit shooting at us." He said.

"Musta broken your heart." I smiled.

"You know me, always enjoy a good fight." He replied.

"Ayep, and Im thankful you do buddy." I told him remembering my rescue and him covering my escape.

"Just sit tight here, when we have a safe place for you Ill come back and get ya. If we need you up in the air Ill come running." He said as he climbed back into the truck. I waved as he turned and drove away.

"Well hell, might as well get comfy." I said as I sat under the wing out of the sun. Manuel sat down beside me as we watched all the activity going on around us. Automatic weapons fire came from our right off in the jungle.

"Must be what Perry was talking about." Manuel remarked as he nervously fingered his forty five in his vest.

"Ahh we'll be safe here. "I assured him. He didn't look convinced. We sat there in the shade under the wing of the MIG watching the activity all around us as different people worked on getting the base operational. I was amazed at all the activity around us. I knew the people in the tower would contact us right away if an air threat developed. We would be in the air in a heartbeat. More transports were landing and unloading material and supplies. We watched in silence as body bags were loaded into the rear of the transports for the return flight back to the base. More evidence that freedom is never free.

We looked over at men in different uniforms being herded into the back of a troop transport. Manuel and I looked silently at each other thinking the same thing. I was thankful I wound up on the winning side and wasnt a prisoner of war, being herded into the back of a transport at gunpoint.

Boner's flight of four A-4s touched down and they were directed to our parking area. Ground techs appeared from nowhere and placed the orange ladders on the sides of the parked fighters. Boner climbed out putting his helmet in the cockpit and walked over to us. His team wandered around as he took a seat next to us.

"Swell day gents." He smiled.

"Hell of a day. They sure are busy." I said.

We all stood up as a fuel truck drove up and two men got out. One by one our fighters were refueled. I looked over at the tower wondering if there was a mission being prepared. It wasn't a good feeling standing there feeling useless not having any info.

"Is there a mission for us?" I asked one of the fuelers.

"No, they just want your fighters ready in case there is an air attack by enemy fighters." He explained. We all looked off into the jungle as more gunfire was heard. It was the constant fire of a machine gun. Heads turned everywhere looking in the same direction at the source of the gunfire. The fuel truck pulled away and a few minutes later two troop trucks drove up and stopped, heavily armed Mexican troops jumped out and formed a circle around our fighters. A lieutenant came trotting up to us saluting. We returned his salute.

"We have orders to secure this area. "He explained. I was glad someone in the chain of command was thinking as more gunfire came from the jungle. The soldier turned and ran back to his men assigning them positions and setting up machine guns behind obstacles. One of the truck divers walked over to us with two canvas bags.

"Perry said to deliver these to you." He told us. We opened the bags as he walked back to his truck. Inside was food and bottled water and fruit juice.

"Good ole Perry, whatta guy." I smiled as the food was passed around. We sat there under the wings of our birds out of the hot sun eating the Pita bread stuffed with chicken and peppers, enjoying the cool drinks. Suddenly explosions surprised us as mortars began dropping around us. We flattened ourselves on the ground. Seconds later two Hinds lifted off turning in the direction of the gunfire coming from the jungle. They flew one behind the other and as they flew over the jungle tracer rounds shot up at them. They circled around and began making strafing runs one behind the other at the source of the ground fire. The ground fire stopped, the Hinds circling like vultures over a fresh kill. I sat up and the rest of the people around began to get up off the ground. Thankfully there was no damage to our fighters from the mortar rounds. We were all in one piece.

A green troop truck came around the corner and pulled up next to our fighters. Perry climbed out of the drivers seat.

"We got a place for you to stay finally." He told us. One by one we climbed into the back of the truck. Perry climbed in and the truck lurched forward. It was a short trip. The building we stopped at was a barracks. There were bunks set up in every room. Down the hall was a bathroom, which surprisingly had hot running water. I figured after the damage we had caused to this base during our attack, there would be little comforts left. I went to the bathroom and gratefully enjoyed standing under the shower washing off the sweat. Back in the bunk rooms we stashed our bags. I changed into a fresh flight suit and wandered down the hallway. There was a small lunchroom surprisingly with cooks from our base working hard in the kitchen. One by one the pilots gathered in the lunchroom after taking showers. We sat watching the cooks set up and drinking coffee.

"I sure hope they feed us as good as they do at the base." Boner remarked.

"You really like their cooking?" Manuel asked him in amazement.

"This guy has a cast iron stomach. He could eat snake meat and think it was a delicacy." I explained.

"Hey I like snake meat." Boner said grinning. I sat there shaking my head. We looked out the windows as the sound of jet engines roared overhead. We walked outside to see four MIG-29s landing, One by one they were directed to the parking lot where our fighters were parked. Their canopys popped open as their engines shut down. Ground techs moved the same ladders we had used to the sides of the 29s.

"Looks like Raul has arrived". I said.

"Looks that way." Boner added.

One by one Raul and Alexi and the other two MIG-29 pilots climbed down. Their heads were on a swivel looking at all the activity around us as vehicles and men were moving back and forth across the base. Perry pulled up in the green troop transport greeting them, they climbed into the back for the short ride to our new quarters. The truck drove around the base and stopped in front of our building. One by one they climbed.

down Raul unzipped the front of his flight suit. We watched them cringe as one as more automatic gunfire erupted from the jungle.

"Sounds like the natives are restless." Raul called to us as they approached.

"Former residents are voicing their displeasure at our presence here." I told him. He grinned.

"Coffee is this way boss." Manuel told him.

"Welcome Alexi." I told him. He nodded to me as we made our way inside to the cafeteria out of the heat and humidity. Soon we were all seated and eating, glad for the refreshing coolness. Later we gathered together, Raul had set up a map of Guatemala City showing the main streets.

"Their troops have been building barricades and there are refugees fleeing the city. They know the entrances to the city. Our troops are going to have it rough, fighting street to street. The plan is to bomb any buildings with stiff resistance." Raul began.

"What about any civilians in the buildings?" I asked.

"Trust me, when the fighting starts, there wont be many civilians running around in the open. We'll have clear radio transmissions from our ground forces. They will pop colored smoke to help identify their positions. By studying this map you will get a general idea of the city."

"So we bomb the buildings where enemy troops are firing from?" Manuel asked.

"Correct. Your fighters will circle the city, radios tuned to the ground troops frequencies so they can direct you to your targets. The enemy will have tanks deployed in several locations. They will be your primary targets. You see a tank, destroy it." He explained. "Our ground troops will attempt to capture the airport so our transports can land troops and supplies during the attack. We expect casualties to be high." We sat there in silence as he continued with the simple briefing.

"Most of the Chinese representatives have left the country. A few die hards have stayed. Discipline is breaking down all over the country under control of the communist forces. There is a fear that the communists will take to the hills to fight a guerrilla war in hopes they will be able to retake the country. If we are able to control most of the country, the idea is to help the Guatemalan people form a new government. Many countries in South and Central America will have to subsidize a new economy to help this country get back on it's feet. That will be difficult as most of these countries are third world nations depending on other countries to aid them. There have been intelligence rumors that the Chinese discovered an oil deposit off the coast. If that is true, it's possible that by drilling for oil, Guatemala will be able to reap the benefits and their economy will blossom."

"Our main concern at this point is to aid ground forces anywhere we can, and to eliminate any remaining fighters they may have hidden away for the final battle. Once our forces take the city, and several other key locations across the country, things should settle down. Then our job will be to patrol the air to help our ground troops fight any stragglers hiding in the hills." To the man we all looked up at the roof as if we could see through the ceiling as the sound of transport engines began to land. The noise went on for a few minutes. I knew with every aircraft that landed, more supplies were available to help end this war."

"As of now I am the CO of this base, Grey here is the exec. We will maintain operational control of this base until the high command deems otherwise. They want to control the airbases in this country. Our fighter squadrons will be deployed as we capture each airbase. Tomorrow we will be flying more ground support missions. Tonight we'll arrange our living quarters here. Perry will Get the fighters ready tonight as usual. Everyone will wear their side arms when not flying. There will be a large contingent of armed personnel around this base as security, along with APCs. Until this war is over, we are still occupying enemy Territory, so I want you men to be able to defend yourselves."

We sat there reviewing the details of tomorrows mission, radio call sgns, flight paths, aerial maps, etc. It was a bit primitive compared to what we were used to at our base back in Mexico. Being flexible was part of the job. We spent the rest of the day reviewing information.

"This will be different." Boner said as we sat in the lunchroom eating dinner. There was rice and chicken with fresh rolls and plenty of hot coffee.

"You mean targeting buildings?" I asked.

"Yeah, not exactly an easy mission." He remarked.

"We can do it." I told him.

"I know that, just not used to bombing buildings, Im used to hitting military targets."

"Well these buildings will have enemy forces in them, so in a way they are military targets." Raul explained.

"We can do it boss, no worries." Manuel added.

"The faster we kill the enemy, the faster the war will be over. Kill the enemy, end the war." Alexi commented.

"Her hear." I said raising my coffee cup. Everyone else followed suit.

"Death to the enemy." Manuel said.

"To a swift end to this war." I added. We all clinked our coffee cups together. I wandered back to the room found my bunk, and stretched out in the green military sleeping bag. The air conditioner was on full blast cooling the room.

"I miss my bed." Boner lamented as he stretched out next to me in the darkness.

"Ahhh it wont last long. Soon we will have regular beds in here and then you will have to find something else to complain about." I told him.

"Yeah, Im sure I can find something to bitch about." He laughed. The base was still busy around us as we tried to sleep. Trucks were driving back and forth, the runway was being repaired, transports were landing full of supplies. There was a steady drone of noise outside the building. I felt grateful to be allowed to sleep, I felt sorry for the men out there working all night. I knew Perry and his crew would be sweating and swearing as they worked all night getting our fighters ready for takeoff tomorrow. Their work never ended. Maintenance on our fighters was a 24 hour job. As soon as we landed, each fighter was towed inside a hanger and gone over by the maintenance crews. Keeping these fighters flying, upgraded as they were, took constant attention. Lying there in the darkness on the padded sleeping bag with the sound of the air conditioner running and the base busy around us made me homesick for Ali. I too would be glad when this war was over and I could return to Cuba. I missed Ali terribly. I longed to lie next to her in our big bed in our house by the ocean. My last thoughts were of her as I slowly drifted off to sleep.

CHAPTER SIXTEEN

The next morning we were awakened by Raul banging a billy club inside an empty metal trash can. To the man we hit the floor prone thinking it was a bombing of the base.

"Drop you're cocks an grab you're socks it's revile. Chow is now being served in the lunchroom." Perry yelled laughing at us lying face down on the floor. I got to my knees glaring at him with blood in my eyes. Alexi jumped up with a sharp curved knife in his hand ready to lunge at Perry. Luckily for him Raul came around the corner dressed in a freshly pressed flight suite, yelling at Alexi to drop the knife. It was not the best way to be awakened.

"Raul swiftly retreated out of sight. I sat on my bunk trying to slow my heartbeat down and Alexi was cursing in Russian as he put away his knife. I looked over to see Boner putting away his 45. He had grabbed it on the way to the floor.

One by one we made our way to the bathroom and took showers. Later I made my way to the lunchroom wearing a clean flight suit and an empty stomach. One by one the small table filled up as we got our food and filled our belly's. We sat there drinking coffee ready for our morning briefing. There were blow ups of three mobile missile launchers.

"They found em." I said as we took our seats.

"Good news. There has been a change of plans. We have located the three remaining mobile missile launchers. Your mission for today is to attack these sites and destroy them." Raul told us.

"Hot damn!" Boner called out.

"Awright." Manuel said.

"Death to the tyrants!" Alexi told us.

"Antonio has finally recieved the coordinates of the locations of the Chinese missile launchers. The high command has made this our highest priority." There was a room full of happy faces as Raul went over the mission. Soon we were walking out to the parking lot where our fighters were lined up. I walked around my MIG taking my time to check every detail. As always I trusted Perry and his team, but checking the fighter before flight was a ritual that dated back to the Wright brothers.

I ran my hand along the smooth glass like surface of the MIG. There were no projections or anything to restrict airflow. The skin of all the updated MIGs out of the factory had been reconditioned with sections replaced with a carbon glass composition, painted, then highly polished. The less metal the harder it was to pick up on radar. There were eight brand new Copperhead missiles on dual rails under the wings. I reached under the fuselage and shook the enlarged external drop tank modified to carry more fuel than the original unit designed by the Russians. There were two anti-missile flare ejectors on each side of the fuselage behind the wings to aid in blinding enemy air to air missiles. I ran my hand over the RWR detectors attached to the rear fin and other sections of the fuselage. All external flight controls had been modified with larger stronger motors to gaurantee lightening fast action in the air. Our MIG fighters were better than they were when they came out of the factory in Russia. They were rebuilt and modernized from the ground up with the latest technology available. I was proud of them.

"Give em hell today boss." My flight chief said to me as I signed the paper on the clip board accepting the fighter for flight.

"You can count on it chief." I told him as I climbed the orange metal ladder. Once inside the cockpit I moved my body around getting comfortable. He helped connect me with the fighter, and yanked out the three pins from the ejection seat. I mentally prayed I wouldnt need it today as I hit the power switch watching the instrument panel come to life. I reached up out of the open canopy and spun my hand around telling the ground crew I was starting the big engine. I mashed the start button and felt the familiar vibration around my body as the engine started to spool up.

Once the engine reached the proper RPMs I closed the canopy and locked it into place. I watched the ground tech in front of me moving his hands using the familiar patterns as I tested the flight controls. When I completed that I raised my right thumb to him, he gave me a quick salute and moved away. I kept my hands up high as they pulled the safety pins from my eight missiles under the wings.

I went through my pre-flight check list, satisfied everything was in order. I looked out the one piece clear canopy and released the brake, inching forward rolling along the tarmac towards the end of the runway. I stopped behind another MIG waiting for the team's flight of fully loaded A4s to take off. I sat there watching the fighters take off. A couple of days ago, enemy fighters had been lined up here. Today our fighters were using it. The scenery was totally different around us. It gave me an eerie feeling sitting there.

Finally it was my turn to take off. I lined up with the runway, locked my brakes, ran the engine up. I released my brakes and rocketed down the runway. The runway noise stopped as I lifted off. My landing gear locked in place. I joined Manuel and we turned east ahead of the A4s. We started receiving data from the AWACs flying north of us. There were no airborne enemy threats. My missiles were armed, I was flying lead position, I was ready for a fight. I was eager to end this war so we could all go home to our lives.

The battle for the capital city had yet to begin. Our ground forces were setting up for the main attack. There still remained the task of conquering the southern part of the country. Once the capital city was taken, resistance in the rest of the country would fold due to lack of a central command. We had control of the air, which would help our ground forces overwhelm the enemy.

I glanced at the map on my thigh board, then back out at the terrain below us. We were on course. We maintained radio silence en route to the target not wanting to give the enemy any warning of our approach. Our job was to come in from the west and eliminate the surface to air radar sites controlling the SAM missile launchers protecting the Chinese mobile missile launchers from an air attack.

Three minutes prior to the target I double clicked the mic button. It gave the order for our attack flight to split up into four different converging elements. Our plan was to hit the site from four different directions seconds apart hoping to confuse the ground enemy controllers. I dove down between the mountain tops and used the valley to hide our approach. We twisted and turned flying nap of the earth invisible to the enemy radars. I pulled up the front of the MIG and turned away with Manuel on my right. I moved the stick and lowered my left wing turning as I looked down at the collection of dark green trucks connected together with long cables. I could see the familiar star pattern of the SAM launchers. Roaring in over the target I locked onto my first target with my helmet's visor sighting system and centered the two boxes on the target. I squeezed the trigger on the stick with my right hand and watched as two of my missiles shot off under my wings. Behind me Manuel was hosing the target with cannon fire. I hit the flare button and flares shot out of their ejectors as I pulled up away from the target. I glanced back over my shoulder rewarded with seeing flames and smoke pouring from the trucks and antenna structure. Seconds later two more MIGs attacked from the south launching their missiles then pulling up into the blue morning sky. Tracer rounds were spitting up into the sky from hopefull gunners trying to hit our escaping MIGs.

The mobile missile launchers were covered with camouflaged netting to hide from aerial detection. Flying this low it was easier to see them. There were three of them lined up their launching arms were moving up, the tips of these deadly killers were rising towards the sky trying to win the race against time. The ground controllers were trying to launch these monsters before we destroyed them.

Seconds after our attack Boner's flight of A-4s came screaming in dropping their bombs right onto the launchers. The entire area was a sea of explosions, flames and thick black oily smoke. Men on the ground were running away from the flames into the jungle trying to escape the inferno. One of the ground controllers had managed to launch a SAM from it's launcher. I watched it lift off into the sky spinning awkwardly in a corkscrewing circle as it tried to rise up, obviously damaged. It managed to gain altitude before it arched over diving into the green jungle leaving a smoking crater. Again and again we dived on the target hitting trucks, small portable buildings and SAM missile launchers. Our missiles, bombs and cannon fire devastated the area. Infective tracer fire continued to reach up into the sky hoping to hit us.

Satisfied the site was destroyed and these three giant missiles were no longer a threat I called over the radio to RTB. I knew there were hundreds of people just waiting for the confirmation from our flight team that the target had been destroyed. I imagined the huge sigh of relief up and down the continent knowing those huge monsters would not be dropping out of the sky killing our people.

We flew away in a different direction than we used for our attack to surprise any one on the ground hoping to pick us off with shoulder fired missiles. I stayed low again screaming between the mountain tops in our escape. Miles away we pulled up, gaining altitude, safe now from any ground threats. I scanned the instrument panel for any warning signs that I had been hit. Grateful that I had escaped without any damage I turned west heading back to base.

"Greywolf requesting landing clearance." I called over the radio as we approached the airbase. The tower called back acknowledging our return. I dropped my flaps and gear and lined up with the runway. I adjusted my engine speed, came in on track. When I touched down I tapped my brakes and released my drag chute feeling the fighter slowing. One by one the team touched down. I pulled up in our assigned space and locked my brakes, cutting my engine. I opened the canopy and slid my helmet off, the sweat dripping down my face in the humid air. I was thankful to be alive. We were one mission closer to going home. Suddenly I missed Ali. I sat there thinking of her and our house on the beach.

The ground tech moved the orange ladder against the side of my fighter with a thunk and climbed up. He started disconnecting me from the fighter. I climbed out and slowly walked around the MIG looking her over. There were black scorch marks from the missile exhaust under the wings. I was amazed there were no hits from all the ground fire we had flown through. One by one we walked into the building. The cool air conditioning felt like heaven. After shedding my G suit and hanging up my helmet, I sat down and wrote out the report of our attack. We had lost one fighter to ground fire. Thankfully our rescue helicopter had found him and picked him up. This war was taking a terrible toll on our pilots. We were losing planes almost every time we flew.

"I sure hope we are getting close to ending this war. Im getting homesick." Manuel told me as we sat there eating our evening meal.

"Well when it ends it's back to test flying for me." Boner added as he shoveled in a fork full of rice.

"I could use some peace time flying myself." I told them. I was missing Ali terribly and longed for our home by the sea.

"Well after this is all over, I'm sure it wont be long before Antonio has another mission for us." Raul remarked.

"Yeah, now that's what I like to hear." Boner said gleefully. "Action means money." I silently shook my head. Being a bachelor he had no ties to anyone, his home was where he slept, and where he flew. I was thankful I had someone to go home to. That night after eating and a long shower I sat on my bunk and wrote a letter to Ali.

Early the next morning I stood outside the building drinking coffee. Suddenly I turned my head looking at the end of the airfield as a green C-47 was making it's approach to the end of the runway. I watched as it landed touching down easily. As it approached the end of the tarmac and began to taxi in, the flag of Mexico was prominent on it's tail. Soon the plane came to a stop and the pilot cut the engines, the props slowly coming to a stop. The rear hatch opened and came down slowly lowered by someone inside. there were steps on the inside of the hatch making exiting simple.

One by one there were men in Mexican military uniforms coming out. A jeep pulled up and the driver stopped, leaping from the vehicle saluting. Three of them climbed in and the driver jumped in throwing the little jeep into gear and sped away.

"Wonder who they are." Boner remarked from behind me.

"Important whoever they are." I answered. I started walking towards the C-47 with Boner behind me. I slowly walked around the aircraft. It was in excellent shape. The paint was new, the tires in great shape. It looked like it was factory fresh. The and co-pilot came down the steps.

"Nice landing there. "Boner told them.

"Thanks." The short one replied. The other pilot stood there looking around the base.

"These guys high up on the food chain?" I asked him.

"You could say that yeah, Head of the Air Force of Mexico high enough for you?"

"Okay if I take a peek inside." I changed the subject? "Help yourself. just don't touch anything." he replied with a smirk looking at the wings on my flight suit.

"Thanks. Ill try not to break anything." I assured him. The first thing I noticed as I ducked my head climbing in was thick blue carpeting on the deck. There was a small but modern bathroom in the rear. There were several new thickly cushioned chairs along each window, one row of seats on each side. The cockpit had been redone with modern controls and navigation instruments. It was impressive. There was a red telephone on the wall.

The Air Force general had flown here to visit the captured enemy air base. There was an awards ceremony that afternoon. We had to stand in the hot sun to receive our medals.

"Can you believe this shit?" Boner whispered to me as we stood at attention in our class A uniforms. It was miserable standing there sweating under the hot sun.

"I would have been satisfied if they gave me a cold beer." I told him.

"Would you guys shut up. I cant take you clowns anywhere can I?" Raul growled at us. We grinned back at him. Soon it was over. We headed back to the building at the end of the ceremony. I went straight to the kitchen. I opened the huge silver refrigerator and hauled out a case of beer. I started passing out ice cold cans of beer. We sat around working on the cold beer.

"You guys need to act more military in front of the brass." Raul told us. I just nodded my head. I thought it was ironic that we were sitting there in our class A uniforms drinking cold beer while Raul was scolding us about talking in ranks.

"No problem boss, can do." Boner told him.

"Ahhh Im just giving you guys shit, you know that. You guys do a great job."

"Thanks Raul." I told him. "I'm ready to go home. Ive had all the fun I can handle."

"It will be over soon. When this is over we will all be going home." He assured me.

"Works for me." I told him.

"I'm sure Antonio will have something for us again soon." He added.

"Hot damn, more money for me." Boner said with a grin.

"Spoken like a true blood thirsty mercenary." Manuel said.

"Guilty as charged and proud of it." Boner said raising his beer.

We were surprised when Perry drove up to the front of the building and jumped out. Two of his mechanics climbed out of the back of the truck and carried in two large boxes. We stood up as they came in.

"Compliments of the general." Perry told us. He opened the boxes and shoved his huge fist into crushed ice. He pulled out a lobser shaking it under our noses.

"Hot damn we gonna eat good tonight." Boner said grinning.

"You going to eat with us Perry?" Raul asked.

"Hell yeah if you're inviting."

"Consider yourself invited." Raul told him. I tossed Perry a beer.

"Elixir of the gods." He said. That night we ate lobster and rice with a spicy vegetable mix downed with ice cold beer. I stumbled to my bunk, and climbed up into the top grabbing both sides as I lay there trying to stop it from spinning.

The next morning Raul woke us up for breakfast. We had a mission. Raul went over the briefing as we sat there at the tables eating. We were to fly backup for Boner's flight of A-4s to hit targets in Guatemala City in support of our troops. The push forward for the capital was finally on. Our MIGs were loaded with four bombs and two missiles each. There would be ample targets to hit today. The brass was expecting heavy opposition from the enemy troops. Urban combat is the most difficult type of combat there is. The enemy turns every building, basement and rooftop into a fortress or booby trap. Heavy casualties were expected and the rescue Hinds would be busy airlifting our wounded ground troops out of the combat zone.

Raul displayed aerial photos of anticipated areas of heavy ground fighting. We were given a detailed map of the city for our thigh boards. The city was sectioned off into grids with letters and numbers along the side to help us locate buildings and targets. The international airport located in the southern part of the city was a high priority target. From there our forces could land transport aircraft loaded with troops and supplies. Once the airport was secured our Hind rescue choppers would be landing there to offload wounded soldiers at the self contained MASH unit that would be one of the first structures set up there. These structures were basically lightweight con ex boxes air transportable easily connected together to form a small but modern aid station.

Air threats were thought to be light or non existent. Taking into consideration Murphy's law we would carry two missiles in case we did encounter any air threats. We went over our call signs and expected entry routes of our troops into the city and the airport.

Once the briefing was over we made our way to the locker room where our helmets and G suits were hung. I slid mine on and walked out to the area our MIGs were lined up on. I climbed the yellow ladder and slid down into the cockpit. The ground tech helped connect me and he slid out the safety pins from the ejection seat.

The brakes were set, I hit the switch that brought the instrument panel to life. I reached my arm straight up and spun my finger in a circle telling the ground tech I was starting the engine. It could hear the slight whine as it started to slowly spool up. The ground tech quickly pulled the wheel chocks away.

I moved the stick back and forth up and down, I tested the rudder pedals and felt no resistance. The engine was turning at the proper revolutions, engine temp was normal, generator on, ADF and marker were on. I programmed the nav computer to the correct GPS coordinates. Internal fuel tank and drop tank were full, there were four five hundred pound bombs and two Copperhead missiles showing on the left panel screen. I checked the heads up display and the images on the inside of my helmet visor. I reached over and set the flaps to 24. I reached up and slid the canopy closed securing the locking lever with my left hand. The brand new MIG was shuddering from the engine vibrations ready to take off.

As usual we were given the green light from the tower using a bright hand held unit. Radio silence was observed. I unlocked the brakes and slowly began rolling along the tarmac to the end of the runway. One by one we lined up ready to take off. When it was my turn I rolled to the end of the runway and locked my brakes. The tower was still giving me the green light, I did a fast cockpit check verifying everything was in order, unlocked the brakes, moved the throttle forward with my left hand and hit the afterburner. The MIG lept forward racing down the runway. I pulled back on the stick and the MIG lifted into the air. I was flying again.

I raised the gear which locked into place with a thunk. When I reached altitude I adjusted the flaps and looked to verify Marco my wing man was at my four o'clock position. He was.

Off in the distance I could see columns of thick black smoke rising to the sky. The battle had begun. We linked up with Boner's flight of eight A-4s. I pulled up and covered them from above. My radar was sweeping but no enemy aircraft were up. I could hear ground control giving Boner's flight exact locations to drop their bombs. One by one they made their approach and dropped them while Marco and I and the other two MIGs flew air cover in a slow circle above the city. We were using the National Theater as the center point. Down below us buildings full of enemy troops were being pulverized by bombs. Seconds later our troops began moving forward along with APCs. Again and again bombs would fall on buildings enemy troops were using to fire on our ground troops. Building after building was incinerated allowing our troops to push forward as they occupied the city.

When it was our turn Boner waggled his wings and rose up to a higher altitude to fly in a circle to cover our six as we made our bombing runs. My headphones came alive with grid coordinates and building descriptions and one by one we dropped onto our targets. Someone on the ground fired off a missile. My RWR began chirping and the right screen verified a missile was coming at me from the ground. The automatic anti missile system kicked in ejecting high intensity magnesium flares to confuse the missile. I jinked left and right quickly changing altitude, diving for the ground hoping the soldier on the ground guiding the shoulder fired missile would lose sight of me. It must have worked because the missile continued on missing me.

Down below our ground troops were pouring into the city in long lines. The airport was under control of our ground troops. Mexican transports were disgorging paratroopers their chutes looking like white mushrooms in the air. Soon supply transports were landing and lining up, armored vehicles and troops running out the rear of their aircraft. The sky was clear of enemy fighters, we had dropped our bombs, it was time to RTB to refuel and rearm.

One by one we turned east and lined up for landing. After landing I climbed out as the ground techs were reloading bombs under the wings and topping off our fuel tanks. I went inside the building took a leak and grabbed a bottle of juice on the way out. Once again we were in the air over the city dropping bombs on enemy positions. The end of the day showed our ground forces in control of the northern half of the city as well as the international airport.

The next day we were in the air again, dropping bombs on buildings. The end of the day our forces were in complete control of the city, TV and radio stations. The TV was full of programming trying to reach out to the remaining part of the country under communist control. Offers of clemency were given to any enemy combatants wanting to surrender. Food stuffs were being trucked in so the civilians could eat. The occupying forces had brought construction equipment in clearing the streets of debris. Electricians were doing there best to restore electricity to the city. The old flag of Guatemala flew from the capital building once again. Military MASH units were set up to deal with the injuries of troops and civilians alike.

"Seems there are transport ships loading up people at Puerto San Jose. Seems anyone who can get there from the opposing side is fleeing there to escape." Raul told us that night.

"Whats the official position on that? Are we going to do anything to try and stop them?" I asked before anyone else could.

"The word from the brass is the less we try and hinder their escape the quicker this will be over." He told us.

"Hear hear. I can drink to that." I answered back raising my bottle of beer.

The next morning we took off armed to the teeth again helping our ground forces fighting south of the city. We dropped bombs on enemy positions in the jungle being guided by radio instructions from our troops deploying colored smoke. On the way back to base, my RWR went of as the radar screen detected two enemy J-11s flying east to west at a high rate of speed.

"Tiger flight, there are two bogeys east bound converging on friendly aircraft returning north." My headphones came alive. Marco and I changed direction trying to intercept the J-11s. They were slightly ahead of us as we roared north trying to catch them.

"Air force General Rodriguez is aboard his aircraft heading north, he is being pursued by enemy aircraft." The tower radioed us. My blood turned cold and I felt my heart lurch as I heard those words. I had no idea where the two J-11s came from, but that was a mute point. Somehow the remaining enemy forces had managed to put these two aircraft up to attack the general's C-47, maybe just as a revenge motive. The slow moving C-47 was ill equipped to escape two J-11s with a load of missiles.

I tuned my radar, lit up my missiles and once I got good tones fired both at the two fighters. They shot off my wings racing ahead to their targets. Marco followed suit right behind me. The two fighters split up and dove for the earth ejecting flares as they did. One of my missiles went after the flares as I was to far away to be able to guide them with my helmet. The other missile flew right up to the target and it fell off the radar display. The other two missiles Marco fired missed the remaining fighter. I hit my after burner hoping to catch that fighter before he engaged the C-47.

My heart gave a lurch as I realized I was too late The J-11 fired off a missile at the slow moving C-47 and quickly changed direction south. I was coming up behind the C-47 and the missile was coming in from the right.

"Marco get that bastard." I called over to him. He lifted his wing and hit his afterburner racing after the enemy fighter.

"Whats your plan?" he called back.

"I dunno Ill think of something." I told him.

"T hats what I was afraid of." He returned.

I cut in between the C-47 and the oncoming missile with my afterburner lit flying northeast away from the general's aircraft. I was hoping to redirect the missile's heat seeking sensor to my hot exhaust and away from the C-47. It was all I could think of at that moment. There was no way I was going to let it hit that slow defenseless plane. My RWR started chirping warning me of the incoming missile. I grinned to myself as it changed direction turning towards my six. I called the tower giving them my coordinates as fast as I could talk hoping they would hear them the first time. I looked left at the Green C-47 flying low off the deck and felt a huge shudder, I felt like a giant hammer had hit my back as the missile hit my MIG. I reached down and yanked like hell with all my strength at the escape handles. The explosive bolts went off with a loud bang and the canopy flew off over my head, the next thing I knew the ejection seat was shooting me up and away from the fighter into the blue sky. I separated cleanly from the seat and the chute snapped open. I looked down and saw the forward half of my fighter rolling in the sky with flame shooting from it's rear as it slammed into the jungle below. Another of Antonio's fighters was now flaming junk in the jungle.

I began to try and locate a landing spot as I floated down. I looked over and saw the C-47 begin to fly in circles around me, the pilot waving like crazy at me as he waggled his wings. I waved back glad to know he saw me. I knew they would be sending a rescue Hind after me soon. Seconds later I was crashing through the tops of the trees branches scraping my body as I fell through them. I bent my knees as I came down and landed in soft mud rolling as I hit. I did an automatic check of my body parts, relieved to find nothing broken.

"Shit!" I yelled out as I slowly stood up my body sore from the force of the ejection. Twice now I had ejected and was lucky enough to talk about it. At least this time I wasn't behind enemy lines. I unfastened the chute harness and found a spot under a tree to sit. I yanked out my survival radio and pulled out the antenna.

"Anyone on this frequency GreyWolf is down, GreyWolf is down, am uninjured requesting pickup." I said into the mic.

"This is Alpha One, we copy your transmission and your position, chopper is inbound your location. The general says many thanks for that stunt, says he owes you one." I heard as the C-47 flew overhead. The sound of those two engines were a sweet reminder of how lucky I was.

"Greywolf copies, tell him buy me a beer and Ill figure we are even," I replied.

"Wilco, cold beer, copy that GreyWolf, rescue chopper is fifteen out, one five out."

"Copy one five, many thanks Alpha One." I called back. I sat there and reached for the little water bottle in my survival vest. I drained it down quickly. The sound of the C-47s engines a reassuring sound as he circled above me. I looked around me and saw I had landed on a hill top surrounded by trees and vines. I wasn't sure how the chopper was going to get me out, but just knowing they were minutes away wiped away any worries I had about getting out of here. I sat there until I heard the familiar sound of the Russian built Hind helicopter from the West. I yanked out my tiny smoke grenade and pulled the pin throwing it from me. It began spewing out purple smoke which reached out from the thick jungle into the sky.

"GreyWolf this is Nightingale we have your smoke, standby for rescue." A voice came over my radio.

"Glad to hear you guys up there." I radioed back. Seconds later I heard a crashing sound as a green metal contraption came down through the branches and landed on the ground at the end of a steel cable. I recognized it as a jungle penetrator. It was a three sided escape seat designed to penetrate even the thickest triple canopy jungle hence the name. I quickly unfastened the nylon belt and folded down the arm and climbed aboard. I strapped the nylon safety belt around me and reached for my radio.

"Im secured you can haul me up." I told them. The Hind began to lift up. I was glad I had left my helmet on as I was raised up through the branches. Tree limbs and leaves were smashing my head as I was pulled up. Suddenly I was above the trees in the sunshine being pulled up to the right side of the chopper. The ride came to an end as a trooper reached out and pulled me close to the opening. A second pair of hands unfastened the safety belt pulling my body inside the chopper.

The Hind changed pitch and angled away heading back towards base. One of the crew chiefs began checking my body for broken bones as my flight suit was in tatters after being pulled through the branches.

"Im fine guys really, no injuries." I yelled above the sound of the noise. One of them handed my a bottle of water which I gulped down instantly. I could see the C-47 off our starboard beam keeping up with us. I figured they were returning back to base with us.

I thought it was an ironic position I found myself in. I was in the belly of a Russian built armored attack helicopter being escorted back to base by the head of the Mexican air force who was flying in an antique American World War Two transport. What a way to earn a living. I was glad to be alive and in one piece. I was wondering how Marco had made out with the remaining J-11.

I looked out and saw the base. The Hind pilot was calling for landing clearance and minutes later we landed. Raul was there standing next to Perry and Boner. The C-47 was coming in over our heads on his approach.

"You must live under a lucky star Grey to survive two ejections. What the hell were you thinking of making yourself a target like that?" Raul began yelling at me.

"It was all I could think of at the time." I explained.

"You ever do something dumbass like that again and Ill personally kick your ass you hear me?" he yelled again.

"Yes sir." I replied standing at attention giving him a crisp salute. Alexi reached over and picked me up with his huge arms giving me a bear hug.

"Put me down you ape I cant breathe." I managed to squeak out. Perry slapped me on the back as my feet touched the ground.

"This isn't funny, do you know how much paperwork I have to do now?" Raul yelled again.

"I know Raul but I couldn't let that old C-47 get hit like that. By the way what happened to Marco?"

"He shot the bastard down with his cannon." Boner said.

"Hot damn! Outstanding." I said with a big smile.

"Yeah he cant wait to tell ya." Perry said.

"Damn I need a beer." I said as we climbed into the small truck. Soon we were rolling along back to the small building that was our living quarters.

"Seriously Grey dont be doing shit like that again, we cant afford to lose you." Raul told me as we rolled along.

"Yeah ok Raul I wont." I told him.

Boner had a huge grin and was shaking his head. Later I was standing under the shower draining a cold beer enjoying the water. Perry had taken my helmet and was doing a diagnostic on it. I told him I wanted to keep it. It had survived two ejections. Marco's killing of the J-11 was the last shoot down of an enemy fighter in the war. Three days later it was all over. Most of the high ranking Chinese advisers along with their disgruntled former Cuban government officials had left. The remaining enemy ground troops had surrendered and turned in their weapons. Mexican military troops were in control of the majority of the country.

Raul turned over command of the base to a Mexican Colonel and a Guatemalan Major. We flew back to our base in Mexico. It was a relief to return to a modern facility again. We had to endure another award ceremony.

We each received medals and awards for our actions. Perry and his crew received awards for their hours of tireless work keeping all our fighters in the air. Our pilots received medals for each J-11 shot down. I felt embarrassed as hell standing up there in front of the whole base to receive my medal for saving the General and his crew from the enemy missile.

Antonio had flown over in his Connie. He and Ali both were sitting in the second row watching. I kept a straight face during the ceremony respectfully accepting the award. There was a celebration after in the main auditorium. It was a large ball complete with uniforms and evening gowns. We sat there stuffing ourselves and drinking expensive booze. I wore my dress uniform with the three sets of wings.

I was standing by the bar when Ali entered. My heart skipped a beat as she sauntered in. She wore a bright red evening gown with a plunging neckline and a slit up the side. Every male head turned as she strolled in. She walked right up to me and we danced a slow dance together.

The Mexican General was grateful as hell and told me if I ever needed a favor he was indebted to me and to let him know. It gave me a great feeling. When it was time for us to return to Cuba, I flew with Ali and Antonio in his Connie. It was great to return to our little house by the ocean. The night we returned Ali and I sat on the beach naked in the dark making love and drinking wine under the stars.

Getting back to work was a nice change. I had more awards to adorn my office wall. There was no threat from an enemy wanting to kill us. We concentrated on keeping our fighters in fighting condition. Flying practice sorties seemed tame and boring compared to the daily war missions we had been flying. At the same time it was pure joy just to be able to fly without worrying about a missile being on your tail. I actually enjoyed doing the paperwork that was waiting for me.

Boner and I went back to work test flying fighters for Antonio. The joint Mexican Guatemalan coalition that was the temporary form of government in Guatemala shared the profits from the oil wells discovered off the coast of Guatemala. Modern schools and clinics were built for people living in the rural areas. Life became better for the people there. American factories moved there and income rose for the workers.

Manuel's wife became pregnant again. We kidded him about it. Antonio expanded his factory to include rebuilding older military transport aircraft. He hired two Russian test pilots that Alexi referred to him. It created a lot more work for Ali.

For me I was grateful to be home, with my friends, not worrying about being shot down. Cuba was safe now that Guatemala was stable. I had proven myself loyal to Cuba fighting under her flag. I was no longer looked at as a gringo. I was now one of them, a native. It gave me a good feeling inside.

Printed in the United States
By Bookmasters